ALSO BY WILLIAM COOK HAIGWOOD

Journeying the Sixties: A Counterculture Tarot

A Time of Unsearchable Things

Davenport

Bonny Doon

Wilder

SONGS OF SURVEILLANCE

Stories of Spying, Watching and Eavesdropping

SONGS OF SURVEILLANCE

Stories of Spying, Watching and Eavesdropping

william cook haigwood

Printed in the United States of America

Published by Cooskie Creek Press

Library of Congress Cataloging-in-Publication Data

ISBN-978-1-7337262-1-4

Cover photographs © 2020 William Cook Haigwood

For Gabriel

Table of Contents

NORA WEPT

1

At a disturbing moment somewhere between bad dreams and prosaic sex, Nora wept. All the frustrations of a difficult year accrued in an uneasy wakefulness. It was too early to get out of bed or to find something to watch or read. She turned over and smothered her sobs in a pillow.

She hoped not to awaken Daniel who sprawled beside her, one of his bony knees rolled into her thigh in a way that made it hard for her to move. She tried to lift her leg and he awoke anyway. He heard her whimpers as she tried to catch her breath.

"You OK?" he asked, alert to her crying but too sleepy to understand it.

She wasn't OK. And she could not expect a lover of barely four months to grasp all the crushing details of her previous year's misery. Especially details never shared with him—and she wouldn't share. It wasn't safe. And it wasn't fair. Daniel was at least kind. He was deferential to a fault. But her onslaught at this hour would be too much for him. There was nothing fair in what had happened to Nora, how a year that began with an adoring, successful fiancée and a happy pregnancy ended with neither and had left her living alone in a spare one-bedroom apartment in a scruffy subdivision of Roseland.

Nora tried by herself to sort out the facts of what felt like a recently broken life. Instead, she succumbed to an acquired index of dreadful and unwelcome verities. She was mired in regret and expelled to a vast, silent desert. Daniel, as nice as he was or tried to be, could not begin to fill so wide and threatening a space.

Daniel turned to cuddle Nora who, for a new and welcome moment, accepted the reach of his arm around her and took comfort from his bare warmth. He kissed her back and she felt the swell of his erection punch the base of her spine. What the hell, she thought. Dull sex was still sex. Daniel rolled against her and did not speak.

She did not need his words, in fact preferred not to hear them as she conjured her own thoughts to feed her arousal. She did not need to face him. She could control him from behind, manage his passion, touch him, tease him, and finally admit him. And this would be enough for the morning. If she could not come she would finish herself off while he was in the shower.

Nora fixed Daniel's breakfast and sent him off to a place of work where he lived a life apart from his barely supporting role as her rebound lover. Daniel was late and did not take a shower and Nora did not finish herself off. Her vulnerable subjectivities fed a piercing disappointment and for the brief time she was able to feel sorry for herself she slipped into her swimsuit and left her apartment to walk to the building's pool.

She had the morning off. She found a chaise lounge and rolled it into a patch of hot, blinding sunlight. She fell onto the canvas, her stomach pressed against the fabric's rough seams and buttons.

Behind her she heard a rhythmic splash of the water and turned to see a young man, a shirtless, muscular boy, push a long-poled net across the pool. She looked at him and he looked back, a dark-haired middle teen with piercing, alert eyes. She was the only tenant at the pool and only woman in sight. The boy's gawking attention startled, even frightened, her.

"You not working today?" he shouted with dauntless insouciance.

It was none of his business but she answered anyway, taken with his youth, his muscular shoulders, his daring way.

"I work afternoons," she answered.

"I'm an accountant."

Her superfluous job description made no impact on the boy who kept skimming the water. Nora removed her sunglasses and dropped her head into the chaise. She felt him looking at her, staring at her body while she pretended to remain unaware. Still aroused from the morning with Daniel she imagined the boy watching her bottom, seeking to see what was between her legs. She stretched them and made a point to open her thighs slightly, listening for any change in his movement, in the rhythm of his net in the water. She turned over to lie on her back, adjusting her sunglasses to peek undetected from beneath them. It was for her protection, she thought to herself, though curiosity was the real motive: was he watching her?

The boy moved across the pool's rectangular lip, looking ahead into the water while occasionally turning to examine Nora.

"Hot again today," the boy shouted at her.

"Yeah," Nora answered without looking up.

"Too hot."

The boy approached as she watched from behind her sunglasses. It was thrilling and also scary. He stopped a few feet from her.

"Where do you live?" he asked.

She looked up at his towering strength, his smooth, olive skin, and into his clear, brown eyes.

"Six. Why?" she responded and then asked, weighing the consequences of answering only after she answered.

"Cool," he said finally and returned to the pool.

Approaching her apartment Nora encountered her neighbor as he limped up a flight of cement stairs carrying two bags of groceries.

"I can help, Jory," Nora shouted and seized a bag from him.

Jory was a war veteran living on disability. His muscular upper body shrunk under a perpetual hunch supported by two weak, shattered legs, one locked in a steel brace that bulged from under a wrinkled pant leg cut at the cuff to accommodate it. His apartment was directly above Nora's.

"Thanks," he said with a shy nod before looking away.

"No, thank you," Nora said.

"It's the least I can do. The ceiling fan is a godsend in this miserable heat."

Jory appeared to blush.

"It works for me," he responded.

"I knew you'd like it. But I just installed it. You picked it out."

"It was your idea," Nora insisted.

"I would never have thought of a ceiling fan. You must have lived in the tropics."

Jory smiled, which was in Nora's memory a rare occurrence.

"A year in Iraq," he answered.

"Not exactly the tropics but all the hotels had fans."

Jory opened the door to his apartment, dropped his groceries on the floor and took the other bag from Nora. He limped to the kitchen and returned. Nora watched his young body tilt and yaw as Jory used the walls of the narrow hallway to support himself. Was he even thirty? It had been seven years since the war. Jory appeared to tire quickly. He struggled like an old man to move.

"You tell me if you need anything else," Jory said assertively.

"I'm the handyman around here. They pay me now."

The building's owner had hired Jory to do odd jobs and ongoing repairs, work that allowed a young, wounded veteran to claim employment.

As she entered her bedroom Nora turned on the ceiling fan. She stripped off her bikini and climbed onto her unmade bed. A light breeze tickled her wet skin. The boy at the pool remained a deep impression; one she utilized, along with her fingers and a splash of hand lotion, to claim her morning's postponed consolation. After a short nap and a shower she dressed, made a tuna fish sandwich with extra pickles and drove to her office.

2

JoAnne insisted oral sex was not real sex.

"At least it can't get you pregnant," she said.

"Not unless you spit into your panties," replied Dorine who drew smirks from the other accountants, all women. They occupied the fat-walled and windowless office of Levenheimer and Company LLC in downtown Santa Rosa.

Jacob Levenheimer was the CPA and the women were the company though none shared in the limited liability corporation comprising members of Jacob's family among which Jacob, his wife and oldest son were the only voting partners.

"Clinton has a point," Dora declared.

"Maybe he didn't have sex with that woman."

JoAnne scoffed.

"Of course he did," she hummed with a kind of sonorous despair.

"Our sexy president. What a hunk. I wish it had been me."

Dorine said it sucked to be an intern.

"Heard it already," said Nora.

She rolled her eyes.

"But did you hear about the President's Day Sale? All men's pants half off."

"C'mon. It's the middle of a stinky, hot July," JoAnne jumped in.

"That's even older than the intern joke."

Talk spun out of a loop of innuendo and into the politics of a sitting president whose extramarital sex life had become the subject of a hostile congressional investigation.

"Will he be impeached?" Dorine asked.

Nora said maybe. But Clinton would never be thrown out of office.

"I thought it was the same thing," Dorine said.

The words vanished from Nora's attention as her phone rang and she answered it.

"Hi sweetheart. Is this an OK time to talk?"

It was Nora's mother whose developing habit was to phone every couple of days. She did not expect an answer to her question and appeared to assume it was always a good time to talk.

"I have a couple of minutes," Nora said.

Her mother told Nora she had something important to tell her. Nora knew she did not wish to hear it.

"Ed and I were at the Ridge winery and we saw Trevor…He was sharing a table with this woman, you might know her…"

Of all things her mother could tell her, Nora did not want news of her former fiancée, did not want her mother's discoloring dust clouds of an inadequately witnessed aftermath.

"No mom. Stop. Just stop."

Nora's insistence silenced her mother for a tediously long moment.

"It's over. Leave it alone," Nora shouted into the phone.

"Really, Hon, I'm just thinking of you. Trevor's acting like a jerk. I thought I could…"

Nora was not going to become the rationale for her mother's obsessive curiosity about her former fiancée. Her mother would not let go of Trevor. She said during the good times that Trevor was the best thing ever to happen to her daughter. Nora hated that her mother probably still believed it.

"Trevor's not a jerk," Nora answered.

"How many times do I have to say it: just leave the whole thing alone. Please. I've got to go mom. I'll phone this weekend."

Her mother's tone switched from a tedious whine to one of choleric hurt while Nora hung up the receiver and walked to the lunchroom to find a napkin. She wiped her wet, red eyes.

Jory was sitting outside when Nora returned home. The fading twilight put them both into deep shadows. Jory held a can of beer pulled from a six-pack resting under his frayed and faded lawn chair.

"Seems to be cooling off," Nora said as she searched her purse for her key.

"Maybe the fog will come in tonight."

Jory shrugged. He said it wasn't likely. He watched the Weather Channel, which he seemed to think made him an expert on the topic of Northern California weather. If television were a resource Jory by himself could have been one of its networks.

"Roseland gets hot, hotter than the rest of the town," he announced.

"I grew up here."

"Why do you think it's hotter?" Nora asked skeptically.

Jory did not know but he thought it was the reason so many Mexicans were moving in.

"Used to be big family farms here," he said.

"A whole piece of county land surrounded by a city that doesn't want it. Now it's all becoming apartments. I hate it."

By her count of his empties Jory had consumed four beers. He didn't appear drunk but might have been.

"Are you locking your windows?" Jory asked as Nora started to walk away.

She had no answer.

"You need to. Burglaries around here are getting bad. I'm not saying it's the Mexicans but...well...you can't be too careful. Three last week and one in the Vista Apartments up the street. Bad scene. Dude was pistol-whipped for what? A wallet and a bicycle. These dudes must be hungry to steal such piddling shit. Hungry or young. Or stupid. "

"Not so stupid," Nora said.

"They haven't been caught. I'll check my windows. Thanks."

Nora moved toward the hallway of her building and strolled across a stained, beige carpet toward the apartment door. She opened it. She expected to see Daniel but remembered he was on a sales trip to Portland which also meant she wouldn't be spending the usual midweek nights in his west county condo.

The stuffy darkness was momentarily welcoming. She knew it well: the heavy air of forbearance and tolerance, the dusty evidence of time passing and the presence of her essential possessions that were for her an inventory of trust. She stopped in the living room to check the glassed, winged frames on either side of a much larger picture window. She began to wind them shut but they occupied a space that appeared too small for anyone to enter. She, like her property, occupied a momentary and delusive security.

3

Most of Nora's accounting work was for vintners and grape growers. Jacob her boss hunted for business among the county's renowned wineries and usually with intrusive courtesy as he stepped into tasting rooms and cellars to sip, spit, buy a bottle of wine and then engage an entrapped manager or winemaker in conversation. Whether the subject was fruit, oak, soil or acid Jacob turned it back to the competition and the security of balanced credits and money in the bank.

Your neighbor does it, Jacob would say as he pointed vaguely across a valley. *Why not you? Do your art and let us do your books.* Jacob knew the bourgeois ideology: that every individual, in his own self-interest, considered himself superior to others.

Jacob brought in a new winery every week, loading his accountants with work and frustrating Nora's plans to work part-time and to return to school. The money was good and she had all the work she wanted. But she wanted something more, something without the frailties of a workweek that was no substitute for real life.

Her town was close enough to the Bay Area to command city rents but far enough away to pay country wages. She thought a job in health care would suit her financial needs and local temperament. At age 34 she wasn't getting younger. She needed to enroll in college and the fall deadline was closing in.

Her worries held her as she strutted toward her office. Crossing the avenue she missed a step to the curb, lost her balance, collided with a light post and plopped inelegantly against the sidewalk. A woman walking with a cane approached from one side.

"You OK, darlin'?" she asked.

A man's hand shot into view. It was attached to the sleeve of a dark suit coat. She grasped it and felt herself lifted like a cloud. She turned to thank her savior and saw a familiar face as surprised to see hers as she was to see his.

"Trev..." she mumbled the word without a salutation.

There was nothing to expect. Her former lover and almost husband said nothing until there was nothing left not to say.

"Nora?" he asked.

It was a question with a much larger dimension for Nora than

Trevor ever could have intended. After a cursive, protecting search of his eyes, Nora let go of his hand.

"You shaved your moustache," she announced.

Trevor felt for his upper lip as if trying to hide it.

"Yeah…" he said.

He asked Nora where she was going.

"Work," she answered cautiously.

"You?"

Trevor, his long, muscular frame buttressed by a brown three-piece suit, was going to court.

"A difficult client," he volunteered.

"He wants justice. I want to negotiate. I never want to let a judge decide."

Nora missed most of his words and heard clearly only the sound of his voice. Trevor continued talking until a billowing familiarity—locked into this single and surprising moment—induced in Nora a creeping enchantment. He asked about her hair. She was letting it grow. As he spoke she twirled a few modest curls that did not quite touch her shoulders. Nora had thought for months how she might address Trevor should she see him again. She had not, and now all she could imagine was that, while their relationship was over, it had not actually become final. A wave of warmth passed through her filter and she stood listening to everything Trevor said until he looked at his watch and said he had to leave.

"Could I buy you a drink later?" Trevor said with no reference to any context.

"What time do you get off?"

Trevor sounded serious.

"Why don't you come by," Nora said without guile and not as a question.

Trevor's eyes widened as if he were on the verge of the smallest step toward pleasure. His arms relaxed as he picked up his briefcase.

"You still live on Rose?"

Nora nodded.

Nora wondered why her mother said such terrible things about Mexicans. She hated that Nora lived in Roseland and rarely visited. Nora enjoyed Roseland, its earthy smells and bright colors and the outdoor life of her immigrant neighbors. Children played in the alley behind her and on the street in front. Their chattering Spanish allowed her to think at times she lived in another country. She bought tamales from a truck on the Avenue and arrived home early. She passed the dark boy who cleaned the pool and who stared at her again and followed her with his eyes as she sauntered into her building and turned briefly to give him a coy, responsive glance.

When Trevor arrived she served him tamales with salsa and poured them each a cold glass of a common white. Within ten minutes they were in her bed where her mind now raced with random and inapposite thoughts as Trevor practiced his familiar touches, which in a previous time would have dissolved her into excruciating arousal but that now felt queerly unfamiliar, even forced.

Eventually she passed through feelings of self-limitation, self-hatred and guilt as Trevor touched at last some inner good thing that lifted Nora out of the silence of her empty words and grew her back into the retraceable and unguarded history of a tender love. She was open again, even if just for the moment prior to Trevor's catapulting and disorderly come. She contained his wobbling thrusts to her seemingly infinite depth and to their flinching, spasmodic end.

Trevor rolled over breathless and Nora giggled to channel restlessly her still unrelieved excitement. There were no words until Trevor made some comment about missing dinner while Nora listened to the children laughing outside. She curled into the bow of his body and waited. Nothing else was said for several minutes.

"I have to pee," Nora announced and slipped out of Trevor's grasp to sit up at the side of the bed. She patted his thigh affectionately and stood up.

"What's that?" Trevor pointed to where Nora had been sitting. A widening garnet stain formed a wet V shape on the sheet.

"Oh shit," Nora sighed.

"I'm starting my period."

Trevor looked at her with an expression of sudden horror.

"It's just my monthlies, Trev," Nora said nervously.

"I'll clean it up."

She waddled to the bathroom, one hand holding her vulva as if it were a leaky milk carton. She mumbled a curse under her breath. When she returned with a roll of toilet paper Trevor was already dressed.

"I'm sorry, Nora. I need to go."

Nora stood naked while Trevor bolted out the bedroom as he had done months before when at a resort hotel near Monterey her germinal pregnancy had exploded into a spreading, bleeding sludge that covered her dress, her legs and the carpet. Only then Trevor was running to call a doctor and this time he was simply running. Nora had no tears left, even as her smallest steps toward pleasure were also steps toward the bitter hardening of her pain.

4

Nora had the night to process Trevor's devaluing repulsion of her simple blood, her regulated stain of potential he could not bear to imagine pouring from its source. She had a dream about Trevor's visit that, however mutilated, still served her. Nora would not be his lover, much less his wife. She wondered if she would ever be any-one's wife or mother.

She spent the warm morning indoors, assembling a light breakfast of eggs, blueberries and coffee and watching the news. Television was all-Clinton-all-the-time though there was nothing new to report about his Oval Office sex. The news was old and it seemed the old-er it got the louder it was shouted. How could so much be said so long about a President's penis without anyone saying the word pe-nis? Nora turned off the sound and watched a chubby, grey-haired senator rattle stiffly, point his finger and frown. The women at work knew more than he did. They all knew men better than men knew themselves. A woman's survival still depended on it.

When Nora returned home, she found her parking space taken by a utility truck. She grumbled a curse and drove out of the lot to park on the avenue. She hiked back past the pool to find Jory again sitting outside in his lawn chair. Beside him was a bottle of sparkling wine resting in a bucket filled with ice.

"You want a glass?" he asked her.

"The bottle isn't open," Nora said curtly.

She was impatient to go inside her apartment and drop her heavy purse. She knew she was an ugly mess and wanted to take a bath.

Jory grabbed the bottle, twisted the cork while tilting the bottle slightly, removed the cork as it made a crunchy pop, took a glass and then filled it with spuming, bubbly wine.

"Here," he said pushing the glass toward Nora.

"I'd invite you up but it's blazing upstairs."

Nora took the glass and from it a cool, frothy sip. She swallowed, exhaled and waited.

"Come on in," she said and walked glass in hand down her dark, humid hall.

Jory lifted himself slowly and hobbled after her. Nora had forgotten about his disability and needed at last to make a nurturing hollow from both time and space to accommodate him. She slowed her stride, opened her door wide and took the bucket from him to set like a trophy on the cluttered, scarred Formica of her kitchen counter.

"You make coming home pretty easy," Nora said after another swig of wine.

Jory was quiet as he lifted his glass in a token toast and then squatted carefully over a kitchen chair before falling onto it.

"There," he said through a squint of relief.

"Present and accounted for."

After twenty minutes and two refills Jory's loquacious history poured from him like the wine from its bottle.

"I guess if you can't find your mother, maybe she never existed," he concluded.

Jory was taken from his parents when he was seven years old and grew up without them. He became the ward of more than a half-dozen foster families and ended his adolescence by enlisting in the Army. His most recent stepmother, a middle-aged woman he referred to as Connie, drove him to the induction center.

"It was hard for anyone to keep me around," Jory said.

"I was angry. Well, at least angrier than they were."

Jory's hard life embarrassed him and he gathered from Nora's wilting and distant glances that it might be depressing.

"You have a good day?" Jory lobbed the question at her like a bocce ball and waited for it to stop rolling.

"I've had a bad day," she answered flatly.

"Actually, I've had a bad year. Perhaps I'll have another."

Jory was slowed by Nora's smug pessimism. He asked what had happened.

"I'd rather tell you about my mom," Nora answered.

"She's the mom I wish I didn't have—at least not now. It's not that I don't love her. It's just that her work with me is finished and she doesn't seem to know that yet. Funny that you would not have a mother when you needed one and I have a mother when it's the last thing I need."

As Jory tried to grasp Nora's meaning, there was a knock at her door.

"I'll get it," said Jory, laboring heavily to get out of his chair.

At the door a delivery boy in a red apron handed him a large pizza box and Jory pushed a twenty-dollar bill into his hands.

"You ordered pizza?" Nora asked.

"When?"

Jory was silent for a clumsy moment.

"Before you got home," he answered.

"I thought you'd be hungry."

Nora wrestled with a time frame that made little sense.

"How did you know I'd be home…I mean why did you…?"

As she struggled to comprehend both Jory's timeline and motive, the door opened again. Daniel stood in the doorway.

"What are you doing here?" Nora asked Daniel.

She was surprised but sounded irritated.

"You said you were coming back Saturday."

Daniel surveyed the scene before him, subdividing the inside spaces into the islands held by its occupants. Nora stood near the sink pouring wine into a glass. Jory held in his large, lardy arms the pizza he had ordered.

"Looks like a dinner party," Daniel said finally.

His sober sarcasm offended Nora who was more than slightly drunk.

"This is not a goddamned party," she shouted.

"If it were, you would have received an invitation."

Daniel's eyes lit up with his own hot epiphany.

"If this is not a party, and I'm not invited, then I think I'd better leave."

He backed into the hallway and walked away.

"Shit," Nora muttered as she marched unwillingly toward the door.

"Dan!" she shouted down the hall.

"Dan. Come back."

She heard a car's engine turn over and the low and lowering moan of a vehicle driving away.

Nora saw herself immediately engulfed in a swarm of miscues. Pizza, wine, Jory, mothers, Daniel, all converging in her kitchen like elements of an eerie transformation. Jory began a slow, lumbering march toward the door.

"You too?" Nora asked loudly.

"You're leaving too?"

Jory shrugged.

"Think I might have ruined your evening," he said timorously.

Nora laughed with a vibrant irony that frightened Jory more than an armed enemy.

"Ruined it? Honestly, Jory. There is nothing to ruin. Men are constantly leaving me. Please be my guest."

She threw the door open and waited through Jory's slow, infirm departure. She poured a last glass of wine and stomped and pouted on her way to the bathroom. She slipped into a thin cotton nighty and returned to the living room where she phoned Trevor, hanging up when she heard the start of his recorded message. That was all. She was at last obedient to a law of denial and the free rejection of desire, even in the face of her life's constant invitations.

5

For many weeks Nora recalled how sounds from the living room woke her that night from a deep sleep. She had peeked over the covers to see light leak under the closed bedroom door.

She assumed it was Daniel returning to her. She fell back on her pillow and pretended to sleep. He would have to apologize for leaving her. And he would. She knew it. She waited for him to turn off the light, open the door and creep mutely toward the bed.

Instead, the sounds in her living room grew louder, as if Daniel were moving furniture around, opening cupboards and drawers, picking up objects and dropping them. Irritated, Nora sat up and turned on her lamp.

"Dan..." she called sluggishly.

"Dan, what are you doing? Come to bed."

The door opened.

"Fuck!" shouted a tall, stocky figure, its head shrouded in a black wool ski cap.

Two addled eyes stared at Nora through the cap's thin eyeholes. Two men clamored up behind the one in the doorway, their heads also covered by black ski caps.

"She's here! What the fuck?" one shouted.

The first ran to the bed and grabbed Nora's neck, cupping his gloved hand over her lips. Adrenalin surged in Nora's mouth as she began to struggle.

"Settle down and you won't get hurt, ma'am."

Nora kicked her legs and tried to scream. She tasted the salty leather of the man's glove pushed hard against her cheeks, so hard she could feel her teeth cutting into her tongue. Another man approached and grabbed her ankles.

"Hold her," the first man said to the third.

"Just relax!" he shouted at Nora.

She stopped struggling even as her heart and mind were flooded with invigorating terror. The third man leaned against her head and shoulders to hold her in place while the first pulled tape and a cloth from his pocket.

"This won't hurt," he said as if he were a dentist probing a broken filling.

He forced the cloth between her clenched jaws and frantically wrapped tape over her lips and behind her head, catching her hair as he looped the tape twice around. The motion was quickly confining and as Nora struggled to breathe she loosened one of her arms and grabbed at the man holding her down. Her clutch caught a wad of his ski cap. She tried to hold on and pulled the cap off the man's head. She recognized him immediately. It was the boy who cleaned the pool.

The unmasked youth looked at her, no longer an alien and drained instantly of his menacing strength. Nora's eyes pleaded with him as she gulped a deep breath and as the first man pulled back her arm, alarmed to see the boy without his cap.

"God fucking damn it! Now what do we do? She's seen you!" the first man shouted. He appeared to be the leader and began to bark orders.

"OK. Tie her up. Tie her up good."

He pulled a short length of rope from his jacket and hurled it towards the second man who caught it and quickly bound Nora's ankles. The boy put his cap back on and held Nora against the bed. The boy pushed hard on her shoulders as his elbows dug into her breasts. The big man bound Nora's hands and wrists and wrapped the tape around her waist, lifting her nighty to make a tight hold.

Once she was secure the three men gathered near the door to talk. Nora thrashed uselessly in her bondage. When she heard the men speak, she stopped moving. Amid their whispers, Nora heard only a few words. The leader was furious and talked rapidly, sometimes in Spanish. She thought she heard him say they would have to get rid of her. Nora again struggled, writhing against her bindings and unable to scream. The leader picked up the clock radio sitting on Nora's bureau and tore the power cord out of it. As the others walked back into the living room, he approached Nora slowly, the cord pulled tight between his two outstretched hands.

In the surprising battle between her fear and the men's greed, Nora realized she was little more than an object. Was she going to die? She was killed constantly by daily deaths but it was too soon, and she was not ready, to accept the end of her existence. As her antagonist approached, Nora squirmed like a trapped rat. She could not even speak, to argue her case against a faceless brutality that appeared ready to execute her simply as an expedience in the commission of a theft.

And a theft of what? Her emptied purse lay on the floor, its contents scattered across the rug. Were the possessions they would take from her worth even a hundred dollars? Was this the measurable value of her life? If she could speak, she would swear never to reveal what had happened. *Take my stuff. I give it to you. I give you everything and promise you anything. I'll sign a note that says it is all yours, that I am the thief to want any of it.*

"Sorry, ma'am," the tall, stocky man said as he sulked toward her with the cord. He was the gang leader of his own self, giving himself the order to pull no punches.

"I have to do this."

He hovered for a moment over Nora's violently resisting body, her every muscle taut as she flailed against the tape and twine that held her. A loud crash boomed from the living room followed by angry shouts and more crashes. The tall man turned and ran out of the bedroom. Nora heard yelling, still more slams and crashes and the sound of breaking glass, and then a voice yelled *Come on! Go! Now!* And then silence, or rather something Nora later recalled as an oddly quiet interlude punctuated by a whimpering, steady moan.

Several minutes passed before Nora loosened one of her wrists enough to leverage in a winding motion the freedom of one of her hands. She used this hand to peel at the tape that bound the other. With two hands free she sat up and untied the thin strand of rope binding her ankles. Survival seemed nonsensical after feeling certain her life would end. It was if after witnessing the end of the world, she had emerged alive from her basement.

She staggered toward the living room and peered cautiously in. The moaning continued. At her apartment door she saw the body of a wounded man spread like a carcass across the rug. It was Jory. Next to him was a baseball bat that blocked like a dam a pool of blood formed from the distributaries trickling from an unseen wound at the back of his head. Nora fell to her knees.

"It's OK," she whispered to him.

"You'll be OK, Jory."

She searched for the blood's headwaters and held her hand hard against its wettest surge. Jory's shallow breaths were all she heard until they were snuffed by the urgent swell of approaching sirens.

6

Daniel found Nora in the hospital emergency room. She did not see him as she stood and spoke with two police officers. Her downcast eyes were narrowly focused like those of the sleepless others on call at any hour. She appeared at home in this refuge for the homeless and injured. She was barefoot and bandaged at her ankles and wrists, which she had scraped while breaking her bonds.

Daniel waited and then approached cautiously as the officers walked away. The time between her phone call to him and his arrival was enough for Daniel to assemble an appropriate quantum of shame. Why had he left her alone? What had been so angering that he needed to walk away and leave her unprotected?

Of course, at the time he had no idea she would need protection. And the details of what happened were still sketchy, still without meaning. He did not yet understand how she became the target of a violent robbery. He knew he should have been there to protect her but did not know how.

"Nora," Daniel uttered cautiously.

Nora looked up.

"I'm so sorry," Daniel said without conjecture.

"I should have been…I mean, you needed me and I…"

Nora listened without expression, unimpressed with his stunted attempt at manly contrition. Virility was a gesture and all virilities now aroused Nora's suspicion. She said nothing to complete his thought, nothing to help him appear the tough guy he wished to appear, if not to her at least to himself.

"Let me take you home," he offered as he touched her shoulder.

Nora squirmed away.

"No! Not home. I'm not going home!"

Daniel again apologized and told her he meant his home, that she could spend the night with him and they would figure out in the morning what needed to be done. Nora's shoulders fell as she slipped back into a brooding resignation. Dan waited.

"OK," she said weakly.

Nora had nothing to say on the ride back to Daniel's condo so he stopped talking. Inside, Daniel found Nora's overnight bag and handed it to her along with his blue terrycloth robe. After she showered Daniel turned down the bed but Nora said she wished to sleep on the couch. Daniel appeared hurt but did not object.

"It's been a rough night," he said finally.

"Can I get you anything else?"

Nora appeared strangely vacated, as if some past life had suddenly been annulled. She listened to Daniel's offer with obvious effort and then said no and walked past him to enter his living room alone. Daniel noticed she was shivering and offered her another blanket, which she declined.

"I think Jory may have saved my life," Nora said in the morning as Daniel drove her back to Roseland.

Nora was to meet a detective who would escort her back into her apartment where she could retrieve some belongings. Her unit, along with Jory's, had become a collective crime scene. It would be a few days before she could move back in, if she even wished to.

Daniel had offered his place to Nora indefinitely. He had never said he loved her, wondering timidly for months if he were simply attracted to yet another woman he overvalued or who, perhaps, overvalued him. With the mention of Jory as Nora's savior, Daniel sank farther into his ponderous insecurity and wished he was, or had been, a more alert and decisive lover.

Detective Sam Perales met Nora and Daniel in the parking lot. In the morning heat he still wore a green sheriff's jacket and tie. He was tall, slightly paunchy and sported a thin, black moustache that gave his round face a distinguished, scholarly appearance. He was cordial and shook the hands of both Nora and Daniel.

"We have the suspects," he told Nora who held her hands tightly together and began to cry.

Daniel sensed her piteous relief and brushed her shoulder with his hand.

"The kid was hiding in the pool house and the other two, well they drove west on Highway 12 and I don't know what they were thinking. Our deputies and the CHP cornered them in Valley Ford. Did they think they were going to drive into the ocean?"

Nora followed Detective Perales into her apartment. The pool

31

of blood that had flowed under Jory was gone and a pile of broken glass was swept into a corner of the kitchen.

"Take anything you need," the detective instructed.

As he walked with her into the bedroom he pointed at the ceiling fan.

"Nice feature," he said.

"Ever been a problem for you?"

Nora looked at the detective who absorbed her puzzled look.

"I guess not," he said.

As Nora collected clothes and toilet articles, the detective asked if she could meet with him Friday in his office. He needed her statement.

"I have a few questions," he added.

"And don't bring the boyfriend," he whispered.

"Daniel?" Nora asked from behind a vacant stare.

"He's not my boyfriend."

The detective nodded and stepped outside.

Nora pulled two dresses from the closet, took three changes of panties and two bras from her dresser and grabbed shorts, tops and a swimming suit. She packed a travel bag with cosmetics and scooped up a near full box of tampons. She took one last look and stepped out of the bedroom.

"What's happened to Jory?" she asked the detective as they walked toward the front door.

"Serious condition," he said officiously.

"I can't tell you much more. You'll need to check with the hospital."

Nora left her apartment, the promise of its protection now an implication of failure. She would never hear the wind against her house—any house—the same way again. Instead of a lovely and furious howling with no power over her, the wind—at least for a while—would roar through the walls to infest her vigilant sleep and bad dreams.

"You can move back this weekend," the detective said.

Nora shook her head.

"Do you have a place to stay?" he asked.

Perales said there was a crime victim fund that would buy her a room in a hotel for up to a week, if needed. Nora said no. She could make it to the weekend on Daniel's couch. He was in no position to push her any closer to his bed and she knew it. If he wanted her, and he seemed to, Nora knew he would humor her, tend to her, but leave her alone at the slightest hint of trouble. It had the feel of a manipulation, but so did survival.

Men rarely modeled reality. She thought herself better than that. If she were not living in reality now, what could reality ever be?

7

Nora phoned her office the next morning and told Dorine to tell Jacob she wouldn't be coming in.

"There was a robbery and I…"

Dorine interrupted her.

"We know, Hon," Dorine said.

"It's all over the front page and the radio. That poor young man. What a hero. God, we're so glad nothing happened to you. We're all praying he makes it."

Nora was speechless. Dorine put Jacob on the line.

"Are you OK?" asked Jacob with unusual concern.

"Take the rest of the week and into next if you need it," he nearly shouted into the phone.

"What a brave boy. We're taking up a collection for him at Rotary today, Nora. What's his name…Jory, yeah. A war veteran. What's his last name? Where should we send the money? And if anyone wants to speak with you, where would we…"

Nora held the phone away, dazed by a new celebrity that kept company with her worst fears. She did not want a story nor did she wish to read it, did not want to be a subject of discussion, did not want to see or be seen. She thanked Jacob without saying for what.

She reached Daniel at work. He was called out of a sales meeting and said he intended to phone her.

"It's news, Nora. The story says burglars broke into your apartment and Jory heard them and came downstairs. He carried a baseball bat and got into your apartment through the open door. When two burglars came out of your bedroom he whacked them with the bat but a third followed and wrestled Jory to the ground. Then the burglar took the bat and pounded Jory on the back of his head. Several blows."

Nora choked on an incipient sob. Daniel heard her and waited.

"The burglars panicked when your neighbor opened her door and saw them. The rest is what you told me. So I guess Jory really did save your life. Has anyone phoned you yet? The detective? A reporter?"

"I don't want to talk to anyone," Nora sputtered.

Daniel said she could stay at his house until things blew over. Nora did not think things would blow over.

She asked Daniel if the story said anything about Jory's condition.

"Sounds bad," Daniel answered.

"They're saying life threatening injuries. The cops are trying to reach his family, if he has one. Do you need me to come over? I can leave work early."

"I'm fine," she answered.

"I'll see you tonight. I'm moving back to the apartment on Sunday."

"You don't have to," Daniel offered.

"Yes I do," Nora responded.

She did have to. The fear of returning to her home was something like the fear of flying. To conquer it she had to do it. She would not be thrown from her life, thrown into the shadows of a dependence on others. What happened was her one encounter with a fateful spin of the wheel. Here number had come up once. It never would again. She had to believe that or she would stop living her own life and depend eternally on the kind indulgence of others.

"And you're going to move back into that pit?" Nora's mother screamed at her.

"Are you insane? Your perfectly nice and considerate boyfriend wants to put you up in his big condo in the country and instead you want to move back into that hellhole in the middle of a slum where you were nearly killed? God dammit, Nora! What's your fucking problem with sweet, successful men? "

Nora held the receiver away to protect her ears, and her psyche, from another of her mother's reproaching assaults.

"They caught the burglars, mom," Nora reported without emotion.

"I'll be OK."

Her reassurance was useless. Nora's mother would always blame her daughter for all the poor choices that appeared to have ruined her life. As if even her miscarriage had been a bad choice. She said once, and only once after Nora stopped speaking to her, that her daughter should have waited to marry before getting pregnant.

Nora reminded herself her mother loved her. There was no father, not in Nora's memory, and the men who passed through the porous walls of her childhood homes fared no better than Nora and few stayed very long to absorb her mom's stormy resentments. Mother's sharp, angry words used to hurt Nora. Now Nora heard them without emotion, did not take them personally and instead forgave in her only parent all that was merely pathological. Nora's circumspect detachment was the slender thread that kept a daughter's love alive.

Detective Perales spread eight photographs across the empty surface of his desk and asked Nora to pick out the suspects. She saw the pool boy's photo immediately and pointed to it. Perales set it aside.

"And the others?" he asked.

"They wore hoods. You know that. I didn't see their faces."

Nora sounded frustrated. Perales said the pool boy worked as a scout for the burglars. Cleaning the pools at apartments gave him information about who was home and when.

"But the others..." Nora shook her head.

Perales said they might have a problem if the burglars could not be identified.

"But you have the pool boy," Nora argued.

"He's not talking," the detective answered curtly.

"*Sureños*, probably. The boy won't squeal."

"What are you going to do?" Nora asked through a tremor of refreshed terror.

"You can't just let them go."

Perales engaged his practiced professional warmth intended to fabricate closeness when he and a subject were miles apart.

"Actually, we have a video recording of the assault on you. We have the suspects' voices and film of the clothes they were wearing. We even have the sound of one of the burglars calling the other by name."

Perales pulled out two photographs from the pile he gave Nora.

"Here they are."

Nora stared at the faces of two frowning males, posed as if in a line-up, their eyes expressionless. They appeared similarly heavy set and jowly in a way that suggested they might be brothers. They appeared much older than the pool boy.

"A video...how?" Nora asked confused.

"First I need to ask you who installed the ceiling fan in your bedroom?" Perales asked.

Nora looked up suspiciously.

"Why?" she asked.

"It's important to what I have to tell you."

Nora said Jory installed the fan. Perales leaned forward as if to affirm his empathic docility in a way that would invite Nora's trust.

"Jory has been videotaping what goes on in your bedroom. There is a pinhole camera lodged in the fan connected through the floor to a video camcorder in his apartment. We have a tape of the entire attack."

Nora's eyes widened in a way Perales expected they would.

"They...you...what?"

Nora tried to visualize her apartment under constant surveillance without placing herself in it. She at first could not, indeed refused, to imagine she was being watched, and recorded, in her bedroom.

"You have...the attack...the...you have it on tape?" she narrowed her line of questioning.

"Then what's the problem?" Nora challenged Perales.

The detective said there were other things on the tape.

"Intimate things," he said.

Nora's eyes narrowed.

"To introduce the tape into court we have to say where it came from and why it was made," Perales said.

"Can you do that?"

Nora asked what she needed to do.

"It would be best if you allowed us to bring charges against Jory. Unless he had your permission, what he did was illegal. And if he had your permission..."

Nora asked how many tapes they found.

"Just two. There are likely more. We need a search warrant to find them and for that we need to charge him. And you would need to file a complaint."

Nora sought a premise for her resistance.

"But Jory…he saved my life…and he's fighting for his," she offered with what sounded to Perales like withering conviction.

"I don't care about any other tapes…"

Perales continued to play the good cop. He told Nora he understood she might need to think about what he had told her.

"Go home, maybe talk it over with your boyfriend."

Perales knew Daniel also was on the tape and would know that as well and not be happy about it.

Nora lashed back.

"No! He's not to be involved. And he's not my boyfriend."

Perales abandoned truth to relativity and Nora to her power.

"I'll phone you tomorrow," he said.

Nora stood, anxious to leave.

Perales apologized for surprising her.

"Surprised?" Nora blurted sarcastically.

Her recent life seemed a constant and perplexing experience of offensive, disrupting surprises.

8

Nora swept. She cleared away the shadows and smells of her apartment. She scrubbed at the stains and dumped the debris that divided her from her home. She stood on a high stool and examined the ceiling fan in her bedroom. She saw a clear globule of glass but nothing behind it.

It was as if she were seeking something under a veil of a nature other than her own. It was hard to imagine the crumpled, limping Jory as an erotomanic voyeur. Did he film her with Trevor the previous week? He must have. At first she wondered what Jory watched of her life, her sleep, her sex. She felt anger rise but not very high. She was a private person up to a point. If such a calculated and unknown exposure had saved her life, who was she to complain?

While she cleaned, the phone rang. It was Daniel. He asked how she was, a question he always asked now as if his perfunctory queries would prove the truth of his caring. She wondered if Daniel really knew how to care, his largest concern appearing to be his own that Nora would leave him, be done with him, no longer take his pleading calls. Could he help?

"I'm fine, Daniel. I don't need your help," she said plainly.

There was a long and enervating pause.

"Is it something I've said? Something I've done…or not done?" he asked.

Nora did not answer. After what she had been through, Daniel's self-absorbed fears appeared trivial.

"I need a few days. Maybe a week. Maybe more. That's all," Nora said.

She hung up the phone and picked up a newspaper, the first she'd purchased in years, to read the latest coverage of what had happened. Passing days were shrinking the space given to the burglary. On page eight she found below the fold a six-paragraph update with the headline *Veteran who saved Roseland woman still critical*. She was not identified this time and wondered if she ever would be again.

The story dwelled on the condition of Joshua "Jory" Sullivan, age 29, disabled Gulf War veteran who apparently heard burglars enter the apartment of his neighbor, a single woman in her thirties, and went downstairs with a baseball bat to stop them. He was assaulted and badly injured. The suspects were captured and were being held without bail.

As she watched a glazier replace the broken glass of the wing window her attackers used to gain entry, Nora saw a county sheriff's patrol car pull into the parking lot. Detective Perales walked toward her apartment. There was a comforting lag between Nora's healing repression and healing recollection and she did not welcome another disturbing conversation with a cop. She walked outside to head him off. He seemed to recognize her resistance. It created between them an empty, paralyzing interval.

"I brought you a copy of the tape," he said from a distance.

He held up a manila envelope stuffed with an object obviously hard and rectangular.

"You need to see what we have, what your neighbor saw," he added.

"Why do I need to?" Nora asked defiantly.

"It might help you decide, that's all," the detective answered cautiously.

Nora let the detective approach and hand her the tape.

"Phone me," he said firmly before turning to walk away.

Perales left the impression of a strong man who at one time might have been a compliant, pleasing youth, the two merged now in the engaging assertion of a dominant male. He seemed to count on force and charm to turn Nora into an accuser. She would watch the video, he thought. Nothing else was needed.

And Nora did watch. Once alone, she popped the VHS cassette into her player. The view was at first strangely distorted, a wide view of her bedroom with the bed in the upper right corner but fully revealed. The grainy image was a mush of bleeding colors that looked more like black and white. She heard her voice though initially she was out of sight. The picture was not entirely clear but the sound was perfect. She heard herself shouting at Daniel from the bathroom as he sat naked on the bed and waited for her.

She remembered the time but not the date. She watched for twenty minutes as she ambled into view also naked in the illumination of the bedside lamp, which was ample to reveal every touch, rub and thrust of her sex with Daniel. She listened to herself moan and come. She heard her encouraging words that at the time were offered anxiously. She recalled worrying Daniel would not finish, would not hold his erection for the long time it often took him to orgasm. She watched amazed at her body—her hips fatter than she imagined, her breasts as perfect as she thought them to be. She watched her performance, knowing how it was one, and now concerned it was good enough, real enough to be convincing.

In an unsettling jolt, the tape switched to another day and time, showing Nora alone on her bed, removing her swimsuit, touching and then rubbing herself into another come, one she acknowledged as more intense than the one with Daniel. She watched through Trevor's visit and their sex, aware now of her clinched eyes and bristling ecstasy while Trevor appeared to watch her cautiously and occasionally turn to check the clock on her dresser. She saw herself ravished not by the Trevor over her and inside her, but by the idea he triggered within her, the particular voice, touch and posture formulated from within and that were irreplaceably her own. She registered the embarrassment of her bleeding and Trevor's quick departure. She saw with graphic and heartbreaking confirmation he did not care.

The last segment showed the invasion of the burglars. It was obvious Jory also thought the noise from the living room signaled Daniel's return to her apartment. She watched in horror as in a very few minutes her groggy awakening became a helpless confrontation with her likely killer, a threat she faced with what now appeared to be uncanny calm. She heard clearly the words of the men in her room as they argued whether and how to kill her.

"This is Perales," the detective answered.

"This is Nora," a woman's voice announced.

"I need a few more days to decide," she said.

"Sure. Sure. All you need," Perales said.

Nora thought he sounded like Daniel.

"Have you watched this?" Nora asked directly.

Perales was silent.

"Some of it," he answered compliantly.

"How long was Jory taping me?" Nora asked.

Perales didn't know.

"But if you press charges we can search for other tapes," he offered eagerly.

"They must be around somewhere."

"Has anyone else looked at the tape?" Nora asked again.

The detective was silent for a moment.

"An assistant DA…a woman," Perales emphasizing the word woman.

He thought that might be helpful for Nora to hear.

It wasn't.

9

It occurred to Nora that making use of another human being could be another way to love. The thought came as she walked along the hospital's shadowless corridor and entered a room where Jory lay on a high, mechanized bed, his head wrapped in heavy bandages, his body covered by a long, white sheet. Nora had described herself to the nurse as a concerned neighbor though the nurse's eyes eventually registered Nora's place in Jory's misfortune. Nora was news: the subject of a current story available to anyone.

Nora stood beside the bed and its motionless occupant. She searched for a recognizable feature and settled on Jory's nose. His nostrils flared with every labored breath.

Why were you watching me? she asked without speaking. *What use did you make of me? Was it for sex?* If so, it was an elaborate seduction for so lonely a conquest. She wondered if what Jory took she might have given freely if he'd asked. She could not say what she would have done before the robbery. Only that she owed Jory her life and now would give him anything.

Nora heard footsteps behind her and turned to face a tall, gaunt man in his fifties wearing a wrinkled blue T-shirt, scuffed jeans and a Giants baseball cap. His pointy leather cowboy boots clacked as he crossed the floor.

"Howdy," the man said ingenuously.

"I'm Jory's uncle. Who are you?"

Nora backed away from the bed to give the man room to approach.

"I'm his neighbor. I didn't know Jory had an uncle. He said he didn't have any family."

Nora answered without saying her name.

The tall man said he wasn't Jory's biological uncle, just the brother of his foster mom. He went to the side of the bed and touched Jory's arms searchingly. He stroked what he could touch of Jory's forehead.

"I love him like my own," said the uncle.

"He spent his last two years in high school at my house. Jory was a wild handful. He wanted to join the army and no one objected. Anything to get him out of here. He was headed for trouble and we

43

all thought the Army would tame him. We didn't know he'd end up in a war."

"The war sure took a toll on him," Nora said, breaking a long silence.

The man relaxed slightly and introduced himself as Uncle Stewart but did not give his last name. He continued to stare into Jory's flat stillness.

"He's not asleep," he said.

"I don't know if he's even in there."

Stewart recalled Jory's last leave before shipping out to Iraq.

"He looked so strong and handsome in his uniform. He loved his new life as a soldier. The army taught him electronics and put him to work in communications. He had a talent for tinkering. I knew that. He was a crappy student but he could fix anything with wires in it."

Stewart said Jory wanted to become an electrician when his duty was up. He was learning photography.

"And then the war. And the bomb that nearly killed him. He survived but what a toll. What a useless waste."

Stewart stifled a sad, billowing groan.

Nora walked toward him and reached to place a hand on Stewart's shoulder.

"Not a waste," Nora said.

"Everyone knows Jory is a hero."

She saw in Stewart's eyes the realization that the nearly dead were not really alive but also the hope that death was temporary.

Nora opened her door on Tuesday morning and greeted Gabriela, the across-the-hall neighbor. Her toddler son tugged at Gabriela's rosy red, floral shift as she handed Nora a warm baking dish filled with two neat rows of enchiladas slathered in a syrupy red sauce.

"*Para usted*," she said.

"You please take these."

Nora thanked her. She liked where she lived. Gabriela had called the police the night of the robbery when she heard the scuffle in Nora's apartment.

"You're a dear, Gabriela."

Nora thanked her.

Her neighbor blushed and lifted her fussy toddler into her arms.

"You take care," she said to Nora.

"We all watch now. We help each other. You see."

Nora viewed the toddler with tender envy. Childhood was a radiant wilderness, unfettered and physically joyful for the child who was cared for, loved, and protected by a faithful mother.

The phone rang and Nora ran to answer it. It was Detective Perales. He asked her if she were ready to press charges.

"Do I have a choice?" she asked sarcastically, set off by the detective's apparent confidence that, presumably offended by Jory's secret videotape, she would now cooperate with his investigation.

"Sure, you have a choice," answered the detective.

"You can help us nail these guys or we can drop the charges and let them go. It's up to you."

Nora did not believe him.

"Jory saved my life. Can't we just leave him alone? He's a gravely injured veteran and if he hadn't been watching me I'd be dead now. He's had a hard time and a hard life. Besides, I don't want this to come out. It's embarrassing for me. Do you care about that at all?"

Perales waited a moment to slip credibly from bad cop to good cop.

"No one will blame you for being outraged by Jory's recordings and also grateful for his coming to save you. You had no control over this. If anything, you are as much a victim of a pervert as you are of the robbers."

"Jory a pervert? He's not a pervert." Nora responded rigidly.

"And I'm not outraged by what he did."

"Oh..." Perales uttered in surprise.

"Really? Not a pervert?"

"Look, I'll testify for you," Nora offered.

"But I don't want Jory's tapes involved if it means I have to do anything to hurt him."

Perales waited again. He was running out of time and options.

"Take a couple more days," he said pliantly.

45

He was still the good cop though he could still deliver bad news.

"If you can't help us we'll need to subpoena the tape as evidence. It won't help us if you're a hostile witness against your attackers. Really, ma'am…"

Perales tried to sound both firm and entreating.

Nora had no response other than to say good-bye and hang up the phone. It seemed farfetched but not impossible she and her attackers might end up on the same side of a courtroom. Nora would need to create a provisional coherence to explain the terms of what felt like a failing life.

10

Sleepless, Nora felt herself on call at any hour. Where did a secret begin and where did it end? She was a secret to herself now, unable to process the difficult aspects of love that in some mysterious but provident way involved making use of another human being. She could not rest, not even lie down, during her first few nights spent back in her apartment.

Her mother phoned one evening to ask about Daniel, and not about her.

"We're breaking up," Nora said directly.

Her mother released a berating sigh.

"What is it now?" she asked wearily.

Nora said Daniel was not who or what she needed.

"I've been unresponsive. He hasn't phoned in a week. I think he's gotten the memo."

Nora's sarcasm was intentional. She wished to provoke her mother into another scolding rant; to hear it again and perhaps for one last time, after which she would run away, find another town and another job and change her name.

"God, Nora, you are such an idiot. Daniel is as rich as Trevor. And he wants to take care of you. Why can't you just go with it? Anything reasonable is so damned difficult for you."

Nora's mother thought of money as life's only reliable currency. She did not register how all its engendered conflicts could extend a polluting avarice into the tender corners of love since tender love was not at all her priority. Her mother reduced all relationships to their material origins and when Nora was a child never missed an opportunity to champion the strength of this reality principle. Now Nora saw her mother as economically impotent and her alleged sobriety increasingly a form of indulgent wrath.

"Frankly, mom, I don't give a fuck," Nora said and then hung up.

The phone rang again and Nora did not answer.

"Well, she may be an unlikable bitch, but you have to admit Hillary got a raw deal."

Dorine defended the decision of the president's wife to stand by him while JoAnne replied with a cynical smirk.

"It's bullshit. They aren't a couple. They're a corporation," she said.

Nora had been in the office for an hour and accomplished nothing. Jacob had told her she could take all the time she needed from work, but after two weeks his calls were more frequent and his insistent interest in her welfare just a red flag that she was needed back on the job.

Nora dreaded a call from Detective Perales. Days had passed since their last conversation and the detective's barely veiled ultimatum that she cooperate with the prosecution.

The phone rang at her desk and she knew it was Perales. She waited, picking up the receiver at the last ring.

"I've got some good news and some bad news, Nora," the detective said.

His tone was distant but laced with enough modulation to sound unthreatening.

"The good news is that the pool boy has cracked and agreed to testify against his accomplices in exchange for a reduced charge. Guess the idea of going to trial as an adult in a murder case was enough to freak him out. A sixteen-year-old boy facing life in prison. He couldn't wait to squeal. Anyway, we don't need the tape. We still want your testimony about the attack and burglary. But we don't need to bring up Jory. I thought you should know right away."

The detective's words grew in Nora the first swell of incipient relief left incomplete by what he had not said.

"Murder? What murder?" Nora asked hesitantly.

"Yeah," Perales muttered quietly and waited.

"That's the bad news. Jory died this morning."

Nora felt the choke in her throat become a full and throttling sob. Dorine and JoAnne turned toward her and approached.

"I'm sorry, Nora," the detective offered with smooth, considerate gravity.

"Not as sorry as I am," Nora sputtered and collapsed onto her desk.

JoAnne wrapped her arms around Nora's quivering shoulders while Dorine hung up the phone.

Nora rested in her bed with the silence of her body until she heard the sound of footsteps overhead. It was late morning of another day off work courtesy of her boss Jacob who was shaken to learn the local hero had died. Jacob likely visualized himself photographed by the newspaper as he handed Jory a check at a Rotary club meeting. Instead, Jacob offered to pay for Jory's funeral until told by Uncle Stewart there wouldn't be one. With no other outlet for his good will he turned to Nora and gave her three days of bereavement leave.

Nora jumped up from her bed and into a pair of shorts and a sweatshirt. Barefoot, she climbed cautiously upstairs and approached the open door of Jory's apartment. Inside she saw the back of Uncle Stewart beyond a stack of empty boxes. He was bent over to investigate the contents of a low bookshelf. She called to him by name and he turned to see her.

"I'm afraid the boy was a bit of a slob," Stewart complained affectionately.

"Can I help?" Nora asked.

Stewart took in the full view of her in a way that made Nora feel watched and examined.

"Well, maybe you can," he answered brightly.

"I've got to get his stuff out of here by Saturday. The landlord is champing to get a new renter. I'll show you around. Tell me if there's anything you can take."

Nora followed Stewart as he toured the apartment. The spare living room was furnished with a VCR and an older 21-inch television along with a small couch and cracked particleboard side table. The kitchen was empty with a few dishes in the cabinets and a few more dirty in the sink.

"I'll wash them," Nora offered.

Stewart smiled and accepted.

She followed him past the bathroom (*God, don't go in there* he warned) and into the bedroom. The curtains were drawn. Stewart flipped the light switch and, instead of the light, turned on Jory's ceiling fan.

"My Jesus. The boy had at least some taste for comfort," he said to himself.

Nora wandered toward the center of the room and saw the rug

pushed back where a patch of floor was under construction.

"Landlord said he's replacing some stained floorboards," Stewart said.

Does he know? Nora searched Stewart's face for something resembling guile and found nothing.

Stewart pulled from the drawer of the bed table a half-full bottle of Jack Daniels.

"Doesn't surprise me," Stewart said as if embarrassed.

"One of Jory's dads started him early. Thought it was funny to give a six-year-old a couple of drinks and watch him bounce around the living room. That might have been OK up to a point, except he also beat the living tar out of him."

Nora had her own regrets about the luck of the family draw but her small life was never at risk. She could not grasp the terror of Jory's early childhood, a terror that might have made the brotherhoods of war appear an antidote to suffering. For a moment Nora's history bled into the artifacts of Jory's and she began to imagine the grounds of a common commencement of their lives that had pushed both to the sidelines of experience. Trauma may have robbed Jory of a social conscience, but not his creativity.

Nora noticed the walls were bare except for an American flag draped and sagging over the unmade bed's headboard.

"I'll clean the kitchen now," Nora said and left the room while Stewart shoveled through the drawers of Jory's large, wobbly dresser.

In the hallway she passed a shelf filled with movie videos, their colorful boxes aligned in alphabetical order down to the bottom shelf where her eyes were drawn to a separate row of unmarked cases. She counted about a dozen and opened a box to see a cassette tagged with a white sticker and the handwritten phrase *Nora 6-13 long night.* She opened a few others and found cassettes similarly marked with her name, a date, and an obscure comment apparently intended to jar Jory's memory of its content.

Nora waited a few moments and returned to the bedroom.

"I've found something I'd like to have," she told Stewart who turned to welcome her interest in anything of Jory's disorderly legacy.

"He has a lot of videos. I love movies. Could I buy them?"

"No…" Stewart said thoughtfully.

"No…no way," he repeated firmly.

Nora froze with fear. Was the good uncle in on Jory's secret? Had he discovered Jory's tapes and watched them? If so, he now owned them and there was nothing she could do.

Stewart looked again at the shelves loaded with cassettes.

"You won't pay for them. Just take 'em. They're yours."

Yes, in fact, they really are mine, thought Nora as she pulled a large empty box out of the living room and began hurriedly to load videos into it, the unmarked videos first. She then dragged the big box out of the apartment and down the stairs, pushing it into her bedroom after locking both her front door and the bedroom's. It was too late for Uncle Stewart to change his mind and, anyway, she would not answer the door. She took the unmarked videos out of the box and wrapped her arms around them as she fell onto the bed.

If love were the encounter of two solitudes, she thought, it was first provoked by the view of one's own experience of desire. This was Jory's view, which was not of her but of himself watching her, caring about her in a way that enriched the cultivation of his loneliness. It was as far as he could take love in his sad, broken state. But it was real love. And of course he acted instantly to save her life, willingly aware it might be the final and full measure of his own life's perpetually subverted promise.

JUST MY
NEIGHBORS

1

"**D**o you think it was something you said?"

Garyn shrugged at his wife's question.

"I didn't call anyone names, if that's what you mean."

Garyn was defensive and his wife knew better than to press him, to challenge his self-owned and absorbing version of events. Nor could she express her dismay he had lost another job. They traveled so far to make a new life: from Seattle to San Francisco with the expressed intent of starting over.

"And this damned apartment. How do we end up with the only sixth floor unit without a view?"

Garyn tried to change the subject of Tania's disappointment—his unemployment—to the subject of his own disappointment—their small Russian Hill apartment, subsidized in part by Tania's father and that had no view other than the wall of windows facing them from the building across the alley.

"Does anything work for you?"

Tania begged for hope from a place of weariness.

Garyn heard his wife's rising exasperation and had the good spousal sense to stop talking. He took another sip of wine and let a long pause gestate between them while he weighed her resentment.

"A computer. Who's supposed to know how to use a computer? I know the keyboard but there's no damn logic to anything else," Garyn billowed.

"I'm a salesman. Why do I have to build my ads on a TV screen? It's absurd. The publisher's a dope to be sold a bill of goods like that. He must have paid a fortune for all those machines and if you ask me, they're useless. I was his most successful salesman. But I couldn't sell because I was chained to his fucking computer."

Tania's quizzical expression suggested if Garyn had been so successful as a salesman why had he been fired?

"I suppose there's a learning curve," she said.

"Our school secretary struggled to learn the computer program. She hated it at first but seems to like it now."

Tania responded soberly, suspicious their conversation was going to get lost, as it did frequently, in Garyn's perpetual life story of failure at the hands of others.

Garyn knew this. He could not have stayed married to Tania without the self-effacing charm that in every argument he invariably saved for last.

"You're right, honey," he answered in a somber tone that moved elegantly into the warbling warmth of supplication.

"I'm sorry."

These were the magic words.

"Jack said he'd give me a good recommendation. I'll hit the streets tomorrow."

He thanked his wife for her support and patience and offered to take her to dinner on Polk Street.

"The Thai place. You love it. My treat."

Tania weighed the consequences of staying out late and staying up later on a Tuesday night. A class of third graders would be waiting for her at 7:55 Wednesday morning an hour away in Foster City.

"We'll be fine," Garyn reassured Tania before stuffing a forkful of noodles into his mouth.

"This town has plenty of sales jobs."

Tania's smile faded.

"It also has plenty of salespeople. And a lot of them can work on computers."

Garyn heard his wife's barely concealed bitterness.

"Now don't go negative on me," he replied.

Negativity got Garyn through much of his life but he would decide how and when.

Dinner was otherwise a success. Garyn drew Tania's attention to her teaching, listening patiently as she described the inner workings of a chaotic third grade classroom. He convinced her to order a second glass of wine and retreated in silence as her loosened lips fluttered volubly. Even if the details bored him, Tania's chance to tell them made her very happy. They glided home tractable and satisfied.

In their darkened living room Tania approached the window to draw the curtains. When Garyn returned from a trip to the bathroom he saw Tania still at the window and still in darkness. He walked up behind her.

"What do you see?" he asked.

His approach surprised her.

"Oh, nothing," she said as if embarrassed.

Garyn searched the skyline's inky shadows.

"Actually, down there."

Tania pointed toward a window of the apartment building behind theirs. Garyn searched a few floors below.

"Over farther—to the right," Tania directed.

Garyn found the warm orange glow of a low-lighted kitchen. He saw what appeared to be the edge of a wide table on which something bounced with rhythmic fervor.

"Are those people?" Tania asked.

"Are they screwing?"

Garyn looked back at Tania. He felt the advancing edge of a sexual curiosity Tania usually hid from him until in times of arousal it was upon her and she could not help being seen. Otherwise Tania's animal was contained and did not peep and in a way that only impelled Garyn's insatiable curiosity about it.

"Let's find out," he said but not too eagerly lest he curb her arable urges with the aggressive advance of his own.

He walked quickly to the hall closet and pulled from the top shelf a pair of binoculars. He returned to the window, lifted them to his eyes to adjust the eyepieces and focus. He smiled and handed the binoculars to Tania.

"Here," he said calmly.

"Have a look."

Tania took them and lifted the eyepieces to her eyes. Her surprise opened her mouth as she looked back at Garyn and then back through the binoculars. Garyn knew what she saw: the bare and widely opened legs of a woman, her body pushed back onto a kitchen table while a muscular young man, his shirt off and his pants at his ankles, stood thrusting hard and fast into her. The angle of access hid the woman above her breasts and cut off the man's face at the chin. But the view, brightened and intensely magnified by the lenses, amplified the action. The sex was furious and seemed to have arrived at its point of no return. Even without binoculars, Garyn could see the woman's legs arch and fidget in hungry coordination with the exertions of her lover. Minutes passed, Tania quiet though Garyn noticed her breathing quicken and her hands tremble slightly.

"Oh my god," she sighed.

Garyn asked Tania for a look but she did not hear him and kept watching. Garyn saw the figures stop, stand and appear to move to the floor.

"What are they doing now?" Garyn asked.

"They're…he's on the floor and she's holding his…no, she's moving…she's on top and they're…I can see her face…oh my god…"

Garyn stepped behind Tania and leaned his chest with gentle assurance into her back.

"Let me steady you," he said as he put his hands on her shoulders.

He felt her short, excited breaths. He let his hands fall to her waist and waited.

"Oh…oh my god…" Tania shouted.

"She's…are they finished?"

Garyn saw the couple separate and leave the kitchen.

"Where did they go?" Tania asked with ingenuous disappointment.

"Probably to the bedroom," Garyn answered.

A light went on in an adjacent window.

"They're in the bedroom," Tania reported.

Garyn saw a naked woman approach the window and pull the

curtains closed.

"Awww…" Tania moaned.

She dropped the binoculars on a chair and leaned back into Garyn's chest. A moment passed.

"Garyn?" Tania asked.

Garyn nodded.

"Take off your pants and get on the couch," she commanded.

"Yes, ma'am," Garyn answered in mock obedience.

"Don't talk, Garyn," Tania ordered as she unbuttoned her skirt and slipped out of her panties.

"I'm yours," Garyn responded frivolously.

"Don't say a single word, Garyn. I mean it."

It was an arousing ultimatum; as if Garyn spoke again he might be sent to the principal's office or given a time-out.

2

Garyn slithered stubbornly from bed. He knew his wife had been up for an hour. From the acute and clanging tones rendered by rattling pots, he also knew she was angry.

"You OK?" he asked as he stood in the kitchen doorway.

She was dressed for school in a tight collared white blouse and billowing blue cotton skirt. He wore only his striped boxers.

"I'm late," Tania stammered.

"Maybe I'll get fired, too."

Her tone was impatient and contemptuous. Garyn retreated into the hall, nearly naked and perhaps fully ashamed.

"Oh, honey," Tania shouted as she ran after him.

Garyn knew what to expect. He turned and hugged her. She apologized. His petulant silence made room for little else.

"You were a good boy last night," she purred.

And then she was gone.

"Bye."

Her last shout was timed to the slam of the front door.

Garyn spent much of his waking life watching people. He poured milk into a bowl of cornflakes and sat at the window. He searched the opposite building and found the scene of the previous evening's performance. Bedroom curtains remained closed but a woman in a burgundy robe marched back and forth across the kitchen floor, disappearing occasionally from Garyn's limited angle of view. He searched the building's other windows and found several open to the lives lived within. Those directly across from his were most accessible and he watched as couples collaborated briefly in kitchens and dining rooms before vanishing, presumably to their jobs or appointments.

A child dashed between a kitchen and a dining room to find his coat and a book. Most windows were wide and long, running ceiling to floor. Bedroom windows were more shallowly framed and hid their standing occupants below the waist, though the open bedroom windows on the floors below him revealed beds and carpets. The farther down he looked the steeper and more narrow his angle of view. On a second floor he spied an open bedroom with a limited view of the upper third of an unmade bed, pillows thrown askew just out of frame.

Without a job, Garyn was free to walk the streets. He loaded a role of Ektachrome into his FM2 and packed it and a long lens into a camera bag. He left his building at the Filbert Street entrance and walked up the hill to Polk. No shower. No shave.

He felt like a vagabond only a day after Jack called him into his office to tell Garyn things weren't working out as he had hoped. Maddy had been Jack's ad manager for four years and in just two months Garyn had her climbing the walls.

"What do you have against her?" Jack asked.

Garyn had shrugged.

"She's the one with the problem…and that uppity god damned attitude," Garyn declared.

But Jack wasn't listening.

"You mean uppity as in uppity black woman?" Jack asked bitterly.

"I'm only saying she could use some manners. And she dresses like a dyke."

Garyn knew immediately it was the wrong response, especially with the OJ Simpson trial in the news and on TV all night and all day. Race was suddenly and everywhere a very sensitive issue but Garyn didn't care. He had been fired before. He would work again. But not today.

Today he was an artist with a camera and with the whole afternoon ahead of him. Tania might ask later about his job search, which he would then promise to start tomorrow. Would she tell her rich dad Cas that Garyn was out of work? He'll go crazy, thought Garyn. He doesn't like me. At 37, Garyn's age fell nearly halfway between Tania's and her father's; giving her dad the concern his son-in-law was either a patriarch or a predator.

When Cas Bryant arrived in Seattle for Garyn and Tania's wedding, Garyn also had just been fired. Garyn told Cas these things happened in the newspaper business. Cas thought Garyn too old to still be bouncing around but then Garyn found a part-time job as a photographer for a community weekly. It didn't pay what sales paid but it was a job. Cas drove back to Marin and Tania began her student teaching. Just take care of my daughter Cas had said to Garyn, the last words spoken between them.

Crouching behind a blind of trees in a park west of Fort Mason, Garyn pointed his camera at a man and woman cuddling on the lawn. The late afternoon sun silhouetted them in the foreground of its blooming radiance. It was a crisp fall day and as a cool wind scuttled over the grass the couple tightened their embrace. Garyn began the day photographing trees, mountains, architecture, withering vines and the curl of waves rolling across the bay. But people interested him more than nature and intimate people most of all.

The couple's posture shifted as they grappled for leverage through a long and muggy kiss until the man looked directly at Garyn who dropped his camera and ducked quickly away. The man flinched and then flared, propped suddenly and threateningly on his knees as Garyn hurried down a path toward the Marina. He heard an angry yell and accelerated his pace without looking back. The reflection of his subjects had been dissolved like a still pool hit with a splashing stone.

Tania found her husband sitting in the living room, watching their window as he might their television.

"What do you see?" she asked.

"What's not to see?" he answered glibly.

"That was quite a show last night."

Tania was not in a mood to reminisce. What they had experienced was an unexpected occurrence. Tania appeared put off that Garyn might be searching their neighbors' windows for another. At dinner Tania asked her husband about his search for a new job.

"Tomorrow. First thing," he answered as Tania stopped eating and sunk back in her chair.

"Now what's wrong?" Garyn moaned.

"You've been in a pout ever since you got home."

Tania began to weep.

"We can't do this again, Garyn. We can't go even a month without your income. This isn't our little bungalow in West Seattle. This is San Francisco. This is Russian Hill. This is the big city where we were supposed to—you were supposed to—finally make it. You said you'd make $45,000 this year. I make $24,000. You do the math. Without your income we're screwed."

Garyn's first response was panic, which he returned typically to Tania as hurt feelings. At this moment he could offer only his helpless and poorly defended resentment.

"We moved here to be close to your dad," he whined.

"Don't start bitching about income. Besides, he's richer than Croesus. What are you worried about?"

"Don't bring Cas into this," Tania answered, her expression turned suddenly cool and bold. She crossed her arms in a way that signaled to Garyn she was serious, or at least to be taken seriously. He would need another approach.

"What do you want, hon?" he asked pensively.

Tania glared.

"I wanted to get pregnant."

Her answer was curt and caustic.

"But that's not going to happen. Not now."

She stood up and walked toward the bedroom.

"You need to find a job," she said before closing the door and falling onto the bed.

Garyn returned to the living room to stare out the window. He heard Tania's sobs and thought to go to her. Instead, he watched through the window as the dinner hour sprang to life in the building that blocked his view of the bay and the hills beyond. Couples and families gathered at tables behind the windows. An aproned older man and woman bussed in their kitchen, hugging and kissing as they cut vegetables for a salad.

Garyn counted more than two-dozen windows through which he observed the intimate habits of other humans. He watched knowing he would not disturb them. It seemed insane to dwell on the meaning of a natural world when he could explore so freely the ways and means of other people.

3

The following morning Garyn was up before Tania. She found him at the kitchen table combing a newspaper's want ads and sipping coffee.

"Three interviews by Friday. That's the goal, anyway."

He spoke with caffeinated exuberance. Tania said nothing but approached from her soporific blur to give him a mild, but encouraging hug. Effort counted for something. Garyn hoped to appear active and engaged but in fact he was an invalid. His default position was one of weakness even as he momentarily modeled strength and resolve. Healing was not likely. Garyn needed to exert an effort only through breakfast and then he could let go of his focus and fall back into the perfection of his imperfections.

It was not a lie. He loved Tania and wanted to please her. He also was an artist, crippled inherently and constantly by the demands of others who did not understand or sympathize with his lonely genius. He was only human, as grotesque and deformed as any. He would not succumb to some cult of completeness lest he lose his heart and soul.

Garyn showered and dressed for the work Tania hoped he would find. When she left, he returned to the window to watch his neighbors. Many of the same people appeared from the previous day, mired again in weekday morning routines that seemed far from any lofty truth of human intimacy but that fed Garyn's rising and demonic eros.

He was astonished at the quantity and simultaneity of behaviors: cups lifted to the lips, chattering mouths, marches between rooms and the grabs for bags and coats. Several front doors opened in near syncopation within five minutes of the hour. Far below in the second floor bedroom, Garyn spied the slumbering faces and upper torsos of a young couple. Amid the other building's throbs of machinating animation they slept, still and lovely, in each other's arms. He imagined them in love, guileless and natural and, like him, unemployed.

Garyn put down the binoculars and went for his camera. He attached his 70-300mm zoom lens to the camera body and tried to focus on the second floor couple. His shaking hands blurred the image and he went for his tripod. With an extended mount he was able to tilt the lens down from the windows' slender, opened right wing. He pulled the lens to its longest focal length and brought the couple in bed into focus, astonished by his magnified proximity. Their quiet faces filled a third of the frame, the woman on her side with one white breast exposed over the blanket and illuminated only by the sun's indirect reflection from the alley outside. Garyn checked the shutter speed, a very slow 1/25th of a second. He was grateful they were still sleeping. He snapped four frames before turning toward the floors directly across from him.

Within an hour Garyn's tripod stood tight against a table, the camera's long lens six-inches from the window's open panel. He used the tripod's joystick to direct the camera from floor to floor and then from window to window. He stopped where a window was uncovered and people moved within its frame. By mid-morning Garyn had finished the previous day's roll of Ektachrome and reloaded with black and white, a faster emulsion that allowed him to raise his shutter speed to 1/250 of a second in the brightest rooms. It was enough to stop movement at high magnification.

He photographed past lunchtime when another flurry of comings and goings brought windows and floors to life and his loving couple on the second floor arose and disappeared from view. Through the afternoon he framed more windows and snapped what he saw: a man sleeping on a sofa, a child and mother reading together on the floor of a cluttered living room, an old man smoking a cigarette on his balcony, an affectionate couple talking across a dining room table.

The sun's long shadows began to appear in the late afternoon and Garyn realized he had been shooting all day. Tania was due home anytime. Reluctantly he closed his window just as lights began illuminating the other building's interiors. He pushed his camera and tripod into the back of the bedroom closet and returned to the kitchen and his newspaper. Ten minutes later Tania walked through the door to find Garyn where she had left him.

"Still looking in there for a job?"

Garyn's nervous laugh in response sounded to him loud and disquieting, but he was prepared for her query.

"Two calls today. Waiting to hear about an opening with a suburban weekly on the peninsula. Let me fix you dinner."

Tania appeared tired and left the kitchen to change her clothes. Garyn slipped into an apron and pulled vegetables from the fridge and raviolis from the freezer. He gazed back at the building that once blocked his view and that now was all he cared to see. Its windows hung in the darkness like a sheet of brightly lit postage stamps, most uncovered and flush with occupants.

The week passed without suspicion or abandonment. Tania said little about work as long as Garyn appeared busy. Garyn avoided danger by cleaning the house, shopping, fixing dinner, and running baths for his beloved. He spent the better part of two days photographing neighbors, and all of another day visiting photo galleries at the foot of Geary Street. He was home each night before his wife; allegedly occupied all day with a job search he assured her was time-consuming but hopeful. She accepted this and returned to the transgression of loving her husband who, she knew, was not all she wanted but still all she had.

Garyn used his time efficiently. Friday he spent the quiet morning processing film in the kitchen and making prints in a makeshift darkroom he created out of their windowless bathroom. His old Beseler enlarger fit snugly under the sink and in a half-hour he could spread trays and pour chemicals for printing. He had time to make a dozen prints that stunned him with their simmering intimacy. Quality was excellent and the tonal values tolerant of the difficult lighting challenges he faced shooting through windows.

He had captured wondrous moments: laughs, frowns, hugs, and other companionable gestures and acts that had no words but needed none. He was impressed. For an amateur photographer with little self-esteem and few scruples he had stumbled on a splendid subject matter: the private course of daily life revealed at the edges of its most unselfconscious expression. The lives of his neighbors opened as an undiscovered frontier. He had seen nothing like his prints anywhere.

4

Garyn was the new owner of a family secret. He purchased it at Gasser's Photo on Geary Street. The secret was a used Nikon 500mm f4.5 lens paid for with $470 taken from his and Tania's savings account.

The cash he handed to the proprietor was nearly a fifth of the account balance and he had not told Tania about the withdrawal. The account held money they were saving for a down payment on a house that, until he found work again, was a distant dream. But the lens, a tool that nearly doubled the magnification of his zoom while providing two additional stops of light exposure, was immediately and for a limited time accessible.

He held the lens in an open box, its fat black barrel nearly as wide as it was long and weighing close to four pounds. He imagined its brighter, closer view through the viewfinder of his camera. He promised himself he would pay back the purchase with the first week's check from his next job. He could not say when that would be but the lens—the glass that greatly extended the reach of his new and ambitious art—would be mounted on his tripod within an hour.

"So you think you have a lead?" Tania asked at dinner.

"What is it?"

She bit into a lukewarm burrito, still frozen at its center.

"This needs another nuke," she said coolly and stood to walk to the kitchen.

The interruption gave Garyn time to compose an answer to her question.

"Oakland," he answered crisply.

"A news group that bought the old Tribune. Papers in the valley."

"That's a long way," she observed.

Garyn knew she didn't believe him.

"Actually, I've been thinking about a career change," Garyn announced with a pose of thoughtfulness.

"Like what?" Tania asked suspiciously.

"Real estate," Garyn said instantly.

"I'm a good salesman and look what it's done for your dad. I just need to learn the ropes. Maybe he could help me."

Tania was silenced by the mention of her successful father and, hoped Garyn, quietly seduced by the vision of the two most important men in her life working shoulder-to-shoulder. It was a hard card for Garyn to play. He knew it would buy him time now but at a high price when time ran out.

"Will you phone him?" Tania asked eagerly.

Garyn said he would need a week to check out his latest newspaper lead. Then he would begin to look into real estate. He would call her dad. He promised.

Tania exhaled, her suspicion muted by the irresistible idea of Cas and Garyn aligned as mentor and pupil, father and son-in-law. A reverie of the future was a welcome relief from her abiding worry. She really did not know what Garyn did all day.

Garyn's new lens provided a suddenly successful pipeline into more of his neighbors' lives. Apartments too far or too dark for the limits of his old zoom were now available in his viewfinder, made crisp, close and bright by infinitely better optics. The increased magnification forced Garyn to weight his tripod to make it steadier. But the results were impressive.

His new accessibility stretched the hours he spent before his window in a way that forced a dissonance in his and Tania's schedules. She fell into bed exhausted by 9:30 and arose before six. He stayed up late, pulling his camera out of the closet after she fell asleep, shooting well past midnight and not arising the next day until after she left for work. Their uncoordinated waking and sleeping shuttled their sex to the weekends and then only when either expressed a frustrated need. Garyn found this new distance from Tania strangely comfortable, as he grew more fully absorbed in making photos of his neighbors and ever less welcoming of Tania's queries about his job search.

His prints with the new lens were beautiful: sharp, revealing and with a wide tonal range that highlighted the proximity of his neighbors in a way that left virtually no distance between viewer and subject. Two young children reached together like chirping chickies for their mother. A businessman just home from work sprawled with his partner on the couch, his tie loosened as he sipped a drink. A husband stood on a chair to hand a bouquet to his wife who laughed uncontrollably.

The expansion of his photo time grew the varieties of intimacy he captured. Arguments and sex, which he found reliably during later hours, became more prominent. A day after purchasing his new lens he discovered the late-waking couple on the second floor did not usually leave their bed without making love. He had acquired two weeks of views: tight, close studies of their faces *in flagrante*, their arms wrapped tightly around their squished torsos that, in thrusting urgency, became a soft, lovely blur.

In three weeks he produced more than 50 prints. A dozen he had shown to Tania, alleging he photographed out the window only an hour or two in the afternoons to kill time while he waited for the phone to ring. He showed her his gentler work and not the hot sex or boozy fighting he caught late at night.

Tania was actually charmed by his image of the older couple aproned and kissing in their kitchen as they prepared dinner. Garyn said he saw them once or twice a week. He noted the woman was often gone from the home and assumed she still worked while her husband did not. Tania asked Garyn if he ever again saw sex. He said no, afraid the wrong answer would arouse more of Tania's interest and end his fledgling new art.

And art it was. He was certain. His brief time as a news photographer taught him to barge into situations and shoot aggressively. He had no qualms probing the secret lives of his neighbors. They were plums for the taking. Some of his sex imagery led him to imagine how Dr. Masters might have felt observing patients having sex though Garyn prided himself on being a better scientist since his subjects were unaware they were being photographed and therefore related exclusively to each other and not to him. Sex was not a dominant subject of Garyn's window photography, but nevertheless characteristic of what Garyn found innovative and interesting. The intimacy of his neighbors was viewed and captured at its deepest and most personal moments, creating images that dwelled loftily at the vortex of his curiosity about the larger human experience. This is what he told himself, still wondering if it was evident in his work.

His best photography, and the scope of its accomplishment, remained largely a secret to his wife. In this way Garyn held some power over the guilt he felt about deceiving Tania, though the price for intimacy with neighbors was his forfeited intimacy with her as their sex grew more disjointed, abstract and fractured. One night while watching Twin Peaks reruns they came at each other like two subjects in a cubist painting and could not find each other at all. It was a sad stalemate that left them both silent and sleepless well into Sunday morning.

At the start of October's third week, Tania alerted her husband to an unhappy milestone: he had been without a job for precisely two months.

"It's not rocket science, Garyn," she said to him.

"I know how you spend your time."

Yes, he thought she did know and was grateful she hadn't said anything until now. The previous Saturday morning while he was out grocery shopping, Tania found his complete portfolio of 11x14 prints featuring his selection of more intimate scenes: couples getting ready for bed, women and men in various states of undress, and couples kissing and copulating.

"You must spend nearly every waking hour with that camera," she said accusingly.

Garyn pleaded with her to see the art he was making, the profound truth experienced in the intimate lives of their neighbors.

"Yes, your pictures are interesting. Maybe even good by some standard," she acknowledged.

"But your obsession is not. Garyn, we need an income. We need you to work. If you don't have a paycheck by the tenth of next month, I'm going to have take money from our savings account to pay the rent."

Her words rattled Garyn who could not risk another baring exposure. He promised to have a job in a week. He promised twice.

"Just don't raid our savings," he begged. "Don't."

5

Garyn considered himself a wounded soul. Were anyone to ask a deeper question, he might confess his contempt for social norms. He hated his sales jobs and usually disliked most of his co-workers. He loved photography and believed he loved Tania. For her sake he summoned enough perseverance and industry to take a job he did not want but could always have.

"You know the drill," the publisher told him.

Paul Prescott owned a chain of community weeklies north of the Golden Gate.

"Your desk is by the window but I don't want to see you there. You're outside sales. Exclusively."

Garyn knew. It was usually the hardest job that paid the best.

For $350 a week plus commissions Garyn might clear $2400 a month. It was not a city salary but his job wasn't in the city. Garyn crossed the Gate under the bridge's orange towers and pondered his drive north to Sausalito. An acceptable bad drive, and against the commute, but still a dozen miles south of San Rafael, the main street of his new sales territory. Tania's father lived in Marin but farther west in wooded hills near Fairfax. It was unlikely their paths would cross. It also was unlikely Garyn would last, though he didn't worry about that now. His first commission check would refill the savings account and even an unfavorable score.

He reported his new job to Tania, who was thrilled. At their celebratory dinner in an Italian restaurant on Polk she prattled ebulliently as if relieved from a test of faith. She called her husband sweetheart for the first time in weeks and urged him to phone her father.

"I'll bet he can help you."

Her words hit her husband like a squandered truth.

I need help, he thought. *Help from a father-in-law that hates my guts.* He chose another topic and wished immediately he hadn't.

"I still can't believe OJ wasn't convicted," he said dryly.

Tania frowned.

"C'mon honey. Let's not start that again."

It had been nearly two weeks since the celebrated verdict and the subsequently bitter fight between Garyn and Tania that followed.

The acquittal of a star athlete and movie celebrity for the murder of his ex-wife and her boyfriend had become for them a contentious issue and a substitute for the intimate ones they would not discuss. Tania thought OJ had been framed while Garyn knew he was guilty. Knew it.

"Because he's black?" Tania asked at last exasperated by their foolish fight, touching the third nerve of Garyn's wounded soul.

"I think it's wonderful that in America anyone can buy justice, regardless of the color of his skin," Garyn had shot back.

"Those people seem to get away with murder. Perhaps that's why they do so much of it."

"What about the people who murder *those people?*" Tania retorted mockingly.

"What white man ever went to jail for a lynching?"

The argument, fueled by a spaghetti dinner and a bottle of Barbera, had ended in a sticky pool of determined resistance and confirmed suspicions. Tania went to sleep certain her husband was a racist. Garyn did not sleep but stayed all night by the window, his camera trained on any lighted apartment until dawn brought into view the first sleepy subjects of a new day. For a while Garyn and Tania experimented with exile, living next to each other but in different countries, their common border patrolled by OJ.

One evening Garyn returned home with Thai take-out and a bouquet of roses. He graciously waved off his OJ comments.

"You're right, hon. No need to go there. I was wrong about all of it."

Tania smiled and while they chewed their spring rolls Garyn sensed from her a forgiving hopefulness he might use to negotiate his art. He was a thief, and encouraged to have read somewhere that all artists were thieves. He would plead to the charge if it brought him recognition as an artist, which he knew he deserved.

He wished to continue his photography and hoped Tania would understand if he set up his camera in the living room to make photos in the evenings and on weekends. She consented even while struggling to accept, if she were to admit it, another signal from Garyn of his careless cravings. *Why must he spend so much time watching others? What is more interesting about other people's lives, more interesting than our own?*

69

She did not ask these questions though her warm, randy mood over dinner was transformed into irritation when after eating and doing the dishes Garyn positioned his tripod and camera while all but ignoring Tania who slipped into the bathroom and then to bed. For Garyn a loving partnership was won once and kept as a lifelong possession. Tania, however, considered love a continual achievement. Garyn accepted Tania's disappointment as a manageable cost of marriage. Tania could not say what was acceptable though in any conflict up until now she thought acceptance was her only choice.

Norman Nance was a photographer for the city's daily newspaper. Garyn had met him at one of the photo galleries he visited on Geary and now was meeting him again at a café on Columbus.

"Tell me again how you made these?" Norman asked Garyn as he shuffled through a stack of his prints.

Garyn set down his cup and leaned in to view the specific print in Norman's hands.

"Must have been mid-morning. I get good light into that side of the building. The 500mm has an f4.5 aperture."

Norman continued to stare at the photo of a young man and woman in a silhouetted embrace in the foyer of their apartment.

"And no one sees you?" Norman asked without looking up.

"No one's looking," Garyn answered.

"Do you think you invade their privacy?" Norman asked.

"You're a journalist, Norman," Garyn answered.

"What is privacy?"

Norman heard Garyn's point.

"Privacy is like property," Garyn continued.

"Some have too much and some too little. The less someone has the less there is to invade."

Norman looked up and smiled.

"You've been thinking about this," he mused.

There was a pause.

"These are pretty damned good," Norman said finally.

"Damned good. The subject matter is unique and you're an excellent printmaker. What do you want from me?"

"I want a show," Garyn answered.

"I want to sell them."

Garyn thought he wanted wealth though what he really craved was fame. He thought he'd been to enough galleries to understand how things worked. So had Norman.

Norman asked Garyn if he any of his work ever had been exhibited. Garyn said no. Norman looked pensively out the window, distracted by a young woman, her hair and skirt pulled and blown by an onshore breeze.

"You're not ready yet for the Geary galleries," Norman offered.

"Forget downtown. But there are some smaller venues in the neighborhoods that might pick you up. One near you. I know the owners."

Norman scribbled a name and address on a card and gave it to Garyn.

"Have you thought of taking some classes?" Norman asked.

"You're not far from the Art Institute. You're good. They'd want you."

"No time," Garyn answered, gathering his prints to leave.

Garyn was too busy inventing the beginning of his story to imagine how it might end.

6

Garyn entered the Vortex art gallery on Polk Street with dismissive disdain for what he thought a shabby interior of empty, grey walls and inadequate illumination. He encountered a short, portly, middle-aged man wearing a white shirt that barely held its place over a rotund belly and wrinkled and too-long striped pants that swaddled his ankles and shoes. The man's sloppy appearance seemed a match for the dirty premises and Garyn wondered if he were in the right place. The man reached toward Garyn who took his hand in a cautious shake.

"You Norman's friend?" the man stated as a question.

Garyn nodded cautiously.

"And you—you're Mel?"

"Yah…Melvin Van Atta. Please, let's sit."

The man spoke with a mild accent Garyn could not identify. He directed Garyn to a table near the larger of the gallery's two and only street-facing windows. Mel apologized for the space's barren appearance.

"Between shows, you know. New one starts in a week. A local artist. Acrylics. Brilliant. So show me what you do."

As Garyn opened his portfolio Mel took out a pair of glasses, polished them with his handkerchief and slipped them over his red, bulbous nose. Garyn sat back as Mel sifted through a stack of his prints. For several minutes Mel said nothing though occasionally he would tilt a print toward the window's reflected light, pull himself back to take in its fully framed scene and then lean forward to squint closely at small details. Several minutes passed without comment while Garyn waited with resentful urgency.

"How long you been a photographer?" Mel asked without looking up.

It was a question Garyn had never before heard.

"About 15 years, I guess," he answered.

There was a pause.

"And these? Tell me about these," Mel asked.

Garyn gave the short speech he had rehearsed with Norman. He mentioned his curiosity, his opportunity, his interest in a photographic rendering of intimate human experience while remaining unseen by his subjects. Mel held up a print. It was Garyn's photograph of the older couple in their kitchen, both in aprons while they prepared dinner. The man stood behind the woman while hugging her with a jolly passion that seemed to surprise her, her mouth opened by a sudden sentience as she reached to hold the man's hand tightly against her breast.

"Zat's fucking beautiful," Mel said directly.

"Lovely. Really lovely."

Garyn relaxed against the back of his chair, enduring another long silence as Mel stood and wandered a few feet away and looked down the hall toward the gallery's rear room.

"So what now?" Garyn asked finally.

"Tell me about your other shows," Mel asked.

"What sells best?"

"This would be my first show," Garyn responded hesitantly.

Mel's round face was pulled into a fat frown of concern.

"First show? Nothing else? Have you studied somewhere?"

Garyn shook his head. Mel paced again, taking more time as he walked in larger circles across the gallery's center floor.

"OK," he said at last.

"Here's the deal. I have three photo instructors from the Institute opening December 7th. My small room is available. I can put you in there with 16 prints. We need a name for the show. Come back tomorrow. Yah, Sunday. We'll be here. You'll meet my wife and sign an agreement. Commission is 50 percent. We'll help you price the work. Write you up. You'll need to leave these prints with me so my wife can look at them. We haff to hurry. I must send out announcements. Zat OK for you?"

Garyn nodded, shook Mel's hand and left. He was two blocks from home before his stubborn detachment collapsed under a warm, privileging rush of elation.

Garyn waited until Sunday evening to tell Tania about the gallery. The details had been hammered out between him and the Van Attas earlier that afternoon. His show was to be called *Windows* with the subtitle *New Work by Garyn Toth*. The term "new work" was intended to get around the inconvenient fact Garyn had never before exhibited his photographs. The 11x14 prints, which the Van Atta's were paying to have framed, would be priced between $250 and $400 each. Garyn was incredulous. Would anyone buy such high-priced work? Mel's wife, Louise, assured Garyn something would sell.

"There are three we want to buy," she had told him.

"And now you can say you've had a show."

Garyn was given second billing to the three Art Institute instructors who were showing older selections from oeuvres much larger than Garyn's and that would fill the front of the gallery. Their show, entitled *Masters by Three Masters*, was intended to play on their reputations as both artists and teachers. Some of their photographs were vintage prints familiar to collectors and were priced in four figures. The show would begin with a preview and opening on a Thursday evening in early December and continue until mid-January.

Garyn described these details to Tania after walking her by the empty gallery on their way to dinner at the Thai restaurant. At first Tania was disbelieving. She scoffed at her husband not to pull her leg. Eventually she grasped from Garyn's inexhaustible excitement as he reveled among its details that the show was, indeed, a reality. That she was not at first thrilled pushed an immediate wedge between them.

"It's—I don't know how to say this, Garyn—can you really display these photos? Photos of people doing private things? Could you get in trouble? It's good work, dear, don't get me wrong. But what kind of people would want to show these pictures in public?"

Garyn sunk into a sullen hulk. It was his finest moment in photography and not only was his wife anything but pleased; she questioned the judgment of anyone willing to display his photographs.

"Well, if the gallery owners think it's OK…" Tania said at last and reached tentatively for her husband, offering a hand that he refused.

Garyn said little more and for the rest of the evening rebuffed her efforts at repair. At home he disappeared into the bathroom to pour chemicals and make prints.

"Got an early day at work tomorrow," Garyn said dryly.

"I need to get these done tonight."

When Tania awoke in the morning Garyn was already gone. She left a phone message at his office but he did not return it. He arrived home at six in the evening to sit silent and solemn through dinner before making more prints in the bathroom, a pattern that continued for nearly a week before Tania apologized tearfully and begged Garyn's forgiveness.

Garyn listened patiently and embraced his wife with a tepid hug that communicated little more than Garyn's determination to proceed at any cost. That morning he had replaced the money he took from their savings. The score was even again. Indeed, in the face of Tania's mortification, Garyn presumed he might have the edge.

A week before his opening, Garyn took a sick day from work to organize his show with Mel. The gallery's interior was freshly painted and track lights bathed the walls in a clear, eloquent glow. Mel determined the placement of his photos in the small, tight gallery, which Garyn now realized was out of sight of the main entrance. A large sign on a glossy signboard hung over the tiny room's doorway. It featured Garyn's name and portrait and the name of his show. For several moments he stood transfixed by the printed herald of his arrival.

Garyn and Tania were an hour late to the gallery opening. Rain and bridge traffic had delayed Garyn's evening commute. They arrived just as Mel tapped a wine glass to quiet his guests and to make a few introductory comments. The small space overflowed with a chattering crowd and after introductions, Garyn pushed past Mel to show Tania his photographs in the back gallery. The crush of people within at first frightened Tania who managed to climb gingerly between two women balancing wine glasses as they clustered at one of Garyn's prints. It showed young children in their underwear, bathed in late afternoon sunlight and framed by an apartment window while they played a game of statue on a carpeted floor.

"What a mob," Garyn said later as he introduced Tania to Louise.

"Your husband's a hit. We love his work," Louise said to Tania who appeared both flummoxed and grateful.

"Press is here tonight," Mel added.

"Two local critics and a reporter for the daily. They came for the Masters but they're spending a lot of time in there."

He pointed toward Garyn's small gallery.

Garyn absorbed Mel's assessment with a cautious thrill. Was he a hit? What did that mean? He glanced at Tania as she pushed her way around the small room that displayed his photographs, hung now in black, wood frames that sealed his views into artifacts of a fine art.

It had all begun with looking, with his curious inquiry into the life lived around him. He watched his wife stare at his photos and then turn to watch others who also stared. He felt himself clasped by a vindicating regard. Tania turned again to see him. She smiled. She blew him a kiss. And another.

7

Garyn wandered Fourth Street in San Rafael as if he were at the edge of a dream. It was Friday. He had been late for work though no one seemed to be watching. He had three advertisers to close before he could slip away into his own gifted reverie. Mel phoned him to say several photos were sold at the reception. Mel had a check for Garyn he could pick up Saturday. Garyn didn't think to ask how much. He was now a success, whatever the stakes or outcome.

Even Tania said so, her rewarding affection the catalyst for a sudden and opening reunion. Arriving home from the reception Tania pushed him into their bed and promised wordlessly to take his breath away. He obliged with a riff of welcoming sighs, her assertion his favorite quality of their lovemaking. She was firm, but respectful, though it had been a long time since Garyn felt from her such a luscious insistence.

Good news traveled fast and filled the weekend. On Saturday Tania walked with Garyn to the Vortex where Mel handed him a check for $2400. He promised more and told Garyn to watch the papers for reviews: both the daily and a regional art weekly.

"They sent photographers this morning to take pictures of your photos," reported Mel excitedly.

Garyn awoke early on Sunday and walked to Polk Street to buy a Sunday paper. Before Tania entered the kitchen he had breakfast ready and the cover page of the G section folded by her placemat. *Probing life's ordinary secrets: the intimate photography of Garyn Toth* read a headline across the center of the page. Underneath was a reproduction of Garyn's photo of the older couple in their kitchen and a review that praised Toth's work as groundbreaking and graphic, the perfection of a photographer as all-seeing while also unseen. A paragraph referred vaguely to Garyn's technique as canny, almost voyeuristic and praised the images as fresh and revelatory. Little was said about the three masters.

Garyn knew his neighbors well even if they did not know him. He waited Sunday evening for their predictable evening routines. He was surprised to see closed curtains in two apartments where before they had never been closed. Lights were off in several other units and he wondered if his luck was changing. He rationalized his views outside were things of the moment but wondered why so many were suddenly missing.

The working week began abruptly Monday morning and passed for Garyn and Tania like a blur. It was Wednesday before Garyn again could turn his camera on his neighbors, immediately encountering a profusion of curtained windows as if a contagion of privacy had infected every floor. That night he did not sleep, uncertain what kept him awake. At 3 a.m. he went back to stare at the darkened windows that had become the source of his subject matter. He could see opened curtains in a few, though through their slatted breaches only impenetrable darkness.

Mel called Friday to report a heavy amount of weekday foot traffic in his gallery, much of it drawn to Garyn's images. The attention surprised Mel, who credited favorable reviews including another that appeared Tuesday in the local arts weekly and included the image of the elderly kitchen couple that also appeared in the daily. That evening Garyn set up his camera and aimed it at his neighbors only to find nearly every window curtained. On Saturday morning they had not opened. Why was everyone closing the curtains? He placed his tripod and camera in a corner and answered Tania's call to come to bed.

Monday haunted Garyn with its burdening negotiations. What he made with his sales was in no way as satisfying as what he made with his eyes and lens. He drove back to his office after lunch to find a phone message from Mel.

"We have a problem," Mel said gravely.

"Your neighbors are coming into the gallery. They are suing us. You. They say you photographed them without permission."

Mel sounded frantic.

"What?" Garyn asked.

"Yah…" Mel turned away for a moment and Garyn heard the unintelligible but overwrought mutterings of Louise in the background.

"Yah…and the cops. The cops came by. Said they were investigating a complaint about a peeper. They took pictures of your photos. Wat is going on, Garyn?"

Mel sounded unhinged. Garyn said he did not know but that he was coming over immediately. Mel struggled to say something else but Garyn hung up the phone. Within ninety minutes Garyn stood in front of the gallery and pounded on its door. It was usually closed on Mondays. Through the window he could see the hulking, shadowy movements of Mel who lumbered forward and opened the door.

Garyn rushed past him like a hard wind. Inside his small gallery all the walls were empty. He turned to find Mel.

"Over here," Mel said somberly.

Garyn saw his photos stacked on a table, each wrapped in butcher paper.

"Keep the frames. Just get them outta here," Mel shouted.

"We don't want no trouble."

He handed Garyn a manila envelope.

"You need to read this," Mel commanded.

"You need a lawyer."

Mel picked up an armload of Garyn's prints.

"Where's your car?" he asked bluntly.

"Let's go."

Dazed and wounded, Garyn drove home. He thought for a while Mel would come to his senses, that he was simply responding to a temporal necessity and that it would all blow over. It was not quite three when Garyn entered his apartment and walked to the large living room window. He stood and surveyed the windows across the alley, some of them with curtains again drawn open. He found his binoculars and searched the windows for signs of life.

In one he saw a man in a chair smoking a cigar. In another a woman entered quickly from a bedroom and closed her curtains. In a third he saw a middle-aged man also holding binoculars and looking back at him. The man turned to call his wife who approached from the kitchen. The man waved wildly and pointed toward Garyn who slipped instinctively out of view and tugged the pull cord to close his curtains. He walked to the center to peek through a slender crack of fabric where the two curtains met.

The windows across from him surged with life, people on phones walking toward the windows as they spoke to each other, curtains opening as in nearly every apartment someone approached a window to search for Garyn's. More fingers pointed toward him, more curtains opened and also closed as those who were once his unwitting subjects discovered together the artist who had discovered them.

Garyn retreated to the couch and tore open the manila envelope given him by Mel. It was a court summons issued by an Eleanor Landower individually and on behalf of her two minor children and eleven others against the Vortex Gallery and its owner Mel Van Atta and photographer Garyn Toth. The complaint alleged Toth had invaded Landower's privacy and "the privacy of others" to make photographs displayed publically without the subjects' permission. The summons asked for an immediate end to the display of what were termed unlawful photographs as well as for unspecified monetary damages for the plaintiffs.

Garyn fell backwards onto the couch. He dropped the summons on the carpet and curled into a thick, fetal ball. He waited. Outside a storm was brewing. An hour passed while Garyn anticipated what he could not say. Tania arrived home at four, surprised to see her husband.

"What are you doing here?" she asked.

"I'm sick," Garyn muttered, barely coherent.

"I had to push through quite a crowd downstairs," she reported.

"Why are the curtains closed?"

Garyn looked up.

"I'm cold," he answered, all his happy circumstances substantively and entirely revoked.

8

Garyn questioned his relationship to reality. He sought a level of awareness somewhere between the thrill inspired by imaginary goals and his countering, deepening despair. The ideal was to find a place between, a place with no feeling. He remained on the couch through the night and into the morning. Tania awoke, checked on him, ate and left for work.

He was relieved by her departure until she phoned to say she was forced to run another gantlet of people gathered outside their building's small lobby. A television crew waited at the end of the steps and had asked her if she knew a photographer who lived on the sixth floor.

"Did you say anything?" Garyn asked anxiously.

Tania said no.

"What's going on?" she asked.

"Are they looking for you? Those people didn't look happy."

Garyn feigned surprise. He said he didn't know but would phone Mel at the gallery.

"Why Mel?" she asked urgently.

"Is this about your pictures of the neighbors?"

Tania released a sonorous gasp.

"I knew this would be trouble."

"Look, it's not what you…"

Garyn did not know how to finish his sentence.

Tania had to leave to meet her class. She would phone later.

Garyn considered opening his curtains but instead turned on the television. He punched the buttons of the remote looking for morning news programs. He landed at a camera's view of a reporter, microphone in hand, standing in front of a familiar building. It was his. The reporter pointed to it as she spoke about the "voyeur photographer" who lived within, whose intimate images of neighbors inside their apartments were exhibited at a local gallery. Neighbors were angry and were suing.

The camera cut away to show the portrait of Garyn displayed

at the Vortex and another photo of the gallery entrance. The reporter said legal issues surrounding the images were "murky" but the gallery was closed indefinitely and neither the gallery owner nor photographer could be reached. Another woman, who identified herself as a neighbor and the unwitting subject of one of Garyn's photographs, described her "shock" at seeing herself in a photo as she sat inside her apartment. The reporter goaded her.

So you're outraged?

"This guy didn't have my permission. He's a jerk. He's dangerous."

"So you're the guy who spied on his neighbors?" asked the flat, nasal voice in Garyn's ear.

It took Garyn an hour to search the phone book for attorneys. It took another hour for him to find one that answered the phone.

"You Mr. Seifert?" Garyn asked.

"And you know about the photos?"

"All over the papers and TV," said the voice that acknowledged he was Seifert.

He could see Garyn in his office at 3 p.m. He was on Columbus near Montgomery.

"It's not what you think," Garyn whined.

"OK," said the attorney.

"You tell me what to think and I'll tell you what to do."

To escape his building and its crowded entrance, Garyn did not take the elevator. Instead, he walked each flight down the stairwell, stopping at the first floor to peek into the noisy lobby still filled with neighbors and news cameras. He continued down to the basement, found an exterior door in the parking garage and dipped into an empty alley. He scurried briskly up the hill, dashing through intersections until he reached a park. No one followed.

A steep wooded path led him to the edge of North Beach and into Chinatown where he slithered along Grant amid concealing clusters of holiday tourists. He passed a newspaper stand and saw his story above the morning edition's fold. *Voyeur photographer sued by neighbors.* The headline blared above his photo of the embracing older couple. Garyn pushed a quarter into the slot and grabbed a paper. He would show it to the lawyer.

"I've read it," said Seifert as Garyn took a seat in his office. David Seifert was a copyright attorney seemingly intrigued with his client's predicament. Was Garyn Toth an artist or offender? Or both?

"They're just my neighbors," said Garyn.

"They're not famous or anything."

The attorney shook his head. He said he wished Garyn's subjects were famous.

"This would be a lot easier if you'd photographed Woody Allen or Barbara Streisand," he said.

"We might have a case. Celebrities don't have private lives. But your neighbors do."

Garyn slumped in his chair.

"There's another angle," Seifert said, his eyes brightening.

"Your work is art. It was judged as art by an art dealer, exhibited as art and sold as art. There are times when art is protected more than people."

"What's this going to cost?" Garyn asked.

Seifert wanted a $2500 advance to get started and would phone in a few days after he read the court documents. He advised his client to stay out of sight, avoid reporters, and do nothing with his photos.

"Certainly don't sell them or show them and by all means don't take anymore!"

Garyn began a slow walk back up the hill. He marched through the financial district imprisoned by the shadows of tall buildings that hid him like a toad in the weeds. He dreaded an evening with Tania. It was the last straw. She would be furious.

He arrived at his building through the alley. Under the sky's cloudy, opaque twilight Garyn walked cautiously toward his building's basement door. He stood outside and searched his pocket for the key. He could not find it. He searched his other pocket. As he used both hands to grapple frantically with his resistant denims, a man approached. He wore an overcoat, his head covered by a creased, navy blue fedora. He walked slowly with the gait of a very old man.

Garyn thought him a homeless panhandler until the man stood in front of him and looked earnestly into Garyn's eyes, which widened fearfully in recognition. The man was a neighbor and a subject in Garyn's most widely distributed photo: the older couple embracing in the kitchen.

"You're…wait…" Garyn muttered nervously but could not find the right words.

"Julius," the man said.

"Julius Burnside. The guy in the picture."

His voice was scratchy and solemn. A restless silence ensued as a truck roared past the alley.

"Are you suing me, too?" Garyn asked sarcastically to cover his guilt.

He never expected to be caught and now thought himself busted.

"Sue you?" Julius laughed.

"Sue the giver of a gift? You must be joking."

Garyn's strained face opened into a confused stare.

"Gift? What gift? Most of your neighbors want to kill me."

Julius smiled and asked Garyn to join him for a cup of coffee at a café on Polk. The old man turned to walk away and Garyn followed awkwardly behind. If Garyn had given the old man a gift, what had been taken?

9

"Don't get me wrong. You've really fucked up my life," Julius said after squeezing into a corner while dropping two paper cups on the table.

He pushed a cup toward Garyn who now appeared frightened.

"Is your wife pissed about this?" Garyn asked.

He had a vague hope of blooming camaraderie if both men had angered their wives.

"My wife is dead," Julius answered somberly.

"Oh, my god…" gasped Garyn.

His culpable mood allowed him to take the blame for everything.

"Dead for seven years," Julius answered.

"The woman in the picture is not my wife."

The woman was the wife of someone else. As Julius explained to Garyn with what felt like an odd, even loony excitement, the woman was married to Julius' best friend on the ninth floor. Since the death of his wife, Julius and the woman had been having an affair.

"Seven years," Julius sighed.

"But I've loved Marion for twenty. What you did was awful. But it has made me happy, happier than I've ever been. And at my age that's saying something."

Julius told how he and his wife and Marion and her husband Ernie met at a neighbor's bridge party shortly after moving into their building in 1957. The couples hit it off and socialized frequently. They went to movies and shows. Played bridge. Ate dinner together twice a week.

"Our best friends ever," Julius said. "Then my wife got breast cancer and died. They took care of me. Ernie played golf with me and Marion brought me food. Then Ernie and I got tired of playing golf but Marion still visited during the day while Ernie was at work. We realized we'd been in love with each other for years and not said anything. The rest, well the rest is in your photo."

"And the photo is a gift?" Garyn asked suspiciously.

"Yeah. We're caught now. We thought no one was watching but someone is always watching. The Lord is watching. Maybe you work for the Lord?"

Julius crumbled under a hoarse laugh.

"After your picture was published we had to tell Ernie. It was terrible. Ernie was crushed. Would you blame him? We all cried. But we're all very old and age brings some wisdom, some patience. Since we don't have much time left we've all agreed to care for each other. Ernie isn't jealous and is gone frequently to visit old college friends in San Diego. Marion thinks he might be gay. They haven't had sex in years. Ernie must be gay or else he doesn't know what he's missing."

Julius gave Garyn a lurid wink.

"Anyway it's out in the open now. Marion and I are free to love each other."

Julius drained a last sip of coffee.

"So you have given me a gift. Really. You are not entirely the cause of my misery and very much the maker of my deliverance."

Julius stood and threw his arms around Garyn and hugged him hard.

"Maybe it's time for you to get a gift?" Julius said with engendering glee.

"Who can say? Be patient."

Julius rose and left.

On the way back to his building Garyn found the missing key tucked tightly behind the wallet in his back pocket. He knew as soon as he entered that his apartment was empty. The low light of a table lamp illuminated a note left by Tania. She had packed some of her things and left to stay with a teacher friend in San Carlos. *I can't say what will happen. I just know I'm tired of this. You're all over the news and it's awful.*

She asked that Garyn not call her or try to see her. She would stay with her friend until the school vacation break and then visit her father for the holidays. If there were any disincentive for contact that Tania might have effectively thrown at Garyn, it was her father. Cas was the last person he would engage with the burden of his new and debasing fame.

The phone message machine blinked in the kitchen. Garyn clicked on a single message left by his boss. *We didn't see you today so I know this can't be a surprise to you after what's in the news. I need to let you go, Garyn. It just won't work to have you selling ads for me now. You're a huge liability. Goodbye and good luck.*

Garyn snickered cynically after hanging up the phone. Liability was Garyn's last consideration when he first wished for fame. He intended initially to explore with his camera the web of human intimacy and not the boundaries and reaches of morality. The intersection of his photos with public scrutiny had created an explosion from which he emerged hurt and disabled. He was more of an invalid now than ever before.

Garyn collapsed on the couch in front of his window. The curtains were still closed. He had not opened them for a week. Racing thoughts wracked his body with nervous pain. Tight breaths became a nearly frantic hyperventilation as his pulse pounded, his stomach burned and his head radiated with a hammering throb.

Garyn sought to reduce the frequency of his thoughts, to bring them slowly into his mind one at a time so that he might confront and examine them. As his thoughts slowed so did his breathing. Eventually, he could see between his thoughts the emptiness of each moment as it came into and left the present. Herein he grasped his place between cause and effect, between getting and giving, between the ticking clock and his ceaselessly active mind.

Perhaps the cure for loneliness was solitude. He was alone and also not alone. He stood and peeked through the curtains, feeling suddenly provisional in his existence. He had thought it a benefit not to be seen until tempted into exposure by the gift of fame. And he was famous now but in all the wrong ways. Instead of the observer he was now the observed. Burnside's description of a gift felt like the master's slap.

Garyn's talent had become his last defense against a cruel and resolute fate. From the time he was a child the world was uncertain and he was incompetent to win and hold its love. Now the narrowing straits of experience were confined to the four enclosing walls of his apartment. For a moment he reveled in the true limits of freedom. Then he wept. All he denied had come into being. All he decried he had unconsciously chosen. He could not move at all and yet could see for miles.

TRICKS OF THE TRADE

1

Chogan Sloat thought the earth itself was alive and wondered what was in it. He surveyed more than two hundred green plants in a clearing far above his valley. He sat on a hill of rocks on land he could not map. He had found the land the old way, by crossing slender trails and leaving them. He had wandered with his senses along slopes and gulches, driving Jorge mad with restless confusion as he searched for a wet, secret place in the sun where his companion might plant his valued secrets.

They had taken two days to find this place, Jorge impatient, even angry, that his Yurok guide wandered in seemingly aimless circles with such certainty and purpose. When it was found, Jorge understood. It was a perfectly useful and also hidden place. Jorge thanked Chogan and offered him a share of the eventual profits. Chogan lit a small fire and thanked the forest.

Chogan watched the skies closely. He also searched a copse of birch trees that hid the single approach to the slender valley where Jorge's leafy sinsemilla grew from its sturdy trunks. He listened for unusual sounds and heard only the wind and the craving cry of an angry crow. He rested his rifle against a rock and stood again to listen, stepping from the shade into the mountain heat of a blazing July sun. He heard the soft murmur of an airborne engine. It grew louder and closer. He retreated behind the rock, rifle in hand, and waited. From behind the trees a helicopter burst into view, its engine now a thundering, whacking fury.

Fear surged in Chogan's throat and he cocked his rifle uselessly. If it were a raid, he did not have a chance. His only way out was to wriggle through underbrush and crawl deeper into the forest. He could not save a captured crop, though he had already counted its earnings. Jorge had shown him what agriculture could do with the rhythms of the sun and not the moon. It was so different to grow a crop, so different from hunting for fish or looking for work. Chogan had never before tamed land. It was a revelation to watch plants grow in rows, to absorb the multiplier effect of seeds, to anticipate as yet unimagined wealth though he had never before plowed anything.

The helicopter pushed westward without slowing and Chogan relaxed the grip on his rifle. He marveled again at the scope of Jorge's operation, recalling how the tight valley had been cleared of grass and weeds, its dirt turned with fertilizer, seedlings planted and water siphoned through a gravity-fed pipe from a tributary of the New River. It was all an intimidating miracle of invention. The sun, wind and rain were the traditional resources of Chogan's people. But he was tired of taking only what was offered and happy to earn a small fortune from a crop he and Jorge could force from the soil. His mother told Chogan a spirit had spread out the earth like a big blanket and enriched it with all his people would ever need. Chogan needed money and he needed it now.

Six weeks were left before harvest. Jorge was sending someone to relieve Chogan who was wanted in Eureka for a meeting with Jorge's buyer. That someone was expected anytime, another reason Chogan watched and listened vigilantly. That someone would signal with three whistles, wait, and signal again with two. Anyone else was not welcome, though Chogan did not worry. The parcel of land he found for Jorge was far off the paths and well beyond and above the boundaries of parks and reservations. Anyone arriving here would have to know what Chogan knew.

It was not a new idea that what the earth grew could be sold. But it was one thing for Chogan to imagine how illicit wealth might grow and another to grasp how it might be marketed and moved under

the white man's nose. Such was trade and Chogan had bad recollec-
tions of the role of commerce, which had hurt his people and him in
the insidious spread of fences and property across the blanket spread
by a spirit. The blooming plants were still a comfort to Chogan.
They grew where there were no fences and would be harvested like
the fish in the fall, all at once and without leaving a trace.

His prevailing vigilance was like a net and as Chogan's eyes and
ears swept across the green gulch he gathered in every detail and
sound. He watched a doe slip noiselessly under a distant branch. He
heard again the cawing crow and, at last, an unmistakably human
whistle beyond the birch trees. Chogan grasped the coded signal
and whistled back, walking cautiously forward to greet his reluctant
replacement.

"God damn. Finally found it…" a young, thin man said, dropping a knapsack.

"He wasn't kidding. Jorge said it was four miles off the trail. It's
farther than that."

Chogan stared. It had been a week since he saw anyone and this
man, his long blonde hair streaming out from under a camouflage
baseball cap, his blue t-shirt dark with sweat, was still a stranger.

"I'm Marty," the man said, aware of Chogan's remote, assessing
posture.

Marty was a gold miner who lived near Hawkins Bar and an as-
sociate of Jorge's for whom he occasionally did favors.

"This is one of them," he said to Chogan.

"Say, are you an Indian?" he asked, rattled by Chogan's stoic
silence.

Chogan gave a short, sharp nod.

"You're one big boy for an Indian," Marty added nervously.

Chogan might have said he had been told that many times before
and that his father was a large white man and not an Indian. Instead,
he said nothing.

"You a Hoopa?" Marty asked anxiously.

"No," Chogan finally spoke. "Yurok."

Marty whistled again as if to marvel at a stunning fact.

"And you're up here just outside the Hoopa boundary? You want
to be careful. Say, where's the water? I'm dead thirsty."

Chogan pointed toward the back of the gulch. He handed his rifle to Marty and walked past him through the birch trees.

"Well, goodbye," Marty said sarcastically and then, as an urgent afterthought, "When you comin' back?"

Chogan did not turn.

"Four or five days," he shouted before disappearing into the trees.

Chogan took short sturdy steps down the sloping unmarked path that led away from the gulch. The route was a clever invention, a traverse of visual cues scratched on tree trunks and assembled in varying piles of stones. A compass was needed occasionally to establish the proper course along a perpetual switchback invisible to anyone not aware of what they needed to see. Chogan relied for orientation on the placement of the afternoon sun, his thoughts drawn reluctantly to a white, dead father he did not mourn, whose existence had been a vicious labor and whose legacy had become Chogan's burden of size, honey skin and hazy blue eyes.

Two hours passed before Chogan emerged onto a trail where his short steps became long, angry strides. For another five miles Chogan stirred under the abasing memory of an empowered man that had caused and also thoroughly compromised his flawed existence.

At the trailhead, Chogan passed four cars to find his '82 El Camino, what he called his Blue Bomb that, nearly ten years old, still ran pretty well and certainly well enough to get Chogan to his mother's house in Klamath Glen. She was full-blooded Yurok, as was his brother. It was for Chogan an essential heritage but one that provided him with a dubious status as half-breed, and the feeling he was little more than a misplaced, if useful fiction.

2

Chogan could be angry with his father without being hostile to the white man, though he liked Jorge because he was not white. Jorge's dark skin and sharp knife of a nose gave him the look of an Aztec warrior, another tribe that, like Chogan's, was native to the land. Jorge was at least a foot shorter than Chogan who bore with a broad, hulking height the evidence of his father's pollution. To tell the truth, he hated how big he was though to tell the truth was to invite denial. Wherever he stood he stood out, aware that people he did not know, would never know, looked at him curiously. Was he a freak? A big Indian, he thought. I'm a big Indian.

And there were those as big or sometimes bigger who would push up against him, shout at him, taunt him. Chogan was no stranger to trouble. He had hurt others and been hurt. He hated what this did to him. He preferred the forest, knew it well, knew the trails between Requa and Doctor Rock and had walked them all.

Jorge met Chogan in the spring while both pumped gas at the Shell station in McKinleyville. Chogan told Jorge his rear tire was low. Jorge thanked him and bought him a beer. Jorge was interested in Chogan, his life on the reservation and his time in the woods. After three drinks, Chogan agreed to be Jorge's guide on a hike into the Siskiyou Mountains. Within weeks Chogan was Jorge's partner in farming and had quit his job at the mill.

Chogan waited for Jorge on a side street near West Wabash in Eureka. He had left his truck a block away and paced nervously at a corner, aware of the awareness of others. He was here to meet Jorge's buyer, a man from Oakland who Jorge said was "loco, man, really loco black dude but all cash…"

Chogan saw Jorge's truck roll toward him from the east and recognized Jorge's much younger brother Jaime in the passenger seat. The truck slowed and turned. Jaime waved. Chogan did not.

"You tell me, monkey," said the skinny black man from Oakland.

"I didn't want this meeting. I didn't want to see your brown ass until the harvest. But I have my concerns."

Jerome was the leader of a gang Jorge called the Izzy Boys. He bought Jorge's pot, culled from the Humboldt growers Jorge fund-ed and represented. The meeting began in the sparsely furnished kitchen of a shabby stucco duplex. It moved to the living room when another black man at the window gave Jerome a signal. As if orchestrated, four more black strangers entered and took seats around Jorge, Jaime and Chogan.

"You have us outnumbered," Jorge observed helplessly.

"This isn't what we agreed to."

Jerome laughed, his forehead bright like shiny ivory in the pale afternoon light.

"We didn't agree to shit, unless you've changed your mind and want to move some speed for me."

Jorge waited a moment and then shook his head.

"You know I can't do that," Jorge seemed to plead.

"Who else gonna move your pot into the cities? And pay you $1500 a pound? Jorge, all I'm askin' is that you return the favor. Light up your god damned world. Meth meets 7,000 college students. It's a gold mine. I need you, bro, and you need me."

It seemed strange to Chogan that Jorge the outlaw, the Chicano dope runner of the North Coast, would stand up to his outlaw buyer. But Jorge shook his head.

"No, man," he said.

"I ain't moving your poison up here or makin' it either. Find someone else."

"Ho, it's poison now?" Jerome chortled.

"Then what's your fuckin' weed, greaser? Health food?"

Jorge endured Jerome's insults with a calm that surprised Chogan.

"It's principle man," Jorge answered.

"I won't."

Chogan knew enough about Jorge to comprehend his choice. It was safer to transport an illegal product than to grow or make it or to supervise its sale. It was why Chogan and Martin guarded the pot patch in the Siskyous and not Jorge. Pot was one kind of product, but speed a wholly other. Meth was cooked in labs amid the attendant risks of volatile chemical reactions and suspicious smells. It left a wicked trail of evidence and, unlike weed, thoroughly and reliably ruined the lives and bodies of its users. Jerome lived in Oakland and what did he care?

Jorge lived on the coast. It was his home and he cared very much.

"Here's a principle," Jerome said.

"It's called the principle of necessity. Let's say we're on a lifeboat in the middle of the ocean—this really happened. We on a lifeboat that will sink if we don't throw ten people overboard. No, it ain't right is it? To kill ten people. But we have to work fast, so who's going over, you or me—or someone else?"

Jerome pointed toward Jaime and waved with his other hand toward the four new arrivals standing in the living room. Three quickly produced revolvers from the pockets of their jackets. A fourth, towering and muscular, lifted Jaime from his chair and onto the floor. Chogan watched incredulously as two more men grabbed Jaime's stubby arms and held him while the tall, muscular assailant pulled Jaime's pants down and then dropped his own. A crowd of Izzy Boys surrounded Jaime, his naked ass visible through the legs of those guarding him.

"You go, Mack," Jerome shouted to the tall attacker who now stroked his erect penis and pressed hard against Jaime's exposed buttocks.

Jaime yelped and Chogan jumped to his feet.

"Easy, you Indian fag," Jerome shouted.

"Your hair is so long and purty. Do you get a lot of cock you fucking Indian bastard? Would you like some, too?"

An Izzy Boy pointed his gun at Chogan who returned to sitting. Jorge did not move, seemingly aware of, and resigned to, the principle of necessity.

"It's a principle that makes explicit what our instincts tell us," Jerome lectured through a pontificating pose. He cheered Mack on as he thrust hard into Jaime's ass while Jaime moaned helplessly.

"Don't want no tears, don't want no jive," Jerome crooned with the rhythm of Mack's thrusts. "Above all things, don't want no lies."

And then Jerome laughed as Mack grunted one last thrust and withdrew. His stout attacker turned to stuff a flopping shiny cock back into his pants and Jaime was released. He crawled frantically across the floor and hid behind a chair where he struggled to get his pants back on.

"Your big Indian ain't much use to you," Jerome taunted Jorge.

"He's like one of those cigar store Indians. He doesn't scare me. Now get the hell outa here. The next time we meet I want to see you and your brother behind the wheel of a truck full of good pot. We'll call you and tell you where."

An Izzy Boy opened the door of the duplex and pointed toward the street. Jaime stood and ran past him, shoving the tall black man aside in his rush to escape.

Chogan walked with Jorge in silence while Jaime staggered ahead like a shamed child. No words were spoken between the men, both mixed-breeds, who knew their defeat to be an affirmation of their ambiguous status.

"We need more guns," Jorge said as he climbed into the driver's side of his truck.

Jaime slumped next to his brother and would not look at Chogan. It had been a brutal loss of face from which he might not recover. Jorge told Chogan to pack a week of food for Marty and to take it to him at the patch. He wanted Chogan elsewhere.

"Phone when you get back," said Jorge, who started the truck and drove wildly down Wabash. Chogan considered Jerome's principle of necessity and weighed it against another: that crimes, like sins, could not be dismissed without threatening the order and existence of all things.

3

What grew in his body began in the heart. Chogan's life emerged from a home where his childhood was for a while a radiant wilderness, boundless and physically joyful as it is for any child cared for, loved, and protected by an attendant mother. His mother's big heart grew Chogan's larger one until it collided with the boundaries of his drunk, bitter father who luckily did not live in his mother's home near the Klamath Glen airstrip but survived between mill jobs in a trailer stored at a mobile home park outside Eureka.

As a toddler, and later a schoolboy, Chogan visited his father on weekends while his mother Hateya waited tables at the lodge. Dad was a wild man and white. His coarse good looks and scabrous character sustained an attractive and dangerous charm. When he stood up, Chogan's dad was taller than his trailer. Hateya had met him while he drank at the lodge and succumbed at last to his strong eyes and potent attentions. They lived in his trailer until Chogan was born and she returned to the reservation, fearful of the father's unpredictable rages but not so afraid she wouldn't later send their son back to stay with him.

Chogan grew up in a two-bedroom house opposite the air strip and shared one of the bedrooms with his little brother Honan, born five years later to Hateya and an older member of the tribal council who eventually left her. His brother was finishing college in Arcata while Chogan was back in their room, at age 31 a native son too old to be returning home. Hateya, alone and nearly 50, welcomed back her older boy as a valued remnant of her incomplete life though she feared for Chogan's uncharted future. Chogan assured her not to worry but could not tell her why; could not say in less than two months he would be rich.

Jorge met Chogan in Redway and told him to park his truck in an empty lot down by the river. Together they drove west to Briceland and swung left onto the Old Briceland Road. A half-mile later Jorge turned into a gravelly, unmarked driveway where he unlocked a gate. Jorge stopped his truck in a shrouded grove of redwoods where another car was parked. A skinny man wearing a navy blue t-shirt and ragged jeans stood nearby and pissed on a tree.

"Tom!" Jorge shouted as the man turned awkwardly and pulled up his zipper.

Jorge introduced Tom Thumb, a Briceland hippie who planted the patch and now, as harvest approached, slept in the woods. Jorge and Tom led Chogan deep into the forest. In 15 minutes they stood at the edge of a half-acre of pot plants that spread like a vast green quilt up the side of a mountain. The patch was at least twice the size of Chogan's and smelled ripe like a stinking pool of dead fruit.

"The Izzy Boys don't get this one," Jorge told Chogan.

"They don't know about it."

Chogan asked who was buying.

"Don't know yet," Jorge answered.

"Jerome gets yours and two others but not this one."

Chogan asked why Jerome got anything after what had happened in Eureka the previous week.

"I owe him," Jorge answered bitterly.

"Last time. Last fuckin' time for that mean snake. We'll be even and I'll have a new buyer."

Jorge said he'd resurrected a contact in Los Angeles.

"Farther to drive means more risk. I'll drive it myself all the way to Guatemala if it means I can dump the Izzies."

Tom Thumb saw something move at the end of the patch.

"Another god damned deer. Shoo!"

He dropped his rifle and ran fifty yards toward the forest and disappeared among the high, green stalks of several maturing plants. Jorge walked Chogan forward, Jorge the member of another tribe but not the white man's though he was an entrepreneur like the white man, someone who understood markets and trade.

"I'd like to make a deal with you," Jorge began.

"Where's Tom?"

Tom seemed essential to Jorge's offer but had vanished at the end of the patch. Jorge cupped his ear.

"Too quiet," Jorge said before pushing his hand over Chogan's mouth.

"Down! Get down!" Jorge whispered frantically.

Chogan struggled with Jorge as they fell to the ground. Jorge pulled him off the path and inside a row of plants before leaning out to see Tom walking slowly towards them, his arms outstretched like a zombie's.

"Shit!" Jorge screeched.

He signaled Chogan to follow him quietly as he slipped quickly back toward the trail. Looking behind, Chogan saw a half dozen armed cops run past Tom and toward them. Jorge pulled Chogan's arm and they tumbled down a hill toward the truck where three sheriff's deputies were crouched and waiting.

Chogan turned and pulled Jorge into the forest.

Up there! he heard a deputy shout.

Chogan dragged Jorge through a thick hedge of thorny brambles that stung his throat and hands as the men fell through the branches. Chogan pushed Jorge to the ground where they felt the pounding footsteps of the deputies run past. When the pounding stopped, Chogan led Jorge quickly through the forest undergrowth to a rocky ridge about fifty yards away. They bounded together toward a visible outcropping of boulders and slipped down the other side.

Chogan searched for a trail. He found tracks, perhaps a deer's, and led Jorge forward along the animal's route. He followed the tracks slowly, aware of the sun through the trees and the need to stay under branches and in the shade. The outline of animal hooves stopped in a clearing where Chogan found the bones of his trail-maker scattered like sticks. Chogan searched for other ghosts to follow and continued to find his way down the entropic fall of a hillside and toward a slim, flush gulch he and Jorge traced until, after another look at the sky, Chogan began his climb up a steep grade embroidered with broad banks of bay trees and poison oak. He dragged Jorge forward who, after his first objections, was too stunned by the totality of their enclosure to object.

"Are we lost?" he asked Chogan who shook his head.

A few yellow leaves appeared as the dying prelude to a new season of dying. Mosses on trees brushed their faces while Chogan continued a slow, steady march through tight, crowded trunks of new growth. A clearing appeared and Jorge nearly burst into it before Chogan grabbed to hold him back. A helicopter was heard everywhere, distant and then close with no predictable range.

And there was no wind; only the subtle sounds of the forest and their own crackling steps that frequently fooled them into thinking theirs belonged to others. A resolute and insistent climb continued and with no path other than Chogan's slow linking of markers: a trunk, a rock, a small clearing, each forming a stepping stone to the next. Jorge, when he wasn't gasping for breath, marveled at his companion's competent traverse of an unmarked wilderness.

After an hour the helicopter sound receded and then stopped. Tall trees made it impossible to know if they were near a summit, both of them sweaty and Jorge dying of thirst and living on hunger. Chogan appeared to have no worries but Jorge's had just begun.

"I'm fucked," he shouted, finally.

"That was a primo patch and it was mine."

"Chinga mi madre!"

Chogan ignored Jorge's complaint and rushed ahead to peer east over an emerging peak toward the rooftops of Redway, still two miles away. He was animate with all the shapes, smells and sightings that pointed their direction home.

4

The dark road passed under Chogan's truck, recurring evidence of motion he did not actually feel. He passed Redcrest and at last thought it likely he was not being followed. Until then he was prepared at any moment to be stopped by a cop, ready to be reeled back in like a swimming salmon caught on a line.

It had taken most of the afternoon to creep down a mountain and hike with Jorge across two valleys, their last quarter-mile an obstacle course of fences and distant houses. After hours of free passage through a trail-less forest, a barking dog might have undone them. They could not walk on the road so their approach to Redway took them through fields and backyards with all the attendant risks of trespass. They made it to the bridge and crossed the river beneath it, wading out at a public beach and then walking in the evening darkness toward the market parking lot.

"Won't see you for awhile," Jorge said.

"They have my truck but they don't have me. I'll be at the border tomorrow night and deep in Baja before they start looking."

Jorge, wet and dirty, reached up to put his arm on Chogan's shoulder.

"Ditch the crop," he counseled.

"It's too risky now. Maybe next year. Leave before anyone sees you."

Jorge entered the phone booth to phone Jaime while Chogan walked to his truck.

Past Redcrest Chogan saw lights from the village of Shively flickering through the trees. He was near the place his father had died when the car he was driving plowed off Highway 254 and plunged into the Eel River.

It was two days before the car was found though by that time no one had missed him. Chogan's father had long since passed out of the lives of his loved ones. Chogan was twelve and the facts were given him second and third hand and as vaguely as possible. Years later his mother would fill in the details. Chogan visualized his father speeding back to Eureka from an all night party in Garberville, flying along the Avenue of the Giants just before dawn to avoid the

Highway Patrol on 101. The car was found turned over in the river, his father's bloated body face down on the river bottom, his hand still tight around a cracked bottle of Cuervo Gold.

Chogan waited three days in Klamath Glen, concealed like a shy child in his room. A story in the local paper described a pot bust in Briceland that resulted in one arrest and the taking of more than 500 mature marijuana plants. It was the middle of September and of course the plants were mature. A harvest was beginning and preparations were apparent in the movement of vans and trucks along forest roads, activity watched closely by law enforcement. The story featured a photo of cherub-faced Eureka police chief Everett Bascomb, regional spokesman for the Campaign Against Marijuana Planting or CAMP, the acronym by which the consortium of police agencies was known. It was CAMP's ninth year of helicopter fly-overs and raids on the area's pullulating culture of pot farmers.

Chogan spent a day hiking to his patch with more food and whiskey for Marty, acutely aware he was at risk. Were he to be caught, he would be charged with numerous felonies. He would also face the opprobrium of his mother's angry tribe, which hated the marijuana trade and wanted it kept far from the reservation's river and forests. Jorge's escape alarmed Marty who was ultimately assuaged by Chogan's offer to share his profits. Marty knew how to dry and pack the plants and it was worth a 10 percent cut to put him in charge.

"With Jorge gone, where you gonna sell it?" Marty asked suspiciously.

Chogan said he had a plan, but Marty knew he was bluffing.

"We should cut this shit down soon," Marty said.

"Real soon. You know why I carry this rifle. It's not to chase off deer. Someone finds this patch, well…it's us or them now."

That evening Chogan's mother sat with him at dinner.

"You afraid of something?" she asked.

"No, why?" Chogan responded.

He avoided her inscrutable brown eyes and long, lined face. Her grey hair was woven in a long straight braid and he stared at it as he faced the woman who lifted him into life, whose vigilance had protected him until he pushed away to search for his own control. Now his own vigilance was most often like that of a dying man who struggled with the enclosing tedium of a great mystery. He was vigilant but as he realized now, also observed, a vulnerable object of observation wherever he went.

Chogan had been parked on West Wabash for an hour. He could see movement behind the window blinds of Jerome's duplex. He left his El Camino and stood in the street. The door of the duplex opened and a tall, muscular black male approached. He wore a navy beret and kept one hand conspicuously fisted in his jacket pocket.

"Who are *you?*" he asked Chogan.

"I'm the Indian fag," Chogan said contemptuously.

"Go tell Jerome the Indian fag is here to see him."

The tall male retreated to the house and in a few minutes returned.

"Come on in," he said to Chogan who shook his head.

"Tell your boss to come outside. The Indian fag is not a fool."

The man's face tightened before he again retreated.

"Hardly recognized you," Jerome said as he approached Chogan. "When did you cut off all your hair?"

Chogan ran his hand self-consciously through the middle part of his short bowl cut but did not answer. He asked Jerome to climb into the front seat. The two sat in gawky silence until Jerome asked what Chogan wanted.

"I think I have something *you* want," Chogan answered.

"Oh yeah?" Jerome snorted.

"Jorge's gone and the cops have his dope."

Chogan offered a meek, weird smile as he looked for any magic behind Jerome's eyes.

"Not all of it," Chogan answered.

Jerome appeared surprised to hear that Chogan had a stash. He asked where it was and how much he had. Chogan offered Jerome nothing but a small cellophane bag filled with dry, pale green buds.

"Try it," he said.

"If you like it, there's more. A lot more. I'll come back tomorrow."

Jerome pocketed the bag and stepped out of the truck.

Chogan drove slowly away, conscious not to appear worried or intimidated, though he was both. Jorge's experience with Jerome left Chogan distrustful. In two weeks Chogan and Marty had converted Jorge's patch into 234 shrink-wrapped packages of dried, cured pot now stored in several cardboard moving boxes in the back of a Blue Lake shed.

Cutting down more than 200 plants had taken two days though Marty's choice to dry the plants in the arid October heat of the mountains saved them a week. Packing out more than 100 pounds of weed took six trips over three days. Transporting it was done during a weekday's morning commute. Marty bought bags, borrowed a sealer from another grower and packaged it all in two afternoons.

When Chogan returned to West Wabash the next day Jerome was waiting for him.

"How much you got?" he asked Chogan as he slipped again into the front seat of his El Camino.

Chogan had 133 pounds for sale.

"Why should I buy from you?" Jerome asked fiercely.

Chogan again looked into Jerome's eyes for any kind of magic. Finding none, he was not intimidated.

"Who else can you trust?" Chogan asked.

Jerome was silent.

"I'll give you $2,000 a pound, but that includes transport. You need to get it to the city for me."

Jerome looked up and down the street suspiciously.

"I'm too hot. This time of year a black man driving a van through the redwoods is a cop stop waitin' to happen."

Chogan was silent. He hadn't considered transport. He visualized briefly the long drive south and thought Marty might help.

"When do I get my money?" Chogan asked.

"When it's delivered," Jerome answered.

Chogan cast him a suspicious look.

"Who else can you trust?" Jerome asked.

5

No one ruled innocently. Chogan admitted to himself he knew next to nothing about deals. He wondered if he were working for Jerome rather than simply trading with him.

Employment was something Chogan thought he understood. In his young life he had found employment more acceptable than initiative though it never paid much. Millwork was his father's trade and easily became his. It was steady work and kept him busy. He never considered critical thinking his strength nor was it ever encouraged. His brother excelled in school and would soon have a college degree. It didn't seem to matter. Both Chogan and his brother were broke.

The drive to Oakland was planned for a Monday morning when traffic was light and police surveillance presumably lax. Jerome left first with an Izzy Boy and drove his Seville. Chogan followed ten minutes later in his truck, the back open and empty. Marty drove last in a rented car. Marty and Chogan carried the pot hidden within the seat upholstery of their vehicles. Packages bulged at the seat seams and anyone sitting in the car would know something was wrong. But the sealed bags concealed all smell.

Jerome said he was a decoy.

"If they stop anyone, it be us," he said.

"You guys just keep goin'."

Jerome appeared remarkably reasonable and cooperative as he planned the transport of Chogan's crop, quite unlike the bestial martinet who had ordered Jaime's ass fucking during the meeting with Jorge.

For days Chogan had calculated and recalculated what he would earn from the crop he inherited from Jorge. The total exceeded a quarter million dollars. How can it be worth so much? Perhaps because he had a bounty in a time of scarcity, and at a time when it was most needed.

He had some experience with impacts of scarcity. He could remember when gasoline was 55 cents a gallon. Were it not for the raid on Thumb's patch, Jorge would be driving south, not Chogan, and with a crop larger and worth much more than his. Instead, Jorge was gone.

"You only get caught once," Jorge told him.

Chogan had not been caught. Not yet.

Approaching Garberville, Chogan saw Jerome's Seville speed up and begin to pass cars. *What the…? He's doing 75.* A highway patrol cruiser passed Chogan on the left, its lights flashing, and raced to catch up with the Seville. Jerome slowed and left the road followed by the patrol car. Immediately two other cruisers and a sheriff's van slid in behind the Seville from an adjacent on-ramp. As instructed by Jerome, Chogan drove on, as did Marty behind him.

Chogan suppressed a surge of panic and continued south, checking his speedometer. He settled into the slow lane and let the needle float between 61 and 64 mph. Marty held his position a quarter mile behind. Chogan rode his brakes down the steep hill that dropped him in front of the golf course near Benbow Lake. He wound cautiously through Cook's Valley and over the snaking mountain pass before reaching the non-existent town of Leggett where the freeway began again.

Jerome said the drug road between Humboldt and the Bay Area was called The Gantlet because there was no alternate route. The cops knew any dope passing from north to south would be on this road. They just didn't know who was carrying it though in a decade they had perfected suspect profiles and a menu of phony reasons to pull anyone over.

Danger points were Garberville, commercial capital of the Emerald Triangle pot-farming community and home to a highway patrol substation, the open road through Cook's Valley and the flat, unfurled highway south to Laytonville. These wide expanses offered grand vistas for surveillance and several checkpoints where officers and patrolmen on radios could track drivers along the route and compare their observations.

As the traffic slowed at Willits, Chogan waited for Marty to catch up. Continuing south, they reached Calpella and stopped separately at a roadside winery just outside the sprawling valley city of Ukiah. They made no contact inside but left the tasting room together to use the john.

"So far so good," Chogan said while standing over his urinal.

"When we cross the San Rafael Bridge, take the exit to Marina Bay Parkway."

Marty nodded.

Between Hopland and Healdsburg, increasing traffic hid Chogan's El Camino within the flow of cars and trucks. Leaving Santa Rosa the traffic was thick and stalled. As he loped along, Chogan saw Jerome's Seville pass him in a commuter lane. Jerome waved and flashed a wicked smile. There were no more worries unless either Chogan or Marty had a flat tire or an accident. With their destination so close, such a liability was all Chogan could imagine until he and Marty crossed the bridge and, one after the other, landed in a commuter parking lot on the industrial north shore of San Francisco Bay.

As instructed, Marty and Chogan waited in their cars. Jerome had said he would meet them but Chogan realized he hadn't said when. He observed a white van at the other end of the lot, a formidably empty space the length of two football fields. Across the vast asphalt plain he could see a fat white fog fill the Gate and spread across the Bay. A figure in the white van seemed to be watching Chogan and Marty. A half-hour passed before the van crawled slowly toward them. Chogan started his engine and for several moments considered bolting from the lot and signaling Marty to follow.

What if this were a set-up to steal his crop? The van pulled in front of Chogan's truck and blocked its path. Jerome signaled from the driver's side for Chogan to follow the van, his face wide with the same ironic smile he flashed when passing Chogan earlier on the highway.

Chogan signaled Marty and they followed Jerome's van over the freeway and onto the choked streets of West Richmond lined by old tract bungalows in varying states of decline. A fifteen-minute journey through several intersections of cluttered streets brought them to a detached wood-framed garage behind what appeared to be a church building. Jerome jumped out of the van to speak with an elderly man sweaty in the afternoon heat and wearing a coat and tie.

The old man approached and directed Chogan and Marty to steer their vehicles past the garage doors and to the rear of the dark, windowless interior. Again, Chogan was seized with apprehension, reflexively suspicious of men he did not know and suspicious always of the non-Indian though he acknowledged while Jerome sometimes behaved like a white man, he wasn't one.

"Welcome," Jerome announced jovially as he approached Chogan.

"We done it. And I know. You want to get paid. One day, one more move, and we're done. Wednesday. Don't you worry. We've got a place for you to stay."

Chogan wore his suspicion like a sign.

"I want to leave soon," Chogan said firmly, though he had no leverage.

His truck and crop were being locked up in a hidden garage and he didn't know where he was. He did not carry a weapon. If this were a community it appeared one rooted in forgetfulness and hiding.

"Yeah, right," Jerome said, leaning hard into Chogan's face as if to occupy every corner of his vision.

"No trouble. Look, I'll front you most of it in the morning—how about $175,000? Bring it to you myself. The rest on Wednesday. No shit."

Chogan was not reassured. He had not known what to expect. If he lost his crop entirely he was out nothing but the gas for the trip and Marty, well he'd just have to eat it. It would be a hassle not to give Marty his money. And dishonorable. Chogan tried to resist the greed he understood to be an infectious characteristic of the colonizer.

The old man introduced himself as Rev. Lamont Tatum, minister of the First Church of the Holy Harvest.

"You boys are our good Samaritans. Praise the Lord and welcome to our spiritual community. We are grateful for your service on behalf of the congregation."

Chogan appeared puzzled while Marty smirked.

"Church of the harvest?" said Marty.

"Yeah, I'll say."

Jerome interceded.

"It's cool. You guys come with me."

Jerome shook the reverend's hand while Chogan and Marty climbed into the van.

Chogan watched through the window while Jerome and his companion retraced their route through dingy streets lined with shabby homes and boarded storefronts. Occasionally Chogan saw a liquor store or a market at a corner crowded with black men sitting or talking. At the freeway Jerome drove toward the bay along the Parkway and turned into an expansive development of bayside condominiums spread out in two-story units among trees and lawns. Jerome approached a gated entrance and stopped to press a code into the buttons of a freestanding kiosk.

The gate opened and Jerome drove toward the bay and parked in a space labeled *Reserved*. Chogan and Marty followed him to the second floor and through a door that opened onto an expansive living room furnished elegantly with leather-upholstered furniture. A floor-to-ceiling window opened like a mouth to the breaking swell of grey fog pushing across the bay. The peak of a tall mountain held its distant view until the fog filled the window entirely with its swirling mesh.

Chogan did not know anyone in the room. Jerome paraded among them, slapping hands with several men and embracing three women. He called Chogan and Marty over and introduced them as "associates." The men, all but two of them black, shook Chogan's hand. The women, who stood together in the kitchen, held up their drinks in an impromptu toast and smiled.

"Hey Jazzra," Jerome shouted, introducing the lightest skinned black woman to Chogan.

"She's the Reverend's niece. She'll drive you back to the church later. Yeah, it's cool. Right, Jazzra?"

Jazzra forced a smile and tossed Jerome a cold, irritated stare.

"First we party."

Jerome returned to the living room, leaving Chogan in the kitchen, a tower of awkwardness now imbedded within the stalled conversation of three aligned women. Two looked away but the woman named Jazzra continued to make eye contact.

"You're a dark man but you ain't African. What are you?" she asked.

The question struck Chogan as unusual and invasive, but not rude. The woman appeared genuinely curious and could not know that Chogan, whatever he called himself, did not know exactly what he was.

6

Later Chogan would remember what he recognized as Jazzra's aptitude for morality. He thought it a talent and also as a special kind of intelligence, perhaps amplified in its contrast with the gathered others. The crowd in the living room grew and shrank as guests entered and left.

At one point a gaggle of young females, too young in Chogan's mind, entered wearing short skirts and tight, sleeveless tops. They disappeared with Jerome into an adjacent bedroom. Amid the smoke, shouts and drinks of Jerome's party, Chogan had taken only a beer and found a seat at the kitchen table far from those passing joints or huddling to snort from straws. Jazzra joined him, sipping for an hour from the same glass she used for her toast.

"So you're half white?" Jazzra asked after listening patiently to Chogan's labored explanation of his origins.

"Suppose that's why you're so big. I'm something near half-white. My daddy was black and my mom was Irish. That's probably why I'm so short."

Chogan thought to say that Jazzra wasn't so short but realized it wasn't necessary. She was seeking an ally and not a compliment. Everyone else had left the kitchen to join the roar of Jerome's party, to do more drugs and drink more alcohol. Chogan's eyes fluttered covertly as he sought to view entirely the woman seated across from him: her surprisingly light-colored eyes, not blue or green, but also not brown; her strong shoulders sleeved in a stern, ochre blouse; her hair a lawn of tight, black curls shaped in a neat bubble that held itself in place; her tapered jaw and long neck. Altogether she held a full suite of attractive features that, amplified by a plangent, soothing voice, captured Chogan's complete attention.

From its sudden opening plunge into a discussion of skin color, their conversation veered guardedly back into more topical subjects of place, time and weather. Chogan enjoyed Jazzra's fluidic voice and let her do most of the talking. She seemed pleased with Chogan's apparent interest and entrusted him with details.

Yes, she was the Reverend's niece. She had lived with him since the age of 14 when her parents died in a car accident. Chogan choked on this news and tried to offer a condolence as Jazzra shook her head to brush him off, a gesture that appeared habitual and timeworn. Her parents' death was not news to Jazzra and she left quickly the subject of their passing.

Chogan made room and asked about her life now. She managed the church office when not attending business classes at Contra Costa College. Her uncle was a religious man. The church was his life, along with a woman who lived with them in the house adjacent to the church building.

"Ruth," Jazzra announced neutrally.

And that was all.

"And the drugs?" Chogan asked openly.

"What about the drugs?" asked Jazzra, appearing immediately cool and defended. "The drugs are Jerome's. My uncle's got nothing to do with them."

Chogan pulled back as Jazzra assessed his confused expression.

"Listen, there's a lot you don't know and don't need to know," Jazzra said.

She told Chogan he and Marty would spend the night in the Reverend's guest room.

"You probably gone tomorrow. The less said the better for you."

"Can I trust Jerome?" Chogan spit his question onto the table.

Jazzra waited before answering.

"You can trust Jerome to be Jerome," she said finally with a jaded sigh.

The Reverend's residence was a single story bungalow Chogan had not noticed when he first drove into the church building's rear garage. Jazzra stopped her Ford wagon near the home's back entrance and she and Chogan helped a very drunk Marty to his feet and into the kitchen and then down a short hall to a large rear room with two double beds.

"Looks like a Motel 6, I know," Jazzra announced.

"The Rev has a lot of visitors."

Jazzra asked if she could get anything for Chogan.

"How about some tea in the kitchen with you?" Chogan replied.

Jazzra countered with a sage, silent smirk, similar to her expression when they first met, only now more friendly and nuanced.

"I only have Earl Grey," she answered as if to set a firm, unspoken limit.

Morning broke in the darkened bedroom through yellow cotton curtains. When Chogan drew them open he confronted rows of long, black bars across the windows. He turned to see Marty still askew on the adjacent bed where Chogan had let him fall. Chogan ran to the bedroom door and turned the handle. The door clicked as it opened and Chogan charged through the short hall, surprising the Reverend, Jazzra and a tall, older woman in a burgundy terrycloth bathrobe. All were seated at the kitchen table.

"Everything OK?" the lanky old man asked. He wore sweats and a black Raiders jacket. Chogan relaxed his shoulders and nodded.

"Need my toothbrush," Chogan answered and then hopped with his bare feet across the kitchen's cold linoleum and out the back door into the driveway.

Chogan looked around to see bars on all the home's windows and those of the church. Houses he viewed across an alley also were barred, including a white-trimmed two-story duplex, it's first floor windows covered by gleaming white bars that matched the trim. For a terrifying moment Chogan had awakened with a feeling of imprisonment, as if surrounded by black faces and barred windows, as if he were being watched constantly while unable to see. He went to his truck and pulled from the rear seat a small knapsack, noticing the seat had been removed and roughly replaced.

He searched beneath with his hands. The packaged pot he had carried from Humboldt was gone. It had been removed and he had not yet been paid. He breathed deeply into an absence that was not yet a loss. Jerome said he would come this morning to pay him. Chogan would wait. There was Jazzra in the kitchen. There was the memory of his conversation with her well into the morning, their disclosures that seemed at some mutual place to spark a yearning. He had hugged her good night. She had welcomed him before turning to climb the stairs to her room.

The Reverend stood at the stove poised and aproned before turning to plop two fried eggs onto Chogan's plate. Chogan looked up to catch Jazzra's smile as he cut into the soft yolks that bled their yellow in a spurting wave that reached to the dark crust of Chogan's toast. He was hungry. He was also fearful.

"All in the service of the Lord," Rev. Tatum announced.

"All this work. All this bounty. We offer it all to Christ Lord Jesus. Amen."

"Aw, c'mon, Uncle Lamont," barked Jazzra.

"We don't know this man's religion. He may not believe what we do."

Chogan attempted to wave off Jazzra, as if to say he did not believe but that it did not matter.

"You know what I say, child," the Reverend announced.

"We can be who we are in faith at all times. Who knows who we might persuade just by example?"

Jazzra frowned. Chogan smiled. The older woman sat watching everyone.

"You might make more sense if you'd invite our guest to Bible Study," the older woman said sharply.

"As it is, he may not be here very long."

"Thank you, Ruth," Jazzra announced sarcastically.

"We'll all take note."

Chogan heard Ruth's voice for the first time, its sultry trill an informational counterpoint to the Reverend's august baritone. Chogan did not care about faith but knew better than to challenge the customs of a host, especially one that might make him rich or kill him.

"It's here, man. Well, maybe not all of it. I need a couple more days."

Jerome did not apologize for the sudden plan to pay Chogan in two installments. As he sat with Jerome in the garage Chogan opened a flat, canvas bag to find several stacks of what appeared to be $100 bills. Each stack was neatly banded and there were 17 stacks, each allegedly containing a hundred bills.

"Go ahead and count it. Shit. You got a couple of days. No fuckin' hurry."

Chogan grabbed a bundle in his fist and held it to the light, as if to see something authentic he could not touch.

"Yeah, it's real, motherfuckah." Jerome answered Chogan's unspoken query.

Jerome told Chogan to make himself at home at the Reverend's house and that he'd return Thursday with the rest of his money.

"Thanks," said Chogan.

"But I've got other plans."

Jerome's tightly managed cool gave way to a querulous gaze.

"Huh? Hey man, you are a guest."

Chogan flashed Jerome a smile, his lips and teeth taut with determination. They were not colleagues. Chogan was not a guest. The radius of wealth that encircled each made brotherhood impossible. They were not enemies but were each nevertheless at risk.

"I'm staying somewhere else."

Jerome asked where.

"It doesn't matter," said Chogan.

"I'll be back Thursday. It's Thursday, right?"

Chogan picked up the bag full of money and strolled from the garage, melting with each step into the frenzy of his possession, frantic with what he had secured from a voluble stranger. It was foreign trade and he strolled as if walking briskly past customs before he could be stopped or searched.

The kitchen was empty, except for Marty who sat at the table and held his forehead with one hand while drinking coffee with the other.

"That was some shit last night," Marty said absently as if through a haze.

"I have your cash," Chogan announced.

"You can leave anytime."

"Cool," Marty answered through a tired voice drained of capacity.

"Next time, man. When you get back, let's talk about next time."

Chogan shook his head.

"No next time, Marty. No next time ever."

7

A gift was like blood in the body, pumped and returned to the heart. Chogan accepted Jerome's money as the gift it was and used it first to protect himself. Thinking he might be followed, Chogan left the destitute Richmond suburbs behind and retraced his route back across the bridge. He found a swank hotel in San Rafael near the Civic Center far back from the highway. He parked his truck, entered the hotel and paid for a good room but not the best.

He paid in cash for two nights. He had gone forward by looking backward, his eyes in his rear view mirror as much as on the highway. Chogan thought he would be followed and made several obscure and otherwise needless turns through town until at last he felt alone.

He carried his wealth into the hotel under his coat and squeezed his 17 bundles of cash into the safe inside his room. He put his jacket into the canvas bag and made a point of giving it to the concierge to place in the hotel's safe. Anyone watching might assume Chogan had secured his valuables with the hotel and would leave his room alone.

In the early afternoon he re-crossed the bridge to Richmond and drove to the church. He wished to see Jazzra again and found her at her desk in the tiny church office. She was speaking with an older black man in a corduroy suit. She saw Chogan and waved weakly. The man turned to see him and left when Chogan approached. He asked Jazzra to have dinner with him. She asked him where. He asked if she liked seafood.

"Yes," she said. "But where?"

Chogan smiled broadly from his face's high place over hers. He laughed.

"Does it matter? I promise to bring you home."

Jazzra smiled cautiously, her eyes again the beams Chogan remembered, the warm rays of an internal light.

"My Uncle Lamont is a lovable old man," Jazzra said as she poked with her fork at the crispy skin of a blackened halibut filet.

"But he's an airhead. If he didn't have his God he wouldn't know what he was doing."

Chogan heard Jazzra say "his" God and not "God."

Did Jazzra believe in God?

Chogan did not ask.

"Seems like a lot of work to run a church," Chogan responded.

"How do you do it and go to school, too?"

He wanted to ask why.

"I don't know how much longer I can," Jazzra stated after a long pause.

Her suddenly pursed lips conveyed a jolt of repressed emotion. Tears formed in her eyes.

"Something wrong?" Chogan asked directly, and perhaps too directly.

Jazzra's eyes narrowed as she felt herself become the exclusive object of Chogan's deep concern. The hint of a secret spread across the table in a way that forced Chogan to give it a wide, untouchable space.

"You don't have to say anything," Chogan said quietly.

"You're safe here. You're safe with me."

At some point Chogan recalled leaving the wharf-side restaurant with Jazzra and driving the ten minutes to his hotel. He bought her a drink in the bar. They talked again of race and remembrance, their childhoods with white parents that neither knew very well nor liked very much. Chogan's easy manner continued to arouse Jazzra's canny charm, a quality she appeared to manipulate comfortably once her tears were shed.

A connecting tendril grew between them, grown perhaps from their unusual racial bond, each half-Caucasian though each claimed not to be white. One was the product of a white mother and the other a white father and each seemed to comprise the unusual half of the other, a half not particularly well-remembered or regarded in its vague abandonment but nevertheless synchronous, syncopated, even concentric as if they together were cradled within a shadow of trauma, hurt or sorrow and, perhaps now, deliverance.

The sex was good. Jazzra caught the gleam in Chogan's eyes and made the first, unspoken suggestion they go to his room. It seemed the natural outcome of an evening that a day before had begun with a smile in a kitchen. He later recalled how large he felt under her small, wriggling frame, as if he held an infant lover to his breast that took such flights of pleasure from his mountainous muscularity.

Her thrill seemed unstoppable by anyone, even herself. She cried, moaned, and called out. He felt her deep spasms and held her close through each unsteadying burst. She sprawled over him, a petite and squirming animal barely enough to cover his thighs and chest and almost like a small lap pet but for the surge of raw, rich joy he felt with her. He was flat on his back when he at last came, Jazzra whispering to him her sultry, encouraging words. It was intimate beyond his capacity to describe though not more than he could grasp.

Morning's call to Jazzra was Chogan's soft touch. It took full possession of her as he awoke to hold her relaxed body with a natural and gracious regard. Her words came easily. He appeared to listen for every one and asked her for more.

"Let's go away today," he said to her.

"Where's the ocean?"

Jazzra knew. She left a message for Ruth. *Not coming in today. See you tomorrow.* Chogan and Jazzra ate breakfast in the hotel dining room before driving west on Sir Francis Drake Boulevard through the villages of San Anselmo, Fairfax and Lagunitas and toward the thick fog beyond the green ridges of Point Reyes. Chogan bought sandwiches and bottles of beer at a store at the intersection of Highway One in Olema and continued driving 10 miles to Limantour Beach.

They walked barefoot along a windless span of sand and arrived at a hill of dunes shaded by an old cypress. The chilly fog evaporated quickly and opened a blue and limitless horizon. They ate a quiet lunch until Jazzra's words filled an awkward, ungathered silence.

"My parents weren't killed in a car accident," she blurted.

Chogan put down his bottle of beer and took her hand.

"Mom killed dad. She's in prison for life."

A tear formed in one eye and bled down Jazzra's cheek. Chogan waited for a story. Jazzra's mother caught her father having sex with another woman and in an alcohol-fueled rage took his gun and shot them both. Her father died instantly and the woman two days later. Her mother was serving a life term in Soledad prison and it was eight years since Jazzra had visited her.

"It hurt too much. I had to stop."

Jazzra's breakdown drew Chogan to her as if he were an unattached electron thrown aimlessly into her orbit. He entered her pain without guile. He wished to see her in a way that allowed him to be clearly seen by her. In such a way and place, Jazzra felt connected to a resonant, immovable strength and, as if speaking into a warm wind, she could not resist her secrets.

"How long have you been dealing drugs?" she asked him.

"I don't deal drugs," he answered.

"At least, I never will again."

He told her the story of the pot patch and how it fell into his hands. It seemed crazy not to accept such a gift.

"I have what I want. I'm surprised to have it. Jerome owes me some money. Then I'm done. One of these is enough for me."

"Drugs support my uncle's church," Jazzra said dryly.

Chogan's eyes widened.

"My uncle is an inept preacher whose small, dwindling congregation nearly disappeared eight years ago."

She waited a moment for her story to catch up with her feelings.

"And then he met Ruth. She took over his church and his household and managed both as businesses. She advertised the church, started a youth group and pre-school, and canvassed neighborhoods to drum up attendance. She took Lamont to speak at AA meetings and printed brochures to give to hookers in the downtown bars. Even though she's a white woman, she is also a Richmond native and could trade on her family's progressive reputation."

Church attendance increased and Jerome's parents joined.

"Jerome dated me briefly in high school before dropping out to join a street gang. And about the time I began working in the church office, Jerome met with Ruth for what she called spiritual counseling."

In fact, Jerome had persuaded Ruth to let him use the church as a transition point for the sale of pot, from which the church would receive a slice of the profit.

"Jerome wants to kick ass," said Jazzra.

"The drug business is like any business and he wants to climb. Jerome's no different from a junior exec at Chevron. He wants to rise, to have benefits. Earn six figures. Be a big shot. Drive a hot car. For two years the church has been a great cover. Lamont didn't know how the church made its money. Ruth said it was increased pledges and big takes from the baskets. He didn't care. He doesn't care. He was flattered and thought people loved him. A few months ago he began putting two and two together. Now he just looks the other way."

Jazzra let go of Chogan's hand.

"What has changed is that Jerome's bosses want to get out of pot and sell meth instead. It's cheap. Easy to make anywhere. A hit costs $10 and lasts just ten minutes. And it hooks you fast. Two pounds of meth can earn more than a hundred pounds of pot. That's all Jerome cares about now. Getting people hooked on speed. Bad for him, for us all, but he's not the only one who cares. The cops do, too. And why shouldn't they? Who wants meth in that messed up neighborhood? As poor as it is, as polluted as the air is by those big refineries, children still live there. Jerome wants to sell it to children. Teenagers, anyway. You see the young girls at his party? Fifteen. Sixteen. They want dope. And he wants them."

Jazzra's words silenced Chogan who sat still at the top of the dune. He thought of an old framed photograph that hung in his mother's home. Made in the 1920s it showed two of his great uncles naked but for loincloths as they threw wicker nets toward waves crashing on a Klamath beach. They were fishing for smelt and the image captured their hunched, springy alertness as they considered how far to walk into the ocean. The greater their hunger the farther they would walk. It was a tricky business to dance along the border of an undertow, to fling a net without drowning, especially when one did not yet know how to swim.

8

The rhythm of lapping waves filled the silence between Chogan and Jazzra, who stood as if to walk toward the shore.

"I'm going to jail," she shouted.

"Either that or I'm going to die."

She held her hands to her eyes and began to cry.

Chogan rose to face her. He held her shoulders. He waited as she told her story. The man Chogan saw in the office talking with Jazzra was a police detective who volunteered at Holy Harvest and assisted Lamont with his Saturday family breakfasts. He told Jazzra his department had uncovered likely drug dealing at the church. He had suspected some marijuana trade but had ignored it. Pot was one thing, but the movement of speed and crack was too much for the authorities to ignore.

If Jazzra helped the police arrest the dealers, he promised the church would not be harmed. If she did not cooperate, Jazzra and her uncle could be detained as accessories while the church was searched and likely closed.

"He said no one wants to hurt the church. He said he likes us. He said I had a week to decide what to do."

Jazzra pushed Chogan away.

"Is it a fucking trap? He doesn't understand. I can't do anything. Jerome thinks it's hilarious that a cop is a member of the church where he unloads his drugs. That's how crazy he is. If I turn in Jerome, I'll be killed."

"Why don't you just tell Jerome about the cop?" Chogan asked.

"He won't believe it. He'll say I'm setting him up. He hates bad news and always blames the messenger."

Jazzra appeared frantic and without hope.

"No one around here seems attached to the truth. We're all probably fooling ourselves and Jerome seems to know this, knows how to turn our fears into his strengths."

The fish in the ocean or the salmon in the streams were not subject to Chogan's will. He was raised to think himself a servant to his gifts. The windfall from Jorge's plants was no exception. Chogan took into his heart the wounding misery of Jazzra's dilemma and included her and her trouble among all he had so far welcomed and received. He held a surplus and embraced Jazzra as someone who could share it. Only how?

Do you need some money?" Chogan asked.

"Do you need to go away?"

Jazzra appeared surprised and also perplexed.

"I would love to get out. But I don't. That drug money supports the church, which supports me."

"Besides, I have no place to go," she answered.

"No other family. I don't own a car. And Jerome would find me. That brother is a mad man. He'd know what happened and send someone to find me. Worse, he'd come himself."

Jazzra did not believe Chogan could help her, did not grasp his vision of a gift, though she seemed warmed by what she termed his "useless kindness."

"You're a funny man with a good heart," she said.

"In the movies it's always a cowboy who rides in and saves the lady," she said acridly.

"Never an Indian. You don't know my world, Chogan. You don't know its wickedness. I'm trapped. If I run I die and so does my uncle."

Chogan asked again if there were anything he could do for her.

"Yeah," she answered through a flaring sneer.

"Buy me dinner and some drinks. Take me back to your hotel. One more night before you get the rest of your cash and get your half-honky ass outa here."

They stopped for dinner in Point Reyes Station. Chogan ordered a bottle of white wine and a shellfish platter. They peeled shrimp for an hour with fingers made gooey by a creole red sauce. And they drank. When the first bottle was finished, Chogan ordered another.

"There's a part of me that's a terrific con," Jazzra said as she finished her second glass of wine.

"I don't know sometimes if I'm fooling others, or just myself."

Chogan thought he understood Jazzra and heard what he thought was a hint of addiction, perhaps urges fed by threat or deep trauma. She ate and drank as if this dinner were her last meal and later, in his room, held onto him with a fierce and athletic fury perhaps driven more by fatality than arousal.

She struggled to come and was surprised when she did in a staccato of convulsions and shrieks. She collapsed on the bed and fell quickly asleep. Chogan examined her pale chocolate face, sublime like a child's with the unmistakable features of a young woman but also furrows under her eyes from restless, protracted worry. He felt for Jazzra a melancholic empathy that seemed to overgrow the attraction already in place. He wanted to help her as a way to be with her.

They drove back to Richmond in the morning, Jazzra subdued and likely hungover. As he stopped his truck in the church driveway, Chogan offered again to help. She shrugged her shoulders.

"You some kind of Indian dream man, aren't you? You some kind of witch doctor? You almost have me. Come see me today before you leave."

Jazzra blew Chogan a kiss. He had run out of words. Perhaps he was already all the gift Jazzra could manage.

Jerome did not have the rest of Chogan's money on Thursday. What he had was a proposition. Chogan assumed the offer, whatever it was, would substitute for the $80,000 he was still owed. He was right. Instead of the money, Jerome wanted to send Chogan back to Humboldt with a pound and a half of meth.

"You keep everything from your sales, man. No fucking joke. You'll make a hell of a lot more than eighty grand."

Chogan's stone face communicated nothing.

"Who would I sell it to?" Chogan asked.

The question flummoxed Jerome for a moment. He scratched his ragged goatee as he pondered a response.

"You got all Jorge's old connections. You got the colleges and some street folk that would love a pipeline to some of this good shit. You don't have to worry. This stuff sells itself. You do this and I know, I know, you'll come back in a month for another pound. You gonna get rich. Capital doesn't increase unless it's used. We gotta get it circulating to make more."

Chogan would rather have his money but knew now he would

not get it. Gifts were not subject to Chogan's will. He had never been in charge of his fate. If this were still a gift he thought again how he might take it, how he might put it into useful motion. He stood and paced the floor of the garage while Jerome took deep drags on his cigarette.

"How you going to give this stuff to me?" Chogan asked.

Jerome's eyes widened as if he were closing a sale.

"Any way you want. I'll hand it to you tonight. You tell me."

Chogan said no, he did not want it handed to him. If he took it, it would happen according to his plan. A transfer would have to occur on Chogan's terms and not anywhere near the church.

"You gonna do it?" Jerome asked.

In a last, lucid moment Chogan saw the emergence of a beautiful opportunity with the power to be much more than an acquisition. If a gift were realized in communion Chogan could taste its vibrant and powerful potential.

"Yeah," Chogan said.

"I'll do it."

9

A dream might be stronger than experience. Chogan's idea crystalized in seconds, a creation of desire and not of necessity. Nothing could speed up the passage of time. He was patient.

The money Jerome took from him was worth more than what was given. It was the nature of gifts, and particularly the gifts of nature, that they arrived obscurely but often just in time. In most instances they were already present and needed only to be seen.

Chogan phoned his hotel to extend his stay through Saturday night. He drove away from Richmond, careful again to take a circuitous route through the hills of El Cerrito and down The Arlington into Berkeley before feeling assured he was not followed. He crossed the San Rafael Bridge and bought a sandwich at a café in the Northgate Mall where he searched a local newspaper's classifieds.

He found a 1984 Mazda 626 for sale for $3500. He contacted the owner and agreed to meet him at 3 p.m. at the Marin Civic Center. The car was clean with 63,000 miles.

"Runs like a dream," said the owner who described himself as a retired Swede with too much time on his hands.

The test drive felt fine enough. Chogan offered $3,000 cash and drove the car back to his hotel.

He checked the ads again and called about a 1990 Honda Civic Coup for $7800. The car had 21,000 miles and was still on warranty. Again, he met the owner, a young attorney, at the Civic Center and after a short test drive gave him cash for the car and paid for a cab to take the owner home. Chogan phoned his insurance company to switch coverage from his truck to the Honda effective Saturday. He parked the truck and his two new cars at the far end of the hotel's vast lot. He went to his room and phoned Jazzra at the church.

"You just caught me," she said.

"You already on the road?"

Chogan said he wasn't leaving until Sunday. Would she meet him again for dinner?

"What do you think?" she said sharply.

"Where are you? Come right now and get my ass."

Chogan asked for 20 minutes to navigate the bridge during rush hour.

"That's all you get," Jazzra sassed.

"Better hurry."

"If it's lady's choice, we're goin' to the City," Jazzra answered boldly when Chogan asked her where she wanted to have dinner.

What Jazzra loved about San Francisco was the way one could cross a bridge and within minutes fall into the heart of a beautiful, soulful urbanity. She wanted good Italian, a particular pesto gnocchi made only at a small family trattoria off Washington Square in North Beach. Chogan was happy to oblige and admitted his surprise that in just twenty minutes after leaving the church he was parking the Blue Bomb in a garage at Vallejo and Columbus.

They started with martinis at the bar and after sliding into their seats at a table, ordered a bottle of Nebbiolo. Their conversation began with the accretion of little stories that connected the particular dots of their attractive commonalities. Chogan and Jazzra together bore a genetic grievance not easily reconciled with race or culture. They were self-named "others," though each grew up thinking of "the other" as others. For Chogan the other was "waugie," which was Yurok for white man, until he learned his father was white. For Jazzra it was much the same. Her neighborhood was full of black people. Her uncle often said Richmond was a town without Negroes because everyone was black, which angered Jazzra whose claim to be black was possible only because, as she said, "a little bit of black was all I needed not to be white."

"But are we white?" Chogan asked.

For him to be anything less than half-Yurok was all he needed not to be Indian.

"I'm called a half-breed by my own people and mistaken for a tan waugie by everyone else."

Chogan and Jazzra found together a supportive and mutual expression of their difficult identities among the confusions of their respective origins. Race, which did not have a scientific definition, nevertheless had grown for each of them into a biological mitosis of warring cultures.

"The wilderness is a kind of home," Chogan said.

"I feel like myself there and don't worry how others might see me. At least others appear smaller among the big trees and mountains.

I can choose when to appear. The land hides me and protects me."

"You have a pretty happy view of nature," Jazzra responded.

"I only see nature's indifference to its precious creations."

Chogan wondered how Jazzra could see nature at all from within the ragged and ravaged landscape of her Richmond neighborhood.

"No trees or mountains," answered Jazzra, "but lots of creatures everywhere and huge struggles to survive. Isn't that what happens in the woods?"

Chogan agreed up to a point. But added it was different where he lived and, almost in passing, asked Jazzra to come with him Sunday and see for herself.

Jazzra put down her fork and took a long sip from her wine glass. She looked into Chogan's face with deep, searching eyes.

"You want me to leave with you?" she asked.

"What are you saying?"

Chogan spoke as if exhaling the momentum of a divine spirit. He had a plan and described its elements. The first, of course, was the removal of Jerome as a threat to Jazzra. This Chogan would accomplish by setting Jerome up to be busted with a large amount of meth. He described Jerome's offer and his scheme.

"You just need to tip your sheriff friend. I'll give you the time and place."

"What about your $80,000?" Jazzra asked suspiciously.

Chogan waved his hand. He could not fully explain why the sum was no longer important, why money itself was not the point anymore.

"I have enough already," he answered.

"It's just a gift."

Jazzra set down her glass and sat up as if to take full stock of Chogan.

"Around here no one gives a gift. They sell it for power. You talkin' about blowing eighty grand to set me free?"

"If you're free, maybe you'll go away with me," said Chogan.

"You can always come back."

"I can?" Jazzra scoffed.

"If there is a hint of suspicion I had anything to do with Jerome's…"

She let the consequence hang in the air.

"Then go with me," Chogan demanded.

"And don't come back."

Jazzra at first recoiled from what appeared to be Chogan's guileless plan. Yet he displayed the metal of a smart warrior and clearly knew something about the mechanics of human trade.

Her affection for him had grown reluctantly over their days together. Now he was saying he would give up tens of thousands of dollars to assure her safety. This was a provocation that at last induced in Jazzra a helpless, viral attraction. Silence enveloped them for several minutes.

"What do you want me to do?" Jazzra asked at last, her open face the offering of an abruptly opened heart.

They left the city and crossed the Golden Gate. The night was warm and Jazzra opened her window to smell the breeze blowing off the ocean. She asked her questions while Chogan looked ahead and gave his answers.

"And you really think this will work?" she asked again and then again.

Chogan could not describe the clarity of his vision or that of a dream more truthful than experience. It was a dream that grew from the Yurok part of him just as Jazzra's caution sprung from an urbanity of expected suffering. Too much or too little—what separately could they really do? And why? It was not a trick to have more primacy together than apart.

10

In Chogan's world common objects were animate and held power. Jazzra heard his plan and while struck with its logical simplicity, heard it as a fable by which good outcomes arrived via a warrior's wise management of inner strengths and outer momenta. They lay in bed as he told her, the details so simple it seemed hardly possible it could work. Friday morning he called a cab to return her to Richmond.

"We can't be seen together," he told her.

The plan depended on Jazzra tipping the detective. Chogan would give her the time and place of the drop-off after talking with Jerome. Jazzra would leave the church during the Sunday service and take a train from Richmond to the El Cerrito BART station where Chogan would be waiting. She would leave a note for Lamont saying she was going to visit an old high school friend in Los Angeles and would phone later in the week.

"They'll be watching me," he told her.

"Once Jerome and I have a plan his boys will try to follow me."

Chogan thought he could elude them.

"It's simple," Chogan told Jerome as they sat again in the church garage.

"I'll park somewhere in town Sunday afternoon. It will be a public place where I feel safe. The vehicle will be unlocked. You'll place the shit under a blanket below the front seat and lock the door. I'll arrive at three and drive north."

"Why all this mumbo jumbo?" Jerome asked impatiently.

"Don't you trust me?

"I trust you fine," Chogan said.

"I don't trust things I can't see. I don't want to see any cops. When I think the coast is clear I'll walk to the car and drive it away. That's the deal."

"When you bringing your truck? When will I know where it is?" Jerome asked.

"It won't be the truck," said Chogan.

"I'm buying a new car. Give me a number. I'll call you."

"Where you stayin'?" Jerome asked.

"Why don't we know where you are?

Chogan said he needed his privacy.

"Is that a problem?" Chogan asked.

"We don't have to do this. You can give me my money and I'm outta here."

It was a bluff. Jerome had purchased Chogan's dope for a third less than the agreed upon price. And Chogan would deal Jerome's meth in virgin territory on the northwest coast. Such a deal, and Jerome knew it.

"No. We'll do it your way. You're one paranoid Indian."

"Indians in this country got a right to be paranoid," said Chogan.

"You can relate to that."

Jerome gave Chogan a number to phone.

"When you gonna call?" Jerome asked.

"Sunday afternoon around two," said Chogan and rose to leave.

Chogan knew he would be followed. He drove north to Highway Four and meandered east toward the valley and the vast multi-lane river of Highway 680. He turned south toward Dublin and San Jose. He could see the two Izzy boys behind him, cruising wildly around cars to keep pace.

Chogan let their blue BMW creep closer before he crossed two lanes in a swift and risky dash that put him on one of several exit ramps to the 580 cloverleaf. He watched the Izzys pass helplessly on the freeway. When and if they returned, they would not know what direction he went or where he was bound among several directions and thousands of cars. Chogan drove through Hayward to the Dumbarton Bridge and crossed to the peninsula to drive north toward the city, the gate and the hills beyond.

Jazzra answered the phone and Chogan heard her cool voice signal caution in the presence of others.

"I can't tell you yet," he said vaguely.

"I was followed today. I don't want to take chances."

"OK," Jazzra minimized her response.

"When?"

"Sunday morning," he answered.

"Will that work? You can call me here after nine."

"I'll make it work," Jazzra answered.

Chogan gave her the hotel number and his room extension.

"And the BART station," Chogan said.

"One o'clock Sunday. El Cerrito. See you there. Yes?"

"Yes," Jazzra answered.

"Yes, you will."

Chogan enjoyed the new motion of money though he did not like to carry its weight. Saturday he drove his El Camino to the Marin City flea market and put a handwritten sign on the windshield that read Free Truck. A stocky teenage boy pulled his father over.

"What's the catch?" the father asked.

Chogan grinned.

"It runs fine. I'm moving. First one to take the pink slip gets it."

Chogan left as the father and son started the engine and high-fived in the front seat.

I'm one rich Indian, Chogan thought to himself as he drove the Mazda across the bridge and scouted Richmond neighborhoods for a secure public place for the meth drop. He found the vast circular parking lot of the Hilltop Mall and drove toward its multi-story retail complex. He parked in a diagonal lane some fifty yards north of Sears and stepped off the distance to the mall where he presumed Jerome would wait and the police would hide.

After exploring the premises, he returned to the Mazda and drove to a nearby residential block where he parked it on the street. He walked back to Hilltop and phoned for a cab to take him to his hotel where he handed the driver a hundred dollar bill. He also left a large tip with his dinner check. He gifted everyone who helped him, circulating his wealth in another kind of forest and reaping its constant return.

When Jazzra phoned him Sunday morning Chogan sat in his room packed and ready to leave. He had driven to Richmond before dawn and moved the Mazda into the Hilltop parking lot. He gave her the car's location and told her what to say to the detective.

"Jerome might bring some boys," Chogan said.

"They have guns."

"You still think this will work?" Jazzra asked.

She could hear Chogan sigh.

"It has to," he said finally.

He would see her in El Cerrito.

As Chogan crossed the bridge he saw great plumes of black and white smoke fill the southern sky, pouring out like a storm from behind the hills of Oakland and Berkeley. At the BART station Chogan drove slowly through a sooty haze. He parked and walked to the plaza under a light rain of char and ash. It was 11 a.m. and he imagined Jazzra leaving church to catch her train. He bought a cup of coffee at a café and assumed the agony of waiting. He realized the air was very warm and that he was afraid.

He tried to bring up some soothing truth to restore his confidence. He envisioned all the dead who lived before him, their bones spread out like the waves of salmon climbing a river's downhill current. If Jazzra did not come, would he leave anyway? She would come. What must happen was now an act of faith. The meth drop needed to look natural to all who would be watching: to the detective and the police, to Jerome and his boys, and even to bystanders walking by. No one must know who was watching and where, something Chogan himself could not know.

He walked from the café in time to see Jazzra standing on the BART platform. He waved and she found him.

"What's all this smoke?" she asked fearfully.

Chogan shook his head as he lifted her suitcase and pushed it into the back of the Honda.

"We're not waiting to find out," he said.

Chogan drove toward the freeway and entered Highway 80 going north.

"Is this the way?" Jazzra asked worriedly.

"You're driving toward Hilltop. The bridge and Eureka are the other way."

"We're taking Highway Five and crossing through the mountains," Chogan said.

"We aren't going anywhere Jerome expects us to go."

Jazzra was silent as Chogan crossed the Carquinez Bridge and pushed through Vallejo as the smoky skies receded behind them. Fire engines passed going south.

"Must be a big fire back there," Chogan said.

Jazzra nodded nervously.

He stopped in Vacaville to phone Jerome. It was just past two.

"You goddamned mothuh, you sure cut it close," Jerome shouted at him.

"Where the fuck are you?"

Chogan told him the Hilltop location of the Mazda and spelled out the car's license plate.

"No bullshit," Chogan demanded.

"Put the dope in the car, lock it and leave."

"Yeah, yeah," Jerome said.

"Not even a kiss goodbye, big Indian man?"

Chogan hung up the phone and climbed back into the Honda. Jazzra gave him a searching look as if to ask both him and herself what exactly they were doing. We are floating away, Chogan wanted to tell her. We are hawks in flight. Jazzra grasped his unspoken meaning and in her uneasy transience felt again like confluent warmth.

It was as scary for her as it was effortless until that evening when they arrived in Red Bluff and found a motel for the night. Dinner at a Denny's was like all the others, their conversation dwelling again on their common childhoods lived as cultural orphans, then turning flirty and teasing until they were gathered up together for the return to their room. She watched Chogan closely. He was an intimate rock and in bed a giant next to her with warm lips and earthy smells. He anchored her wary thoughts.

"There is no place else I can go," she told him through suddenly hot, wet tears.

"No place else I want you," he answered, his arms tight around her.

No place else in a mean, ravenous world.

11

Wet wreathes were a remnant of the vacated holiday season and as the man in charge of maintenance Chogan began to take them down. He slipped out of a drenching downpour and huddled in the building's foyer where he climbed a ladder to reach a row of drooping pine and holly. It was an early January morning, still dark in the rain, though gamblers were arriving, as they did at all hours, to play games at the Trinidad Rancheria's new casino.

Chogan did not need the job but he was glad to have it. His mother found it for him, perfect for a big Indian and his new girlfriend, who also was hired as a part-time bookkeeper. And his prospects were good. He was training for a position on the casino's security force, which meant in a few weeks he would have a gun.

The gun seemed less important now as the old year faded away and with it the abiding fear of Jerome's unknown whereabouts. For days after their easy escape, Jazzra and Chogan searched what newspapers they could find for information about a drug bust in Richmond. But there was only one story anyone was reporting: a great fire that destroyed hundreds of homes in the Berkeley and Oakland hills, a fire that killed more than two dozen people and on a single warm and very windy October weekend became the most destructive blaze in the state's history.

Chogan and Jazzra took their first refuge in Hateya's Klamath home, hiding in Chogan's childhood room while waiting to confirm Jerome's arrest and the end of the Izzy Boys. After a week Jazzra phoned her Uncle who said Jerome and his boys were gone and he and Ruth didn't know where.

"Cops all over the place now," he told her.

"They sit in their cars at both corners and watch us like god-fearing hawks. When you comin' home, darlin'?"

Jazzra said she didn't know. She wanted to ask about the detective but Chogan thought it too risky to talk to a cop.

Chogan went to work, more as a cover for his fortune than to pursue a career. He was probably the richest Indian on the Klamath and wanted no one to know it. A job would help him divert his cash into a bank account from which he could pay his mother's mortgage and the rent on his new Westhaven house that overlooked the ocean. Picked up by the tribe in a foreclosure, the three-bedroom vacation home stood at the edge of a plateau at the west end of Sixth Avenue. Rent was $650, high for the area but affordable for Chogan.

A high wooden fence along the road gave Chogan and Jazzra a common feeling of security and in late November Chogan drove by the old Izzy Boys duplex on West Wabash in Eureka and saw a For Sale sign on the lawn. Whether Jerome was in jail, in hiding, or dead, it didn't seem to matter. He was gone. And that meant a new life finally could begin for Chogan and Jazzra. Time no more was the echo of fearful reckoning but more what Chogan understood it to be, the experience of night and day, the phases of the moon and the living breath of summers and winters and not just the passing of years.

Though life was hard for Jazzra and becoming harder. She loved Chogan but hated that few if any black people lived in her new community.

"It's the goddamned sticks," she said in frustration one Sunday morning.

"Not a sister or brother anywhere. I don't know if I can do this."

Chogan at first fought with Jazzra who for a couple of weeks was ready to go home, whatever the risk. It was a tribute to either their love or their desperately entwined conspiracy that Chogan suggested they go farther north and live in Portland or Seattle, real cities of diversity. They looked ahead to a spring trip into Oregon and Washington.

Gamblers walked past Chogan's ladder, mostly white men with money to burn. Even if they didn't have it, they burned it. There were no clocks in the casino, which presented no problem to the Yuroks who had little use for measured time. Chogan had noticed that Indians did not gamble. It was white people that used the space obsessively to pull at slot machines, play craps and cards, bet on spinning wheels and sporting events, to try to beat the rhythms of time and overwhelm what they called the "odds" that in a Native understanding were only unorganized moments.

Time seemed to change nothing despite hopes for progress, success or good luck. Time was an eternal moment inhabited by ancestors as well as the living. It was secure in its recapitulation of natural processes but made more dangerous by the insertion of lineal expectations, by the idea it went somewhere. Instead, Yuroks occupied their casino as if living at the back of a cave into which the children of old white settlers were invited and lulled into timeless preoccupation, where past transgressions might be balanced and compensated and the conqueror's children thoroughly fleeced.

Their journey north had held Chogan and Jazzra in mutual grace, their escape a vital and cooperative practice. A week of such work had converted their attraction into affection with touches and glances that shaped a hearty and urgently reliable trust met both in body and mind. In creating the terms of their new existence, Chogan offered to Jazzra both his wealth and protection while honoring Jazzra's freedom to decide at any time to do what she needed or wanted to do, even if that were to leave him.

It wasn't necessary. Jazzra's mother had abandoned her. Her uncle deferred to Ruth who intimidated her.

"I have never had any standing," Jazzra said.

She did not know where she would end up in her life but what and where she was now was good enough and, in any event, she was never going back and Chogan showed in a willingness to move to a northwest city his deep and unfamiliar but very welcome regard. She needed no more words for time.

One afternoon while they were shopping in Arcata, Chogan saw Jaime leaving Toby and Jack's. He waved and walked him back to his car, reaching under the seat for a stack of bills.

"It's $10,000 from the dope," he said to Jaime, who reeled in surprise.

Jaime could not find words to thank his brother's friend.

"You take care of yourself," Chogan told Jaime.

"And tell Jorge hello."

Slowly a future seemed drawn into the present in a way that offered increasingly bright glimmers of hope even as the weather shifted into its wet, wintry and mildewing dissolution.

"How long will you be with us, Mr. Rivers?" asked the hotel desk clerk as he handed back to Jerome his fabricated ID.

It was a driver's license in the name of Marcel Rivers, an alleged resident of Encinitas. Jerome smiled with the confidence of a burglar who had just found a hidden key.

"Two nights," he answered.

"Leaving early the last morning. I'll pay now."

The clerk apologized for the wet weather while Jerome counted out several twenties.

"Eureka—it's winter, you know. We get a lot of rain," said the clerk.

"Yeah," said Jerome, distracted as he took his room key and climbed a stairway to the second floor of the Red Lion Inn.

Jerome lay on his bed. He was suddenly comfortable in a place he no longer belonged. He recalled again the Sunday afternoon that changed his life, that gave him strength and power in accordance with his dreams and only because he had some second sense that saved his ass.

Was it his anxious response to the wind-blown ash of the big fire? Was it the security guard driving slowly up an aisle of parking spaces in the Hilltop lot? He couldn't say but at the last minute, instead of giving the boys a pound and half of meth to leave in Chogan's car, he stuffed into a bag a sweat suit and a pair of smelly tennis shoes taken from his car trunk. As one of the boys opened the driver's door, a dozen cops surrounded him and grabbed the bag. The Izzy boys were pushed to the ground while a detective emerged to search the bag and them.

While Jerome watched from the Hilltop's second floor food court, he nearly threw up. His test run had begun as an afterthought. It became a reckoning of his inadequate understanding of places he could not see. He walked to the back of the Sears store and hid for a half-hour in a bathroom stall where he tucked a wrapped 24-ounce sack full of meth vigorously into his pants, tightening it under his belt in a way that made him look simply paunchy and not guilty.

The cops, who were called immediately to the huge fire in the hills, released the Izzy boys. Jerome emerged after the police cars left and met his troops at the mall's north exit. His apparent good judgment won him his boys' loyalty and raised his profile with the gang bosses who counted. He was given a new and larger territory and also time to take care of Chogan.

Jerome drove through a driving rain toward Westhaven. He had called in his last favor from a local dealer and learned the address of the big Indian. As he drove, Jerome considered the people he had killed, far fewer than the people he had threatened. As a youth he shot two members of another gang but only one had died. As a drug gang gofer he was called on to take out a street dealer who had broken the rules.

The previous year he was hired to kill the wife of a colleague when she tried to leave him and take away his children. He picked her up to run an errand and left her body deep in the hills of north Tilden Park. He never left a trace and was never caught. This would be no different.

12

Jerome believed at any moment in what he pretended to be. Tonight he was a warrior determined to reclaim his honor. All that was left was to scout his antagonist's property and to decide how best to kill him.

Jerome found the highway's Westhaven exit and through a pounding downpour followed directions back across an overpass that dropped him into an elevated meadow lined at its perimeter by a looping road and several homes. He parked under a tall redwood tree and rushed across the meadow to a fenced residence he had been told was Chogan's.

Lights were on in the split-level house though a high fence blocked its entrance and the gate was locked, forcing Jerome to feel his way through the darkness of an adjacent forest. He found a back gate that opened on a wide yard overlooking a road below and, beyond the road, the stark cliffs of a barely visible shoreline. He heard the clamorous smash of surf above the roar of a furious wind and the pounding clatter of rain against the ground. Jerome crawled behind a tree to view the home's wide downstairs window filled out by the warm flickering light from a fireplace. He saw Chogan's back in a chair as he sat and spoke with a woman sitting on a couch. Jerome crawled closer for a better view and staggered to his feet when he realized the woman was Jazzra.

Jerome had not accounted for enough empty spaces in his version of events even to imagine that Jazzra would be with Chogan. She had left Richmond. He knew that. But a connection to Chogan was unimaginable, until now as it grew from a surprise into a revelation and then became an irrevocable and angering conclusion. Jerome would have to kill them both.

Driving back to Eureka Jerome savored the details. The next night he would park again under the tree, which was too far from other homes on the loop to be viewed by anyone. He would climb again into Chogan's back yard and slip along the side of the house to knock on the door. He would wait in the shadows thrown by the fence and when either Chogan or Jazzra emerged, he would shoot. From there he would enter the house, likely to confront the other who would be caught by surprise.

Once both were shot and killed he would leave as he came, run to his car and in a minute be back on the highway headed south. By the time their bodies were found, Jerome would be in Oakland. He thought of wearing a mask but decided against it. It was an important and essential quality of Jerome's vengeance that Chogan know who had found him and would kill him.

The rain continued into the following day. Chogan and Jazzra drove to the casino to work their shifts, canceling a lunchtime walk along the trail north of Trinidad to Omenoku Point. It was enough to plan dinner and an evening alone. Together they were becoming increasingly non-existent in their individuality, feeling more between themselves like the alternating rhythms of a tiny, vibrant community.

They had new names for each other, cute and unique and chosen like Yurok names from the personalizing circumstances of their new lives. A black lab pup would soon join their family, delivered on the weekend by Chogan's brother. She, too, would be given a name.

Jerome spent the day in his hotel room. He thought the fewer who saw him the better. Eureka was a town as white in its way as Jerome's own town was black. There would be no witnesses but Eureka was a small enough place that a resident who could not positively identify a black man might still remember seeing one.

Jerome loaded his gun and rehearsed his moves. He watched television in the afternoon and ordered a burger and fries from the restaurant around 3 p.m. By six he had packed his small case and left the hotel. He wanted an early start. He wanted to surprise his targets after their dinner, which he would watch them eat until they appeared satisfied, relaxed, even soporific. He would watch and then surprise them like a cheetah on the savannah ambushing its exposed, forsaken prey.

On the way to his car Jerome stopped a bellhop to ask the location of a nearby liquor store.

"Three blocks up. Fifth and Myrtle. You can't miss it," said the bellhop.

Jerome would want a drink after the killings. He would buy a pint, at least, of something strong. Bourbon or tequila. He couldn't decide. Something he could sip slyly as he drove home. Jerome found the intersection and turned his BMW into a vast and mostly empty parking lot behind the store.

Jerome climbed out of the car and scuttled toward the door, his head down in a driving downpour, until he felt someone bump into him. Jerome looked up.

"Hey, watch it, dude!" the other said until, peering into Jerome's face, he pushed an arm out to stop him.

Jerome stared at the man, a small Mexican he vaguely recognized.

"Hey…you the fuckin' nigger that jumped me last year," the man shouted at Jerome.

Jerome stopped and looked at the Mexican he quickly recognized as Jaime. A stolid silence held the two men in their places for a moment until Jerome, bolstered by his cultivated rage, smiled wickedly.

"Yeah, we sure did fuck you in the ass you stupid little prick," he shouted at the small Mexican.

"You know you won't forget it. Still sore you dumb cocksucker?"

Jerome laughed.

"You need to get your ass out of here before someone fucks it again."

Jerome continued to laugh in a way that expressed his fully realized aggression. Jaime backed off and began to walk slowly away.

"Yeah, get out of here before I fuck you in the goddamned ass myself," Jerome shouted.

He watched Jaime disappear into the darkness.

Jerome entered the store and weighed his choices, settling on a pint of Jack Daniels and another of Hornitos. The bottles were pulled from the shelf and bagged by a brusque store clerk. Jerome walked back out to the parking lot and approached his BMW, his head again down in the rain.

He opened the side door and rushed to sit in the driver's seat. As he started the engine he looked up to see his windshield smashed, a large hole at the driver's position radiating a cascade of infinite fissures.

"What th…?" he muttered and jumped back out of the car, looking first toward the street before hearing a shout.

"Hey nigger, over here!"

Jerome turned to see Jaime standing on the other side of a blue Chevy truck, its engine running. Jaime aimed a large rifle at Jerome. Two loud shots shattered the rainy night, Jerome blown back as his body sprawled across the pavement, his bloody head instantly detached and rolled toward a puddle.

Jaime climbed back into his truck and drove down the alley, turning right at Myrtle. He went two blocks before reversing his direction, ending up on Fourth Street in a sea of cars traveling Highway 101 south through town. He turned west on H Street and drove to the wharf where he stopped near an empty pier. He got out of the truck and carried the rifle under his jacket, hunched against the heavy rain. He looked behind him once before dropping the weapon into the bay.

Jaime heard the sound of sirens roll like a loud wave from south to north. He climbed back into his truck and turned on the radio. The voice of Ana Gabriel warmed him with the embrace of her latest hit song.

> *Pero yo te aclaro de una vez*
> *lo debes de entender*
> *es demasiado tarde*

"*Es demasiado tarde…*" Jaime sang as he started the engine and drove cautiously back toward the highway. He turned his truck away from the distancing sirens and again rolled south and out of town. He would be at the border in 16 hours. Jorge would be surprised to see him.

HEARING
VOICES

1

The reasons Wendy gave birth to a child did not occur to her until after she lost it. Wendy remembered her husband wanted a baby, wanted the smell and touch of an infant almost more than the smell and touch of their sex. Wendy enjoyed sex though it was hard now to recall in either smell or touch the experience of either her baby or sex. Her husband, too, was lost.

It had been three months since the accident and as she sat in the bedroom shrine arranged neatly to memorialize both her daughter and partner, Wendy emerged briefly from the fog of her grief. *I wanted love,* she thought. *I wanted love and also to stop thinking about love.* Sammy provided Wendy her purest, most unalloyed object of unconditional love, while her husband ended entirely her search for it.

Both daughter and husband were gone and while she still loved them, they could no longer love her. Three months after losing Sammy and Joe in a crosswalk two blocks from home, together and in the same slashing moment, Wendy was just now finding space to breathe. She thought it might be a good sign to be able to survey the damage without crumpling, to ask questions without anymore needing answers. She still spoke to them, still chatted Sammy up in the mornings as she dusted the bedroom's furniture and photos and argued with Joe in the evenings, usually after a second glass of wine. These were her most interesting conversations. To living friends, neighbors, co-workers and family she rarely had very much to say. Most by now had stopped calling or trying to elicit anything but general information about her state and health.

There had been no funeral. Joe and Wendy were not religious and she knew few people well enough to invite. Joe's parents wanted a service but it would not occur until Wendy was ready. And she could not imagine ever being ready. Two boxes of ashes remained stacked and sealed in the back of a closet and could stay there forever as far as Wendy was concerned. Martha, an elderly widow and her immediate neighbor said over the fence she worried about Wendy, which seemed superfluous since Wendy did not worry. Such a loss had dropped worry completely from her awareness. For three years Joe and Sammy were all she had ever worried about. Without them she was without fear and could not imagine ever again being afraid.

Each day she spoke with Sammy first, addressed the color photo of a happy toddler with straight honey hair standing in the yard, a face open and broad with the smile learned from her father. Sammy had Joe's blue eyes and open face and her father made her laugh so hard at times, so hard she would start to pee, her relentless giggles echoing away as she ran for the toilet.

Sammy's life arrived out of Wendy's deep desire to extend her own, to make a life that would be and become something better, what Wendy wanted in her life and had not yet known. Wendy spoke to Sammy in the stunted sentences of a child barely three-years-old. She spoke to Sammy in a way she thought her daughter would understand, aware there was nothing more to teach.

With Joe she was more reflective and sometimes severe. Wendy described her day's quotidian, discussed money and sometimes gossiped about family though after enough wine she could become angry, plead for answers and, when none were forthcoming, accuse him of a painful, gross ineptness, though she wasn't present and did not see the accident. Witnesses agreed Joe had thrown himself in front of Sammy's stroller as a car rushed toward them in the crosswalk. He was bumped high in the air and thrown back head first onto the pavement as the car plowed forward dragging the stroller and child under its wheels for twenty feet before stopping. Sammy's beautiful teardrop of a face was smashed, flattened and left lifeless like a chunk of Play-Doh. The driver was a college sophomore who was applying makeup while speeding in a school zone and who was gravely remorseful and in big trouble in ways that seemed useless to Wendy who had given up her anger with the woman when anger finally gave up on her.

A sloppy drunk or murderous psychopath would make more sense to hate. The previous week an unemployed shopkeeper in Scotland had walked into a grammar school and gunned down 16 children and their teacher. That was someone Wendy could despise. But a ditzy student, a young woman whose promising life was ruined, could not serve adequately as an object of loathing. Wendy had attended a court hearing to witness the driver's arraignment, the young woman bawling uncontrollably like a baby in a way that left Wendy to imagine a grown-up Sammy in the young woman's place. In her darker, more disorienting moments of self-doubt Wendy sometimes thought she should phone the girl and apologize for Sammy and Joe and their temerity to cross the street in front of her.

The central living space of Wendy's home had moved entirely into Sammy's bedroom. The home sat low on a hillside street in west Petaluma, it's vast living room angled with a view of homes, hills and mountains out its wide picture window. The family had gathered there in the evenings to talk, play games and watch television. But it was Sammy's bedroom where Wendy spent her waking time now. She sometimes ate her dinner at Sammy's changing table, surrounded by her daughter's favorite clothes and stuffed toys and an ever enlarging collection of mounted photos scavenged from sheaved negatives and drugstore envelopes filled with 3x5 prints.

The rest of the home had become an afterthought, including the master bedroom where Wendy no longer slept. Instead, she fell asleep each night on the living room sofa and under a lamp she never turned off, the master now a dark repository for Joe's clothes, tools, cameras and books. The home remained hers as long as she could pay the mortgage.

Beyond the home was a neighborhood that until the accident had sustained Wendy's good feelings and good will. She knew her immediate neighbors and had waved at and greeted others as she and Joe walked Sammy each morning and evening within a half-mile perimeter of streets, lanes and cul-de-sacs. This small universe also contained the intersection where Sammy and Joe were killed, a place Wendy drove thoroughly around and no longer approached on foot. The accident occurred just before the winter holidays and Joe's and Sammy's unopened presents remained under the tree until the middle of January.

Wendy eventually returned Joe's, but gave away Sammy's, the experience a numbing trauma and another marker of the wearying engulfment of her loss. It was unreal to her, absorbed as she was with brutal things she could not let reach her all at once. She felt alive only in a world of zombie neighbors that saw her but that she could no longer see.

Beyond her neighborhood was another deeply changed world. Her work still commanded enormous attention. She was the office manager for a local real estate office. Wisely in her first year she had become indispensable as a planner and organizer, but to the point where her allowed week of bereavement leave turned into a crisis for the company's owner. Helpless without her, agents phoned incessantly until she gave up and returned to the office two days early.

Work was still the hardest part of her day in the way it seemed merely to refresh the quality of her time prior to the accident. She walked into the office each morning where nothing had changed and each morning for the first hour or so did not think of anything but work until, struck suddenly by an urge to phone Joe or to check on Sammy, she would need to leave her desk and wait in the bathroom for the tears to stop, stop, stop, why won't they stop.

Tears no longer came, at least not as they did. Nothing any longer came to her and Wendy had stopped waiting. At age 32 she might have made her way without Joe, if Sammy were there to care for and love. Or, if Sammy alone were lost, she might have survived with Joe and likely had another child. She had neither Sammy nor Joe, and no energy to imagine another husband or baby. It seemed impossible to touch anyone again in such a way, with such unrequited affection, to ever again risk such a vulnerable exposure to the wounding mechanics of relationship.

It was the spring of a new year that as yet had no distinguishing features. Wendy found herself begging, criticizing, apologizing and expressing deep anger over the easy disappearance of her husband and daughter. She envied their joining a majority in a way that left her alone in a life that was the visceral and insufferable experience of loss, and apparently nothing else.

2

Wendy's memories were becoming ever more an invention of her unfulfilled hopes. It was the first Saturday of spring and she chose this day to do what she had told herself to do. She pulled the last of Samantha's baby things from the garage to sort and dispose. It was a chore she no longer faced with dread. She imagined her daughter clearly and thought it a triumph to awaken with her death and still feel alive herself, to resist at last the urge of many parts of her to succumb and simply dissolve.

She carried cardboard boxes into the kitchen and set them in a circle on the floor. She pulled a stepstool toward them and sat bent over on its first step, opening the first box and scooping from it an assortment of baby accessories: towels, paper diapers, a plastic infant tub, a few dirty bibs, and a baby monitor. The unused towels and diapers she would donate but the monitor might be worth something.

To think of selling one of Sammy's things was itself a triumph and Wendy took strength from this sudden exertion of practical thinking around the once treasured relics of her daughter's brief childhood. She found both the monitor's wireless transmitter and receiver and plugged the receiver into the wall to see if it still worked. A bright red light flickered and Wendy left the unit on the kitchen table to open another box.

As she tore at another box's flaps she heard a child's pouty cry. It was a small child's cry and very much like Sammy's. Wendy turned instinctively toward the sound, which rumbled from the speaker of the baby monitor. Wendy jumped up and ran to Sammy's room, as she always did when she heard Sammy's cry. She searched aimlessly with the dizzying hope she would find her daughter and at last give up her long and endured experience of loss. She searched among a pile of stuffed animals and reached anxiously behind the bed as if her precious baby were simply lost, until she heard the monitor crackle again with a baby's cry coupled now with the soothing voice of a woman.

"There, there, little darlin'…time to get up? Oh, there, there… let's have our snack. Does baby want her snack?"

The soothing maternal voice quieted the child who Wendy presumed was now cradled in its mother's arms, perhaps nursing, as the mother—wherever and whoever she was—likely gazed at the child affectionately. Or so Wendy imagined as it became clear no baby existed in her house and that the monitor was broadcasting another child's life. But how? And how cruel that this apparition of her own life as a mother could be transmitted so graphically and in a way that touched the core of her deepest hurt.

Wendy ran to the monitor and turned it off. She went to the living room to sit on the sofa, rank with the smell of her unwashed sleep. She sat to absorb the reverberating consequence of absence; a sensation she took in as another's perpetual departure, in this instance that of her baby Sammy. She spoke to her child.

"I am motionless and left in suspense. It is so hard to live with an always-absent you."

She might as well have been herself one of the boxes in the kitchen, a container opened to the truth she would henceforth and always be loved less than she loved.

After an hour of relentless tears, Wendy returned to the kitchen. She refilled the empty box with everything but the baby monitor. She carted all the boxes back to the garage and pushed them onto a high shelf where she would not easily see them. She wasn't yet ready for this next step of her discourse with her dead beloveds. Not ready to reconstitute memories. Instead, she buried them once again in the dry, yellow darkness.

Wendy had left the baby monitor on the table and two days later, after finishing her evening glass of wine, switched it back on. She braced herself for the sounds of the baby, worn down by a bittersweet attraction to the child's cry, though she heard nothing beyond the speaker's flowing hum. She waited through the evening and was about to switch off the monitor when shortly after ten another voice crackled to life.

"My doctor says we gotta use a condom. And I believe her. I don't like 'em, either. But I want to be safe."

It was a woman's voice again, but not the same woman. Wendy hovered at the speaker.

"Yeah…" mumbled a man's voice that sounded more distant.

"Not a problem for me. Course not. We can use some KY, too. It will make it better."

A silence followed.

"Better? I guess, though I don't come from fucking. I hope THAT's not a problem."

It was the woman talking again. Wendy turned up the monitor's volume.

"You don't?" the man replied.

"You didn't know that?" the woman asked.

"I'm a little new to this," said the man.

"Listen, I gotta go home now. I'll call you tomorrow."

Wendy heard the woman say "OK" and then a click.

The experience of absence for Wendy had become an active practice. Being left behind was the task at hand that kept her from doing anything else. Arms once raised in desire were now arms crossed in protection. The monitor's new voices intrigued her, though, and briefly interrupted her grieving. What had she heard? It sounded like a phone call. How was her monitor picking up the intimate lives of others? It was like listening to a radio.

She reopened a box to find the monitor's instructions and combed through them. She read that the monitor was set for broadcast and reception at a particular frequency. It seemed possible other people's devices, baby monitors and cordless phones, could be set for the same frequency and with the monitor's transmitter turned off she was receiving other transmissions. For the rest of the week she left the monitor on. The happy mother returned several times to feed and sing to her baby. The couple Wendy heard talking about their sex also returned and spent an hour reviewing their latest tryst in a quality of detail that Wendy found arousing. She heard other conversations, a few by neighbors whose voices she recognized.

"Wish I had a dollar for every customer that complained about a monitor," said the appliance salesman as he leaned over his sales counter to examine Wendy's receiver.

Wendy reminded the salesman she wasn't there to complain. She just wanted to understand what was happening.

"Of course, a lot don't complain. They don't mind listening to their neighbors."

"Tell me how this works," Wendy asked directly.

The salesman, a tall, older man wearing a wrinkled white shirt with a pocket protector filled with pens, seemed suddenly shy.

"Don't get a lot of women in here with that question," he answered.

"You're right about the monitor. It's a kind of radio set to receive signals from its transmitter in the range of 43-49 megahertz. Trouble is, a lot of monitors and cordless phones are set to transmit at the same frequencies. Receivers can pick these up if the monitor's transmitter isn't on or the batteries are weak. So what you're hearing are monitors and phones in your area that are on the same frequency."

"Is that legal?" Wendy asked.

"Let me show you something," the salesman said and went to a back shelf.

He brought back a handheld device with a stubby, rubber antenna and turned it on.

"The Realistic Pro-34. It's a police scanner. Listen."

He turned it on and showed Wendy the display. Long numbers flashed by in an apparent random order, stopping occasionally when she heard a voice reading off a driver's license or giving brief descriptions. Wendy gave the salesman a puzzled look.

"You're hearing police calls. Cops on duty reporting to a dispatcher or talking to other cops. This one is programmed for 17 local police and fire agencies. Well, this baby can also be programmed to receive phone and monitor frequencies. I sell a lot of them."

Wendy continued to listen as the salesman handed her the scanner. She held it lightly, embarrassed to behave as an eavesdropper.

"So you can hear....?"

The salesman nodded knowingly.

"On sale this week. $99 plus tax."

Wendy cleared the desk in the bedroom and set her new scanner down, loading its batteries and attaching its antenna. She checked the list of frequencies given her by the salesman and read the directions for loading frequencies for scanning. She found she could select a range and the scanner would stop at any active frequency. She was suddenly and obsessively interested in probing for the words and dialogues of others.

For too long she had been engaged only with herself, listening to the words she sent out to her lost husband and daughter while hearing nothing back. She would be fine now to listen to conversations that passed every moment through her walls. She would be fine to know the thoughts and feelings of anyone but herself.

3

Wendy's new receiver became a gently despairing obsession. Dozens of conversations poured through its speaker as in the evenings she tuned through the cordless phone band. She was surprised at how quickly she succumbed to a compulsive interest in the private chatter of others. There was so much and the twenty or so frequencies reliably tuned by the scanner were a chorus of local voices, some of them familiar and all unguarded.

She frequently awoke in the cold darkness of early mornings, her body aching from its bent sleep, her head against the desktop as an empty frequency's noisy hash filled her ears and she at last turned off the scanner.

Standing away from the desk she could feel regretful, even ashamed that an interest in eavesdropping on others appeared out of her control. She rationalized her listening as simply the capture of radio waves that passed through her property and body and that in some sense belonged to her. Still, she felt at times like a drunk with a hangover whose only saving virtue was her ability to keep a secret.

Her days at work became a carefully clocked blur, broken by a lunch hour and two twenty-minute breaks. She was an employee of the company owner and not chummy with the agents who paid her boss to rent their desks and phone extensions. She provided crucial office services without which advertising, open homes, purchase offers and closing documents would be chaos to manage. So she was appreciated, if not always liked. Her reluctance to share deep feelings with others allowed her grief to exist without notice. Hers was a private, hidden sadness as was her new life as a fervent monitor of other people's lives.

And what lives they were. Tuning her scanner during the first week Wendy heard a teen girl worriedly tell her best friend she might be pregnant. She listened to a single woman across the street have loud, eloquent phone sex with her new boyfriend. She eavesdropped on a drug dealer arranging a sale, a sick cancer patient describing stoically his discouraging prognosis, a mother confessing to a friend she had searched her 13-year-old son's room and found a stash of gay porn. She heard the teary voice of an anguished lover, the hilarious banter of two neighbor wives as they ruthlessly bashed their husbands, the strained encouragement of an older woman as she comforted her tired, convalescing sister. A drunken nurse slurred graphically to a colleague her lecherous interest in a new hospital surgeon.

Conversations started and stopped without warning, sometimes one interfering with another in a way Wendy eventually determined was caused by the distance of phones from her receiver, a distance she learned quickly to gauge as those closer to her became regular subjects of her monitoring. Wendy felt boldly charmed to witness the secret lives of others in a way that allowed her to remain unconnected and disengaged.

Throughout her life she had been a shy, private person with an insatiable and unsatisfied curiosity about what people really thought and did. As a young girl her parents moved frequently, leaving Wendy with the wearying task of finding and making new friends every year or two. By adolescence the work of befriending others had become a daunting travail from which she finally withdrew. Yet her interest in those around her was unbearably vital. Wendy determined to simply watch and wait, though this strategy left her unattended and frequently friendless.

Her scanner gave Wendy a surprisingly direct engagement in the lives of those around her and in a way that permitted her to remain unconnected, undetected and unthreatened by whatever she heard. Much of what she heard was boring and routine. Appointments made, services scheduled, sales confirmed and concluded. But after a few weeks she had identified several callers by name and began a notebook in which she scribbled details of their lives and the names of those to whom they regularly spoke.

One Saturday she loaded the scanner with batteries and slipped it into her purse. As she walked the neighborhood's streets she listened through an ear bud as several conversations revealed the exact locations of her most active subjects. She added addresses to her notes and after a month of listening created a hand-drawn map that indicated exactly where certain callers lived.

"I can't say I love you, Ted. Please stop it. Please give me some goddamned room…"

The words rolled through Wendy's scanner, alerting her to a new subject. She checked the clock. It was after midnight and the signal was a distant one, faint and fragile in a way that suggested a range of a quarter-mile or more.

"You keep putting me on, Connie. You keep this crap up. What the fuck? You tease my fuckin' ass with all this friendly jive and then you pull back. Fuck. What am I supposed to think?"

Silence ensued for at least a minute though Wendy could hear the woman's heavy breathing.

"Charles, I don't think this can work," the woman said finally.

"Oh yeah?" the frantic male voice answered.

"Oh yeah? We'll see what works. I'll show you what works. Who do you think you are?"

Silence again.

"I have to go, Charles."

The woman's voice sounded farther from the phone.

"You'll be sorry, Connie. You are going to be goddamned…" and the phone clicked into an empty hiss.

The couple's hostile intensity, especially the anger of the man named Charles, startled Wendy. She heard many conversations fueled by anxiety and tension but nothing about love that was so thoroughly mean. Charles sounded threatening. In a way to rationalize her eavesdropping, Wendy had constructed the idea of what she termed indirect friends. These were people she listened to and cared about and who, of course, did not know her. She used this construct as a way to justify the rich new dialogues in her life, especially those that aroused her strong feelings without personally exposing her to hurt or loss.

The people she heard were real, though her versions of their lives probably were not. She heard what they said and the way they said it, but nothing else. Not who they really were. But it was enough for Wendy, even at times when the lives of her indirect friends could appear fearfully disturbing. Wendy wrote Connie's name in her notebook and added the frequency of the call and the time it occurred. She penciled the word Charles and a question mark.

On Sunday morning Wendy's phone rang. It was too early for a work call, though agents sometimes bothered her on the weekends for open home signs or to give her the name of a prospective buyer. Wendy at first flinched, worried in her drowsiness that one of her scanner subjects might be trying to reach her. Cut it out, they might say. Get out of my life. Instead, it was her mother who had not phoned since early February. Wendy had told her not to call.

"It's been awhile, Wendy," her mother said cautiously.

"I thought I'd try again."

"Uh-huh," Wendy muttered neutrally.

"Everything OK?" her mother asked.

It was her mother's usual question, her careful way to pry open a daughter's heart though she understood it to have been closed to her for many years. She could at one time satisfy, protect and comfort Wendy but in time her daughter's accrued disappointments grew between them an irresistible estrangement.

"I've been worried about you. You don't call and we don't know if…"

"Mom, mom…it's not a good time," Wendy interrupted.

There was a time as a child Wendy was merely the sum of her appetites and needs and her mother could rush quickly to her and meet them. For many years now Wendy's conflicts and desires had grown beyond her mother's reach or understanding. Mother tried vainly and persistently to reunite with her daughter on old terms. Wendy firmly and consistently resisted.

"I only meant…" Wendy's mother tried to interrupt.

"Gotta go, mom. Gotta go now."

Wendy hung up the phone.

Feelings were easily mistaken for reality and for quite a long time Wendy and her mother found it difficult to tell the difference. By the time of her middle adolescence Wendy's misbehavior had grown into an offensive rebellion. Her mother, though she smiled patiently and tried to soothe her daughter, would eventually walk away. And when she left, she took their relationship with her. Too much time passed in this disconnected state while each tended her own garden. Too much time until now there was no time. Wendy's loss was her own and she would die herself before sharing its wormy core with an ancient adversary.

4

As she listened to the scanner, Wendy thought her life was becoming less a narrative and more an abstract painting, dripping with blotchy incongruous and out-of-order impressions. The teenage girl, who thought she was pregnant, erupted with ecstatic relief when she got her period, phoning several friends immediately and swearing never again to have sex without a condom. The boy in question was no longer an item.

"He's such an asshole," she said.

It would not be her last asshole, thought Wendy.

The couple actually using condoms continued to talk about sex, the woman now ready to broach the full discussion of her orgasm with a partner she had begun to trust.

"You were so thoughtful yesterday when you rubbed my neck and back," she said warmly into his silence.

"You did it without asking," she added, as if to affirm his best qualities.

More silence followed as the woman waited for an encouraging response.

"You touch me so sweetly."

Wendy could sense the woman's gentle but earnest effort to direct the conversation to the touches that really mattered.

"Yeah," the boyfriend said as if distracted.

Wendy sometimes thought herself the only person crazy and at fault until her time with the radio introduced so many others who were impoverished, incomplete and equally to blame. The not-pregnant teen restored Wendy's memories of her own childhood sex play with friends and how she emerged from a stormy pubescence into a defiant, also guilty, adolescence that was imperious and unformed for far too long, lasting well into her twenties. Joe, she knew now, had come into her life as the returning father. And he did, so earnestly, erect for her the missing structures that allowed Wendy to accept love and then nurture it in another.

The older woman continued to comfort her dying sister, which

Wendy finally understood was the woman's only family. The couple trying to walk a walk of intimacy remained cautious, stuck and searching. The lovers in torrid conflict surprised Wendy with an intense passion as one night they talked each other into loud, lovely comes. The man dying of cancer tried hard to put his best face on things, increasingly taciturn the sicker he became.

"Damn, don't say anything to John," the tipsy nurse told her friend who had called to report a spectacular and nearly perfect act of adultery.

The friend had spent an afternoon with her lover who had made her "come twice" and ended their sexy afternoon by preparing a pasta dinner for her. She was driving home and had just spoken with her husband.

"He says he's feeling frisky," the friend said.

"You'll have to fuck him, Gina," the nurse answered.

"But I smell, I mean, I really stink of sex," said the friend.

"Tell him you're horny, you've been horny all day."

Laughs. Hearty laughs of women, like those Wendy heard complain about their husbands. Fat laughs of angry women not resigned to bitter disappointments but also not able to step away from them.

One evening Wendy began a scan of the 800 Mghz cellphone band, picking up mobile phone conversations that were more varied and plentiful but often cut short as moving signals were passed among cell towers. She heard an astringent conversation between two women as one helped the other with the words to best express her frustration with a boyfriend's inattention to her needs. The two agreed on what the woman should say to him, how she could remain calm while speaking her truth, how to rebut his objections or listen to his concerns in a way that would build on their relationship. She heard the woman hang up and then phone her boyfriend who answered and spoke cheerfully until the woman delivered her first troubling thoughts.

"I think you need to find someone else," he said coolly to the woman.

"I don't seem to make you happy. Goodbye."

In 30 firm and civil seconds, the relationship was over.

Wendy listened in the evenings to the rolling rhythms of conversations that rebounded and flowed with joy, anger, sadness, boredom, humor, confession and occasional insights.

"Men are always, in their varying ways, soldiers about something…"

Wendy could not name the woman who said this, but wrote down the words.

"I feel guilty thinking of myself," another woman confessed.

"I try to reduce the load of my loving and it is just so hard when I can't know how much, or whether it even weighs on him at all."

Voices of her various narratives would come for Wendy, then go, disappear, overlap, and return. Conversations and voices sometimes confused her though she made an effort in her more obsessive moments to seek out her subjects' physical identities. They were really hers, since the comfort and fullness of their voices were a pipeline to Wendy's own undistracted intimacy within. The voices flowed like a stream over her deep, rocky depths. She was strangely soothed and moved along, though toward what was impossible to say other than it felt like the direction of every river: unmistakably downhill.

Living without contours brought a reliable relief though it sometimes caused Wendy to pass through shadows, to awaken from dreams of a hardened mother. I would call her, Wendy thought, but her mother was only a specter now, a vanishing shade. All Wendy knew was what she could or would remember and it was usually an accumulation of dark experiences, words shouted down a hallway, admonitions to a vagrant daughter and premonitions of her failure.

"You'll see," the lonely abandoned woman shouted at her daughter.

What Wendy's mother wanted for her was college and a successful husband. And she had pushed her daughter ceaselessly toward these unattained goals. Unlike her lonely mother who worked for a quarter century as a librarian, Wendy was never a serious student. She found part time office work after high school and ended up clerking for an insurance agency. After moving to Petaluma six years before,

Wendy was hired at the real estate office where she worked now.

Wendy's father left when she was ten and the daughter was all the family the mother had. When two of Wendy's high school class-mates married, her mother became obsessively worried. Wendy was an only child and bore alone the neurotic parent's pestering anxiety. At age 26 Wendy met Joe, a junior college student studying graphic arts. He was a regular at one of Wendy's after-work party bars.

Tall and gawky with wavy dark hair and bright brown eyes, Joe was immediately arousing. They connected physically and spent the first two weeks together almost exclusively in bed. Joe's bohemian lifestyle and casual attitude attracted Wendy but put off her mother. Wrong college. Wrong career. Or said her mother who, after years of begging her daughter to find a husband, ate one dinner with Joe and then tried to wave him off. When things grew serious between Joe and Wendy, her mother seemed to lose all control.

"Marry that man and something bad is going to happen," her mother pronounced ominously.

Within another month Wendy was pregnant. Another month passed before she and Joe were married. Wendy's mother did not attend the small ceremony at the county courthouse. Joe's father, a building contractor, gave the newlyweds a down payment on the Petaluma house while Wendy's mother vanished petulantly into the background until Samantha was born. Mother then returned to reach cautiously for her grandchild while her daughter cautiously guarded her mother's access. Nothing was kind or easy again between them. And then, as if her mother were the uninvited bringer of a curse, something bad did happen.

As she listened to other people's phones Wendy tried to remember when her own stopped ringing. Contact for Wendy came through the overheard lives of others. The image of a telephone's ring as a welcoming alarm was gone. Her telephone, whether or not it rang, assumed a trivial and useless existence. Was it also a measure of her existence? Very few phoned. And those that did, and notably her mother, she wished not to hear again.

5

Wendy was living through a catastrophe and not a crisis. She still had her home and most of her income though she would trade it all in a second for the return of her imperfect loves. Loss was an impasse, in its own way like the amorous trap from which lovers feared they would never escape. Her hours of eavesdropping gave Wendy continued evidence of love's inescapable agonies and limited consolations. Those who said they were lonely at least had their freedom. Those who were hurt and disappointed at least had their lovers.

Wendy listened to otherwise happy people who constantly complained, who mourned all the delights of the earth because they were not their delights. Fulfillments were rarely spoken in these dialogues. Needs were more the subjects at hand and always there were so many. How did anyone hope for any tangible fulfillment? At times Wendy took relief from thinking happiness to be unattainable and therefore unimportant. If people were ever happy, there was always a culpable party waiting to intervene.

Connie and Charles continued their teasing, violent dialogue. Late into an early morning Wendy heard Charles confront Connie.

"I could abuse you," he said boldly.

Connie laughed.

She laughed? Wendy thought it weird and scary that Connie would laugh at what sounded so clearly like a threat.

"I'd like to see you try," she pushed back.

"We can arrange that," Charles answered in a husky whisper.

"Sounds like it's time to go for a hike."

"Yeah…" Connie answered.

"Thursday afternoon."

Charles was suddenly reluctant.

"Got the kids, godammit."

Charles was married to someone else and the father of two school-aged children.

"Friday?" he asked petulantly.

Connie said the afternoon would work for her.

"The big park in the hills?"

Connie said yes.

"What will you be driving?"

Charles said he would be in his Toyota truck.

"OK, you fucking asshole," she shouted at him.

"Oh God, Connie, you are really asking for it," Charles answered.

"I know," said Connie and hung up.

Wendy turned off the radio and spent a sleepless night worrying about Connie. At dawn she arose to go to work and while taking her shower realized she knew when and where Connie and Charles would meet. She could be there, she thought. She could be visible in a way that would prevent Charles from hurting Connie. She could intervene if there were danger. She could. She pictured herself close to them, perhaps behind a bush or tree, and lurching forward, plunging fearlessly into Connie's path at any sign of danger.

It felt useful as she said it. It was the first hint she might once again become a public citizen after so many months behind closed doors. She would find them and follow them. She would act as a rival to Charles in a way that would protect Connie, perhaps augment the two of terror into a three of survival. It was a thought that thrilled her until it brought her back to the endearing math of her lost family life.

A fact of Wendy's eavesdropping was that she succumbed easily to a pleasure of complicity, of connivance with her listening subjects. She had her favorites and after several weeks had identified many. This, however, was the first time ever she had thought to act on anything she heard. She decided to feign illness so she could leave work early Friday and drive the 20 minutes to the park, a large regional semi-wilderness west of town. Charles and Connie were to meet at two. Wendy arrived 10 minutes early and cruised through the sparsely filled parking lot.

She drove to the end where a blue truck waited, the white letters of the word Toyota on its tailgate painted out neatly to leave only the expression "YO." A husky man sat behind the wheel, the driver door open. Wendy turned and parked her car several spaces away. She watched as the man, she guessed his age as mid-thirties, took out a backpack and spread it on his lap. He reached behind his seat and brought up a folded length of blonde nylon rope and slipped it into the bag.

As he closed the top of the pack, an older model red Volkswagen chugged past Wendy's car and pulled in next to him. A woman got out. She was slender and wore a bright green, one-piece shift of a dress that hung just above her knees. Combined with her fluffy cotton sox and white, flat tennis shoes, the skimpy dress made her body appear younger than what showed in her fixed, weathered face. She ran to embrace the man as he leapt from his truck. He gave her an affectionate shove and after exchanging words that appeared to Wendy as both argument and enticement, the couple began to walk together toward the park's trailhead.

Wendy's first thought was to rush to a nearby pay phone and call the police. A rope? What did the man, whom she was now certain was Charles, what did he intend to do? But to rush to the phone would mean letting the couple out of her sight and risk losing them completely. Wendy entered the trail and followed, attempting to maintain a pedestrian and unsuspicious distance as the man and woman diverged from the main trail to climb a slender, worn path toward the top of a hill. Wendy waited for them to move out of sight before climbing after them.

The trail wound for a mile through deep brush, breaking into sunlight near a rocky overlook before disappearing into a thick copse of oak trees that hugged the hilltop like a fat, forested crown. Wendy stood at the overlook, caught by the sight below of a field thick with mustard flowers. The blossoms were fading under April's early heat but their vast and aureate color still shimmered in the wind like a hot, golden wave. Wendy had missed the mustard this year, had remained inside her house and not seen its growth and flush for the first time since she could remember. It said something to her of her missing life but not enough to ponder. She turned back to the trail and realized after several more turns she had lost Connie and Charles.

Alarmed, she retraced her steps but found no sign of them or another trail to follow. She ran back toward the hilltop where the trail folded abruptly into a deep ravine. She looked for footprints in the dust, finding none but her own. Confused she worked her way back slowly toward the crest of the hill. She heard a muffled cry. Then another. These were followed by a woman's rising voice. It sounded annoyed and angry. She followed the sound to a wall of trees and probed for a place to slip between them. The voice grew louder and Wendy climbed quietly through weeds and bushes to approach it.

"Fuck, fuck, fuck! God damn fuck!"

Wendy heard the woman cry out and followed the sound of the voice. Through the trees she saw what she thought were fleshy limbs moving furiously.

"No you can't. No. No. No."

The woman's voice was firm, if suddenly subdued. Its angry tension Wendy heard as fear.

"I sure as hell can. You can't stop me. Ever!"

The man sounded angry and determined. Through the obscuring branches Wendy could make out two hands reaching high above two wrestling bodies. The hands were bound together by yellow nylon rope.

"Yes, yes, yes," she heard the man cry. "Yes I can, you goddamned slut!"

Wendy charged into the clearing to throw herself between what she presumed to be a victimized woman and her rough, angry assailant.

Instead, she saw the man, naked from the waist down and lying on a blanket, the woman straddling him as she squatted awkwardly to contain the man's wet erection while she rode hard against him.

"You can't, you can't, you can't" the woman yelled.

"Not before me. Not until I tell you…"

The breathless urgency of the scene stalled Wendy in her tracks. It was sex: violent, theatrical, and risky, but sex and only sex. Wendy did not see the man peer over the woman's shoulder to see her.

"What the fuck?" he yelled.

"Who the fuck are you?"

The woman turned and the couple looked toward Wendy as if terrified, the woman jumping quickly away to drop her shift back over her bottom while the man, bound helplessly by the rope, remained fully exposed.

"I'm sorry," Wendy stammered.

It was all Wendy thought she could say until the woman began to approach her.

"You goddamned…Are you just going to stand there?"

Wendy heard the woman's threatening tone and turned to run.

In ten minutes Wendy was at the parking lot, breathless and confused. She started the engine and drove recklessly out of the park and did not look back.

Until that moment, listening had been an amusement for Wendy, a rich and secret pleasure. She had been a fly on innumerable walls while reveling among the many identities she assumed. She listened for hours to people she thought she knew intimately and whom she had never met. These identities had been big enough and loud enough to swallow hers. Driving home she felt the inept emergence of her own. It was feebly entrapped at the back of her throat where tears grew like pods she prayed would never burst.

6

Wendy raced home certain the world was full enough without her. She pulled her Subaru wagon into the driveway and opened the garage door. She cleared away laundry baskets and boxes and drove the vehicle cautiously into the narrow remaining space, pushing the car's bumper against the washing machine before stopping. She leaped out to check her clearance and then dropped the garage door, looking up and down the street for a sign of anyone approaching. Inside the house, she switched on her radio and searched apprehensively for the voices of Connie and Charles.

She waited and waited, frozen by a feeling she was continuously falling outside herself. Two hours passed before she heard Connie's familiar nasal squawk burst through in mid-sentence.

"...more careful. It was fuckin' freaky. I thought she was your wife..."

"No way," Charles interrupted.

"My wife's a lot prettier than that."

"Yeah?" countered Connie.

"Is your wife a lot prettier than me? That woman wasn't so bad lookin'.

"No one's prettier than you," Charles sputtered.

"But keep my wife out of this. And that lady—thirty-five or forty? Those ugly bangs, who wears bangs? And she was fat."

"What was she doin' up there?" Connie asked.

"She wasn't dressed for a hike. Who goes hiking in a wool skirt and silk blouse? It was like she was spying on us. Maybe she's a friend of your wife."

"Damn, woman!" Charles shouted.

"Keep my wife outta this. She hasn't a clue."

"You sure? How can you be sure?" Connie shouted back.

"Anyway, we're not going up there anymore."

"Oh baby," Charles mocked a pleading tone.

"We can go somewhere else. To the beach. Let's go to the beach. I know a place..."

Connie ignored him and laughed.

"You looked so funny—all tied up with your pants pulled down, your big cock sticking straight up. How much do you think she saw, I don't…"

The frequency was suddenly filled with the loud clacking of someone in closer range punching up a call.

"Fred? Fred is that you?" a voice yelled at high volume.

"I need a quote for…"

Wendy shut off the radio. She left the bedroom and walked to the hallway where she stood before a full-length mirror hung at the T where the hall intersected with the kitchen. She looked at her reflected image, black hair combed back behind her ears and her bangs, appearing to her stringy and uneven as she turned quickly for a side view.

Was she fat? She ran her hands across her abdomen and felt for its familiar bulge now evident in profile, a shape she blamed on her pregnancy. She sucked hard to pull in her gut. She removed her pale green blouse and stared at her breasts stuffed tightly into a beige bra the straps of which cut into a rounded plumpness at her shoulders and under her arms. In minutes she stood before the mirror in nothing but her panties, which she also removed to examine her full body. She posed, squatted and twirled, her eyes vigilant for any fleshy bulge or shimmer. Was she fat? The encroaching evening shrouded her in shadows. She had asked Joe this question many times and he always said no.

Wendy was overcome with a sentiment of absence and withdrawal. She was inert and in the gathering darkness content to melt fully away. She walked to the living room to lie naked, her legs open, one draped across the back of the sofa. Anything left of her was expended in an urgent discourse, her pleasure more an encountered object than the achievement of a goal.

At her office Wendy increasingly was among associates and not friends. Her link with those who needed her assistance felt like a contrivance that at the surface level of public conversation became boring and unsatisfying. As much as she tried to listen to clients or customers, it was becoming harder to hear them. Her boss noticed Wendy's undifferentiating ennui and called her into his office for a conference.

"Are you OK?" he asked her.

"You seem distracted. People have noticed."

"No, of course…I mean yes, I'm fine," Wendy answered.

"I mean I'll do better…"

Her boss took an avuncular tone.

"Wendy, you've been through a lot. We understand. If you need some time away…"

Wendy's eyes widened.

"No…no, no. I'm fine. I'll be fine. Please. Let me go. I want to go."

Her boss flashed a smile of mild frustration and told her she could leave.

Wendy did not want to move from her small house on one of the city's low hills and she needed her job to keep it. The home comforted her with its ghosts, those of her deceased family and also those new and compelling phantoms that burst through her radio and brought her their endless intimacies to consider and imagine. Wendy was not finished with something, though a life with her husband and child was finished.

At first the confrontation with Connie and Charles had frightened her, then wracked her with guilt. Later, after hearing them again, she relaxed more deeply into the pure expenditure of her obsession. Exuberance was the equal of some far-fetched beauty and the range of feelings she heard, feelings not her own, were the only ones that mattered.

Wendy searched through her copy of Police Call, the fat volume of frequency listings she purchased from the appliance store along with her scanner. The album-sized paperback contained endless tables of numbers, radio and police frequencies for every one of the nation's states and well-sized communities. She found an article describing the use of antennas to improve radio reception. The article gave a formula for calculating the length of an antenna for particular frequencies.

"You don't have to go to all that trouble," the appliance salesman told Wendy as she stood at the counter.

"I got something that works just fine. Sell a lot of 'em, too."

He went into the back of the store and brought out what appeared to be a portable metal pole about a yard in length.

"Attach it outdoors and run this lead wire to your receiver. Connect it to the antenna input. The higher you place it the better. Improved reception guaranteed. I'll take it back if you aren't satisfied. $49.99 plus tax."

On a warm June Saturday Wendy dragged a wobbly wooden ladder from the garage and leaned it against the house. She took one of Joe's screwdrivers and her new antenna and climbed to the roof. She balanced herself against the roof's stiff incline while taking in the wide view of her city and the mountains beyond. At the valley's end she could see the regal, profiled peak of Mount St. Helena, the region's largest mountain. A light wind rustled the hanging branches of an old oak tree that brushed the roof with a rhythmic scratching. Wendy staggered carefully toward the chimney where she attached the brackets and then slid the antenna's base into them. She tugged the antenna, which seemed firmly attached and then ran a wire to the roof's edge above the bedroom.

"My stars and garters, Wendy, what are you doin' up there?"

Her neighbor Martha spoke to Wendy from her backyard.

"Repairs. Minor repairs," Wendy said briefly and descended below the fence line and out of sight.

"Be careful, darlin'" Martha shouted.

Wendy did not answer.

She went to the bedroom and opened the window to grasp the wire hanging outside. She pulled it in, stripped the wire as instructed by the salesman, and attached its exposed bristles of copper under the radio's external antenna screw. She turned on her scanner. A flood of words filled her ears. Her radio had become a machine that ran all by itself, its crank turned magically to produce ten conversations where before there had been only one. She punched her way through frequencies to hear a cacophonous concert of voices as if the valley below her were now a choir of singing frogs after a hard rain.

It was Saturday and she listened to a vast and unrelieved flood of words and inflections. She recognized the flirty, accommodating voices of dating couples building together their hopes for the evening. She heard teen boys plot their parties, vandalism and sex while girls confirmed with each other the terms of their resistance and the limits of their fun. She heard angry words and sad reckonings. She heard the weary voices of frail victims and ponderous lectures of nascent sociopaths. She heard proposals and confessions, accusations and apologies. She listened as two women planned a meeting of a sex positive women's group they had named the Organauts. The group planned to attend a male strip show at a local nightclub with some time left over to trade sexy stories.

Wendy prepared to embark, to submerge into a fever of language, a possibly endless stream of idiosyncratic and largely anonymous lives. Love makes me think too much, she thought. Now there was too much love even to think about. Wendy went to the kitchen to heat a frozen dinner in the oven. She set the stove timer and went back to the bedroom. A multitude of other voices would do her singing now since the sound of her own voice only made her cry.

7

Day or night Wendy occupied a perpetual darkness out of which emerged the words and emotions of her accumulated bonds. She understood that all whose lives she heard were not attached to her even as she grew deeply attached to them.

Weeks became months as spring became summer and when she was not at work Wendy stayed close to her new source of all experience. She heard long distance phone sex between a college co-ed home for the summer and her humanities professor, an older woman. The nurse who had counseled a friend to fuck her husband after sleeping with her lover now had a lover of her own. Her graphic descriptions of their wild sex seemed overwrought, though still entertaining. The man with cancer became more laconic until all calls ceased. Wendy's search of the newspaper obituaries turned up nothing conclusive.

Wendy worried about a teenager in an abusive relationship with an adult gang member. The girl spoke frequently with a clueless friend who couldn't grasp the thought of anal sex, much less why anyone who hated it would endure it. She heard family members gossip wickedly about each other, then address their scorned subjects directly with saccharine regard. She spent half her time tuning out business calls to tradesmen, the dreary chatter of phone sales, tedious discussions of homework or home repair, invitations to parties or dinners and bromidic descriptions of vacations and travel.

Emotions drove her interest and while an evening did not go by without at least a handful of graphic sexual discussions, she was especially drawn to any honest and vulnerable confession of feelings. There were more stories available than she could ever care about or hear. Broken-hearted lovers were the most loquacious subjects though loss appeared in many ways. Love and death were the main attractions in every life and Wendy waited earnestly each night for the latest news.

Over time she was able to use a city map to plot the addresses of particular callers, aware of an obvious pattern of signals that revealed a sweet ray of reception that extended northeast approximately two miles to Western Avenue where signals seemed quickly to drop off. Her curiosity led her to an article in Police Call about the electromagnetic spectrum, on which she plotted the relatively long frequencies of AM radio transmissions. The spectrum suggested a larger reality that fascinated her. All energy, including all that could be heard and seen, arrived on a wavelength. She learned that if the electromagnetic spectrum were a piano keyboard, the visible spectrum of light would occupy the width of a single key in a piano's fifth octave. What light showed her was merely the rainbow tip of a vastly larger reality. All was length and frequency and rumbling up from the lower keys were the signals she heard each night, that she quickly realized were like rays from the sun, and without that source of experience there would be no experience at all.

One night she heard the sounds of sex; moaning, loud sex between a man and woman that led her at first to wonder if they had left their phone off the hook in the middle of a call until it occurred to Wendy she was picking up another baby monitor. It was probably in a child's room that, she quickly realized, might also serve as a guest room. Someone else—someone who lived in the house—could also be listening. At first she was amused to think of herself eavesdropping on an eavesdropper until she became aroused by the idea that hosts might purposely spy on their guests. She listened closely, enraptured by the clear words and sounds of the couple and piqued that she could be sharing these private moments with another listener. It was too much. As the couple finished, so did Wendy, her ravenous timing perfect and palpably satisfying.

In evenings that followed she searched for other baby monitors, finding briefly and again the monitor of the familiar mother and child that first introduced her to her radio world. The monitor was itself a labyrinth of sounds within the labyrinth of signals that decorated Wendy's darkness. So much of what she heard was about sex, alive with sex, expressions of emotions and urges that could be happy or angry or fraught with worry. They were all animal expressions that brought Wendy closer to her own mortal awareness. Girls and women spoke to each other constantly about their menstrual periods as if their cycles could clock arrivals and departures in both the body and the heart. After the birth and death of a child, periods seemed to have no more use or meaning for Wendy, other than to remind her of what she presumed was a wasted mortality. Should she be having more babies? She could not imagine how.

Hungers hemorrhaged from her subjects' unsatisfied languor while dumping into the airwaves vast chants of sadness, some irredeemably maudlin and self-absorbed and others more heartfelt and even poignant. In one conversation Wendy heard a woman's ageless voice describe to a friend her worries about a dead son buried in a nearby cemetery. Winter rains each year pooled near his gravesite forcing her to clear away refuse and garbage. The woman also worried that during floods water seeped into her boy's grave and made him wet. Could she have afforded it, or known the cemetery's topography, she might have chosen another plot. Her friend listened quietly and offered the maladroit observation that *little Billy Palmer is an angel* now in a way that Wendy knew was not helpful.

Later in the night, Wendy awoke from a terrifying dream of mud, ash and fire with no clear residue other than her tearful remembrance of the poor radio mother of a dead Billy. The woman's quaking voice haunted Wendy all through her morning at work. During lunch Wendy rushed out to buy a bouquet of lilies. She drove to the cemetery and had an office attendant direct her to the boy's grave. Wendy descended a long hill toward the property's east fence, finding at its edge an older marble grave marker. She approached by stepping charily among the stones of other, older graves. She read the stone: *William Harvey Palmer March 11, 1948—May 19, 1955 Our Little Billy.* The boy had been dead for more than 40 years.

The son's death, in a way Wendy tried not to imagine, was as fresh to his old mother as if it had happened yesterday. Wendy set the vase of lilies in front of the small, rounded stone and picked up any random refuse she could find. She was standing among what were clearly the cemetery's cheap seats, crowded into a patch of withered lawn flat against the storm drains of an adjacent boulevard. Little wonder it got wet in the winter.

Would this also be Wendy's fate; to carry grief for decades and to embellish its sad and multiplying details through a relentless echoing of her loss? She thought of the boxes in her closet, the ashes that were not yet mud, and of the fire that condensed the flesh of her loves into a white, sparse residue that began with her desire and grew from her blood; that was irretrievably lost and also forever embedded.

8

Wendy could not remember when she fully grasped the potential for good acts anonymously given. It might have been an evening Wendy heard the despairing mother describe in a call to her disbelieving friend the miracle of the lilies.

"They were fresh and in a rose vase. I brought two home. They're beautiful. Who remembered Billy this way? Only an angel could."

Wendy's world heaved for a moment with the news of her own intervention. She thought boldly she might do more. She had considered herself too shy to intervene, even when someone was in trouble. But like a spirit she was now omniscient. She knew so many lovely and troubling secrets. She knew, knew, knew it all; wrote it down in her notebook and kept detailed descriptions of the many private lives so completely in her view. For months she had postponed events with friends, refused her mother's phone calls and messages, arrived for work late and left early, so as to stay intimately connected with the lives she heard but did not touch, would not touch because it might hurt too much to make contact.

But good acts—these could be done without contact, without recognition, which seemed to her the holiest of ways to give back to those whose suffering reached deeply into her. She pictured herself leaving bags of groceries on doorsteps, sending anonymous presents, buying gift certificates and flowers, lots of flowers. She would listen for every heartfelt need and determine each day what she might do to address it.

She thought herself an angel and perhaps in some unconscious pursuit of ethereal grace, ate and drank less often. She stopped buying wine and by mid-summer was shopping infrequently. Her colleagues at work noticed she was losing weight and asked about her.

"I'm fine," she said.

"I'm really doing well."

It was convincing until Wendy heard a radio voice talk about her. It was a neighbor she had seen recently in the park.

"She's not healthy, if you ask me," Wendy heard the woman say as she described Wendy's dour, detached appearance.

"I wonder if she's suicidal," the neighbor speculated.

"She's certainly not very friendly. That husband was such a sweet-heart…and the poor baby, the…"

Wendy shut off the radio.

Wendy's acquired knowledge of her neighbors' lives sparked a realization that, like the visible light waves of the electromagnetic spectrum, human needs occupied a narrow niche. There were few callers that discussed anything but health, children, sex, or comfort. These were the same needs of any animal though Wendy's phone subjects appeared deliberately to intensify them into rich narratives of pleasure and pain.

Wendy picked through them and, where she could identify her subjects, sought ways to reward their success or to assuage their grief. Flowers were easy. Wendy bought and carried bouquets to graves and memorials and left them without cards. Listening to her radio she would at times hear her gift mentioned in tones that suggested it to be an assuaging, if occasionally disquieting, mystery.

Happy news was harder for Wendy. A young and pregnant woman was to marry the father of her fetus and, already defensive about the circumstances of her new family, reacted with rage to the appearance at her doorstep of an anonymous dozen white roses.

"Someone making fun of me? Like I'm not a virgin, right? It's Pete. I'll just bet. That jerk. Just because I wouldn't fuck him."

Happy gifts Wendy offered were usually lost in a pile of accumulated others, and ignored or left because they were nameless.

"I am not a giver," Wendy said to herself.

"I am not a giver until a gift bears my name."

It appeared after awhile that her anonymous contributions to happy people created more confusion and suspicion than they did good will.

Summer drew to its close, Wendy aware of cooler evenings but little else beyond the range of her radio. She maintained a maximum efficiency at work, driven harder by the concerns expressed by her boss: that she appeared distracted, even fraught. All of this he said he understood but, like her mother's ceaseless imploring (which by the end of August had ceased entirely), his kind queries irritated Wendy who, she thought righteously, should simply be left alone to do her job. Realtors and agents spoke breathlessly about politics and the economy and in a worried way that frightened Wendy. She had lost track of the news. There was an election coming. Would Clinton win another term? Wendy had no opinion and could not name the president's opponent.

Instead of an angel, Wendy's gifting led her to feel more like a ghost or perhaps a witch. She was a brewer of brews, a spinner, a secret agent inserted into the largely circular scheme of her subjects' experience. She was a sparking candle, lighting other candles with her invisible mercy. Her intimate knowledge was a power for something and she thought always for something good. But at a critical moment in her relentless, sleepless, sometimes meal-less days, she assumed the full measure of a secret power.

And as it did whenever she heard it, the voice of an anxious mother left Wendy thunderstruck.

"My boy! They're taking my boy! I can't come to work today! God, it's my fault. All my fault. Oh, God, forgive me. OOOOhh-hhh...."

The words pounded through the radio's small speaker, warped into a sibilant moan that passed over Wendy's own unattended despair and into the unreal, the disreal, zone of her aural imagination. A child lost. How? She heard the mother hang up on her baffled boss. Wendy felt her heart come close to breaking as she registered the mother's wailing terror and desperate self-blaming. Wendy listened for more calls. A conversation emerged between neighbors.

"...and there's some question who left him...it's so sad...was he even three?"

And then silence until another caller opened with a question.

"What's going on at the Iverson's?"

And a response.

"Hell if I know…but it doesn't look good…cops and an ambu-lance…"

Wendy opened her notebook to the penciled map she had made of the neighborhood. She did not know the woman's home but guessed its location.

"Did you hear about the Iverson child?" another caller shouted.

"What happened?" was the ingenuously returned query.

"An accident…that's what Anna says…but…"

Wendy disconnected her radio from its wire antenna, attached its portable rubber pole and raced outside. In an ensuing twilight she could see the flash of red and blue lights bouncing off low clouds of incoming fog. She ran toward them, covering two blocks before turning a corner to see several police cars and an ambulance parked like a random bulwark around a small bungalow of a home. Two officers stood at the sidewalk and asked small clutches of curious neighbors to please move on.

Wendy heard a loud siren and watched as the ambulance pulled abruptly out of an adjacent driveway and roared down the street. She switched her scanner's search to the police band.

"Has anyone talked with the parents?"

From the sound of the siren in the background, Wendy knew it was the voice of someone in the ambulance.

"The parents will meet you at the hospital," an officer responded.

"This doesn't look good. Do they know that?" said the voice from the ambulance.

"We're talking with them now. Over."

The officer signed off. There was nothing else to hear.

Wendy walked toward the house. She passed a small mob of neighbors beginning to disperse.

"Nothing to do now," said an elderly man.

"Poor little guy."

Nothing? thought Wendy. There was always something, always something to do.

Wendy would do something. No, she would not make the same mistake she made with Connie and Charles, not simply charge in without understanding what had happened. She would ask first, ask what had happened and what she could do.

She approached the gate of the squat redwood fence that surrounded the bungalow's shallow front lawn. She opened the gate and strolled through. Others might stand around helplessly but Wendy knew what was needed. She would talk with the mother and learn the depths of her loss and suffering. She would give her deep comfort and hold her close. She would let her own broken heart break open the seal of this woman's unbearably contained grief. It was the least she could do. Wendy had become the visiting angel that had never visited her. And now it was time. It was.

"Hey, where you goin'?"

A police officer approached Wendy and grabbed her.

"You can't go in there!"

Wendy pulled away and continued walking toward the front door, ignoring the officer's question. The officer reached for her again, holding her arm behind her back as another officer approached.

"Are you family? Tell me who you are and I'll tell them. But you need to wait here."

"You're hurting me," Wendy shouted at the first officer.

"I have to go in there. I can help them. They don't know it but they need me. They need me."

The officers looked at each other and the first strengthened his hold on Wendy's arm.

"Come with us, ma'am," said the second officer.

"No, no!" Wendy shouted.

"I'm the only one who can help. The only one..."

The first officer pulled out his handcuffs while the other held Wendy's arms tightly together. The snap of the cuffs bit into Wendy's wrists. Her arms were behind her back and she could not move them. She began to fall, and then to scream.

"I am the angel. You don't understand. I'm the one. The only one. I know. I know. I know!"

Departing neighbors turned to watch as the officers struggled to lift their screaming prisoner and move her quickly back down the walkway.

"It's a lady," said the elderly man.

"Say...I think I know her..." said a woman who lived at the end of the block.

The two officers stuffed Wendy hurriedly into the back seat of a police cruiser while a third came over to take her purse and radio. Barely three minutes had passed between the moment Wendy walked through the gate and the conclusion of her arrest. As the cruiser left with Wendy, the neighbors continued to shuffle away from the white bungalow. What had happened did not appear real though no one said as much. Unreality was surprisingly abundant and unutterable.

9

Wendy waited somewhere for what she dreaded the most: an intervention by others in the private life of her uncoiled anguish. She still could not grasp how an attempt to help a wailing mother led to her arrest. Or how her arrest led to a further investigation of her living situation, her recent history, even her mental health.

"It's not their business. None of it," Wendy muttered to herself.

The sad story, sadder than hers, was the outcome of the crisis that drew her into her current predicament. The wailing woman's son was indeed lost. He died while taking a bath that, through a misunderstanding, both his parents had left unattended. The mother in the kitchen, the father in his workshop, each thought the other was with the boy in the bathroom, until the parents collided in a hallway and in a mutual panic ran to find the boy's limp, naked body, still and floating in the tub, his head face down near the drain. The first EMT to arrive attempted mouth-to-mouth resuscitation until the boy could be put on oxygen. He was taken to the hospital and left on life support for a day while the parents came to terms with the reality of his death and agreed to let him go.

Wendy learned all this from a therapist who interviewed her for a probation assessment. The therapist was a woman near her age and who seemed sympathetic to Wendy's attempt to offer the mother angelic support. But there was the matter of Wendy's interference with the police (a misdemeanor) and that she carried a police scanner, which implied premeditation.

"You were listening to police calls," the therapist told Wendy.

"You walked up to the house deliberately. You knew you were interfering in a police emergency."

Wendy had no response. She had been listening, and for months hearing much more than police calls which, gratefully, had not caught the attention of authorities. She did walk up to the house. She did resist the officer who stopped her.

If convicted Wendy faced up to six months in jail and a large fine. The therapist used this as leverage to move Wendy into treatment.

"You've had a big loss yourself," she said.

"Have you ever sought help?"

Wendy said no.

The therapist told Wendy if she completed a recommended course of treatment, the misdemeanor charge would be dropped and her arrest erased.

"Do I have a choice?" Wendy answered resentfully.

Wendy waited through the therapist's patient silence as a familiar and painful rock grew in her throat while her eyes, suddenly bleary and wet, opened a window to all her wounds. The therapist offered Wendy a box of tissues.

The therapist knew Wendy was not an offender and that her effort to reach the mother was an attempt to heal herself, to join her loss with another's and to create a psychic solidarity of suffering that would hold her through what had not yet been addressed. It resulted from a pathological isolation corroborated in the therapist's investigation by other noted behaviors: time missing from work, lack of appetite, delusions of engagement while for months she spoke to no one.

Wendy heard her name called. She rose from her chair in the clinic waiting room. She passed a mirror and saw what appeared to be her. She could not remember when she stopped looking into mirrors. Was she pretty? Was she fat? The questions posed by all mirrors returned to her and she remembered immediately why she had stopped looking into them. She had become a missing person: from life, from work, from any real or shared connection. As long as she remained immersed in her vague ether, she likely did no harm. It was when she decided at last to act that she ruined her charade and grew into someone she could no longer manage.

Dr. La Belle, a tall, lithe woman in her 40s, bent forward to reach for Wendy's hand and welcomed her into the small room where seven others sat within a circle of chairs, one empty and waiting for her. Wendy took her seat.

"Let's all welcome Wendy to the grief group," said the doctor.

Wendy counted four women and three men who introduced themselves by first name only. Wendy nodded feebly as each said a name and looked deeply into her eyes with what felt to her like prying. Had it not been for the shock of the new, Wendy might have collapsed instantly. Instead, she held on through the end of introductions and, when asked, said her name and thanked everyone for welcoming her.

The group discussion began, Wendy listening as she might to her radio, now with faces as well as voices, all aligned and present with her. A woman named Elena appeared to continue an ongoing report of her struggle with cutting. Another woman talked of still feeling relief at the death of her husband of forty years that she said she never really knew or loved, but for whom she had provided care through a long and painful illness.

A hefty sixtyish man named Gabby drawled on about his fond memories of children who had not spoken to him in 15 years. Another man, also older, had lost to cancer the woman he had loved for half a century, a woman he fell in love with in high school but never married. Another man was the father of her children.

One of the last two women to speak was sitting next to Wendy. She reported on her latest effort to get the army to release details of her son's death in the Gulf war. It had been five years since he was killed and the mother suspected the army was covering up his death by friendly fire. She spoke through a brittle anger, pouring forth more details of her fight for justice than anyone in the room could fully absorb.

Dr. La Belle interrupted her kindly but firmly and moved the conversation on, eventually landing again at Wendy.

"What can you tell us, Wendy?" asked the doctor.

Wendy felt a sudden unity of disguise and disclosure. She would try to offer some version of her loss that might still conceal her still unraveled feelings. She searched for proper words.

"I have…that is…I am the mother, was the mother, the wife…"

Her struggle for words froze her. This is what death is, she thought. I am hopelessly separated from everyone else. She looked up at all the faces looking back at her, expectant, waiting, eager. It felt impossible to say anything that might reach inside of these others or reveal to them anything that was inside her.

The whole complex process of living—its agonizing, boring, and frightening tumult—appeared as a ridiculous waste of everyone's time until, until in a sweep of the room she saw seven imparting mirrors of this tumult: faces that concealed not very well the qualities of her suffering but also showed a visceral, poignant hunger for whatever she might know that they did not, whatever she might share that they had not yet considered.

"I suppose we're all in this together," Wendy said, expecting to sound as aimless and indirect as the words she spoke but eliciting an affirming nod from Dr. La Belle as well as a shuddering sigh from the woman next to her who reached over and draped an arm over Wendy's crouched, tense shoulders. Wendy felt the woman's touch like a caress, the first in too long and nothing like the rough cuffing by police that took her into custody.

Wendy wanted to say she had lost her daughter and her partner and now drifted painfully and without any attachment to her existence. She wanted to confess a dreadful hatred of the life she was trapped into living since its most wonderful angels had been taken from it. But in her unspoken words she heard a deprivation that felt also like a cure. Her loved ones were now dream creatures that did not speak. Her grief for them had exhausted her, had become like an obstruction to whatever else might be possible. She was weary and without words, weak and collapsed.

Sex had been interesting over the airwaves as an indirect apprehension of death's animal reality without the necessity for her to experience it, though death emerged always to stalk her. She thought she had cleverly turned her back on grief though now she felt the incipient crumble of her body into a deep and postponed experience of a despair that burned her deeply.

And the touch. The touch, the releasing touch, was electrifying. It exposed her to the vast emptiness of an enforced, disconsolate solitude. How alone she had been, how she had used her loneliness and the lives of others to fill the vast range of her sadness with things that would interest but not hurt her. It was one way to manage grief. It was also a way to go completely mad. She could not touch her own life and yet could not leave other lives alone.

A harrowing moan rose out of her, as she shook under the tender weight of her neighbor's arm. Wendy would not move forward before falling back though it had seemed until now impossible that any pain could be enriching. And the fall was mercilessly severe, though it had at last implanted the barest hint of her dormant strength, and the need—if not yet the desire—to live.

NINJA
HOTWIFE

1

Looking and being looked at were his earliest sexual experiences. As a child he could not know they were sexy until as an adult he understood that having complicated desires and discovering ways to gratify them gave him the power to make more of life than simply the achievement of pleasure or avoidance of pain.

There were no limits to his imagination or to that of his wife who, as he watched the video she had sent, told him not to touch himself.

"Oh dear, am I distressing you?" Maria asked as she looked into the camera.

"I'm sorry, dearest. You are such a good boy to let me have Tim's big cock. So much bigger than yours. He's going to come hard in me, very hard. I wish you were here to clean me up. I'll tell you all about it when I get home."

He watched as a large black man, his muscular buttocks filling half the frame, shoved hard against Tania's reddened ass. As he drove deeper into her, Maria gasped.

"Oh...yes, oh yes...oooooohhhh..." she moaned in a long, hurdling cry that leaped into a breathless scream.

"I am so coming, so so coming..."

Her eyes were shut while her ecstatic loss of control for a small, helpless moment returned him to the odd, old thrill of watching her drop again into a covert place of thorough arousal.

The video was all about her though her sex was truly about him.

In their relationship it could not be any other way. He loved her and provided well for her. He was the best husband and she said so. But she wanted, indeed needed, more than he could provide. Needed more sex, more fucking, more cock than he could ever give her. More than any one man ever could give her.

After the first year of a loving but uneasy marriage, he and Maria came to terms with all her relational needs. The good news, at least at first, was that he met most of them. He was kind, attentive, and intelligent. He earned good money as an attorney. He loved her slavishly, but could not fully or solely satisfy her vast, varied and still developing sexual desire.

So he agreed to make room for it, ultimately clearing space for the powerful, firm bodies of other men (bulls, they called them) who would come to their home or hotel and fuck her while he watched, watched and serviced them together. He would provide drinks and food, make a movie, and, in his boldest surrender, lick her vulva clean after a bull ejaculated inside her. It was humiliating but in a shaming way that thrilled him to his core.

His arousal was unwelcome at times and he tried hard to obey Maria's command that he remain soft and disengaged. His penis was too small, she said. It needed to be hidden and contained. She wanted him to be obedient and subdued in the presence of her palpable excitement. He found he wanted this, too. Her pleasure was all he needed and the sight of her ecstasy in the clutch of others, large muscular men—mostly black males with very large penises, a kind of "bull royalty" they spared no expense to find and which they were surprised to discover was marketed on the web— for years were a source for him of a loving, sublime fulfillment.

But something was changing. As he watched Maria's latest video, sent to him while she was on a business trip to St. Louis, he grappled with a decision. He could not say when he first sensed something needed to move. There was an irresistible truth in the elaborate constructions needed for Maria's sexual satisfaction and the circumstances of their cuckolding marriage.

Over time the terms of his satisfying humiliation opened him to a further truth by which the context of his pleasurable suffering was squeezed into a larger, wider view of himself, of Maria, of the fabric of their lives and a still wider and imagined map of human hope and suffering. It was a big picture, drawn from his small and obsessive life that had suggested to him his first big idea: that he could make a larger difference, engage a larger suffering with a meaning larger than Maria.

It was meaning, and not necessarily satisfaction, that was important now. And perhaps that was what he needed to grasp, and should have wanted all along. He watched Maria in the aftermath of an explosive come, her chest writhing, breasts shaking, her legs wobbly and her eyes glazed and half-open.

"Oh sweetie, I wish you were here with us, to see so well what you can't do. Anyway, feed the dogs, pamper the plants and check the mail and I'll see you Saturday. Thank you love, I...."

Maria's large, hunkering bull massaged her thighs before jumping up and out of sight to turn off the camera, oblivious to Maria's spousal love talk.

Maria's husband sat alone in the darkened living room. He was not jealous, though it might cause him less suffering to care more for himself. He was not abandoned. He knew that. He was loved as a husband but felt for a moment he was in mourning, and for an object he wondered might herself be in mourning. He needed her desire, in fact was addicted to it, even if hers was never returned to him. He was thrilled when she withdrew for no particular reason. He loved her contemptuous gaze at him and its astonished, suspicious, demeaning expression. He was lacerated by her beloved disdain and felt like he might always be ready to die for her and her infinite, insatiable and perpetually re-invented needs.

The phone rang and he walked into the hallway. Was it Maria? The ring sounded a recall for him of his first cuckolding sex with her when she left her hotel phone off the hook so he could hear clandestinely all its rapturous shouts and vulgar words. It was before their mutual cultivation of bulls. Her first cuckolding lover was a half-hapless school administrator from Wisconsin she met at the conference she was attending. He said very little in response to Maria's over-modulated arousal, unaware that by fucking him she was

187

making love to her earnest, eavesdropping husband.

The phone continued to ring. He decided not to answer. He checked his pockets and the snaps on his case. He slipped into his overcoat and lingered at the door, finished with his preparations and with nothing left to do. He was not concerned. Where there was no future there was no worry. It was time. He felt like his father talking to himself. It's time, son. It's just time.

2

Maria was tired, and happy to be home. Her key turned in the lock of the door. It was late, all of Saturday gone with the travail of travel. Bumpy turbulence and the long wait for a connecting flight had melted her tedium into a bar of solid boredom. She stood in the foyer and dropped her bags in the darkness.

"Elgin..." she called tentatively.

"Honey..." she yelled.

"Why are all the lights out?"

The darkness didn't answer and she felt up the wall for a light switch that illuminated the hallway in an auroral glow. She wandered into the living room and back through the hall via the dining room, switching lamps on as she went. She wondered where he was, why he wasn't waiting—as he almost always was after one of her trips—with a bowl of pistachios and a pitcher of vodka martinis. They would talk and he would quiz her about her business and her pleasure and the way she boldly mixed the two.

She had looked forward to getting drunk. He loved to hear her reports and, of course, they would look together at the video she had sent. Her commentary would arouse again his obsequious gratitude and precious, darling disgrace. She loved his meek, helpless and inadequate way with her.

She heard scratching at the back door and, approaching through the kitchen, the yelps of their angry dogs. She let them in, two black labs that nearly tumbled her as they sniffed and leaped wildly.

"Haven't you guys been fed?" she asked, almost expecting an answer.

She found their bowls under the sink and filled them from a kibble-filled plastic bucket in a broom closet. The dogs scrambled and drooled, shoving their snouts into their bowls as they gobbled furiously.

"Apparently not," she muttered.

"Where's poppa?"

She worried for a moment, as if her husband were a child, perhaps humiliated by mean friends at a birthday party and now in hiding. She continued her search of their large ramble of a home, the dogs running ahead. Finding him nowhere below, she climbed the stairs to the bedrooms above, checking first his home office at the end of the hall before returning to the master bedroom where there was no sign of him anywhere, no sign of him having been there at any recent time. Their big king bed was made, the closet doors closed, the adjoining bathroom empty and unused.

His apparent absence surprised her, though she was still more disappointed than concerned. He was an attorney with a crucial court appearance Monday morning. He could be at the office working. He could be on his way home. She hoped so. She hadn't bathed since her bareback session with her bull Friday night, wondering all day Saturday if her fellow passengers could smell the musty, decomposing wash of sex all over her. She could smell it each time she lifted her fingers to her face. She wanted him to smell it, to rub his nose into her skin, to clean her up with his mouth and tongue, to taste her ecstatic transgressions and make them his own.

She found the video she sent him in the VCR player, its manila mailer torn open and empty on the coffee table.

"He's been watching," she said to herself, reassured by evidence of his recent attendance at home and to her.

She thought to phone his office and did not. She knew no one would answer. She would wait in their home at the edge of a canyon, a cavernous house paid for by their good jobs.

She opened her suitcase and pulled out a bundle of documents gathered from her conference. Nothing had much value to her. She knew more than most of the presenters, knew by heart the rigors of educational administration. As an assistant to a school superintendent it was her work to manage the tedium of learning, to interface (the popular word now for obsequious attention) with teachers and staff and, above all, to protect her boss.

It was funny work for a woman who used her out of town travel to engage strangers in wonderfully adulterous sex. That had been the real life of her business travel, the peak experience that she waited now to share with Elgin. She loved Elgin for his enraptured misery, his reliably eager suffering on her behalf. There was nothing more important to her than a satisfaction derived from the deeply violating touches of her bulls and the comforting, affectionate acquiescence of her pitiable partner.

Maria took off her clothes and slipped naked into a loose-fitting ter-rycloth robe. She settled into the evening and made her own mar-tini. Looking into the garage she noticed Elgin's car. Was he out walking? Had someone picked him up? Why no message? It did not make sense and, as tired as she was, she began to worry though not excessively. It was too soon to panic. What if he didn't come home, though? Immediately she imagined him in bed with another wom-an. But why on the night of her return? It made no sense he so easily would become someone else's slave.

The phone rang and she answered it, expecting to hear Elgin's voice.
"Yo mama Maria," shouted a husky baritone.
"What's happenin' wich youuu?"
She recognized the loud voice and its affected inflection.
" Pete…" she answered indifferently.
"So, baby, we on for Friday night?" Pete asked.
"Yes," she said thoughtlessly.
"I mean, I don't know…say, have you heard from Elgin?"
"Me? Elgin?" the baritone voice broke into a fat laugh.
"Me hear from your cuck? Honey, that's never the way this works."
He laughed again.
The house's silence pushed her out into the back yard where she gazed at a waxing moon just above a large water tank at the crest of a hill. She stared into the dark shadows of the canyon below their home. A trail led down to a seasonal stream, still dry in October. There had been no rain since spring. Was Elgin down there? She thought of all the places he might be stashed, stored or hidden. It was easy for her to think of him as an item.

He was her cuckold husband, a fixture in her needs like a house-hold appliance, a suppliant to her sexual pleasure. It was easy for a while until the darkness aroused her awareness of the unloving as-pects of her impression and the truth of his husbandry, his devotion, his determined love for her. In a moment he was again indispensable and deeply and worriedly missed.

3

A pasty grey dawn awoke Maria. She searched vagrantly for Elgin and he was nowhere, at least nowhere she knew.

It requires love to know what is different from you, she thought as she sat up in bed. A fading dream blended into a reverie of new fear. *Where is he?* she asked herself again. She thought after breakfast she might ask her nearest neighbors if they had seen her husband. As she brewed her coffee she thought better.

"It would expose a contradiction," she whispered to herself.

She was supposed to know her husband better than anyone, and certainly better than a neighbor. To ask a neighbor his whereabouts, well, what would that suggest?

And though her neighbors were cordial they were not at all friends. It would be all over that she was detached from her husband in some stupid, mysterious way. It would give the appearance of a vast crevice between her and Elgin and fuel a venerable flood of local gossip. She decided to wait. She hoped the opacity of his absence was not the screen around a secret or some gaming of reality and appearance.

She drove downtown, dropping from the treeless Benicia hills, past the oil refinery and onto the city's quaint, historic First Street. Shops were closed but the Captain's, an old restaurant near the pier, was open for lunch. She parked and walked in and sat at the upstairs bar to take in a sunny view of the wide Carquinez Strait and the bridge beyond, under which the strait flowed into San Pablo Bay.

"Lovely day, Tom," she said to the bartender.

"Make me a Margarita," she commanded and Tom, a tall, vested attendant with a tightly trimmed beard covering a stern, thin chin, turned to pull a bottle of Cuervo Gold from the shelf.

Looking out the window and toward the east beyond the water she could make out the roof of the Martinez courthouse. Elgin was due there at 10 a.m. the next day and what would happen? He never missed court, was never even late. And the case—a huge and contentious lawsuit—promised a notable triumph, enough perhaps to move him into the limelight of potential candidates for district attorney.

She looked farther east and north toward Fairfield, the town where she worked as an administrator in the Solano County Office of Education. County employment had brought her and Elgin together, even though they worked for different counties. They met in Benicia during one of the town's street fairs and shared drinks at a local wine bar. When they married, it seemed romantic and also practical to buy a home in Benicia, nearly equidistant from the two county seats where each was employed.

"Where's the hubby today?" Tom asked as he set her drink on the bar.

She ran her finger along the salt-dipped rim of the glass and licked her long, painted nail.

"Away…" she answered vaguely.

Futile trails opened to nothing she could know or say. Sensing an unresolved tension, Tom moved down the bar to take another order.

Maria remained locked in a routine of relief that was in some uncertain way intended to ease her through the unknowable. There was yet no evidence of wrongdoing or even foul play though by now it would not have surprised her to receive a call from a hospital or the highway patrol. She waited at the bar because it was somewhere familiar she could wait with others while anesthetizing herself in preparation for the worst.

She saw the strait's bridge silhouetted by the setting sun and for a frightful moment imagined Elgin throwing himself off it. But why? He was not depressed. He was not despairing. He was a sober, solid man who seemed to love his life and also love her.

"Another, Tom," she shouted and held up her empty glass.

By late afternoon she was drunk and barely able to drive home. Walking into the house she checked the message machine and there were none. She took out her purse and found the phone number for the bull she met in St. Louis.

"Did Elgin call me??! Are you serious, bitch? Why would your slut call me?"

She hung up the phone. She poured herself a brandy and sat in the dark, imagining both the best and the worst in a multitude of dimensions. He might have died in an incident yet to be discovered, in which case he was an accidental saint, her loyal lover boy to the end. Or he could be with another woman, happy and satisfied in a way she could never make possible, but now a disloyal asshole she should hate forever.

She hadn't felt this crazy since her adolescence when out of her childhood she grew into a great longing for a nameless something. She loved giving to others but needed something large and great for herself. At first she masturbated, probing through arousal to its compelling, conclusive release; so compelling she did it a few times a day, in the morning, at night, in the bathroom at school. She rattled like a can at the edge of what she realized now was a churning, desperate libido many of her friends could not, or would not, discuss.

By age sixteen she was having sex with several boys who were serially charming, intelligent, and abusive. She marveled at the miracle of their hard, slick cocks of all sizes and her ability, with her hand, her mouth, her pussy, even with words on the phone, to reduce their sturdy hardness to a wet, flaccid pool. Unfortunately, when they lost their erections they lost their interest and so her life took a cautious shape by which the ebullient assertion of her passion grew into a palpable danger.

And then she found Elgin, a quarter century after the onset of her dangerous puberty. Her true love, and the sex was awful. But he wasn't. He was kind, generous, loving, successful, intelligent and deeply in love with her. He would do anything. He did. At first she didn't care about the awful sex: so quick, premature, spastic, and without any elegance at all. She could get herself off and he loved to watch her and to help as he could. Maria tried to help him, to teach him. But his passivity was ingrained, perhaps made innate by his childhood, which she understood vaguely to have been traumatically oriented around a repressive religious orthodoxy. He was smart, though, and solicited her to talk about her imagined desires in a way that opened her to the possibility her needs could be realized.

And he was willing. He sang an ephemerally popular song from the Sixties, "Bend me, shake me, anyway you want me…" and she would laugh. Until there was nothing left that was funny. The night they met her first bull in a bar downtown was the end of their laughter and the first expression of a serious, compelling, and addictive eroticism.

Maria stood Monday morning in a sea of school children playing at recess, a principal trying to shout at her over the din of their noisy fun.

"I said, we need another surfaced play area—we have more children and they're running out of room. One of our PTA parents made a drawing. He did it on his computer. Say, are you worried about Y2K? Are all our computers going to crash?"

Maria ignored the principal, thinking again why she didn't have children and using the playground's cacophony as a rationale for never wanting them.

Back in the principal's office she was handed the phone receiver by the school secretary.

"Where's my daddy?" the voice shouted.

It was Doreen, Elgin's barely adult daughter by his previous marriage, and the other reason Maria decided not to have children.

"What's the problem?" she asked Doreen, alert to her biting hostility.

She would not have phoned Maria unless she was angry.

"His office is calling. He didn't show up in court this morning. They're trying to find him and you won't answer your phone. What the fuck did you do with my father?"

Maria strained to look professional though she could see from the embarrassed expressions of the principal and her secretary they heard Doreen's every word.

"Can't talk now. I'll call you later," and Maria hung up the phone.

She told the principal she would call again for more details and then left the school to return to her office where two messages awaited: one from Doreen, the call already taken, and another from her husband's law firm, which had come in before Doreen's.

"I'm feeling sick," Maria said to her secretary just before noon.

"I'm going home to rest awhile. Hold my calls. I'll check back with everyone tomorrow."

She stuffed some papers into her briefcase before slinging it over her shoulder.

I'm in charge of nothing, she thought. *I can't control even my own madness.*

She felt suddenly severed from her existence. If others expressed their needs of something, she was the repository of nothing. Her otherwise wide world was now confined to a small space dominated by a private libidinal crisis that seemed, inexorably, to be growing like a wild vine into her visible life.

4

For a single day, Maria nuzzled into a cryptic void. She did not answer the phone, though it rang several times. Messages were left
from work along with another one of Doreen's tirades.

"Goddamnit, Maria, what is going on? Where's my dad? You're
hiding something and you…"

Maria shut off the machine.

She turned on the VCR and watched again the video she had
sent Elgin. There she was, in regal display, spread like a slaughtered
sow across a hotel bed, breathily mouthing her pleasure for what she
presumed was Elgin's pleasure. The hips and cock of a large, athletic
black man slammed vigorously against her as she struggled to hold
herself up. She watched closely, transfixed by her rapturous body
and its aggregate imperfections: moles, cellulite, a ring of incipient
wrinkles at her throat, infirm breasts that flopped like pendulous
bags in a breeze. Still, not bad, not bad for a woman in her early
forties. She waited for the precise moment of her first come and then
turned off the monitor.

Maria did not dress. It was not true that the more she loved the more
she knew. Elgin's unexplained absence was without precedent and
she lounged in its anesthetizing mystery until mid-afternoon when
she poured herself a drink. Several minutes later she poured another
and prepared to sit again to watch the video, this time with a plan to
use it for her own relief. She hiked up her nightgown and spread her
legs, anchoring the soles of her feet at each end of the coffee table.
She was well into her pleasure when the doorbell rang. She stood
instantly and dropped her gown, shaken away from her rapture by
the return of an intractable, irritating unknowing.

Looking from a window she saw a man in a policeman's uniform
pace on the porch.

This is it, she thought. *They've found him. Oh, God. Oh, fucking God. I
don't think I can stand this.*

She wanted to phone someone quickly. She did not know whom.
She could not face this alone. Brought nearly to the peak of her

pleasure she opened herself instead to a fountain of grief and, with tears welling in her eyes, opened the door.

"You Mrs. Harper?" the officer asked.

Another man in a blue sports jacket and cotton slacks stood behind him.

"Yes," Maria said.

"You OK?" the man in the jacket shouted toughly.

Maria waited a minute and wiped her eyes.

"What is it? What do you know?" she very nearly shouted.

"We wanted to ask you the same question," the jacketed man stated.

"I'm Sheriff's Detective Cameron and this is Deputy Schilling. May we come in?"

Maria looked at them quizzically, her eyes quickly dry as she grasped the existence of still more questions than answers. The detective opened a folded leather wallet to show her his badge and identification.

"Yeah, I guess..." she said absently and not certain at all she wanted company.

The first questions were simple, even as they became personal. The detective leaned forward from the fat lounging chair where Elgin usually sat. He asked if Elgin had enemies.

"No," Maria answered, "unless you count the attorney he's opposing in the Contra Costa case. But he's an adversary and not an enemy. They went to law school together...and why? Why enemies?"

Detective Cameron sighed as if to convey both the unknowable and the obvious. He ignored her question and asked another.

"Has your husband done this before?"

"Done what?" Maria responded

"Leave. Just disappear."

As he spoke Maria noticed him staring at her drink glass half full of bourbon. She moved it slowly to the end table behind her and out of sight.

"Who said he's disappeared?" Maria asked.

"Your daughter," answered the detective.

"I don't have a daughter," Maria said through a bite of irritation before thinking for a second.

"You mean, Doreen? Doreen is Elgin's daughter, not mine."

Cameron nodded while the officer took notes.

"She reported him missing yesterday. Says you won't tell her where he is."

Maria stared absently ahead.

"Jesus H. Christ," she stammered.

"That bitch has a lot of nerve."

A glass and a half of alcohol was having its effect, saying things for Maria she wouldn't otherwise say herself.

"Do you know where your husband is?" the detective asked.

His questions were calm and deliberate, one following the other like moves across a game board.

"No," Maria answered after a lengthy pause.

"I was hoping you knew."

She began to cry.

Cameron waited. He had more questions.

"Do you have any recent letters, phone calls, suspicious communications...?" the detective continued.

Maria said no, thinking immediately of the video in the VCR in front of her.

She had mailed that to Elgin and he had watched it.

"Why didn't you report him missing?" the detective asked.

It was the question Maria might have expected, but still it surprised her.

"I think...I've just returned from a trip, I mean..."

She heard herself make no sense at all.

Nothing made sense: Elgin's disappearance, her avoidance of it, her useless responses to a detective's questions. She was a spouse and not an informer. Spread beneath her worry was the truth of her rabid sexuality and Elgin's groveling support of it, her numerous fucking bulls and Elgin's slavish devotion to her. These were not things to share with a police detective, as hampered as she was by what remained unknown and sick with worry her husband was gone. She could not describe Elgin's state of mind before she left, aware she hadn't paid that much attention. He lingered in her intimate life and waited often in the background of her interests and energies.

Sex was shared always with bulls and rarely between them alone. She did not worry, assured by his earnest participation that he was riveted, excited, or so she thought. This cop would not understand any of it. Nor would her employer, if word got out. Maria decided to say nothing more.

"Is this going to be in the papers?" Maria asked anxiously.

"We have a report of a missing county attorney," Cameron stated dryly.

"He did not show up in court Monday for an important case. His daughter reported him missing. You don't seem able to tell us where he is. If he is really missing, then it is a police matter and public information. And we may need the help of others to find him."

"Will you talk to my boss?" Maria asked, wishing at once she hadn't.

"Does that worry you?" the detective asked.

"More than the disappearance of your husband?"

Flummoxed, Maria asked the detective and officer to leave.

"You can always phone me," Cameron said as he rose from the chair and reached into his coat pocket for a business card.

He was tall, thought Maria, taller than Elgin, and big. She mentally measured his broad shoulders and watched with acute interest as he turned toward the door with an athletic swish, almost as if he intended to dash for it, his strong thighs pumping ahead of the stolid, waddling deputy.

Maria returned to work the following morning. Nothing appeared in the papers and her boss asked no questions, in fact didn't ask to see her. The week ended without further calls or questions. Even Doreen kept her distance, though Maria still waited for something from Elgin. Where was he? With whom was he? The detective was a worrisome intruder but he had not returned. She needed to wait. She could do that, was used to waiting. Holding still was a womanly art. Perhaps it was merely a pose but she could hold it until something moved her. So far nothing had.

Pete arrived Friday at six, surprising Maria who had forgotten.

"What the hell. Come on in," she told him.

Together they fixed a dinner and drank martinis. He played the bull but Maria spoke only of Elgin, which was tiring for Pete who played one part well, but only one. For the first time, Maria felt everything from outside as a threat. She attempted sex with Pete but without Elgin there was no provocation, no excitement in the way she had grown accustomed. Pete sensed this.

"You not into this, babe?" he whispered as he unwrapped himself from her, took his body back while she covered hers with a towel.

"Guess not..." Maria admitted.

"It's not the same...Elgin..." and she started to cry.

Pete held her before dressing and leaving. An hour later, Maria's phone rang.

"Come bail me out, sister," Pete shouted into the phone.

Driving away from Maria's house, Pete was stopped by police who found an outstanding warrant for petty theft from Orange County. Pete was arrested and his car impounded. Maria dressed and drove to the police station. She found a bail bondsmen and wrote a check to cover bail.

"They asked me a lot of questions," Pete said.

"What's happened to your old man?"

Every fact had something hard about it, some science that put fragments of reality to work organizing the narratives of desire. Maria's was such a narrative and appeared now to be a growing source of concern of others far beyond the orbit of her peculiar marital sexuality. Was there wrongdoing? If so, atonement, repentance and punishment would follow.

5

As a child Maria had only her mirror as a credible reflection. By age 11 her parents were useless, either praising her lavishly or scolding her severely in ways that had little relation to her attributes. At the dawn of adolescence she knew, even if unconsciously, that she was their child/object, their scapegoat and trophy.

Friends were no help, either. Maria's spunky wildness and precocious sexuality were more than most could understand, much less accept. As her pubescent buddies probed cautiously to mold themselves to each other's voiceless insecurities, to cover their bodies, their fiery thoughts, and especially their feelings, Maria held nothing back. She was an outlaw, but an uncovered one for whom the mirror provided a private partner, a trusted and frequently naked opposite that both complemented and amplified what she thought of as her lovely and satisfying desires.

Maria found and viewed previously recorded videos of her bull sessions with Elgin, most made by him. She rarely watched them. When the sex was over and the bulls had departed, she and Elgin settled back into their spousal swaddle and the cassettes piled up in a cardboard box in the study closet. Elgin did seem to enjoy watching the videos. She was too critical of her appearance in some of them, though the recapitulation, especially as a prelude to the next bull session, could animate her.

She searched the videos for Elgin, as if to confirm some missed clue to his whereabouts. There was none, though in many shots, many more than she remembered, her husband wandered naked in the background, his small penis occasionally in view as his arousal took its own course. In one long shot she was spread on the bed to receive Pete for the first time, his monumental cock impressive and, she recalled, scary as she watched herself hold up a hand to his rippling abdomen as a caution to go slowly.

The penetration was tight and deep in a way she had never before known and, at first, was not exciting until his slow, steady thrust found her depth, a depth she didn't know existed until he touched it.

The recollection aroused her, even as she probed the video for some clue to Elgin's mood or sense of things. Did he really enjoy his cuckolding? He said he did but his expressions in the videos appeared dutifully attending. At times he seemed, if not bored, at least distracted from the action that excited Maria beyond words.

Was he tired of all this and just did not tell me?

Maria assumed from all other aspects of their life together that a dialogue existed solidly, that Elgin had become her reliable and opposite mirror, the partner she loved and who, undaunted by the realization of her wanton and specific hungers, offered his love in return. In this state she continued to see something disquieting in Elgin's retiring demeanor, something completely out of synch with the hard sex of her bulls and the aureate performance of her pleasure.

What appeared at first to be his enthusiasm seemed to melt into the background. A kind of off-screen reluctance took root as Elgin made fewer video appearances. Was she loved in all this? A shudder of fear replaced the bewilderment that had supplanted her feelings of pleasure. The video, too, was a mirror that displayed to her the equivocal details of an experience not fully known at the time it was lived.

At mid-week Detective Cameron phoned Maria. She was in her school district office finishing a budget report for the next board meeting.

"I'd like to meet with you again," he said directly.

"Sure," she answered before cautiously asking why.

"Some new developments," the detective reported.

"Have you found him?" Maria asked anxiously.

"No. We're still looking."

Maria said she would be home by six and Cameron could come by then.

"I need you to come to the sheriff's office," he said.

Maria waited for more but the detective said nothing else.

"I have lunch at 12:30. I'll come then," Maria answered and hung up the phone.

Cameron greeted Maria and guided her down a hallway to a small cubicle with a table and two chairs.

"Tell me more about your friendship with Pete," he asked Maria after she sat down and set her slim leather purse on the table.

Cameron showed Maria a mug shot of her reliable bull and stated his request with a studied confidence that threw Maria off as she sat across from him in the spare, unadorned space.

"I don't know what I can tell you…" she equivocated.

"He's just a friend of ours."

"A good friend?" asked Cameron.

"Yes," Maria answered curtly.

"What's this about?"

"Pete's a convicted felon," the detective stated as if to surprise Maria.

But she wasn't surprised.

"He said you have other friends, friends he's referred to you including a man named Paul you recently spent time with in St. Louis. Is that right?"

"What else did Pete tell you?" Maria asked, a panic rising in her throat.

She could feel the heat of a blush in her cheeks.

"Quite a bit," the detective said firmly.

"What can you tell us?"

Maria thought herself at once odious and in danger. She was stifled by a lover's discourse, what she thought her personal property but that now appeared to be the subject of a search by the authorities. And why? Because her husband was missing and other men populated her life and had sex with her. She had little doubt the detective knew this, that Pete had given up her secrets to spare himself big trouble.

"Just friends," she answered weakly.

"These men are all black men," the detective asked.

"Do you have other black friends?"

Out of her fragile embarrassment, Maria felt the surge of an imminent fear and then the rise of a fierce, unfiltered anger. She would resist this authority as she resisted all authority: no secret frightened her. Any truth could be told as long as it was the truth. Everything else followed. It was her childhood's first truth and still the most important.

"Yeah. But I fuck the men. Elgin helps me. He's such a dear. He insists on it. He finds the men for me and we have a party with them and they absolutely fuck me into orgasmic oblivion in a way that Elgin always finds arousing. I love to please him and he loves to see me pleased."

She watched the detective's eyes bulge and felt the rollers of his chair scrape the floor as he pushed himself back from the table.

"What the hell does this have to do with anything?"

Maria nearly spat her words at him.

"And why do you care?"

The detective, as if consulting his aptitude for morality, remained still and seemingly thoughtful. He did not owe her an answer, this subject whom he might or might not suspect of what? Of something, certainly, related to the disappearance of her husband. His quiet eyes tried to hide the likely thought he had assumed too much and that his first friendly, searching, non-specific interrogation, usually so effective in arousing a suspect's guilt, would open Maria's veins and expose her fears. It did not. She was transparent and guileless. She hid nothing. At least that was his first impression and it was enough for now, enough to close one line of investigation and to open another.

"Did any of these men have a reason to dislike your husband?" he asked.

Maria shook her head.

"He found them. He paid them. They fucked me. Why would they dislike him?"

The detective nodded in vague agreement.

"OK," he said with a tone of closure.

"Where is my husband?" Maria asked directly.

The detective did not know.

"It's suspicious he hasn't phoned anyone or made contact. He didn't pack a suitcase. His credit card hasn't been used anywhere. That usually signals to us the likelihood of foul play. But we don't yet have a suspect. Unless..."

"No," Maria said.

"Don't even go near it. I'm not involved.'

"But you are," Cameron answered.

"You are here and he is not. You are the only one who speaks for him. You are involved."

Maria arrived home without her appetite. She was curious and not hungry. She was also afraid. She searched Elgin's study for a box of recent photos. What pictures they made and printed they kept stored away. Some were photos taken on trips and visits but most were photos of their sex.

One showed Maria wrapped in a Ninja gi, opened at the top while she wore a black mask and no pants. It was used to advertise her availability as a Ninja Hotwife. It was a clever pose, really Elgin's idea, and it created quite a stir. Elgin interviewed a dozen applicants through which he found the bull royalty that so excited Maria. There was a certain type of man: large, muscular, dark-skinned and fiercely confident, that she could not resist. It was not anonymous—she knew the men Elgin brought into their sexual fantasy—but it was safe because Elgin also knew them and stood by while they fucked her.

Another voicemail arrived from Doreen, an obscenity-laced threat that had no real substance. No one would believe her. Doreen's pathology preceded her wherever she went. Elgin traced Doreen's madness to the death of her mother, killed by a lymphoma within two months of its discovery. Not enough time for any child of any age to understand what had happened but especially for one that had spent her assailable youth in the grip of crippling nightmares and irrepressible demons. Maria sustained a protean empathy for Elgin's grown and broken daughter. But Doreen's brazen hostility did force Maria to wonder how she could keep a private life from becoming a public one. If her missing husband was news, what was she?

Maria was under suspicion. Why else would a detective continue to question her? She considered a bundle of immediate regrets. Why had she not been the first to report Elgin's disappearance? Why had she ignored Doreen's addled anger? Why had she burst forth with a frank and angry revelation of her debauching sex with Elgin and her bulls? Why had she said nothing to her boss about her husband's disappearance? She owed him that, a school superintendent with high public visibility.

Was she now a potential suspect, and of what? Elgin's murder? It was unthinkable. And now that she had told the detective about her sex life, would he seek more control over her? Seek to police her or, worse, to protect her? Her desires had no chance of being understood by anyone in authority, had no chance to exist simply for the pleasure they were. Instead, they would be seen as the likely evidence of a vile betrayal and a repudiation of moral codes that were a community's last protection against the railing threat of enchantment.

6

Maria spoke to herself at the end of a wicked week. The telling of her life felt different from its living. The consensual sex that had felt luridly thrilling now threatened her with the idea she had taken a stupid risk. Elgin not only served her, he protected and defended her. It was absurd that his absence, which made her the subject of a menacing police inquiry, also left her without his refuge.

He was ambiguously gone, leaving her unambiguously sad and also afraid. Friday night under a full moon she wandered down the canyon's slender trail to search for him. She felt ridiculous and was frightened in the darkness that was too dark to reveal anything to her. She ran back to the house and locked all the doors. *Is he dead?* she wondered uselessly. *Then everything will have been for nothing.*

The morning brought a phone call from a man asking for Maria Harper.

"Who wants her?" Maria answered suspiciously.

"A news reporter for the Ledger. Name's Tim. Say, how long has Elgin Harper been missing?"

Maria was startled by the man's casual presumption, as if his were a normal question any stranger might and should ask.

"News reporter?" she asked.

"Yeah. Police say they're looking for Harper. Where is he?"

Maria froze.

"Wish I knew," she answered before hanging up the phone.

The phone rang again, rang all morning and she let it ring. At noon she dressed and drove down her hill to cross the Benicia Bridge. She turned off Highway Four west to Port Costa, dropping down Bull Valley to a vast, dusty parking lot at the strait's southern shore. She entered a warehouse-sized building to sit at a long bar with an oblique view of the water. The bartender approached and she ordered a beer. Then another. After a third, she paid and left and climbed a trail into the parkland hills above the tiny town.

She hiked furiously toward the hill's crest where, exposed suddenly to a fierce wind she fell backwards on a bluff to stare dizzily at the white, fluffy wakes of boats sliding east along the shore. Beyond she saw the hills that hid her home and the tip of the water tank that dominated a closer, opposite view out her kitchen window. She squatted under an oak tree for a long, urgent piss.

She felt for a moment like a dumb animal, obscene and stupid. She might be a kitten in the window of a pet store, on view and naked and mocked by loud laughter. Her world was shrinking, the freedom to move increasingly limited. Her view from the hill grew into a long view of her life as a small, bordered nation. She could see rooftops rise in the important capitals of this country: her Benicia home, equidistant from two county seats where she and Elgin worked as respected agents of two respective governments. But her nation was shrinking and, within it, her freedom to move.

Returning home in twilight, she passed her house to see two cars parked at the curb. She did not recognize them or the two men sitting in each. She drove around the corner and, out of their sight, parked near a culvert that led into the canyon. She climbed the slender trail to her yard and entered her house through the back door. Immediately after turning on the kitchen lights, her doorbell rang, and then rang again. It rang several times and she ignored it until it stopped. The phone began to ring and she ignored it, as well, turning off the downstairs lights and climbing the stairs to the bedroom. The ringing continued for an hour, and then stopped. She turned off her light and parted the window curtains to look outside. The cars she had seen at the curb were gone.

Maria awoke early to the thud of a big newspaper hitting her driveway. It was the first Sunday in November. Elgin had been missing for exactly three weeks. Sleep was over and she wrapped herself in her robe and went downstairs. Without Elgin, the house felt like a vast and empty cave. She peeked through the window then rushed to the driveway. She brewed coffee and slathered butter on a slice of toast. She sat at the kitchen table and opened the paper's first section.

Her eyes passed absently over headlines with little meaning. The century was coming to an end and no one seemed to understand what it would mean. Nothing, she thought. But this century ended a millennium and that might mean something, as arbitrary as that was. God to her was some rich, spoiled brat who had no business meddling in the lives of his creation. Regardless, her life and every other life were on some god's time and this morning she regretted her lifelong enslavement to clocks and calendars. She missed Elgin, and not just his willingness to get her pleasingly and deliciously fucked by bulls. She did love him in all his brilliant attention and physical meagerness. She did miss him, more so for not knowing where he was.

She turned the paper's broad, unfolded pages and searched the headlines for nothing in particular. Politics and education drew her attention. It was a critical part of her job to know where local power intersected with local schools. She found little of interest until on page A-8 she saw a peculiar headline: *Cold trail in search for missing attorney.*

The first paragraph described her husband, Elgin Harper, Esq, as a "prominent, local attorney" whose "mysterious disappearance" was now the subject of a police investigation. The five-paragraph story described how Harper had been reported missing by his daughter who had been unable to contact him or the attorney's wife, Maria Harper, assistant to the Solano County Superintendent of Schools. A police spokesman said Harper had been missing for more than two weeks and appeared to vanish without a trace. When asked where her husband was, Mrs. Harper told a Ledger reporter, "I wish I knew" and then hung up her phone. Efforts to reach her for further comment were unsuccessful. An investigation was underway but so far provided no clues to Harper's whereabouts.

"It's odd," Detective Joseph Cameron was quoted as saying.

"He apparently packed nothing, hasn't used his credit card, and hasn't contacted anyone."

The detective said investigators were questioning a number of Harper's friends and family acquaintances. Harper's disappearance first came to light when he missed a court appearance in Martinez on October 4th. Reading her words in the paper shocked Maria. Were they cold and uncaring? Did they make her appear insensitive and mean?

As she was dressing for work on Monday, Maria's phone rang.

"I'm sorry," she heard her boss say.

"Your husband, he…"

"He's missing," Maria answered coolly.

"That's all anyone knows."

"It must be rough on you," the boss said.

"Well, yes, I'm doing my best."

Maria did not feel the words she spoke and did not understand at all why she was speaking. It was her boss. It was the one person from whom she most wanted to hide her personal life. But the newspaper had ended that. Her own life, or at best only a part of it, was now a kind of public property, an asset of curiosity as the terms of an awkward mystery began to define it.

"Don't worry, dear."

Her boss rarely spoke to her with such intimate endearment.

"Take some time off. I'm giving you a couple of weeks of paid leave. You need to look after yourself. I hope everything is all right."

The last words rang with a hollowness informed perhaps by the corporeal terms of business that haunted every Monday morning. Maria had no response.

"OK?" the boss asked tremulously.

"Yeah…I guess…when do you want me back?"

Maria was dressed for work and immediately ready to return.

"I'll check in," her boss said with an evident sense of relief.

"I'll phone you. We'll be fine. Take care of yourself."

Maria hung up the phone. Was she angry, disappointed or afraid? She felt a heat so warm her emotions were indistinguishable. She was hot with a cry intended to prove her grief was not a chimera, not a ghostly fancy. She welcomed a heaving sob. It would speak for her, would tell her story. Her tears felt like a certain kind of black-mail, intended to present her as indebted while she worked behind them to secure herself.

7

Maria was unsettled to think herself an exile. She was not friendly enough with any of Elgin's few remaining relatives to connect with them. Certainly not Doreen, the stepdaughter from hell whose mental illness kept even her father at a distance.

There was an uncle somewhere in the northwest but he was very old and very far away and she had never met him. They were too rich to need neighbors and too busy to keep up with what remained of their distant families. She had few friends of her own and none close enough to bear her tears or terror.

She wondered why Elgin's friends or business partners hadn't phoned. Perhaps they tried and she missed their calls amid the queries she tried for weeks to ignore. It still seemed strange. Why had Doreen stopped phoning? As relieving as this was, it was also disquieting that Doreen had ceased to harass her. Did Doreen know something?

Maria phoned her brother in Pennsylvania. They rarely spoke. Geoffrey was her older brother—much older—and her only sibling. Five years before, the two children were forced together into the lingering care of their elderly parents, though Geoffrey seemed relentlessly to resent Maria's sudden and perplexing arrival so late in his life. He was nearly twenty when his mother gave birth to Maria, which was a joyous occasion for his mother but a disgusting and threatening experience for the son. Since their mother's death, Geoffrey and Maria had avoided contact. The division of their family's modestly substantial estate, a division Geoffrey resented deeply, left the siblings acutely and, at least from Maria's perspective, unnecessarily estranged.

"He's missing? What do you mean? How long?"

Geoffrey was surprised by Maria's news, nearly as surprised as he was to hear from her.

"About three weeks. The police are looking for him. No one seems to have any idea."

Geoffrey was silent, too silent for Maria's comfort.

"I think the cops suspect me for some reason," she blurted.

"They keep asking me questions. I know they've spoken with

my…uh…some of our friends."

Geoffrey was silent for another long moment. Maria sensed her distant placement barely within the circle of her brother's concerns.

"Did something happen?" Geoffrey asked at last, certain there was a cause and likely one created by his sister.

"Did you do something?"

Maria knew immediately the call was a mistake.

"No. I'm just worried. There is no reason," she answered.

"There's always a reason," Geoffrey said.

Maria ignored Geoffrey's summary judgment.

"So are you and my nephews coming out this year?"

Maria's abrupt change of subject met with no objection from Geoffrey.

"No…don't think so. Joanie's mom isn't well and so it's summer in Maine again. Maybe next year."

Maria said she needed to go. She could no longer imagine why she phoned, nor could her brother who offered a curt "hope they find him" and hung up the receiver.

Maria had stopped paying attention to what was true and what was not true. Four years with Elgin, two as his wife, had altered her destiny. Of course, she loved Elgin's willing acquiescence to the terms of her sexual fantasies and his grasp of how crucial her desires were to her experience of living. She should have, but had not, anticipated that the wind of lovely change, which brought Elgin around to become her willing and obedient cuckold, would keep blowing beyond their time of sweet arousal and move them somewhere else. Jealousies and appetites were an irresistible unknown and for the first time she imagined that Elgin might have left her.

But why was she left to feel the heat? She had stopped communicating with her bulls, all of them including Paul driven away by the police investigation. The police seemed also to be watching and following her. It was subtle and nothing she could firmly ascertain. One evening, and then another, she noticed a white sedan at the end of the block that arrived around 10 p.m. and left before dawn. Home alone with no job to go to, Maria drew her own circumference around the neighborhood, placing herself and her fears at its center. Everything that entered the circle she examined with a nearly hallucinatory vigilance.

She was not working and so stayed inside where in the mornings she became frantic, then relaxed as the day made no demands, then grew resentful and, finally, angry with a husband who would leave her in this pit of exposure and threat.

After a while of burning resentment she pictured Elgin in a ditch somewhere, alone and cold to the touch. Why would anyone blame her? It was someone else's job to find him, not hers. She was not culpable, at least not in the ways a detective might imagine. In all of this she was the injured party, despite her once satisfying role as the injuring wife.

Maria returned to her mirror, a lover to her as much as any and both subject and object of her affections. She thought of her mirrors as others might think of past lovers, relying on them to form the terms of her pleasure and meaning. It was a relationship and hers was a history in which questions of identity at first yielded to formations drawn from skirts and mascara, later made more complex by the appearance of crows feet and belly fat.

She could not remember when she stopped looking at herself naked. The videos were one thing: an objectification that allowed her to see her body in relation to another and to visualize its visceral pleasure. The nakedness she now encountered in a mirror was too raw with the ravages of passing time and she was old enough to see that her face, breasts and limbs had passed the prime of their once lovely and integrated prettiness. She was no longer a Pygmalion in progress but, rather, a fading old crow, at once bony and chubby in all the wrong ways. Her mirror, like Elgin, was no longer the lover she wanted but more the only lover left to her. She tried to make the best of it while feeling herself sink with the chains of an addiction, the need to look, always to look, at the warped, crooked mistakes that multiplied with every viewing.

The next morning Maria phoned an attorney and hired him. Rich-
ard Roper was a criminal lawyer close to Elgin and regarded as one
of the region's toughest. Within days he found a cab driver that remembered picking up Elgin the night he disappeared. A day later
Roper had a flight manifest listing Elgin as a passenger on a plane
from Oakland to New York. Roper also learned the scope of the
sheriff's investigation.

"They got your St. Louis guy to talk," he told Maria.

"He was frightened and said a lot of trash he thought they wanted
to hear. Obviously, you didn't kill your husband. He's alive somewhere. We just don't know where. But the detectives have swarmed
over your life like a hive of bees and asked a lot of people a lot of
questions."

Maria asked if she'd caused all this.

"Didn't help to tell the detective about your sex life. Wish you'd
called me first."

Too late, thought Maria. It didn't matter anymore that she was
innocent. She wasn't. In addition to being a bag of bones and fat she
was also a nasty slut.

8

Of all the reasons for Elgin to leave, infidelity seemed to Maria the most absurd. She tried to imagine when and how Elgin could manage another lover. His cuckolding devotion to her had been all encompassing, even obsessive. She could not think of any long stretch of time that permitted a transgression or how her wobbly, inadequate and introverted partner might ever have connected with someone, ever extended or invited an exposing intimacy free of the obeisant shame that drove his apparent arousal with her.

Was Elgin a secret he-man waiting to bloom? Was his miniscule penis irresistibly attractive to someone? If so, the mystery of her husband's disappearance contained the qualities of a miracle. Maria was relieved to think he was not dead, if for no other reason than to lift the fog of obscene suspicion that whirled around her. The damage was wide and she could not know how far it carried. She had only her hands and her words to protect her.

Maria searched again through Elgin's desk and bookcases, moving into a closet to invade dusty boxes stacked against a back wall. She cut into the cardboard flaps of a taped up box the size of a small hassock. Within she found another box, wooden and secured by a small lock. She tore the lock from its hinges and pushed open the lid. Inside were a sheaf of letters, a rosary and a worn, black Sunday Missal.

At the bottom were two photographs of Elgin as a child, one in which a hard-featured but smiling priest held tightly the arms and shoulders of a young Elgin as each faced the camera. Her husband appeared surprised by the priest's embrace and his expression was vacant and confused.

In another photo Elgin stared into an undefined distance. An anonymous hand reached in from somewhere, fingers curled at Elgin's neck as if to adjust his collar and prepare him for something, an event that Maria, judging from Elgin's age in the photograph, might have been a first communion. The letters, all written in Elgin's rough, quick-stroked cursive, described the guilty return of his faith following the death of his wife from cancer. They included detailed descriptions of her funeral and the power of her death over his will to live.

I find only in my humility the meaning I cannot otherwise find in living. He described his inadequacy in the face of so many mysteries beyond his understanding. Several letters read like love poems and Maria was struck by one particular phrase directed apparently to another woman. *I am your loving mystery, dearest lady of so many sorrows. I am someone else's creation but yours alone to use.*

Maria absorbed the confusing details of what appeared to be elements of a secret life. While his words suggested a deep spiritual devotion, they also made specific reference to a woman and Elgin's feelings of earthly ecstasy. Perhaps he had a lover but one he could not touch or did not even know. It would be like Elgin to experience love at a distance, to find his most wondrous joy while in the orbit of something unobtainable.

Roper phoned Tuesday. He had news.

"Did you know $50,000 was drawn from your husband's retirement investments?"

"When?" Maria asked as she absorbed another shock.

She and Elgin held a joint mutual fund to which each donated generously from their salaries. But Elgin's own investments remained his separate property.

"The end of the week he went missing. Another clue you're not involved. But it's a lot of money."

Maria waited.

"Not so much," she answered.

"Elgin has at least five times that in his account. He must not have gone very far."

"He didn't take it with him," Roper said.

"He gave it to his daughter."

Maria's mind stalled for a dizzy moment.

"Doreen?"

It explained why Doreen had stopped phoning.

"Maria, the cops are dumb douches," Roper pronounced.

"Not only can't they dig up evidence under their noses, they've also been slobs about this investigation. They've spoken with your neighbors and your co-workers and boss. I hate to tell you this, but there isn't anyone they've interviewed that doesn't now know something about your sex life with Elgin."

Roper's assessment was not a surprise. A tone had settled around Maria's life in town that suggested she had been culled out of the pack and isolated. A neighbor at the corner who for years had waved at her every morning now disappeared behind his fence when she passed. Acquaintances that usually greeted her warmly were now absent from the paths of her daily routines. None had called to offer concern or condolence. For at least two weeks she had felt alone and thought, of course, it was because she had retreated into her private world of grief. Instead, she saw now that the public world had been retreating from her.

A letter arrived Thursday. Elgin's name was scribbled in the top left corner of the envelope but there was no address. Maria crushed the envelope to her chest and ran into the house to open it.

My Dear Maria,
I hope you can understand what has happened. What I once took on faith I have come to know through experience. And in this way I have at last found the truth of my life. I have served you well and I don't regret it. But in the course of the last year I have become subservient to another mistress, another Maria.
I wish I could have told you about this. As it was, I could tell no one and for a long while not even myself. In many ways this isn't new. My life as your cuckold offered me a celibacy that, while at first agonizing, eventually became my preferred way to feel. As I watched your pleasure grow from the rigors of my humiliating service to you I began to hear a call to a larger, deeper service that reconciled what I thought were the logically irreconcilable opposites of spirit and instinct. Your orgasms were divine. Your pleasure with the bulls became my delicious pain until at an intersection of thoughtful reckoning I accepted my neurotic symptoms fully as evidence of a greater obligation. As I've often told you, my childhood and early adult years were spent in devotion to a church and its scripture, to the dolorous mystery of a sacrifice that saved the world.
Where I left that path I cannot say. But in this poignant year of lovely and

enlightening denial all the roads I've wandered have returned me to the source of an indelible faith.

I am grateful for your affectionate humiliation and the training that has freed me from desire and accustomed me to the frailty of all human suffering. It has made me eligible again for the real pleasures of living, those derived from a pure and devoted suffering among the tragic, inescapable torments of conscious human existence. There are sins but you, Maria, were not the sinner. I was. I am.

You have been a midwife. You have brought me, however unknowingly, to a resurrection from a dark death. I could have died but, thanks to you, I did not. Now another Maria calls. It is the Maria in whose name I do the worshipping work of salvation. Et incarnatus est de Spiritu Sancto ex Maria Virgine: et homo factus est.

I've found my other, real life, Maria. I won't tell you where I am but I work now with a band of brothers and sisters who in your name care for orphaned children, many with fatal diseases or disabilities that make them unwanted to the rest of the world. Relieving their suffering is the ecstasy of our lives and we, like you, are midwives of deep, abiding love.

As for the house and our savings: keep them for yourself. A portion of my investments has been given to my sad, lost daughter. The rest goes to my new family of loving friends to support our work to relieve the suffering of innocents.

The sacrifices of God are a broken spirit: a humble and contrite heart.

Dear Maria, what I saw in you was something that really belonged to myself. The ambivalence you projected towards me obscured the fact of my own ambivalence. Your delicious infidelity pointed out my own unacknowledged desires. Our time is short and for a small moment I have forsaken you, though great mercies remain.

I'm sorry. Of course, I'm always sorry. This is a parting without a proper goodbye. I did cling for a long while to the ecstasy sustained by your degrading love. But I have moved on. I have exchanged that ecstasy for paradise.

Maria dropped the letter on the kitchen table and went to phone Roper. She felt held in a bad lover's last, hysterical embrace and wanted it to end as soon as possible.

9

"The letter proves Elgin is alive," Maria told her attorney.

"The letter proves nothing," he answered.

"It's typed and isn't signed. It could have been written by anyone and mailed by anyone."

Maria frowned.

"What about the writing on the envelope, and the postmark?"

The letter was date-stamped by a post office in Bangor, Maine.

"Could have been written anytime. Could have been forged. The ink is a runny blotch that won't stand scrutiny. One of your so-called bulls could have written it."

Maria looked at Roper, angry and puzzled.

"Well, what then?" Maria asked, exasperated.

Roper was an expert on the naming of things.

"Of course he's alive," he said.

"And of course this is his letter. It's true. We just need to prove it. Do you want a divorce?"

The attorney's comment, replete with what seemed a non sequitur stalled Maria's response.

"You mean from Elgin?"

Roper said yes.

"Who else? I'm not joking, Maria. Elgin has been a friend to me but I'm your attorney and he's offering you all his assets to free him from his marriage to you. Are you going to do it?"

Roper was moving fast and it was difficult for Maria to keep up.

"Yes, I guess. I mean, of course. But how?"

"If Elgin signs a marriage settlement agreement, you get both a divorce and proof he's alive."

Maria asked how that could happen.

"I'll take the papers to him," Roper said.

"I'll find him. I need a week and $5,000. A hospice for babies and foster children near Bangor, Maine? That shouldn't be hard to find. And I have a cousin in Boston I haven't seen in years."

Maria thought she knew Elgin better than anyone but now realized his motives were intractable and impenetrable. She could wear herself out trying to understand what had happened and still not know. Instead of defining Elgin she turned to herself.

What do I want? she asked. To no longer be defined solely by the suffering and pleasure provided by Elgin. She told Roper she would cover his costs and asked when he would leave.

Thanksgiving was approaching and Maria had nothing to do and nowhere to go. There was no family without Elgin. Though he was forced by her wretched insults the previous year to ban Doreen from their holiday dinner, Elgin usually found a cousin or aunt willing to share a bountiful feast and lots of wine. There would be no dinner this year. Elgin was gone and Maria had nothing to exalt. She could not be grateful for loving someone unknown and who would remain unknown forever. She at least knew what she did not know.

On Monday of the holiday week Maria phoned her office to talk with her boss. Her call was transferred to Human Resources.

"We're letting you go," said the HR director.

She was direct, but not gruff.

"It's a budget issue. It's forced us to restructure your department. It's certainly nothing to do with your performance. Fred said he would give you a great recommendation."

Maria tried to object, to query the director, but could not find her words.

"A check to you is in the mail, along with COBRA instructions. You can keep your health insurance for a year."

The director's informing tone flushed away Maria's silent outrage.

"OK," she answered obediently.

"Goodbye," said the director.

An hour later Roper phoned to report Elgin had signed the agreement.

"He wasn't happy to see me," he told Maria.

Elgin had joined an obscure sect of Catholic brothers that called itself Men for the Martyr. They worked together with a group of Canadian nuns to manage a home for displaced children outside the city of St. John in New Brunswick.

"I told him the trouble he left you in. He said he was sorry."

Of course he did, thought Maria. As Elgin had stated in his letter, he was always sorry. That was his role with her: to apologize for his lame sex and to reward her patience with humiliating supplication to her strong, virile bulls.

"He provides legal support for adoptions. He loves the work and wants nothing else from you or anyone. You're pretty lucky. He's left you just about everything."

For a vague time during the call Maria lost track of her desire. What Elgin enjoyed was to go away from her precisely at the moment her desire took shape. At first he had watched her with an interest Maria found flattering. She realized now that at the height of her pleasure, when she needed him close, he was often his farthest from her, usually at the end of the bed while one or two of her bulls filled her and fucked her.

The sensations were incomparably delicious even as they formed a wall between her and her husband. It was a wall of loving sexual enforcement; one she thought locked Elgin into something equivalent to a prisoner's cell for which she felt a deepening empathy. Now she sensed that the cell actually was hers and that her husband, freed by her heat from any responsibility, stood clear, free and away from her slavish intersection with ecstasy.

"Anyway, I've got the agreement and I've phoned the sheriff," Roper said finally. "It's a good thing. He heard about your videos. The D.A. was set to subpoena you and them for evidence. That's on hold. When they see the docs and Elgin's signature, they'll drop the investigation."

The Wednesday afternoon before Thanksgiving Maria drove down First Street to the yacht harbor. She parked her car and climbed the stairs to the Captain's bar. She took a seat and asked the bartender for a margarita. He was unusually attentive to her, stopping by every few minutes to check her glass. When she finished her first drink he offered another…on the house. Maria ordered a platter of fried calamari and a small Louis salad.

She felt the hidden powers of fire in the pleasant comfort of her food, the warmth of her digestion and the hot, burning pleasure of her drink. The bartender, whom she had known for years and who tonight appeared to serve her with notable consideration, took his break and asked to sit with her. His forwardness was also warming. She liked him. He was tall, strong and attractively attentive. She felt a heat rise, the familiar hot wife heat she hadn't felt for months. He looked into her eyes.

"What are you doing later?" he asked.

Maria recoiled. Behind his flirtatious question she sensed something suspiciously premeditated.

"Why?" Maria asked directly.

The bartender struggled for a reason in a way he did not intend would reveal the truth.

"You're a hot lady," he answered awkwardly.

"You must…"

Maria stopped him.

"Tom, for chris' sakes, you too? Is there anyone in this town that doesn't know?"

The bartender swallowed a guilty gulp of air.

"I just thought that…"

"That I'm a hot wife who is now an ex-wife but still in need of a good time?"

The bartender shrunk low in his seat and looked away. Maria was filled to repletion. She needed nothing.

"Let it go, Tom," she said as he turned back toward her.

"Just make me another drink."

Maria stayed past midnight nursing her one last margarita while the bartender considerately avoided her.

"I'll move to the City," she said to herself as she gazed out the bar's bay window toward the lights of the Carquinez Bridge.

"An ad agency. I'll sell the house. Doreen will be pissed."

There was a long indefinite pause.

"Maybe I'll meet someone."

An undefined future fit perfectly Maria's imagined hope for something that would again burn bright, that would feel fiercely and frightfully hot.

SONS OF GUS

1

Magic hopes and secret rites ran the life of Gus Slaughter-beck. He was a man held in place by fatherhood in a way he loved and could barely manage. Though no one providing him with services had the time or money to make a clinical diagnosis, it was generally agreed by all of us that Gus was a narcissist. But narcissists have rights and, despite his reckless, self-absorbed life, Gus was entitled to a chance to keep his kids.

I entered the life of Gus some years after the sons of Gus. They arrived first, the offspring of a serial mother conjoined with the father through a three-year meth binge ended by another man with better drugs. Gus hung around, though, his sense of self augmented by a new proprietary interest, what he termed with unctuously announced affection as "mah boys," his emphasis made in an Arkansas drawl and placed on the word "mah" as he battled to keep them.

And there were plenty of people who wished to take his children away. Young Richie and younger Dalton, ages 7 and 5, had spent the previous year circulated among three foster families while their mother slithered on with her sex life and Gus looked futilely for a job and a home. The mother lived in a trailer park off the Avenue in southwest Santa Rosa and every year kept a man there just long enough to get pregnant whereupon she would throw the fool to the curb before giving birth to another child.

Invariably the new children were lost or neglected, would turn up on a street corner or in someone else's trailer, until the police were called and Child and Family Services would get involved. By her tenth serial pregnancy, Family Services was seizing the woman's infants immediately after their births at the hospital and placing them for adoption. But not before Richie and Dalton were born and, thanks or no thanks to the California courts, were given a year to visit with their father while he battled for custody.

It was an old story for me, a social worker employed by a private non-profit agency that took the state's money to work with dysfunctional families and at-risk children. Sometimes I made a difference. Mostly, I didn't. But it was something, if not enough. Few outside my field appreciated how hard it was to shift lives of misery, poverty, ignorance and poor nutrition into a functioning family experience. Though good sometimes triumphed and, in the case of Gus and his sons, I had for the briefest moment and also the longest year, the illusive conviction I could make a difference.

"It's a dad," said Patrona Mona, the affectionate name for our agency's voluble director of parenting services.

Fiftyish and feisty, Mona sat at her desk and fanned herself vigorously with a manila folder despite the office's December chill.

"You're great with dads," she said to me encouragingly.

"Besides, none of the women here want to go near him. He came on pretty strong to a CFS caseworker and the word is out. Anyway, he has a year to prove he's dad enough to keep his kids."

I asked her what the chances were. We'd been here before.

"Gus is homeless. He's a player and unemployed. He was a drug addict and maybe still is. But he's tested clean for nearly a year. He'll start with supervised visits and probably get tired of the tedium. Besides, the boys' current foster family loves them and wants to keep them. Family Services would prefer adoption now but needs to go through the motions with the dad. He has his rights. I give him a month, maybe two."

I told Mona she probably wouldn't say that about an estranged mother. She did not laugh.

"Yeah," she answered.

"You're always saying dads get a bad rap. But where are they when we need them?"

She swiveled her fan with increased urgency.

"Maybe this will be different," I said.

"Let's hope for a miracle," she answered and with her free hand gave me the case folder.

My first task was to talk to Gus. My second was to watch him. The holidays approached and I wanted everything handled before leaving for a two-week vacation. I arranged a meeting in my office for the middle of the month, hoping to have a visit set up for Gus and his boys by early January. Gus had other ideas.

"What about their Christmas presents?" he asked.

"I got gifts for mah boys."

Gus spoke in a small, quiet voice that belied his monstrous frame. He was tall and burly, a large gut spilling from under his shirt, his long legs pushed nearly against mine as he sat across from me sprawled out and barely contained within a narrow leather recliner.

"I gotta see mah boys before Christmas. Ain't this what it's all about? Shit! I'm their goddamned dad."

Gus was impatient. His short hair stood up straight on his balding head like a flattop cut gone wrong. It amplified his moony face by giving his head the look of a gawky gnome and made Gus appear much older than his 37 years. He was impatient and also mistaken.

No one in my field worked that fast. Weeks were required to prepare for his involvement. I had papers he needed to read and sign before I could begin the process of scheduling a room for a visit or setting its time. We were all about process and part of the test for Gus was to understand this, which he did. He was simply not accepting it.

"Hey pal," he pleaded.

"Don't give me the runaround. Mah boys. Damn, I need to see them and they need to see me. It's Christmas, pal. Where's your spirit?"

Gus said he was a father and for this first moment he credibly acted as one. His impatience appeared heartfelt and even poignant, given the time of year and his narrow passage through an encroaching seasonal darkness. Gus said he was a father and I felt immediately the need to understand what that meant. And he had said "please," which was an unusually contrite gesture for a narcissist. I agreed to take a day from my vacation week so Gus could have his first visit before Christmas.

"But you have to read this parenting book and sign these papers and bring them back tomorrow before five."

I was cleverly firm. In 10 years I'd heard every failed parent's version of trouble, every preventive emergency or bad piece of luck that interfered with a cherished urge to take care of his or her children. But if I asked for nothing in return, too often nothing was all that came back. To my surprise, Gus returned the next afternoon with the signed papers. He had read the book, a slim volume that extolled the strategies of positive parenting. He had even taken notes.

As I was to learn, Gus stood as a 19-foot tall Titan before his children. The boys were caught in the headlights of a busy highway, parents coming at them from all directions. These included their foster mom and dad, with their vision of a bright, lovely future of love as long as everyone would just behave. This attitude competed for the children's loyalty to their father and their thrilling acceptance (as well as threatened rejection) by a lovable wag, a character without boundaries who passed his time submissive to the apathy of the stars and who infected his sons with the disorderly pleasures that were their birthright. How could they resist being seduced?

I helplessly watched all of it. For nearly a year I wandered with Richie and Dalton among the ruins of their incipient lives, amid all the structure and wealth imaginable and also the instability, danger and unrequited experience of a child's love for a parent that existed as a dazzling, irresistible danger. How can children deconstruct a parent's grandiosity? It is beyond their measure. They are left only to incorporate it as best they can. To feel love they must give love and are too young to do so wisely. Without restraint they also are without protection.

The charm of Gus was spread wide. To meet him on the street or in a bar was to connect with what appeared to be an ingenuous, imploring common man, a lover of life and—for the moment—yours, especially. His own life was a complexity of battling forces he would not readily discuss though when he did he lifted a volatile lid that too often, and with the assist of a drug or alcohol, might blow him sky high.

Men were his fellow travelers and women always his best friends, except when they were not. The social worker at Child and Family Services that referred Gus to us, that limited his time with his boys and wanted it all observed and documented, was a demonic, old and frigid bitch and Gus didn't mind saying so, that she lived to strip men of their manhood and fathers of their children. She was an angry old witch and lots of other things that I listened for with an attention so cautious Gus finally caught my drift and let it go.

"I know," he said.

"She's just doing her goddamned job."

To which I thought to ask, but did not, that in all this what was the job of Gus? It was the unspoken question that for months and months would become the unanswered one as Gus tried with all his charm, skill and luck to become his children's father without ever having to be their parent.

2

A man may be only his hands and words as he builds the works and loves that shape his life. In this way I was no different from Gus. I had my work cut out for me, as he did his. I waited with my clipboard in the lobby of our agency's therapeutic services department. I had placed Gus in one of our larger visitation rooms where he waited for his boys.

Through the outside window, I watched the foster mother arrive, a short, corpulent woman in her mid-40s and wearing a navy blue suit. Her name was Greta. Greta Dehlinger. She reached back to unstrap the restraints of two bulky child seats, releasing two quiet and well-dressed boys who with her marched cautiously toward the building.

Inside she introduced me to Richie and Dalton who remained expressionless as they stood waiting for the next steps of what must have seemed an uncertain journey.

"This is Mr. Finney," the woman said dryly.

"He will take you now. I will return at five."

Her words were spoken with a firm, solemn assurance. She then kneeled to hold the boys' hands, which she squeezed tightly before struggling to her feet to leave. The boys watched her disappear through the door and then turned to me.

"Where's our dad?" Richie asked, his arm around his younger brother.

I told them to follow me.

We entered the room where Gus hid behind the door to surprise his boys, emerging bombastically in a rough and doting assault.

"Hey, dudes!" he shouted as he rushed Richie.

"Hey, boy! You wanna piece a me?"

Gus thrust his fat fist into Richie's tummy as the boy folded his hands over his face. Gus laughed.

"You're pretty slow. Where's the cross punch I showed you?" he shouted.

"What's this cover-the-face crap? That's no way to take a punch."

Dalton backed away as Gus turned to face him.

"And you? Hey, little squeaker, let's go a few rounds."

Gus made both hands into fists and waved them under Dalton's chin as the boy bobbed and ducked to avoid them.

"Way to move, little squeaker."

Gus grabbed both boys by the hands recently squeezed by the foster mother and led them forcefully into the room. A bookshelf stood at one end filled with board games and children's stories. Two mats were spread across the floor in front of a high sofa. A wide table held a play sculpture built from Legos. Two large crates contained stuffed animals, toy vehicles, and three or four spongy balls.

"We got two hours, boys," Gus announced.

"What a gas! I brought you snacks!"

Gus fell onto the sofa beside a small knapsack, which he opened to remove a bulging, greasy bag from Burger King.

"Fries and burgers, your favorite!" Gus shouted.

The pungent, gross odor of cooked fat wafted through the room.

I sat on a small chair in the far corner and balanced the clipboard on my knee. I wrote in the date, Dec. 20, 1999, on the visitation form. It was to have been the first Monday of my holiday vacation. I reviewed the form's numerous categories of evaluation, it's checklist of parent strengths and weaknesses, its spaces for narratives and a section for rating compliance with the parent's visitation plan. Within minutes it became apparent there was no plan.

Gus filled more than a room. He crowded out the aspirations of anyone else inside it and as I tried through the afternoon to measure a father's capacities to parent, I was blocked constantly by the anarchic reality of Gus' smothering love, how the boys adored it, how they responded as if no one before or since knew them, got them, loved them as much as Gus. Their father began at the beginning to do everything wrong, which, for Richie and Dalton, felt like everything right.

Richie overturned a toy crate to form a pile of cars, blocks and art supplies that became immediately projectiles in a battle with their dad, who hid behind the couch and laughed wildly as the boys threw at him anything they could get their hands on. As I tried to write my observations, a toy train caboose passed within inches of my forehead and bounced near the windowsill.

"Whoa! Wait! Hold on! Stop!" I shouted and stood up to get everyone's attention, waving my clipboard like a flag of truce.

The boys scattered as Gus rose from behind the couch, his tall, heavy frame like an erect statue hovering over all of us.

"This is Jason, boys," he said.

"Good ole' Jason."

Gus winked at me.

"He's going to help us get back together. He's going to help us be a family, aren't you Jason?"

I remained silent while the boys looked toward me expectantly. I had no words in response so said something vague like "We'll see what we can do…" which meant nothing to the boys. And then I urged Gus to get out a game.

"I know…we'll eat. You boys hungry?"

The greasy bag in the knapsack came out again and Gus gathered the boys around the small table. He pushed the Lego sculpture to the side and set out tissue-wrapped burgers, a cardboard container of French fries and three small sodas.

"Dig in dudes."

And all three began tearing into the food as if they had not eaten in a week. I had to turn away: open mouths chewing, including Gus' wide grinning, masticating jaws, the boys hunched over their food like hawks protecting kills. I looked at my clipboard while they ate. There was nothing to write about what I could not watch.

Gus' love appeared unconditional but something in me felt I had not yet grasped its real terms. His presence with the boys was exhausting and absorbing. At the end of the meal he brought out two small presents, wrapped tightly in bows and ribbon. The boys seized them and tore off the wrapping. Richie received a small box of baseball cards. Dalton was given a gift card at Toys R Us for $15. The boys appeared interested, if not thrilled, while Gus searched their faces for signs of both gratitude and loyalty to him.

"Merry Christmas, boys," said Gus.

"You are the best. You love your daddy, right?"

Richie nodded and Dalton looked away. I searched Gus for his own relational truths, already put off by his attempt to enlist me unwillingly onto his side. He was a smart man in a kind of stupid way.

I watched Gus carefully as the presents were set aside and a flurry of affectionate touches at the table turned into pushes and then slaps and then a game of chase around the table and then around the room. The interaction between father and sons grew again into an interstitial cacophony that, at just the point the noise reached an unbearable volume, Gus jumped up and grabbed both boys, one under each arm, and marched them around the room once before throwing them playfully onto a flat mat.

"It's story time," he shouted.

He told Richie to find a book on the bookshelf while he cuddled Dalton who squirmed disagreeably within what appeared to be a choking embrace.

"Aw, c'mon," Gus shouted into Dalton's ear.

"Give your papa a kiss. It's been forever, squeaker. Gees..."

Dalton continued to squirm, pressed to the mat.

As I jumped up to intervene, Dalton pecked his father on the nose and then scrambled away.

"That's better," said Gus.

"That's right, boys. We love each other no matter what. Got it?"

Dalton nodded through a distraught, cherubic smile and ran to stand with his brother at the bookshelf. I called Gus over to me.

"You can't do that," I whispered.

"What? Can't do what?" Gus asked with flummoxed sincerity.

"You can't force them. Don't physically force them to do anything," I answered.

Gus weighed my words behind a vacant stare.

"Well then how the hell am I supposed to get them, I mean make them..."

"Ask them," I answered.

"Ask them and listen."

Gus let his shoulders droop in frustration.

"But I'm their goddamned father..."

"Ask them...and wait," I said again.

Gus had many empty places that he assumed were fully devel-

232

oped. His demanding affection was, he thought, his most evident virtue. Who could argue with a father's incessant and inveigling love?

As it turned out, I could.

I must have worried the boys who, as they watched me make furious notes, might have thought in their own wordless ways that some jig was up, that their father—and by association them as well—had been caught. Their voices, their words, their clean new clothes that enveloped their small sizes, presented an artifice of cautious security. They were happy to see their dad but guarded in their remembrance and response.

When their foster mother returned, calm and restrained, they slipped from their father's anxious hugs and walked slowly back to the lobby where the woman gathered them together in a wordless, functional hug.

"You're OK now," Greta said presumptively as if suggesting anything other than being with her was definitely not OK, and as if all that might be thought of as out of control was now firmly contained.

She had not seen, as I had, how the boys ran from her predictable containment and toward their father's daring, unpredictable embrace. We may all think our own empty spaces to be the most developed ones; so empty and painful is our untapped ineptness.

Meanwhile Gus passed his aggression off as his fight for something he believed in, though the beliefs at hand were so obviously unexamined. It was still a quandary for me. The desire of a man to be a father is something I never dismissed lightly. So many men ran from fatherhood, ran from their children and the tedious, endless and always vulnerable accountability of a parent's love, and Gus certainly was not doing this. Though his means were limited, his huge, implacable presence made it hard for anyone to dismiss him.

3

My journey with Gus would become a voyage over his deserts and desires, his appetites and lacunae. He could not see what about him was on constant display. It was a secret he kept from himself. Of all he learned from living and thriving on the streets there was little he had acquired about forming trusted paths.

But he was a man who embraced the fatherly entitlement of offspring. In lieu of an estate, he had his boys. They made for him a future and even though it was theirs to live it was for Gus to own.

I had lots of notes. I asked him how the visit went.

"Great…god damned great! You see how those boys love me? Goddamned great!"

Anything he wished had gone differently?

He searched my eyes for the right answer.

"Maybe…not so rough?

He was guessing.

I nodded.

"Maybe less horse play. But, damn, aren't they cute when they go at it? *Wanna piece a me?*"

He mimicked Richie's pouty stance and laughed up a deep, growling chuckle that sounded almost like a moan.

"Could be a problem," I observed neutrally.

"Could start a fight. What do you think? Aren't those fighting words?"

Gus's grin shrunk as he considered my observation. A wave of light wrinkles formed across his forehead and he pondered my words.

"Well, c'mon…he's only seven years old!" Gus at last responded.

"He won't always be seven," I said.

"And what's to keep another boy from taking him on?"

Gus laughed.

"My point, exactly," he answered.

"He needs to be tough," responded Gus.

"He needs to show everyone he won't take no crap or he's going to get side-wound into the next goddamned county by some stupid punk."

The principles of non-violent communication would have to wait for another session together and that wouldn't be until after the holidays and my vacation. To keep his visits with the boys, Gus needed to consult with me each week for an hour of parent education. Since he was homeless, I agreed to meet him downtown at the main library branch near the St. Vincent Shelter. We set a date and time in January and he left the office to find a bus back to town.

I wrote my first visitation report and sent it to Mona and to Jasmine, the Family Services caseworker. Jasmine was a new hire, a young LCSW in her mid-twenties just out of graduate school. For Jasmine's benefit, I focused first on the positives: Gus' affection, his playfulness, his engagement with the boys and their enthusiasm with him. He brought Christmas gifts. I also mentioned Gus' rough play, my need to calm things down and my two interventions when safety was a concern.

Nevertheless, I maintained a positive tone, knowing that too many negatives risked ending visits. Family Services seemed to be looking for an excuse to push Gus away in favor of the seemingly stable foster couple anxious to adopt his boys. Gus wanted to remain their parent and I needed more time to determine if he could. And I wanted my vacation. That's all I thought about with an hour left in the year's last day of work.

My divorce was final on the 26th and my girlfriend's on the 27th. We booked a big room in a hotel in Calistoga and spent New Year's alone together, our children in the custody of our ex-partners. During the week we rarely left the room. Looking back, it was a rebound relationship for both of us and after years spent with the wrong people we were hungry to make up time. And we did. I thought nothing of Gus or his boys until the first Monday in January after Y2K arrived without incident and I could still read my e-mail.

A message from Jasmine told me Gus had been in a fight over the holidays. He was arrested but not charged. The fight happened in a park where St. Vincent's homeless men usually gathered during the day. Gus said it was self-defense. After a night in jail he was released and no charges were filed but a search of Gus' criminal history turned up another arrest three years before for aggravated assault.

"Any convictions?" I asked.

Jasmine said there were none.

"Then his visits will continue," I said.

"Yeah…" Jasmine said in a voice of cool detachment.

"For now."

A son is an ancestor reincarnated and Gus was someone's son. He arrived for our meeting with a transparent bandage covering a row of stitches over his left eye.

"So what happened?" I asked.

"Not easy being homeless," Gus answered weakly.

"Meet some woeful customers out there on the street."

He waited to emphasize that was all the detail he would share.

"Have I fucked up my visits?" he at last asked.

I shook my head vaguely.

"No," I answered.

"At least not yet."

Gus sighed as if relieved. I had become an authority figure and he adjusted his responses to what he thought were my judgments, though he seemed not to know—or care—that I held only one vote in the decision that would decide his future as a father.

"What was your father like?" I asked Gus.

A newer, thicker silence settled over the library table.

"My father? Which one?"

He asked his question from a deep and rippling stillness.

"Who raised you?" I asked.

Gus began to describe his Arkansas mother's life of alcohol abuse and casual prostitution.

"She fucked a lot of guys but she didn't turn tricks. A guy would support her for a while and when he left, she'd find another. That changed when Reggie showed up."

Reggie was a black man from Searcy who did odd jobs and arrived one day at their run down Little Rock apartment to fix the leaky toilet.

"Landlord sent him. Mom threatened to call the city the stink was so bad. Not that the city would have done anything but my mom had fucked the landlord already."

Reggie ended the night in bed with the mother of Gus.

"He left in the morning but I saw him. Unlike some of the others, he came back that night and the night after that. Then he moved in and mom just let him. Never asked me about it. A black man, for Chris' goddamned sakes. I wasn't against a black man but I was surprised she'd do it. Neighbors and all. But Reggie was a big guy and if anyone didn't like it they never told me."

Gus was an only child, which surprised me given all the casual sex his mother had.

"My boys' mom—she's constantly havin' babies. I've stayed around and I've warned her but it's no use. She's like my mom but not as smart. She can't say no to a guy who gets her high. Ever. She can't take care of herself, either. She just keeps pumpin' those babies out. And those family service women just keep takin' em. Not my boys, though. I'm here for them."

I asked Gus to tell me about his biological father.

"Saw him once. He came by when I was four and paid the rent. Never saw him again."

Reggie, though, showed Gus how to box.

"Saved me a mess of trouble where I grew up," Gus pronounced proudly.

"Mah boys are gonna know how to fight."

I asked Gus if he still saw Reggie.

Gus stared back, incredulous that I would ask.

"Noooo…." he answered in a low, knowing moan.

"That man left my mom five years later. Went to Chicago with another girlfriend. Never saw him again. No more dads after that. Just my mom's boyfriends and a couple weren't very nice to me. I didn't care. I was gettin' bigger and they sure didn't want a piece of my angry teenage ass."

"And your mom?" I asked.

Gus stared at me as if I'd stepped in shit.

"She's dead."

His plain, quiet words had a heated sting to them. My only and surprised response was to say simply I was sorry. I could not connect with him, could not cross what appeared to be the shallow frontier of a vast, hidden tangle.

Gus lived immediately and, to the degree one day passed into another, successfully. Success was measured by whether or not he opened his eyes in the morning and could consider himself alive. He held little close to him but his small sons and he boasted to anyone who would listen how much he loved his boys. He taught them his best moves and his worst words. The world was a mean place but not yet so mean for Richie or Dalton.

I knew Gus sensed immediately when we met that I held a special kind of power, however soft-spoken. It was the power to influence whether he would be the father to his children, perhaps ever see them again. My evaluations of his parenting, and my instructions to him about how to improve it, were typically resented but nevertheless heard. And for a while, I could report improvement. Gus was a loving man and could have been a much more loving father had his own father and mother loved him.

I made more notes and gave Gus another handout, two pages of tips on how to praise a child's good behavior and encourage cooperation. He took them without looking and stuffed them into the frayed pocket of his denim jacket. As he shuffled out of the library his long, slightly bowed legs gave him the look of a strolling cowboy, his hands in his pockets while his big boots struck a stolid rhythm on the linoleum. I noticed from behind how much his ears stuck out, reminding me of Richie's ears and reminding me that in this case biology was very much involved.

Gus was defensive, though not good at stifling his emotions. Hurts affected him. More than once in our work together his eyes watered with the mortifying tears of the sincere man I sometimes thought he could be but wasn't certain he was. It was doubt enough to benefit Gus who would earn more chances to build on his successful failings. He worked every moment that came into his life as if it were the final and definitive one that could help him recapture his boys. He feared my power to take Richie and Dalton away but seemed confident that as long as his love did not retreat, such a power would not advance.

4

By early February I understood more of what was possible for Gus, and what was not. I had watched the boys through several visits with their father and had written enough to confirm a few essential trends. Gus loved his boys but seemed not to know how. Parental love for Gus was a successful entertainment. He arrived plundering and ready, even when his boys—sometimes tired and listless—clearly craved quiet time.

I realized my observations were skewed by the confining space of the visitation room. The room was like a cell in the way it limited physical movement, and activity was all the boys wanted when they entered to see their father who regularly grabbed them, poked them, lifted them, wrestled them, tickled them and assailed them constantly with what always appeared to be his overbearing affection.

Yet the boys, at least and always at first, loved these assaultive attentions from their dad. Consistently they arrived in the starchy flannel shirts and pressed jeans provided by their foster mother. By visit's end the clothes were wrinkled and sometimes torn by their father's rough play, or smeared with the greasy residue of their burger snacks, or wet from spilling or throwing water when snack time went awry with more careless, goofy fun.

Gus was cocky and tough and made more so by his contact with Richie and Dalton. He laughed boisterously as he encouraged their playful but also transgressing antics. He created a wobbly tower of stacked chairs to help Dalton touch the ceiling. He urged them into rapturous collisions with him, the furniture and each other without relief. Gus knew the boys craved activity and offered few boundaries, or attempted to extend the ones I set for him, in a room that was tightly and dangerously bound.

The boys, though, were perishable and I noted in their play the strains of more than just their double life of loving one parent while living with a surrogate other. Richie arrived initially protective of his younger brother and threw himself first at his father.

"You wanna piece a me?" Richie shouted at Gus who always laughed wildly at the child's useless challenge.

The wrestling would start with Richie while Dalton wandered

toward the bookcase and a basket of toys and games at the farther end of the room. Frequently he found doll babies and clothes, which intrigued him for several minutes until Gus noticed and then left Richie to intervene.

"C'mere, Dalton," Gus would shout.

"That's girl stuff. C'mere, boy. Let's wrestle."

I intervened and tried to explain to Gus the importance of letting his boys explore, giving them time to decide what they wanted to do, expressing interest in their interests.

"Remember what we talked about?"

I must have said that a hundred times. Gus would remember and then make an inefficient effort to comply with a parenting strategy, an effort intended to impress me with his good will but that came through as resentful tolerance.

The first team meeting to discuss the sons of Gus and their futures was held at the Family Services office in early March. I walked into the building's windowless room where at a large particleboard conference table sat seven people, all of them women. They included Jasmine the caseworker and her supervisor, two attorneys and two therapists (one each for Richie and Dalton), and an administrative law judge to represent the court. I was the only male but, as it became apparent, the team member who had spent more time with Gus and his children than all the others combined.

"She should get an Oscar," one of the women said.

"Oh my god yes. What a performance," responded one of the therapists.

"And what a story. Who could…"

And then silence. I was interrupting something.

"Have you seen *Erin Brockovich?*" Jasmine asked me in an effort to appear inclusive.

I had not.

One of the therapists, referred to by the court administrator as Dr. Janice, talked about her interviews with Richie.

"He's scared," she said pointedly.

"There is a primary defense at work and I can't say where it begins."

"We don't have to wonder too much," the Family Services supervisor interjected amid collective sighs of agreement.

"No, I'm really worried," the therapist responded.

"He's deeply fearful and thinks someone will kill him."

"Someone? Who? Who would kill him?" asked the court administrator whose name was Georgia.

"His father?"

The therapist couldn't say but had noted high levels of anxiety in Richie that in her opinion could move quickly into fear and even trauma.

"The foster mother reports Richie's loss of bowel control that seems to follow within hours of a visit with his father."

The discussion continued as I tried to reconcile Richie's reported behaviors with what I had witnessed during his visits. Tension, yes. There was always a high charge of anticipation in each visit between Gus and his sons. But fear? Trauma? How could that derive from his father?

I pictured Richie, small for his age, his toothy smile and bright freckled cheeks. Playing with his Dad was not easy, but it was familiar and affirming. Despite their rowdy misbehavior I could see at least that. It was hard for me to view Gus as the cause of Richie's challenges.

And I said so. Despite the murky beginnings of his life, both within the womb as a drug addicted fetus and without as a neglected child, Richie held on to the love of at least one parent. And there was no question in my mind that, despite his sometimes obvious lack of capacity, Gus loved his sons.

"There are problems, I grant you," I said to Georgia.

"But why blame the father exclusively if these behaviors occur in the care of the foster parent?"

In the ensuing silence no one at the table answered my question.

"The foster parents are busting their butts to care for these kids," said Jasmine's supervisor, an older woman with bright, brilliant eyes who looked directly at me.

"It's hard to see how they have any responsibility."

The silence at the table suggested Georgia was speaking for everyone. The quiet strength of her conviction nearly silenced me, as well. I had my concerns about the boys and their rough and relentless father. Surely the early lives of these boys were potentially brutal experiences that their father had no capacity to fully grasp or attend.

I was working with him, or at least I thought that was my job. As the provider who had seen the most of Gus, catalogued and critiqued his parenting through hours of visits, I spoke with some authority, however unwelcome my honest opinion.

"He means well," I said of the father, which was entirely the wrong thing to say.

It was not something I could actually see, and the others at the table knew it. What I saw I could not easily describe: the joy masking fear, the aggression indulged as a release from unbearable anxiety, how the boys hung tightly together but also fought separately for their own identities, using each other for aggressive relief and, with the unwitting encouragement of their father, would turn on each other to prove to "him" how powerful and effective they really were (but did not really believe themselves to be). Or how I tried to nourish Gus's primal love into something parental, something with doors and windows that would allow in the light and air of a nurturing protection.

And love. What was the love I was trying to talk about? The women seemed to have some understanding of what a parent's love should look like, as did I. It would be both assertive and supportive. It would set firm, calm boundaries while opening the child like a flower to its singular promptings. These were the ideals, though the work we were doing here was not to grow a pretty bloom but to save and nurture its rooted survival.

"No, I'm not rooting for Gus," I answered to one of the therapist's sarcastic sounding questions.

"I'm rooting for the boys. And in your own funny words I have to say the boys are rooting for their dad. He is not a perfect Dad."

I did not describe my fight with Gus's efforts to keep the boys involved with their biological mother, how he shared photos of her latest baby with them at a visit before I could take them away; the photos of a baby born with a meth addiction and that, once removed from the delivery room, would never again see its mother. I did not say that Richie and Dalton were two boys poised and held over two equally undesirable pits.

"I need time," I said directly, knowing that my one strength in this discussion was the vast amount of time I had spent with Gus and his sons; more time than anyone at the table could or ever would wish to spend with him or his boys.

I said nothing further about my concerns regarding the foster family.

Later I told Gus I had some good news and some bad news. He wanted the bad news first.

"Unless you can get a job and a place to live in the next 60 days, it's likely you'll lose any shot at custody of Richie and Dalton."

I said this without an inflection that might suggest judgment.

Gus shrugged.

"Then what?" he asked with fatal resignation.

"The foster family will seek to adopt them," I answered.

As we sat in the library reading room, Gus looked away. His eyes caught the long legs of a young high school girl walking with agile, athletic strides toward the rest rooms.

"That's fucked up," he sputtered.

"What's the good news?

"You have ninety days before the next court hearing. It's been moved from April to June.

"And that's good?" Gus asked.

I told him to make of it what he could. It was the best anyone could do. If anything changed between now and June, if he could create any kind of stability for himself, it might influence the court to extend a hearing farther into the future. The immediate metaphor I could imagine was of someone walking a plank. Instead, I said inexplicably, that parenting was a weary combat, a sometimes destructive deadlock, a fierce and exhausting mayhem. Gus looked at me as if I'd lost my mind.

5

A warm, onshore wind blew the first week of April through a city park where Jasmine and I sat together watching Gus play with his boys.

"Wanna piece a me?" Richie kept shouting as Gus rode Dalton on his shoulders and taunted his older son.

"I can't HEAR you," Gus shouted loudly as he hopped backward and instructed Dalton to cover his father's big ears.

Richie gave chase and wrapped his arms and legs around his father's log of a thigh and held on tight as Gus, laughing loudly, dragged him in heaving limps across the playground.

"The apple doesn't fall far from the tree," I observed.

"In this case, the farther from the tree the better," Jasmine responded bluntly.

She leaned forward on the park bench and stretched enough to remove her denim jacket in such a way that her yellow cotton blouse flew up with her jacket and, before she knew it, revealed her bare midriff up to the vortex of a pink sports bra. Promptly, she pushed her blouse back to her waist while looking fiercely at me as I turned away. She was a young woman who would be considered attractive in most settings and who seemed conscious of this, even alert in the way this posed a threat as great as any assumed advantage.

Jasmine's remark surprised me. I thought she would have seen some improvement in the father's parenting. I had seen it and written about it. He was more engaged with his sons and measurably more attentive to their interests.

Then I remembered this was the first time Jasmine had seen Gus play with his boys. At all other times she either faced him alone from across her desk at Family Services or stood beside him in court.

"He's so rough with them," she added while releasing a sonorous sigh of disapproval.

"The boys like a little roughness," I answered.

"Especially from their dad. They know he won't hurt them." Jasmine turned and gave me a withering stare.

"Oh really? Not hurt them? Then why is Richie afraid, so afraid he might be killed?"

"Really?" I replied in a way that mocked Jasmine's dismissive tone.

"Killed? By Gus? Haven't you been reading my visit notes?"

Jasmine appeared stunned by my sarcastic temerity and did not answer the direct question.

"The therapist doesn't think there's anything funny about this," she declared from a slow and mildly rising anger.

"The therapist says these boys—well, Richie anyway—is convinced an adult parent is trying to kill him."

I reminded Jasmine the boys had more than one parent. In fact, they had nearly a dozen if she counted all the foster parents they were with during the past two years.

"None like Gus," she answered derisively.

"No one is as rough with them as he is. No one else has been so physical with the boys. So hard on them."

"Well, he doesn't want to kill them, or even hurt them. He barely sees them and only for a couple of hours a week."

My answer was sarcastic, even as I admitted Gus played rough. But it was play and not pathology.

"Wanna piece a me?"

Jasmine returned to me my mocking tone.

"Far from the tree?"

The question was asked as if it were an accusation. I did not respond. The tree of life, sooner or later, was also a tree of death. Which mattered was for each of us alone to decide.

Jasmine left early. Another appointment, she said, but I knew her mind was made up about Gus or she was bored, or—I fantasized—embarrassed that in the tumid course of her professional work she had exposed her bare body. It was an unintended intimacy, and certainly not welcomed by me. But it left her vulnerable in the midst of our disagreeable discussion of the boys. Together we were pushed beyond all viewable horizons.

Ten minutes before the visit's end, Gus gave a skulking look toward the park entrance where he seemed to recognize an approaching vehicle. He flashed me a concerned grimace and left the boys on the swings to approach me.

"I got a job interview in 20 minutes," he nearly shouted and nearly in a panic.

"Whoa, slow down," I said.

"A what?"

The car approached cautiously, stopped in the first, distant lot and waited.

"Gotta go. Like right now."

"But the boys?" I asked.

"Watch them, would you?" he begged me.

"The old lady's going to be here soon. She's always early. And this is a big chance for me."

I looked toward the car where the shadowed profile of its driver was unrecognizable.

"Who's that?" I asked.

"A friend," Gus said, impatient to leave.

"A goddamned friend, OK? Listen, I got a chance here. You don't understand. I'll explain next time. Gotta go."

Gus dashed toward the car, a scratch-raked and faded blue Buick smoking clouds of black exhaust. Gus jumped in the passenger's seat while the car slowly backed up and left.

The foster mother arrived just as the Buick was passing out of the park.

"When did he leave?" she asked suspiciously.

"Is there a problem?"

No problem, I reported, though I was furious with Gus for violating the terms of our visit and leaving me to cover for him.

"He had an emergency. The boys are fine and I've been here the whole time."

Greta took a moment to review my words and mood for a clue to unknown facts on the ground but gave up her query as Richie approached.

"Where's my dad?" he shouted.

When Richie learned Gus had left without saying good-bye he was nearly inconsolable. Dalton shrunk into the shadow of his brother's noisy grief and took Greta's outstretched hand while I scooped Richie into my arms and bore him away to Greta's car.

Gus was what was his. His strange and ebullient incapacity was a certain kind of property, his broken personality a borderless estate. He phoned the next morning with what he said was good news. I decided to wait and hear him out before telling him more bad news.

"I got a job," he announced proudly.

"Yeah?" I answered skeptically.

"Caretaker. It's a property up in the Dry Creek Valley. Woman owns it. Wants me to take care of it for her."

"So you're a property manager?" I asked doubtfully.

"Oh, more than that," he said.

"I'm in charge of the place."

"What does it pay?" I asked again.

"Well, enough. About $2,000 a month."

"We're still working it out," he said, creating more doubt.

"Well maybe you can get a place to live soon," I responded glibly and in a way to challenge Gus and his quaky credibility. I was impatient and momentarily tired of Gus and his games.

"Oh, I got that, too."

He answered directly.

"The house has a downstairs apartment with two bedrooms. It's included with the job."

Gus gave me the address of the house and the name of the woman and I drove there before lunchtime. I wanted to get there before the social worker, attorneys, and therapists heard the implausible news. I did not want to be surprised.

I arrived at the edge of a large vineyard in a small canyon cul-de-sac east of Healdsburg. The property stretched across a dozen acres ending at a large three-story house nestled into a shallow hillside where more grapes grew at the opening to a large forest. I drove up the property's single lane dirt driveway and stopped the car in a circular parking strip overgrown with weeds and bushes. I climbed the stairs to the house's front porch. Boards were missing on two of the stairs. The old front door was covered with gouges and scratches.

One window was cracked and the white paint on the house's siding was chipped and tarnished.

I rang the doorbell and eventually heard a clatter of footsteps and then glimpsed the face of a dark-haired woman peeking through the side window before approaching the door.

"If you're here about the job, it's been filled," she shouted.

"No, no. It's something else," I shouted back.

The door shook, rattled and then opened a crack's width.

"What do you want?" she asked.

I could see her mouth, nose and one eye as she formed her question.

"I'm working with Gus Slaughterbeck and his children. Do you know him?"

The door opened farther.

"Yeah, he's the guy I hired. What do you want from me?"

The woman, tall and willowy in a grey sweatshirt and black stretch pants, pushed the front door out of her way. Her stringy hair was tangled and unwashed and her face appeared fatigued. It was hard to guess her age but she was certainly younger than forty.

"What is Gus doing for you?" I asked.

"Who wants to know?" she responded suspiciously.

"Is he in some kind of trouble?"

I told her no and gave her my card. She invited me in. Her name was Jenifer Abbadelli.

"Of Abbadelli Wines?" I asked.

"That Abbadelli?"

She nodded affirmatively.

"My grandfather," she snorted.

"I married a fool against my father's wishes, but now he's gone. I still have the house and a kid and a tangled, junky vineyard in need of work. That's why I hired Gus. He's a good fit. He said he has a couple of sons that need a place to live. I saw their pictures. Cute kids. He adores them."

"You're getting divorced?" I asked.

She frowned at my impertinence but answered anyway.

"We have attorneys working out the details, including child support and visitation. No worries. I have money. Plenty. Dad's always taken good care of me."

I didn't doubt this. The Abbadelli wine business was one of the county's largest, with as much old money as new. Her boy was named Harold and he was ten years old.

"And Gus can live here?" I asked.

"He'll have to," said Jenifer.

"There's a ton of crap that needs to get done. He'll be busy all week. Seven days. He was the only applicant who said that wouldn't be a problem."

I asked how long the job would last.

"Oh God," Jenifer sighed as her eyes rolled upward in search of a divine answer.

"At least a year. Probably longer if all goes well. I need a working vineyard here and there's a lot to do."

Jenifer invited me in and we climbed down some rickety basement stairs into a separate living unit below the main floor. She led me through its bedrooms, bathroom and kitchen—neat and furnished—and then out a separate entrance that came up stairs beside the front porch.

"All ready," she said.

I asked when Gus would start work.

"Tomorrow," she answered.

She confirmed his salary and I left. I don't know what surprised me more: that Gus had been successful or that he'd been truthful. In any event he was newly incarnated into the pursuit of a rescue that might hold him high above all surfaces both solid and dead. In the truth of this single moment all were one and the same.

6

Among the parents I worked with, most lacking any capacity to love much of anything and especially themselves, I confronted constantly the absence of morality. I recognized it as a consistency of psychic inconsistencies: a way their failed efforts to love became proof for other failures they refused to own. All outer events were merely the parables of an inner life where the existence of emotions signaled the presence of an uneasy and constant yearning.

Gus had briefly broken through this absence by gaining in one lucky swoop both a job and a home. This achievement fit specifically the Family Services goals created for his case. Now the agency was forced to acknowledge the terms of Gus's success while covertly wishing his failure. As Gus moved onto the Dry Creek property, a caravan of social workers and county attorneys trailed him and swarmed Jenifer's estate in search of a loophole. They hoped to enlist the woman's assistance by persuading her that Gus would bring only trouble. Absurdly they sought to give her a drug test, not realizing she had the money to enlist one of the county's star lawyers to oppose them.

The agency's obviously prejudicial scrutiny of Gus turned Jenifer into his loyal ally in a way that embarrassed Jasmine.

"I have to admit that Family Services is really looking for some trouble in all this," she said.

"And if they can't find it, they'll try to make it."

A Family Services attorney did find an open holding pond in the hills above the house that would need to be made safe before the sons of Gus could visit the property. In a single weekend Gus enclosed the pond's 300-foot perimeter in six-foot field fencing, an achievement that served only to convince his benefactor he was, indeed, the right man for the job.

"I'll do anything for those boys," Gus said to me later.

"They're my goddamned life," he gushed ineloquently to anyone who listened.

Jasmine scheduled Gus's first visit at the house for the second week in April, in time for Richie's eighth birthday. Jenifer allowed Gus

the use of her home for a party, arranged as a visit I would supervise. If all went well for a few weeks, then Gus would be entitled to
overnight visits with his boys, notable as the first step in the process
of reunification. Gus spent his first week clearing half an acre of
Jenifer's land in preparation for a new vineyard.

I arrived one afternoon to talk with Gus about the visit and found
him in the field, his shirt off in the valley's hot spring sunshine as he
raised a hoe to attack a stubborn patch of underbrush. The late light
silhouetted his bulky arms and large, long body and gave him the
look of a wiry Gallic gleaner.

"I invited ten people," Gus said.

"Richie's friends and mine. Is that OK?"

I nodded affirmatively.

"And Jenifer's boy will be there. Harold. He's ten. Cool kid."

I told Gus it was fine. It was all just fine. I reveled quietly in the
pleasure Gus took with his new position in life, the gift of Fortuna he
offered first to his oldest son.

"OK, boy, you go for it!" Gus shouted from across the living room
as Richie, his eyes closed, took a deep, hyperventilating breath and
then blew hard at the lighted candles of his birthday cake.

"Yeah, yeah, yeah!" hooted Gus as those around the table cheered.

I watched from a chair placed at the room's double doors leading
into the hall. Richie opened his eyes to see all the candles extin-
guished as well as the array of his and his father's friends. Jenifer
stood at the door to the kitchen while her son sat next to Richie at
the table.

Richie smiled widely, looking thrilled and also comfortably helpless as Jenifer approached to remove the candles and cut his cake. I
saw in his face the relaxed pleasure of a boy momentarily without
vigilance, caught in a singularity built from his own and suddenly
confident joy. Of all the gifts received on his birthday, this was to my
mind the most useful and poignant.

It was a Thursday afternoon and the party, planned originally
for the property's sizable side yard, was pushed inside by the threat
of rain, a threat realized moments after Richie blew out his candles

when sheets of raindrops pecked loudly against the living room windows. The guests comprised seven adults and three children, not counting Harold.

Gus invited more of his friends than Richie's but it wasn't for me to judge. Most of Richie's current pals were schoolmates from his foster parents' neighborhood and while Gus asked me to issue an invitation to them via Greta, she was having none of it.

"Why are we being put through this?" she asked me when she dropped the boys off and they were out of earshot.

"Why are these children being allowed to love such a bad parent?"

I had no response since her question wasn't mine to answer. Who is in charge of allowing love? I thought to myself.

"Let's have a meeting," I said to her before she drove away.

She shrugged her shoulders.

"If you think it will help…"

Then she turned and left.

The party was a success and the first visit of many over weeks that wove the boys into the emerging fabric of Gus's routine at the Dry Creek property. Further visits seemed to offer the first experiences for the boys that I might have classified as real fun. Harold led Richie and Dalton on explorations of the property while Gus jumped with them on a trampoline set up in the side yard.

"Wanna piece a me?" Richie shouted wildly, his challenge now offered more as a celebrating whoop and without the hostility previously released during claustrophobic visits in the small rooms of my agency.

With his weekly pay, Gus bought gifts for his boys and purchased a disposable camera that allowed him to take photos of them together. I was impressed, though I could not help but recognize the role of Jenifer's big house as a harbor for Gus and his boys. Without it, they would all again become refugees.

To construct an embracing family system that begins even to approximate the useful forms of unconditional love is not only extremely difficult but also requires generations of concerted effort and cooperation. It was a lot to ask, and even more to expect, that

Gus could in a few weeks establish the codes of a broad and supporting trust.

I met Greta and her husband Alfred at their modest condominium in a neighborhood of mostly larger homes on the city's expensive northeast side. Alfred, short, gaunt and bearded, emerged from one of the unit's three petite bedrooms, which he used as a study. He worked at the local college as a counselor. I met them in the morning while Richie was in school and Dalton in day care. Their home was neat, but very small. Greta showed me the boys' room, barely large enough for two single beds separated by a slender, unpainted bookshelf. Light filtered in from a high, unreachable window in a way that cast dark shadows throughout.

"We thought we'd have them by now," Greta said as we sat together at the kitchen table.

"It's been a year. This can't be good for the boys. We love them."

I heard her sincerity.

"So does their father," I said.

Greta bristled.

"Whose side are you on?" she asked pointedly.

I waited to answer while deciding whether to answer at all. Gus was an exuberant and cheerful failure. Greta and her husband were solvent and sober but managed the children as if they were on parole, paying so much attention to the risk of a wrong move they struggled at times to make the right one. Hearing Greta's annoyance, Alfred offered a warmer outlook.

"We've never had children before," he said.

"We've learned a lot this past year. They're good boys. Greta and I think we know how to care for them. We've certainly done our homework."

And they had. They had filled out all the forms, read all the books, and boasted numerous community references. As if parenting were simply a matter of homework, I thought. Put all the county's children in a huge nursery at their births and make them available only to the parents who pass their exams. Both Greta and Alfred found it easy to dismiss completely the role of Gus in the boys' lives. If anything spoke more to the fact they had never before had children, this was it. Why does a child love a troubled parent? Why not simply excise Gus, send him packing and the boys, of course, would forget they ever knew him?

No, of course not. A child's first impressions are the most arousing and the ones that last a lifetime. Am I welcome at birth? Who and what welcome me? There were no words of assurance that could fully change or heal the primal link with the boys that Gus possessed and Greta and Alfred did not.

Meanwhile, the father and the foster parents charged with the care of Richie and Dalton hated each other. And though no words were shared between them, the boys sensed instantly they were in a fight of sorts to the death. One family would survive and the other would not.

Richie, especially, feared what the cost would be to him for loving his father, the one parent if he could choose would always choose. He did not say this, could not and would not know this until his father either was established in his life or banished forever. Richie did not need to fear a parent to worry he might die.

"We just want to make it simple for the boys," Alfred said.

"This must be so confusing for them."

I weighed his words and not my own.

"It must also be confusing for you," I responded, not meaning to suggest they were more concerned about themselves than the boys.

But that's how they heard it. Greta and Alfred yearned for a family life. Gus might fear the presumed security and strength presented by the foster parents because he did not know their fragility and the weakness that drove them to seek children to parent, children that might become a welcome distraction from other, more dire and secret struggles. Family love excluded the world, though a bloom of disturbing inner life could always wreck its assuaging fidelities.

7

I don't remember the first time I realized when Gus searched anyone's eyes he was looking for a parent. He looked into my eyes for permission and into Jasmine's eyes for approval. As I watched him and Jenifer together I saw how he looked into hers for affection. She at first appeared flattered by his deference to her feelings; his acute sensitivity to any need that for her might feel immediate and transient but for Gus was persistently and vitally a touchpoint of his survival.

In this way Richie was not far from the tree. He, too, searched the eyes of any adult who came into his life. And there were many. There had been too many. My hope for Richie and Dalton was that their father had at last landed, had at last reduced for a while the number of eyes his children needed to search for the terms of their security.

Seven weeks of visits had established a clear trend of ease and warmth for Gus and his sons. The boys now came to the Dry Creek home three times a week, with weekend overnights to begin at the conclusion of the school year. Gus was so confident about his future he walked down the road to the country schoolhouse to enroll Richie and Dalton for the following September.

"It could certainly happen," Jasmine said to me during a meeting at CFS.

"Things are better, but we need some time. Richie still has his bad dreams and the therapist worries about him. But visits with his Dad are a highpoint. No question."

I asked Jasmine what it would take to grant Gus custody of his sons.

"That's tricky," she answered.

"The foster parents—and CFS—are heavily invested in the adoption option. Frankly, my supervisor doesn't think Gus can last at the Dry Creek property. He has too many fuck-ups already. He needs at least six months of stable living and income for the court to reconsider. But I give it to him. His success so far has pushed his court date back to August. And the foster parents are nervous. But, of course, I didn't tell you that."

July's dose of blessed summer seemed to build on all Jasmine described. Richie and Dalton now visited their father in a paradise of land and love, as if thrown from their suffering and into a dream, as if they had not known they suffered until for a dreamy month they did not. Visits with Gus continued and in their playful, exuberant ease became a pleasure to supervise. The boys appeared increasingly at home on Jenifer's vast property, though the woman's estranged husband had heard about Gus.

Assuming Gus to be his ex-wife's new lover, he petitioned to end spousal support though even Family Services, still eager for any complication that might ruin Gus's success, realized the husband had no case. Gus collected a paycheck, had a job title and description, and lived in a self-contained apartment on the property. Jenifer's attorney fielded the ex's threats and summons in a way that kept the noise of conflict subdued like the feint thunder of a distant storm.

Richie and Dalton arrived three days a week, delivered petulantly and reluctantly by Greta who on Fridays had a particularly hard time letting the boys go since they would spend the night and not be returned to her until Saturday evening. When her car door opened, Richie slipped out quickly and ran to hug his awaiting father.

"Wanna piece a me?" he shouted as Gus laughed.

Dalton, less eager to leave Greta's orbit of care, followed slowly but was easily subsumed in the strong undertow drawn from the exuberant reunification of his brother and father. I sat in on the two afternoon visits and the beginning of the weekend overnight and only took notes if something concerned me.

"Visits are going fine," I said to Greta when one afternoon she asked.

"That's hard to believe," she answered coolly.

"When the boys come home they're a wreck. We can't do a thing with them. Richie is very angry and Dalton won't speak for hours. What is happening over here?"

My first thought was to ask what was happening over there, but I said nothing other than to mention that transitions were difficult for any child who had to travel between two households. I experienced this regularly with children of divorced parents and in a similar way Richie and Dalton were living in two households now. Two households at war with each other and though I left out this comment, my answer did not satisfy Greta.

"It's not right," she stated firmly, her small body erect and pushed angrily forward.

"These boys are in deep trouble and this isn't helping."

I shrugged my shoulders; certain Greta's bitterness was the real issue and that more than anything she feared the inevitable loss of the boys after spending nearly 18 months making a home for them.

"The boys appear to be fine during the visits," I said to her.

"We just want what's best for them. They love their dad."

My last words were not helpful. Greta flashed me a fierce and angry look, her mouth twisted in a slight but weirdly ironic and unfathomable grin. She climbed into her car and drove away.

My first hint something might be wrong came during an afternoon I noticed Gus leave the boys outside twice to go back to the house.

"Watch 'em for a minute, will ya?" he asked me each time.

And then he left abruptly. During one of his trips I saw him through the kitchen window making animated gestures at Jenifer who stood at the sink and did not turn to look at him.

"Everything OK?" I asked when he returned.

Gus appeared preoccupied.

"Yeah. Yeah, sure," he answered unconvincingly.

Another time a fight erupted between Harold and Dalton while Richie sparred affectionately with his father. Dalton's tears brought Richie running. Unhesitatingly he slammed into the older Harold and threw him to the ground.

"Wanna piece a me?!" Richie shouted in a fierce rage as he mashed his fist into Harold's nose and prepared to swing with the other before his father swept him up and away.

Harold, tears streaming, stood and ran into the house. Jenifer emerged and drew Gus into an open field where they spoke in harsh, subdued tones out of the range of my hearing. Gus seemed to plead with open arms as Jenifer stood impassively, her arms folded tightly across her chest. Toward the end of the visit, Harold returned though he appeared flummoxed and violated, as if this single rip had pushed his friendship with Richie beyond repair.

257

During my drive home I wrestled with an emerging cynicism, aroused more by the recent break-up with my rebound girlfriend. I pretended to have known all along it could not and would not work. Her middle daughter loved her dad and hated me. Her oldest daughter was diagnosed with borderline personality disorder and intruded unpredictably when her mother and I were feeling connected. Neither daughter cared for my son. Still, I had hopes I wouldn't admit were much like the hopes of Gus. Ultimately, the baneful loops of misplaced family love held us apart and, when our children did not approve, prevented other love from growing.

Gus had his sons' approval, indeed he had their famished hunger, and especially Richie's hope that a tide would carry them all toward a shore while pushing the foster parents Greta and Alfred farther out to sea. Richie could not grasp the stakes but held tightly, perhaps too tightly, to the trappings in his midst and the dream he considered his new reality. Enough had been subtracted from his life already but never before had he been made aware how great was this lack, how intractably harsh it was…and unfair. Or was it? Perhaps he deserved to hope and to lose. As tension grew on the Dry Creek property so did Richie's earnest search of adult eyes.

One afternoon in the first week of a very hot August and following a subdued but happy visit with his sons, Gus approached me as I climbed into my car. He waited for Greta's car to vanish at the driveway before turning back to me.

"Can you give me a ride to town?" he asked.

He stood over me like a sheepish giant, a stuffed backpack slung over his muscular shoulder.

"How are you getting back?" I asked him in the car as we drove out to the highway.

There was a long silence as Gus gazed absently at the passing vineyards and trees along Westside Road.

"Not coming back," he mumbled weakly.

"What will you do?" I asked in the harsh light of his vagrant exposure.

"Go somewhere else," was his resigned answer.

"What happened?" I also asked.

Gus searched my eyes for a judgment he thought should be rendered.

"Didn't work out," he said from a voice rehearsed in a tone of stiff dismissal though his words emerged cracking under the weight of deep loss.

8

Gus had no capacity to assume a posture of wealth from his life lived in thorough poverty. He had slept with Jenifer, pulled into her web of rebound by his sturdy body and close proximity. He allowed it, even if he didn't at first seek it. I knew what he would not say, that her brief interest in him as a lover was a tantalizing hope for a great deal more.

In the moment he may have thought dreamily of a possible marriage and subsequent wealth for him and his boys beyond anything imaginable. He was tough and street smart and here was his big chance. He knew he pleased her. One evening led to another and another and for a week, maybe two, Gus grew confident in the way a blooming intimacy might manifest as security.

He did not realize he was the ingénue, the innocent consumed fatally in a web of inconclusive needs and then dismissed. The memorable life and time of Gus would be limited to nine wondrous weeks in a wine country mansion, ending in the bed of its owner when his heavy frame was lifted like a feather by a woman's soft, firm voice and then kicked down the stairs and out the door.

The rebound was over before it began. And before Gus could realize his error, Jenifer was tired, bored and finished with any interest in his salvation. Her rich father would bail her out of wicked involvements, anchor her to his property, and hold her lovingly above any serious wreckage caused by her mistakes.

I dropped Gus at the bus station in Santa Rosa.

"What about your visits?" I asked as he pushed himself onto the sidewalk and grabbed his pack.

He gave a sad shrug.

"Want me to tell Jasmine?"

His small, sullen pupils widened into bright brown dots of terror.

"I'll call her," he answered quickly.

"And then you'll phone me," I instructed.

"Right away."

A week passed before I heard anything more about the sons of Gus. The first to phone was Gus who had been accepted into a new homeless shelter in Petaluma. His reunification status with Family Services allowed him to live on the shelter's family floor where he acquired a room with two bunk beds.

"One step forward and two steps back," Jasmine said caustically when she phoned about the next visit.

"Yeah, the boys will see him twice a week and spend Saturday night. That's the court order. But we go back to the judge in three weeks and you have to know, Jason, that things don't look good for Gus."

I entered the shelter and found Gus waiting in the lobby. Through the window I saw Greta's pallid green Subaru wagon pull into the parking lot. I ran outside to meet her and the boys. As she exited the car I caught the return of Greta's regal mien, as if she knew what awaited and now was generously willing to wait.

Everyone waited, and especially the boys. Gus would fail and, even if he did not, Greta knew he would be failed by Family Services and within weeks likely dismissed by the courts. The little boys would be hers though I did not envy Greta's bracing pride. The boys might become hers but they would not always be little boys.

Dalton entered first and ran to his father. Richie came next and lingered at the door as if to take in the abjection of his father's new residence: smells of Lysol and boiling potatoes, people vagrantly asleep on couches, a young, earnest and half-dressed woman sputtering madly at a receptionist, a line of fidgeting older men waiting for the bathroom. Gus called to Richie who at first ignored him before drifting vaguely across the room, his eyes everywhere but on his father.

"You mah man! Wanna piece a me?" Gus shouted at Richie, though the boy seemed barely to hear him.

"What is this place?" Richie asked

"Home for now," Gus answered in subdued retreat.

Richie at last looked at him, still and unmoved but for a slouch and sigh that suggested he was afraid this was the case.

Gus took the boys to an outdoor play area where he photographed them with his camera and, while Dalton waited his turn on a swing, made futile attempts to recapture Richie's attention.

"C'mon, son." Gus appeared almost to beg.

"It's OK. We'll be OK."

Richie turned cautiously toward him but said nothing. For the next two hours Gus played with Dalton while Richie stood off to the side and refused his father's ravenous attention.

And so went the week's visits: Dalton immediately absorbed in the moment, even happy to have so much of his father's care, while Richie vacated the play spaces occupied by Gus and either found something else to do or sat to wait for the visit to end. He often wandered where he wanted and only sometimes where he was told. When Greta came to pick up the boys, Dalton ran to be close to her while Richie sauntered behind as if seeking to stand farther away.

It felt to me as if everyone were simply waiting, even the boys, for what must happen. Gus volunteered in the shelter's kitchen as a cook and hoped a job would come of it. He spoke wistfully of ways he might extend his time beyond the upcoming court date or complained bitterly about his bad luck. I had nothing hopeful to tell anyone, so I said nothing.

One afternoon at a park, Richie found a plastic shovel and sat down in a sandbox to dig with it. At first he made modest, methodical scoops that he dumped in a neat pile until, as if bitten by bees or seized by a demon, he slashed wildly at the sand, hurling shovelfuls at Dalton, then Gus, then other children in the sandbox and then anyone who passed. His fury was shocking. He scooped as if he were excavating a foxhole, scooping out a womb for himself, digging a canal that might lead him back to unbirth, to the source of his experience before suffering.

Gus worried only about being on time for Greta, about the boys getting dirty, about the disapproving looks of passersby caught in the spray of Richie's shoveled dirt. Gus at first tried to coax Richie away from the sandbox by approaching him humbly.

"C'mon, son," he whispered lovingly as he reached for the shovel only to get his face splashed and mouth filled with a fat shot of sand.

"You little SOB," Gus muttered from a sudden and incendiary wrath and staggered toward Richie who, laughing with mad glee, continued to fling shovels of sand at his father's eyes.

"I'm going to…just wait you little fucker…" Gus yelled as he fought through Richie's torrid barrage to get at him.

"Stop, Gus!" I shouted and ran toward the sandbox where I approached Ritchie from behind, catching him in a tight, firm embrace and then turning to shield the boy from his father's approach.

"Back off, Gus," I said firmly.

"Just back away and leave us alone."

My use of the word "us" seemed to relax Ritchie who dropped his shovel to squirm his small body more tightly into the protective fold of my chest. Gus, his red face and fierce eyes alight with rage, took several slow steps backward, nearly tripping over the wooden edge of the sandbox before going to the bench to sit with Dalton.

I saw Greta's Subaru slide deliberately into a parking space. Gus, dazed and spent, took Dalton's hand while I held Richie and leaned to whisper in his ear.

"It's time to go," I said quietly and firmly.

"Shall we go?"

His body shrugged with what felt like a destitute surrender. He pushed off and stood alone for a moment to watch his father and Dalton shuffle ahead. I began to walk toward Greta's car and Richie followed.

There were no good words or good-byes. It was the last visit of Gus and his sons before the anticipated day in court and Gus watched his sons slide into their car seats as if he were experiencing the end of time. He was absorbed in the fact of loss with no strength to rise above its primitive projections. Loss was his old, dear friend; so old he made certain to experience any loss before it happened.

9

"Late forties?" the judge asked. "Seems old for foster parents of a couple of young, rowdy boys."

Jasmine shifted in her seat next to the judge, as did her supervisor at the end of the table.

"They're solid people," Jasmine responded.

"Really. They've been great. And they really want them."

The judge, a retired court administrator brought into family law court for this one case, asked about the father.

"He's incapable of parenting the boys," Jasmine's supervisor responded.

"He's unemployed and homeless and has been for nearly two years."

It was mid-August and the community's control over the sons of Gus was moving into place. The county, represented by its legal team, its therapists, its caseworkers and supervisors, prepared to take full control of Richie and Dalton, to structure their futures and pin them down in a new existence, advocating all along the hope their lives would get better while knowing it was likely they would not.

The judge understood adoption to be risky, hence his questions at the court's preliminary meeting regarding custody. I sat and listened skeptically to the county's case: that the parents were "awesome" and "insanely in love" with the boys. They had spent more than a year caring for them.

As the plan unfolded, the boys would have two final visits with their father in early September before their legal adoption by Greta and Alfred. Gus would be stripped of his father rights and his sons would take the last name of their new parents. A court order would be signed at the next hearing stipulating the terms of adoption. Gus would be barred from contacting or seeing the boys.

The plan was designed to address the needs of the foster parents who hated Gus for his influence over the boys and who wanted nothing to do with him. Family Services, its therapists and attorney argued that, over time, the new arrangement would eventually dissolve the boys' link with their biological father.

"No, no way," I interjected.

"You can't simply dissolve so deep an attachment."

Jasmine flashed me an ugly glare while the judge leaned forward.

"And you are…"

I gave him my name and told him that for months I'd been watching the visits between Gus and his sons.

"Please keep Gus in their lives. Just two visits a year, but something. Keep them connected. Too much of who they are still belongs to their father."

"So you think they need their biological dad?" the judge asked.

"They may not need his care, which is not the point since Gus has shown he can't take care of them. But they need him—they need to grow with him in order to grow *through* him, to be relieved of him in a way all children leave their parents."

The senior therapist interrupted me.

"The boys are afraid of their father," she said coolly.

"Richie, especially, fantasizes that a parent is trying to kill him. It's not safe or appropriate for the boys to be with Gus."

I knew the boys did not fear death at the hands of their father but might fear for their lives without him. He was their numinous creator, the leader who entertained them and commanded them to him, who swept them up in charming flurries of thoughtless grandiosity. He had been since their births. The boys would have to be older to understand this and to let it go. They would have to see and grow with Gus to know and accept his failures in ways that might keep those failures from becoming their own.

"I've witnessed nothing in their visits that suggests either is afraid of his dad," I told the judge, ignoring the therapist.

"They will be cared for in their new family but I know they will never accept the absence of their father. In their hearts and thoughts the boys believe the foster parents exist for the sole purpose of keeping them in contact with Gus."

The supervisor stood to get the judge's attention.

"What Mr. Finney proposes is completely unworkable," she stated without looking at me.

"We have a foster family for these boys. The parents are good people and they love Richie and Dalton. They will never consent to visits with the biological father. Frankly, visits with him have already created disruptions in the foster home. If you want these boys adopted successfully, we need to cut off their contact with Mr. Slaughterbeck."

I felt immediately an excruciating solitude. The table had become a cavernous hollow. No face I looked into would look back at me. The judge alone offered a sympathetic glance though he appeared constrained by the bitter silence around us. What I knew about love and boundary was rich but inapplicable. Knowledge was either healing or poisonous and what I had suggested burned like a fury beyond what was immediately in view. There was nothing left to say. I sat and awaited the inevitable.

The last visit with Gus and his boys occurred on a Monday. The father was allowed to bring presents but the visit would last just an hour and needed to take place in one of the small rooms of our agency. Gus wanted to tell his sons he would fight for them, would hire a lawyer and go to court and would never let them go.

I told Gus that if he said anything of the kind I would be forced to end the visit immediately. I urged him to express his love, of course, but also to help them let him go. It would not be easy but the boys needed to be left with his approval of this big and still unrealized change. How did he wish to be remembered? The question caused Gus to sob for several minutes in the hallway before the visit could begin.

The boys were well dressed and calm, Dalton spilling the fact they were wearing their good clothes for another party later on. Gus offered his gifts and wrestled half-heartedly with the boys who also appeared half-hearted in their play, as if waiting with their father for some inevitable and difficult ending. Dalton seemed to lose himself in a game of nerf darts while Richie meandered at the room's tight, encircling margins as if waiting to be called. With ten minutes left, Gus gathered the boys on the couch and read to them the Golden Book version of Pinocchio. They listened raptly until the end of the visit.

By prior arrangement, it was agreed Gus would leave the room first. The boys would stay for ten more minutes while Gus disappeared and the foster parents arrived. I sat with the boys and offered to read another story. Dalton nodded. Richie picked up the Pinocchio book but, instead of surrendering it, he calmly stroked its binding and looked hard at me.

"It will be OK," I said without thinking and before I looked into the boy's hard, feral eyes. They radiated a steely, impenetrable glow, so cool and fierce it shut me out and I was forced for a moment to look away. When I turned back, Richie was calmly and methodically tearing out the book's pages.

"No, no," I called urgently as he ignored me.

Before I could approach, Richie had ripped out the book's every page and had begun tearing each page into a pile of infinite, small pieces. I tried to take the book but Richie growled and held it tighter.

"Wanna piece a me?" he shouted as he continued confidently to destroy each page. I went back to my chair and waited with Dalton who sat in my lap. Richie finished tearing the book pages and piling their shreds in orderly rows on the rug. His expression was aloof, as if he were again scooping something out of the sandbox, a scooping that again felt like an excavation of his young life's shifting attachments. A wall or a parapet, I did not know what he would build first.

Seven months passed and with it the seasonal markers of fall and winter that pushed my work with the sons of Gus to the very dimmest recess of my consciousness until one early spring morning I received a phone call from a local agency that provided adoption services. The woman who called said she was a therapist working with the family whose name I didn't recognize until she mentioned "two boys—Richie and Dalton?"

Dalton had been adapting reasonably well to his new family, but Richie appeared to be having none of it.

"He fights a lot," the therapist said.

"He runs away. He's seriously defiant against authority. And lately, well…"

She was hesitant to continue.

"Lately, when he's given a time-out in his room he has been forcing a bowel movement and then spreading his feces all over the walls."

The therapist got my phone number from a Family Services caseworker.

"She says you worked with the boys. Saw them with their biological father. She thought you might have an idea what started all this."

As I feared, without Gus in his life, Richie was becoming Gus. He would fight like Gus. He would run away like Gus. He would defy all authority the way Gus showed him. It was his rightful inheritance. Richie's excavations were fast becoming demolitions and for him to survive nothing else could.

"Is their father still prohibited from seeing the boys?" I asked.

"Yes," the therapist answered.

"That's pretty much a given."

"I'm sorry," I answered.

"He should still be there with them in some way. Why can't he see them and, more importantly, the boys see *him*?"

The therapist had no answer. And I could not bring myself to tell her how loving and also risky their father was. But if the boys did not see their biological father who, however else he might be viewed, was still the source of all exuberance, they might live forever with the suckers grown from their blemished, harming roots, live with them in a way that would produce the need to constantly repress and to destroy them.

"I would suggest they see their father; that Gus be allowed to be Gus for them in the years that bring the boys into maturity."

They would then have a chance to grasp a life that surpassed their father, I thought but did not say. Not the life forever beholden to Gus and forever indentured to primal and unrealized suggestions.

"I don't think that would be possible," the therapist answered.

"Any other suggestions?"

I remained silent and absorbed by a cynical feeling of failure. Gus was not killing Richie. The boy was dying in the cradle that could not rock him, dying at the hearth of a love that was conditional and without approval, and offered by caregivers that wanted, really, another child and not Richie. And Richie understood this, rebelled against the reality no one would acknowledge or even make known but that was his pure

268

and only truth. All his deathly and self-injuring behaviors were the expression of something lost and his intention to replace it with something drawn from the source of all engendering danger.

The therapist hung up and I recalled an adolescent male I had worked with ten years before. He appeared to me now as a grown-up version of Richie, a boy attempting to become a man after being thrown by a drugged mother and criminal father very far from his tree. He weathered a childhood of violence and insecurity to arrive at the county's Juvenile Detention Center. At age 15 he had long before outgrown every foster family that attempted to love him, forcing with unexpected and violent outbreaks of rage and hate the constraining limits of his trust.

At age 19 he responded to the pestering and ultimately disappointed love of a young woman by murdering her. Like everyone else in his life she had left him. Sentenced to decades in prison he arrived at San Quentin and within the first week encountered a familiar face in the recreation yard. The face belonged to his biological father, also serving a long sentence for homicide.

The reunion was a noteworthy coincidence, of course, but more notable for the way it appeared to turn both men into model prisoners. When not in their cells, the two were inseparable yard mates. Together they organized a prisoner prayer group, enrolled in classes and did research in the prison law library. I last heard the son had helped with an appeal that would reduce his father's sentence by seven years.

When again would Gus encounter Richie? The appearance of failures beyond their control was a legacy passed from father to son. Who owned these failures? Or were failures something anyone owned? I once believed my work was to help people live their lives. As I considered the consequences confronting Gus and Richie I thought it better to imagine how life lives through us and takes so much without any assurance of return.

Wanna piece a me? I am a piece of you.

There was little hope for any future that had lost every link to its past.

QUIET HOME
IN THE WOODS

1

Through an acceleration of time Virgil lost contact with his previous life. It began as what he and Josie thought would become emancipation. He wondered now if it weren't just a costly squander to move to the mountains and to those of another state where they knew no one but Tessa.

Virgil read the abstract of an article in the *Journal of Sex Research*, weighing whether to continue. The article concerned the nature and frequency of men and women's sexual fantasies. Tessa had given him the journal after a conversation about her developing thesis on human sexual behavior as distinguished by cultural, sexual and racial factors. He was a biologist and while her graduate studies interested him, he also could speak to her in the tongues of science, which she seemed to enjoy even if he were simply her mother's latest husband.

Tessa was visiting and he could not know for how long. Josie either would be cured or linger and die and while no one was saying any of this out loud, Tessa was Josie's only daughter and present for the duration. For the past two weeks she had stayed in the airy guest room of their quiet home in the woods, driving back to Eugene on weekends to consult with her graduate advisor and to see to her boyfriend.

The abstract described substantial gender differences in the salience of sexual fantasies and this was no surprise to Virgil who knew enough about sex—and science—to understand the obvious, though he admitted to not knowing why. Women were a mystery and men were not, though women sometimes said the same of men. He set the article aside and stood to feed the wood stove another log.

Already April and still the long rains poured down daily, rattling the gutters and spouts of their allegedly quiet home. He walked the squeaky hall floor into the master bedroom where Josie sat wrapped in her rocker, vaguely asleep though not enough to miss the sound of his boots over the howling torrent outside.

"Everything OK?" Virgil asked.

"You hungry?

Instead of speaking, Josie nodded.

A yes by any gesture was still a yes, though Virgil noted with silent alarm it had become in recent days easier for his wife to nod than to speak.

Was she weakening? Tessa would know this and certainly would have said something. Tessa kept nothing to herself, especially where her mother's health was concerned.

"How does a healthy woman in her young fifties have a god damned stroke?" Tessa had shouted at Virgil when he first told her Josie's diagnosis.

He had backed away from Tessa, her pale chocolate face suddenly a mask of roiled fury, her words sharp and painful, as she seemed to probe him suspiciously. She was the tall, fearless daughter of two educators, a white and blue-eyed mother who taught high school English and history and a black father who administered an ethnic studies curriculum for the Oakland schools. Her parents divorced when she was 12, giving up their spacious home in the Piedmont Hills for modest apartments blocks apart in south Berkeley. Tessa could walk the encroached, car-filled streets from one to the other and while her parents tried to remain friends, for a while Tessa hated them both.

"Yeah, I'll come out to see her," Tessa said after first hearing about her mother's stroke.

She needed time to work on her psychology thesis and the quiet home on Sweet Creek was only an hour from the university in Eugene and twenty minutes from the ocean. She said the quiet would do her good and what else could she do? It was her mommy.

"And I love my mommy. Every daughter should love her mommy."

Virgil thought he heard sarcasm in Tessa's response but not enough to raise the issue. And he never asked what Tessa thought of *him*. He was merely a messenger most of the time so it was enormously important that one evening she shared her thesis.

He had given up a good teaching job to work for the forest service but he could still truck in the academic lexicons. Tessa appreciated this quality, enough to come to Virgil and to offer him journal articles he sometimes read.

"Just tired."

Josie at last spoke to her husband.

"No, not more tired," she added, anticipating his worry.

"I'm doing better. Really. See?"

Josie threw off a brown, shaggy shawl and steadied herself to stand. She wore blue jeans that hung loose at her waist, covered by the hang of a green flannel plaid shirt that gave her the look of an elfin logger. Josie held the rocker and twirled like a dancer.

"See?"

She laughed as Virgil tried to imagine the small, thin body swaddled in bulky clothing. Did she still weigh even a hundred pounds? He watched her make a weak reach with her left arm into the air, appearing now much older than 54 as she wobbled and nearly lost her balance. Virgil rushed to hold her.

"Yeah," Virgil agreed, trying to convey a convincing optimism at odds with the facts on the ground.

"I'd like to teach again next year," Josie said, recovering her footing in Virgil's arms.

She waited for some encouraging words to form, which they did not. It had been three weeks since Josie was found in her classroom, flat and face down on the floor after the last bell. The principal was walking by and saw her feet under the desk. An ambulance arrived in six minutes during which the principal, a small woman like Josie, crouched and attempted an improvised resuscitation that at the very least shook Josie into stagnant wakefulness. Emergency techs still in their firefighting gear applied oxygen before carting her to a medical center in Florence.

"It could happen," Virgil added at last.

"I know how much you like teaching."

And then he changed the subject.

"Would you like a sandwich? I'm making one and I'll share it with you."

Virgil knew Josie would not return to teaching this year. While she survived the stroke, there was damage to her heart and, in particular, considerable damage to one of its valves. He would not be trapped into giving his wife any false encouragement.

"I wish this rain would stop." said Josie.

"I miss our walks to the falls."

Their quiet home was set near a forest trail that led up Sweet Creek to a two-mile stretch of turbulent and wide, white waterfalls. It was the primary attraction when Josie and Virgil found their property near a bubbling creek that flowed into the wide Siuslaw River. After visiting Tessa for vacations during her first two years in Eugene, they had at last made a summer drive to the coast, passing through Mapleton on the way to the flowing dunes of Florence.

They loved the ocean beaches but not the fog. For a year they enacted the fantasy of selling their home in El Cerrito and, for a fraction of its value, buying property in the coastal hills of Oregon where between storms they presumed the sun would shine. Two teachers in their early fifties would still need jobs and so it all seemed a preposterous though lovely dream until a chance inquiry brought Virgil an offer from the Siuslaw National Forest for a job as a forest scientist.

Josie, after a lengthy phone call with the Mapleton schools superintendent, accepted a teaching job at the 50-student local high school. Both thought themselves lucky to find work, though their new employers no doubt thought themselves luckier: to have employees with city skills willing to work for country wages.

All that remained was to find their quiet home in the welcoming woods, which was easy. Almost too easy, Virgil now thought. Ten wooded acres. A thirty-year-old cabin set back at the end of a wide, sunny meadow: three bedrooms, two baths, and with windows everywhere. The property featured a detached garage and workroom, suitable for conversion to a granny unit and access to the waterfall trail on an easement across land owned by their nearest neighbor on the other side of a shallow, sylvan ridge. And the ridiculous asking price was so low Virgil checked to be certain the home didn't sit in a flood plain.

The realtor said the original owner had died and his children, who did not live nearby, wanted a quick sale. And it was Oregon where, unlike California, land was plentiful and, with the exception of resort areas like Sun River or the valleys and hills of the Willamette wine country, still very cheap.

Gunfire aroused Virgil's first concerns. The weekend they took ownership, he heard the crackle of gunshots from the other side of the ridge. The shooting continued at unpredictable times and in the way all unexpected sounds eventually become annoying. Virgil climbed his side of the ridge to find the sound's source only to be pushed to the ground by bullets whizzing just overhead.

He drove down his neighbor's long driveway and jumped angrily from his car just as a tall, bearded man wearing wrinkled khaki camouflage emerged from a nearby barn with a double-barreled shotgun cradled in his arms.

"I'm your new neighbor," Virgil said.

"What's all the shooting about?"

"What's it matter to you?" the bearded man asked as if incredulous such a question would ever be asked.

"It's my land."

"Yeah…and you nearly shot me while I was up on my ridge."

Virgil pointed toward the hills behind the barn.

"Your ridge?" the man asked in a querulous drawl.

"Think that's my ridge, mister. You know the property lines?"

Virgil didn't but had a vague recollection the real estate agent said the line separating their properties ran along the ridge.

"Nope," said the bearded man.

"Previous owner made the same mistake. Check the deed. You'll see."

"But why all the shooting?" Virgil asked

"Starlings. Sparrows," the man answered.

"My sons—got three—my sons and I try to clear them out every summer. Build their nests in those trees up there. Messy birds, they are. Come back as fast as you kill 'em.

Virgil introduced himself.

"And you...?" he asked timidly.

"Traxler. Jedson Traxler. Now I need you to get the hell off my property."

The man cocked his shotgun.

"OK. Shit..." Virgil said as he climbed back into his Honda wagon.

"We're neighbors...maybe some other time," Virgil offered before backing quickly toward the gate.

Later on a walk to the falls, Virgil and Josie encountered three teenage boys, also in khaki and carrying rifles. They seemed busy patrolling the easement to the trail. Virgil waved. The boys giggled and pointed at them before disappearing into the forest.

Virgil was forced to admit his quiet home was not emancipating. If anything he had taken on more chores, more worries, and too many unexpected fears. Still, he could not deny an intoxicating and indescribable interest manifest as some pleasure he derived taking slow country time to explore his ethereal and most important interests. The first of these dealt with empty space, which Virgil increasingly believed to be the first principle of experience.

2

Virgil hoped Josie would heal. Tessa drove her mother to Eugene for physical therapy and doctor's visits. Josie usually returned tired but managed after a day or two to rally again, which was all Virgil needed to recall their covenant of the quiet home. He could not remember who first proposed the idea of moving to the woods. Likely, it was Josie.

Virgil's life with her had been a loving adaptation to her changing nature, to her walk through some forest of emotions that most men might be afraid to explore but that Virgil willingly and lovingly entered. She was not his ideal of a woman any more than he was her ideal of a man. They liked things this way. Through inevitable conflict and loyal devotion they found their meeting places in the woods until one day it seemed like such a good idea to find a mountain where their lives would feed on the perpetual bloom of a real and common nature.

Virgil read another article in the journal, this time left by Tessa in the bathroom. He usually found the abstracts more interesting than the articles, in this case a study of changing cultural attitudes about sex among immigrants to the United States. There was an intimate pleasure Virgil took in reading something Tessa had just read. She was his stepdaughter and though it was never acknowledged between them, Virgil held paternal feelings for the daughter of his dear wife. It did not bother him that his feelings appeared unrequited. His own son barely spoke to him so to have Tessa nearby and now in his presence renewed a nurturing, parental interest.

As a scientist Virgil was used to abstracts and enjoyed them. Afternoons spent in Eugene for Josie's doctor visits gave him time in the university library to research his wife's symptoms. When he tired of the speculative consequences of ischemic strokes, he turned to the latest biology periodicals or searched for astronomy books that gave him insights into the vast heavens. Before the fall rains he explored the stars by mounting his reflector telescope on a cement pad beside the garage.

From there across their meadow Virgil had a sweeping night view of the southern and eastern skies. He used his telescope, and an old classroom microscope, to explore otherwise hidden, living worlds that since childhood were the subject of his obsessive interest. He measured searches in decimal distances and sought to extend his personal view of space from an atom in a leaf to the edge of the universe. His microscope had brought him as close as 10 to the -5th power where cellular structures were revealed. His explorations of space brought into view vast nebulae at enormous magnitudes of distance and size.

He understood that if he went far enough in either direction, large or small, he would arrive at a place of pure, vacuous nothingness, empty of everything and even light. It was a theoretical horizon beyond which his eyes would never see but one he enjoyed testing with every available instrument.

Shortly after Virgil's meeting with his unsociable neighbor, Virgil and Josie were driven inside by the first of many pounding storms. It was their inaugural wet season in the mountains and it did not disappoint. It was enough for them simply to get to work and school and back home, or to drive over to Eugene to see Tessa or to shuttle over to Florence for groceries. The rain and cold did shut out any sound of their neighbor's gunfire. By the holidays Virgil and Josie had made friends with other residents to the west and farther up the creek.

"Jed's an ornery guy, that's certain," said Bob Ferris who met Virgil as he passed his mailbox one morning and stopped to say hello.

"His dad's still alive and lives in the back. His three boys don't go to school. Home-taught by mom. I guess you can do that now."

Bob said Jed was active in the militia movement.

"Some guys in the county like to get together and march around in khaki," he said.

"Pretend they're soldiers and play with guns. I don't get it but you've probably heard the gunshots."

On the first sunny day in April Tessa drove to Mapleton to pick up toothpaste and ice cream from the mini-market at the end of the town's tiny highway strip mall. She returned in a rage, slamming the screen door so hard it fell loose from one of its hinges.

"What's the matter?" Virgil asked as Tessa assailed a kitchen drawer and lifted from it a long paring knife.

"Next time I go to town I'm taking this," she yelled.

"No motherfucker's gonna call me names again. No goddamned way."

Virgil asked Tessa what had happened and then waited apprehensively as she turned to face him, her eyes red and wet with rage.

"Two jackass boys behind me in line. Start smartin' off about my curly hair and brown skin. I gave them one of my hard looks and it just got 'em going. So I shouted 'You got a problem?' and they backed away and started laughing. 'Oh, the ape lady gonna go jungle on us,' one shouted. And that was it. I went at them and the checker threw us all out of the store."

What did it mean that Tessa "went at them?"

Virgil asked for more details but Tessa ignored him and continued.

"They followed me to my car, yellin' their nigger stuff all the way. I jumped in to come home and they headed for a truck—it was dark green—and followed me. They road my bumper the whole way and then stopped when I turned into the driveway. I think they might live around here."

Virgil had no insight to share. He knew the boys and was sorry to know he knew. They were Traxler's sons with time on their hands on a Tuesday morning and with nothing else to do but to harass his stepdaughter. As described by Tessa, the racism was a daunting assault and Virgil said he would phone the sheriff.

"Don't you dare," Tessa shouted as she set the knife down on the counter.

"I can take care of myself."

"I don't think that's a good idea…" Virgil began.

"You really don't understand, do you?"

Tessa interrupted in a scoffing tone.

"I've been dealing with this kind of bullshit all my life. No one takes you seriously unless you're serious. This is serious."

Tessa held up the knife.

"Yeah. I'll agree with that," Virgil answered.

"Let's at least not tell your mom."

"And why not?" Tessa asked mockingly.

"You all moved up here to live right next to me. Don't you think she'd care? She's been trying to run my life since I was born. I tried for years to get away and just when I think I'd done it, you guys surprise me. *Hello,* you say on the phone. *We're your new neighbors.* Anyone care what I thought about this? Course not. So now that she's here let's give mom the truth about the place where she lives. It's filled with a bunch of crazy crackers."

"Your mother's sick," Virgil said quietly which was enough to quiet both him and Tessa who took her silence from the kitchen and left the knife on the counter.

3

Virgil did not know if he were able to relate in a different way to his life in the woods or if it were better to oversimplify everything. Nothing kept him farther from the forest than his job with the forest service, which required that he sit in an office in Mapleton all day and shuffle piles of paper. There was always something that needed doing, even when there was nothing to do.

The move to paradise had engendered certain anxieties, not the least of which was Josie's untimely stroke and Tessa's confrontation that, as his with his neighbor, might portend a future filled with deplorable troubles. In such a big and lightly inhabited place, a neighbor was everything; even a neighbor who lived so far from Virgil that in his old suburban city Virgil might never have met him. Such a neighbor was in the quiet woods his nearest neighbor and if he could not make peace with him Virgil should at least establish their border.

In the experience of time, happiness and heartache advanced with very different velocities. Virgil knew he needed to confront Traxler about the harassment of Tessa but did not know how. He accepted the dead space that held such a proposition until one morning he passed his neighbor's driveway and saw Jed Traxler opening the mail box, his tall, old body bent like a bow as he searched the box's deep reaches for remnants of lost mail.

"That woman's your daughter?" Traxler asked incredulous and not at all defending of himself or his sons. It was as if the assault was assumed, that a dark woman alone and exposed in Mapleton would, of course, be bothered and made to feel unwelcome.

"She's black," Traxler said.

"How can that be?"

Virgil resisted the nauseating dynamic of an explanation, something he thought Traxler expected.

"Well, it just fucking is," Virgil answered.

"Tell your boys to leave her alone. She's not here to make trouble. Nor are we."

"Then don't," Traxler shouted.

Virgil shrunk away from the tall man's voluble aggression.

"Race-mixing...you know, it's another sign of every civilization's decline."

Traxler's calm declaration sounded for a moment mellifluous and nearly reasonable.

"We're tryin' to protect a way of life up here," Traxler stated as if he were building the fence Virgil knew would always be needed between them.

"Hope you don't give us any reason to feel threatened..."

Traxler let his words swirl into a diminishing and suggestive silence like water running down a sink drain.

"What?" Virgil asked.

"What way of life?"

"We're God-fearin' folk," Traxler announced.

"Lots of us here. We stick together and we don't take kindly to threats."

"Sounds like you're the one making a threat," said Virgil.

Traxler stiffened and took a step back, his eyes wide and piercing. It was a response that appeared to Virgil to have the shape of a well-defended terror.

"No, don't get your gun," Virgil offered with a city slicker's self-assurance and for at least a few minutes as the man with the snake oil.

"I'm leaving. Just don't bother my daughter again. Ever. I'll get the sheriff if I need to."

"Well, you just do that," Traxler answered with a vivid surge of self-assurance.

"You tell him ole' Jed T. sent you."

And then Traxler laughed a loud, gut-rocking chuckle as Virgil walked to his car and, without looking back, started his engine and drove to work.

The hike to Sweet Creek Falls took 25 minutes but Tessa wasn't in a hurry. She wandered away to visit the budding spring flowers beyond the trail. A profusion of fern leaves grew lush and fat and were greener than an Irish hillside.

"Not too far," Virgil shouted after her.

"Don't want to get lost."

From a distance Tessa flashed him an animated shrug as if to pantomime exasperation. She turned to peer into the dark shadows of the deepening forest before walking back to the creek where Virgil stood waiting. She was not a child, but child enough for Virgil that he could not state to her his real fear.

"Is mom going to die?"

Tessa was nothing if not direct and in a way that usually surprised Virgil, as he was surprised when Tessa offered him the sex journal articles. He had no answer but shook his head.

"She's a strong woman," he said, realizing immediately he was not answering her question.

"It's going to take some time."

"To get well...or to die?" Tessa asked again.

"What do you think?" Virgil asked, the experienced teacher able to return a student's flummoxing question, thereby forcing some amount of studious reflection and critical thinking that would leave him the hell alone. He wanted Tessa to hold his hope for him and to hand it over to her as a prosthesis he might be wearing like someone missing a leg.

"I asked because she seems weaker now," said Tessa.

She reviewed two recent trips with her mother to Eugene, lurching through a memorable accrual of symptoms: dizziness, exhaustion, and trouble speaking clearly when the exhaustion set in as it did increasingly.

"And her water colors...do you look at them?"

Painting in watercolor had been Josie's relaxing avocation, her expressive engagement with key moments of a quotidian she tried hard to make into something lush and unforgotten. Moving to the woods inspired her to work more and harder to perfect the constituents of a germinal style. Her easel became a permanent fixture at the porch and her palette a sea of splendid and festering shades.

"They're unfinished," answered Virgil.

"But they usually are...and often for months before she decides how to finish them. That's not strange."

"They're incomplete," Tessa responded.

"All the color is gone. She splashes water and paint and then nothing. Something's wrong."

Yes, it was. As they approached the falls, Virgil reached to give Tessa an avuncular hug and tried to voice his empathy though his words were smothered in the sudden thunder of the first falls. Tessa rushed forward, again the child he could see but that she wasn't, suddenly a curious and enchanted explorer eager for the rush of the noise and the power of water running downhill.

Tessa climbed the trail ahead of Virgil, entering the space of each subsequent fall as if climbing through the circles of paradise. With each climb, the falls grew more rapid until at the final pool she walked into the water to feel with her hand a long cascade pouring fifty feet from the top of a rocky wall, its channel hidden behind a bramble of thick and unapproachable vines.

All words were muted by the thunderous splash of water, leaving Virgil to think on a man's concern about his standing with other men, which was his concern with Jed Traxler, whom he fought for the protections enforced by boundaries. Whereas through his love of Josie he lived in a world of emotional response, of unnamed things that flowed through his hands like the waters of Sweet Creek and which were only delicately captured, if at all.

Josie was the first woman to be for him both a lover and a wife, to be a partner and also a friend. And instead of speaking, he found it always more rewarding to listen, to hear Josie's deep feelings, which were not objects but the qualities of experience that most affected him.

Tessa was quiet on the return walk until the loud roar of the falls retreated behind them and gunshots could be heard beyond the ridge.

"What's all that?" she asked Virgil, who knew but would not admit to knowing.

"Neighbors," he answered.

"You've heard them. They do some shooting from time to time. It's the woods, you know."

"Let's go see," Tessa said and ran ahead.

"Let's not," Virgil answered firmly, again feeling the urgency of a parent.

"Your mom's waiting for dinner and we're already late."

Tessa did not at first obey, though as the gunshots seemed to grow louder she at last turned away from the ridge to follow Virgil home.

"Can I have my boyfriend come visit?" Tessa asked as they stepped together onto the front porch.

"You need to ask your mom," Virgil answered, imagining briefly what this would mean: a boy hanging around the property, for a day…or a week.

"She said to ask you," Tessa said.

Virgil shouldered the ineffable weight of his love for Josie and all she brought him, including Tessa. He felt again the effect of inchoate emotions that needed no description or assignment.

"Of course, dear," he answered. "Of course. Anytime."

4

It was not easy for Virgil to choose a future. There were too many to consider but the one that recurred had him sitting alone in their house as endless rain pummeled the roof and windows.

Did Josie bring me to the mountains to leave me here?

His thought did not hold Josie accountable. Even if the knowledge of disease had existed, for a very long time it lay buried deep in the cells and, even if visible (which it was not) was never something they wanted to see.

Poor health might be the reason he no longer had sex with Josie, though Virgil recognized their sexual life ended a month before her stroke. The bewildering work of making a new home in a new place, and of doing their respective jobs and chores to support it, halted for a while the luxury of sexual friendship. It was to be only for a while, and each understood this, even if they did not say it.

Teases were still welcome as was the occasional attempt, though at these times one or the other was usually too tired or not in the mood. Love continued—the agape of their lives was never stronger and they were deeply committed partners. But the passion they shared in the making of their new life did not translate easily into arousal.

A bell rang and Virgil put down Tessa's latest edition of the *Journal of Sex Research*. He had meant to ask her about her studies when they walked to Sweet Creek Falls. He did not and now responded to Josie to whom he had given a small crier bell with which to ring if she needed anything. She was not bedridden but rest was prescribed. And since she seemed weaker each day than the day before, bed rest was the operating principle of her care.

"Just some water," she asked quietly.

"And maybe one of those chocolate cookies Tessa bought."

Virgil approached the bed where his wife lay wrapped in her blue terrycloth robe, art books and sketches spread around her.

"Working?" Virgil asked.

He made a point of describing any activity she performed as work. It was drawn from his need to feel they still did work, were still together a team forcing forward the achievement of perpetual constructions.

"You might say that," Josie answered with tepid diffidence.

"I won't."

Virgil found Tessa in the kitchen and asked her where she kept the chocolate cookies.

"Gone," she said.

"All gone."

"Your mother wanted one," Virgil answered.

"Shit!" Tessa mumbled.

"Am I going to disappoint her again?"

Virgil's face reddened as he felt himself pulled among the ties that bind, which Tessa registered immediately as a man's unwarranted judgment.

"You wouldn't understand," Tessa declared.

"Mothers and daughters are helplessly linked and most often victims of the best intentions."

"She's always been proud of you," Virgil answered weakly.

"What the fuck does that have to do with anything?" Tessa blustered.

"A positive model—she was my proud mom who still modeled surrender, weakness and self-suffering. She wanted me to be strong and independent, and also thin, pleasing and never selfish. She shaped me to be the success she wasn't, which taught me only to succumb to criticism. I don't do criticism now. The cookies are gone. I ate them. Tough shit."

Virgil was silent. He walked to the cupboards and searched for something else he might offer Josie.

Tessa began to weep. Virgil approached her and placed his hand firmly on her shoulder.

"She can't die," Tessa howled faintly.

"Too much left and too much work to do. She can't know what damage her sweetness has caused me. It's not her fault she's white and I'm black. But it's not mine, either. She's never met me where I am and maybe she never will. Maybe it can never happen. But I need her now. I need her to need me. It's not a race thing. Race doesn't exist. But tribes...tribes are a tyranny."

Virgil found a Hershey's chocolate bar in the drawer where Josie stashed her secret treats. He undid the wrapper, broke off a chunk and placed it on a saucer. He filled a water glass from a cold pitcher in the refrigerator.

"Take these into your mom," he told Josie.

"She's waiting."

Virgil took his Thursday lunch break and drove to Florence to withdraw money from their savings account. On the way he mentally calculated how long they could survive on his one salary and still pay the mortgage and save for retirement. His mind filled vast empty spaces with nothing but available probabilities.

He considered his existence in the forest and on the surface of the earth and felt nearly claustrophobic within the limits he perceived to be in place. He could travel as far as possible in any direction and, while anchored by the curvature of gravity evident at any of an infinite number of horizons, always arrive at the place he left. To free himself from this wheel he would have to leap off the planet, which for a moment he visualized as a grain of sand. This compression of space was still no comfort since by his calculations the earth as a grain of sand placed the Sun's nearest star neighbor at the edge of the Grand Canyon. For a man several sizes smaller than a molecule that would be a long journey, indeed.

As he withdrew $500 from the bank, it was clear to Virgil that, either as destination or return, he and Josie did not have enough money to go back to California. The cost of the move, the loss of their old jobs, the terms of a new mortgage and, most of all, the aggravations of Josie's illness, would not permit it. He thought they might as well be astronauts stranded on the moon without a way home. He tried to resist a feeling of fateful encroachment, though it was impossible not to succumb again to oppressive anxiety over what he could not control.

Virgil kept despair in the background, helped at night by his surveys of an occasionally cloudless night sky. As the sun set he watched Jupiter rise; a bright, colored orb he explored across space, always dazzled by his direct experience of the largest planet and its scattered moons. Did Galileo see the big red spot? Did he turn as Virgil did to explore the binary stars and galaxies clustered in Leo? A sliver of moon was slipping backwards out of the west, waxing each night into an ever brighter beacon that eventually hid the dimmer stars. The penumbra of a partial solar eclipse might be present the morning of May 10th. Virgil absorbed the apparent calm clockwork of the heavens aware that it was moving at speeds he did not feel and barely understood.

As he watched the sky one evening, Virgil thought he heard something move in the woods. The trees sometimes swayed with the wind and four-footed mammals broke into runs through the meadow. But this sound was different. It had the lumbering rhythm of footsteps, likely something or someone bipedal that seemed to move and stop near the bushes just under the ridge. Virgil found a flashlight and one night waited until the stepping rhythm was engaged before pointing the light toward the sound and flipping the switch.

Nothing. He walked across the meadow and shined his light deep into the shadows. For a week he waited and flashed his light and saw nothing. Yet the subdued crunching sound of steps was unmistakable and unsettling.

"You don't have a dog?" Bob Ferris asked Virgil.

"You should have a dog. This gal is a beauty but she needs a home. I can't keep her."

"What's her name?" Virgil asked.

"Pepper," Ferris answered.

"Cute and black and full of spit. If you need a watchdog, she's perfect. Doesn't let a thing get by her."

"And she's up to date on shots and stuff?" Virgil asked.

"Got the vet papers. Here, take a look. She's a healthy girl and not too old."

Virgil shuffled through a file of veterinary bills and got down on his knees and yelled into the yard "Pepper!" His command summoned a lanky black lab that nearly knocked him over.

"Good Girl. Are you a good girl?" Virgil asked Pepper who tilted her head curiously as if to ask if Virgil were a good boy. Her tail wagged furiously while she nuzzled Virgil's cheek and licked his nose.

"Yeah. OK. The price is right," Virgil said.

"Wish I could keep her," Ferris said.

"I gave her to my son as a pup three years ago and now he's getting divorced and has to move her out. Damn. What am I supposed to do?"

"She has a good home now," Virgil assured his other neighbor.

The two men shook hands and Virgil called the dog into his Volvo.

Pepper took her place in Virgil and Josie's home in time for a weekend visit by Tessa's boyfriend, a UO senior named Marcus who majored in psychology and also played tight end for the football Ducks.

"God, she's a beauty," Tessa shouted when she saw the dog.

"Can she sleep with me? Are you a good girl, Pepper?"

As expected, Josie was more subdued but still easily taken in by Pepper who, instead of joining a new family, seemed to assume that everyone she nudged, licked and nosed was a new member of her pack. Virgil planned to have Pepper spend a week inside and asked Tessa to manage her while he worked.

In the evenings he sat outside to view the stars, Pepper attached to a long leash and curled up beside him. The noises he had thought he heard seemed to vanish while Pepper responded to other sounds she heard but that he could not. She was a smart dog, alert and pleasing and happy. Virgil relaxed into the evening's cool concealments, in love again with a new and loyal and very best friend.

5

Josie could be tough and unstoppable, qualities that inspired Virgil to move with her to Oregon. She was the impetus of their adventures, which Virgil loved though never suggested. He was a quiet worker in their relationship: the soothing gardener who prepared the soil, nourished the growth, or pruned the bush.

Josie ignored limits while Virgil constantly gauged them. Together they made a life of balanced opposites that, through a lucky range of coincidences, brought them to the realization of several goals that included ultimately a new life in a new land.

Now Josie was ill, very ill, leaving Virgil to serve as both caregiver and decision-maker, as the planner and custodian of both their lives and the anxious witness to her fading enthusiasm for living. How had this happened?

This life in the woods was intended to revive and lift them, to conserve their strength and feed their open hearts with something they thought of as Nature's brilliant, unvarnished splendor. They had not reckoned that their life together in time could be subject to forces they hoped to elude: the vulnerability, transience and mortality of a relentless and efficient Nature always in sight and yet easily discounted and forgotten.

It was not a decomposition of love. Virgil sat with Josie, spoke with her, served her meals and rubbed her back and feet. Tessa, too, engaged her, held her and despite the pull of unresolved grievances loved her mother deeply and refused to imagine living without her.

Virgil thumbed through a sex journal to find a study by a Dr. Schwartz outlining recent findings in a survey of college co-eds. It was another article given him by Tessa. She would ask about this later, since he had taught classes filled with teenage women. Josie said Tessa's interest in sex began early and that she was a confident and precocious child. She masturbated as a preschooler and while it seemed to concern her father, Josie allowed it, especially at nap times when it could be done in soothing privacy.

Tessa's graduate work moved her into comparative cultural

studies of sexual behavior and a thesis was taking shape, which she worked on most nights but not this weekend since Marcus was here and staying with her in her room. They spent many hours behind its closed door, reminding Virgil of Josie's comment about Tessa's childhood naps.

Marcus was tall, slim and strong with a deep coffee coloring that gleamed in the light like a smooth, wet beach rock. His bright, attentive eyes caught Virgil off guard as Tessa introduced him. They radiated cautious warmth but offered also a completing trust.

"Glad to make your acquaintance, sir," Marcus announced simultaneously with an athlete's firm handshake.

Virgil felt the fullness of the young man's self-assurance, afloat in his well-conditioned body and aligned with every flickering movement. He was efficiently himself, a fit and handsome figure that moved without resistance.

Virgil knew enough about football to ask Marcus about his game, though Marcus pointedly switched the topic to Tessa's psychology research and his regard for it. He described her intellectual qualities with colloquial reverence.

"Damn, she's smart," he said.

"She's helped me more than anyone can know."

Virgil was charmed. Marcus was mature well beyond the terms of sexual fantasy or innocent romance and seemed guided in his affection for Tessa by feelings and relatedness that drew creative power from a rich well of wise interest.

For two days Marcus and Tessa took long morning walks along Sweet Creek to see the splendid fury of its many falls, grown white and turbulent in a flush of spring rains. On the third day they returned anxious and discomposed.

"Those damn boys again," Tessa shouted.

"Launched rocks at us from across the creek. Hid in the bushes like the cowards they are. But I heard their laughs. I know them. A rock just grazed me and Marcus caught another. Where do they live? I want to pay a visit."

Marcus was silent behind fierce and angry eyes.

"Nothing I'm not used to, sir."

He spoke directly to Virgil.

"Young punks. A local nuisance but I'm not scared."

Virgil lied and said he didn't know where the boys lived. He thought about phoning the sheriff and decided against it. The next morning Virgil and Tessa left for the beach and traveled only as far as the end of the driveway when Marcus couldn't stop the car. A check underneath revealed the brake line had been cut.

"You don't have a gun?" Bob Ferris asked.

"You should at least have a god damned gun. This is the back-country, boy."

Bob slapped Virgil on the back, arousing an awkward look of pain.

Backcountry appeared to be Bob's appellation for what he presumed was primarily a man's world. It had been awhile since Virgil felt the slap of male bonding—a way for one man to touch another without suggesting a physical affiliation.

"You'll like this," Bob continued.

"A Remington 870 shotgun. Perfect for whatever you need to chase down. Everyone needs a gun."

Virgil might have argued this point, but did not. He held the rifle to his shoulder and let Bob move his hands and fingers into position. They walked outside where Virgil discharged the rifle and nearly fell over from the recoil. After several more shots, Bob praised Virgil's form and control and then sold him the rifle for $200.

A discernible decline in Josie's functioning coincided with a call from her physician in Eugene. He asked for a meeting with Josie, Virgil and Tessa on Tuesday when Josie was scheduled for another weekly exam. On a recent afternoon Josie tried to walk Pepper in the yard before the dog dashed forward after a rabbit and toppled Josie to the ground. Tessa was the first to find her as she struggled futilely to stand.

"I'm tired...so tired," was all Josie would say.

Virgil arrived and carried his wife into the house. Love was not decompensating but Josie certainly was. Love was still love but for the first time Virgil saw himself in a limiting love that certainly no one wished to see as terminal but that was becoming the unnamed ghost in a marriage increasingly engaged with unspoken and irrevocable loss.

"The heart is weak," said the good doctor to Josie.

"The damage is severe."

Virgil and Tessa sat on either side of Josie and listened.

"We've waited with some thought she might rally," the doctor continued as he looked away from Josie.

"But there is no improvement. In fact, as you may have noticed, her condition is worsening."

Virgil had taken his only earned sick day from work to attend this meeting. He asked if the doctor was suggesting heart surgery.

"It's all that's left, I'm afraid."

The doctor frowned.

"It's a difficult choice because I cannot say what Josie's quality of life would be after surgery. She has congestive heart failure. A lack of oxygen would be a persistent threat to her sentient function."

"Then what?" Virgil asked through an encroaching bloom of anxiety.

"How are you going to save her life?"

"That's the point," said the doctor.

"Surgery is our last best hope and it comes with considerable risk."

In the breathless silence that followed, the doctor offered a referral for a second opinion but warned Virgil it would likely produce the same conclusion.

"I don't want surgery," Josie said weakly.

"But mom," shouted Tessa. "You can't die."

"We're all going to die," Josie said as if speaking to them from some quiet, peaceful distance.

"This is not a surprise."

Tessa burst into sobs, her head and arms falling to the office table where she hovered like a wounded animal before covering her face with shaking hands. Virgil sat still, for several moments unmovable as what moved within him grew into something nearly impossible to bear.

"I'm sorry," the doctor said in a solemn voice likely perfected for just this use.

"Very sorry."

On the ride home Virgil and Tessa fell into the silence created by Josie's exhaustion. There was nothing to say, no more spurious cheer, no more strained efforts to instill hope or to engage the sleeping and worn out wife and mother. Virgil had no defense against what was dying at the core of his life: Josie's wondrous disjunction as a living and loving being. The doctor had given everyone the freedom to speak about the inevitable. But no one was saying a word.

6

Virgil often felt threatened to name things that passed through his hands like water, things he could only hold lightly, if at all. As he focused his old classroom microscope, a patch of specialized cells came into view, forming the cylindrical xylem of a pine tree that ferried water and essential nutrients from its roots to its needles.

Virgil's small specimen was itself the door to an internal world and in its swirl of blue ovals and green spindles a revelation of the otherwise invisible. The small, interconnected objects were lined up like so many salami slices. In their dead, still state they revealed another story of life.

He longed to look into the crevices of these cells while they were alive, to grasp their mechanical operations, to watch mitochondria process fuel, as he might lean over the open hood of a car to observe its running engine. The exercise of seeing so much and so far or so close was reliably thrilling in a way that kept him from the things he could not see and only feel.

He no longer located the inner world of emotional response and deeper transmission he shared exclusively with Josie. He could not quell the passing of time that rolled through him like a wind. He could not explore despair as he might a specimen. It changed, flowed, and also ran through his hands. He could not vanquish water, though he still searched every corner of the cosmos with the secret hope he might find a universal truth that could save his wife.

Virgil scanned the abstract of another journal article. It highlighted a study of American women and race-specific attitudes about pre-marital coitus. He found this one in an edition left under a stack of newspapers in the laundry, the article folded out as if to be saved. He knew enough about Tessa's studies to understand her interest in this particular problem of arousal and race. Perhaps she had misplaced the magazine and so he left it conspicuous and open on a table in the hall. Virgil was a steadfast scientist but science accomplished only so much. He accepted that the more the universe seemed to function coherently, the less it appeared to make any sense.

His wife made no sense. Her dynamic decline was so far along and so quickly and indisputably at its crisis Virgil thought only that they were subjects of a great fall from paradise by which all tenderness and trust might be destroyed. He had at first resented her decision not to try surgery. But within days felt remorse for his selfish desire to keep her sick and suffering body for himself.

He kept her near him, even if only one day at a time. And for now her eyes still met his. Each night he entered the house and whistled loudly. Josie rang her bedside bell to let him know she was still there. He slept next to her, but over the covers so as not to interfere with her catheter. Her deep snores, which he had never heard before and which increased with what Virgil presumed to be an increasing congestion in her lungs caused by inefficient circulation, kept him mostly awake.

When morning arrived, he leaned over to kiss her and stroke her hair until her eyes fluttered and opened enough to see his eyes. A weak smile signaled her link to this last available gesture of their once robust intimacy. Virgil looked deeply into hers, searching for something beyond the emptiness that cradled all natural energy.

It was Friday night after Virgil had finally fallen asleep that a loud pounding on his front door, the catalyst for Pepper's frantic barking, shook him back into a vague wakefulness. He staggered to the front door as Pepper circled wildly behind him and opened it to greet a deputy sheriff, his wide belly girdled by a black gun belt and holstered revolver. These were the first things Virgil's downcast eyes saw until he heard the deputy's voice.

"You the resident and owner?" the deputy asked, drawing Virgil's attention to a square face supported by a fat neck that gave the deputy's head the look of a top heavy marble bust.

"Well, yes…" Virgil answered in a moment of trust.

"Say, what's this about?"

The deputy ignored Virgil's response.

"Do you know this boy?"

The deputy pointed with his flashlight into the darkness, illuminating the face of Marcus, who stood between two other deputies.

Off to the side, Virgil saw Tessa.

"Course he does, you old pig!" Tessa shouted at the deputy who ignored her.

Virgil nodded in agreement.

"Yeah, that's Marcus. Marcus Butler. He's staying here with me. The woman is my daughter."

"Your daughter?" the deputy gave Virgil a suspicious look. "Really."

"Stepdaughter, if you want to get technical. What's going on?"

The deputy explained that Marcus had been involved in a fight with two youths, one of whom had taken a punch from Marcus that broke his jaw. Marcus said the boys ambushed him while he and Tessa were leaving the Mapleton store. There were no witnesses and the boys denied it, saying Marcus rushed them and they fought him off.

"Your Marcus says he was acting in self-defense but the boy's father wants to press charges," the deputy answered tersely.

The true story emerged instantly for Virgil. He knew who the boys were and what had happened.

"I bet the boys live next door."

Virgil pointed toward the ridge. The deputy followed Virgil's pointed finger before turning again to face him.

"Sounds like this has been going on awhile," the deputy surmised.

Virgil told his story, cataloguing incidents of harassment experienced by his daughter and Marcus, and identifying their tormentors.

"I told you. I told you," Tessa shouted at the deputy.

"Now leave us the hell alone. We aren't bothering anyone who doesn't bother us."

"Marcus is a student in Eugene," said Virgil.

"Plays football. He's a good boy."

"Plays football?" the deputy asked.

"Yeah. Tight end for the Ducks. Right, Marcus?"

Virgil looked toward Marcus who nodded.

"Oh....," the deputy responded.

"THAT Marcus Butler. "

"And you are...?" Virgil asked the deputy.

"Gooch," the deputy responded.

"Mel Gooch."

The deputy stared again at Marcus as if to sort out some affirmation of the boy's alleged celebrity. A long moment passed as the deputy weighed all the visible elements of his situation as well as the still invisible consequences of any action, including the likelihood that an arrest would keep him busy until morning, and longer once the newspapers learned a star college athlete had been taken into custody. In the end, he decided to do nothing.

"You keep the boy here," Gooch said to Virgil.

"Let's not have any more trouble. OK?"

He instructed the other two officers to release Marcus who with Tessa scurried to the front porch.

"Go Ducks," the deputy mumbled with mocking reverence as Marcus passed him and did not look back.

Virgil arrived home from work on Friday to encounter a van full of khaki-dressed men in his driveway, rolling slowly toward the house. Virgil pulled in front of them and stopped.

"Where's the posse?" the driver shouted at Virgil as he jumped from his car.

"The what?" Virgil asked.

"The soldiers, the troops! We're here," said the driver, as he began to look around suspiciously.

He appeared younger than Marcus. An older man sat next to him and whispered in his ear.

"Say, who are you?" the young man asked Virgil, tugging at his camouflage stocking cap.

"I was going to ask you the same thing," Virgil answered defensively.

More whispers from the old man to the boy. His eyes notably wider, the boy put the van in reverse and began to back up.

"Sorry, pilgrim," the driver shouted as he drove.

"Wrong address. Shit!"

The van rumbled backward faster than it had arrived, disappearing just beyond the gate. Virgil ran after, watching as the van turned back on Sweet Creek Road and disappeared again down Jedson Traxler's driveway.

By 6 p.m. the sound of gunfire rose from Traxler's side of the ridge, louder and more constant in a way Virgil had not yet heard.

"What's that jackass doin' over there?" Tessa finally asked in exasperation.

"Sounds like a goddamned firing squad."

Virgil said he would go see but only if Tessa stayed in the house with Josie.

As he cautiously climbed his side of the ridge Virgil knew there was nothing he could do. He had a country neighbor who had no grasp of neighborly reciprocity, no abstract sense of community that would engender even a grudging acceptance. Virgil approached the north end of the ridge where two large boulders formed an outcropping behind a copse of trees. From a narrow slot between the rocks he had a nearly complete view of the Traxler property and could remain unseen and protected from stray gunshots.

Below he saw a line of some twenty men, all dressed in khaki or camouflage as they fired rifles at paper targets pasted to the trunks of several trees. Through his binoculars Virgil saw the targets were enlarged photos of President Clinton and his wife Hillary, blown out and torn by hundreds of fired rounds. Several colorful and unfamiliar flags flew in a light wind from a flagpole in front of the Traxler residence, one bearing the phrase *SO Militia* against the blue background and seal of the Oregon state flag. Virgil also recognized a Confederate flag. As the firing stopped, hoots went up from the men while Traxler appeared in front of them to lead a cheer.

"For Ruby Ridge and Brother Randy," Traxler shouted as the men waved their weapons.

"For the brave martyrs of Waco and brother David," he shouted again to the men's louder and seemingly angrier acclamation.

Thereafter the men appeared to break ranks and gather in a circle near an outdoor fire pit. Traxler's sons carried two large coolers from the house, digging inside each to grab and pass around cans of beer. Virgil recognized one of the khaki-clad men as Deputy Gooch.

Throughout the weekend, Virgil climbed to his secret perch to watch Traxler's guests shoot, circle, march like soldiers in improvised formations, and party. A serious meeting seemed to take place Sunday, the men again gathered by the fire to talk and drink beer. Virgil heard the anger again rise in Traxler's voice as he led the men in what seemed a final, solemn prayer, the men on their knees before they parted. Traxler's visitors climbed into several vehicles and drove away.

All afternoon and evening Virgil sat with Josie, her thin frame like the delicate webbing of a new spring leaf. Her eyes brightened as Virgil held her hands and Tessa rubbed her feet. He and Tessa did not speak through a strangely comforting silence that needed nothing but contact with Josie's small, still warm body.

After Josie fell asleep, Virgil carried his telescope into the yard to watch again the rise of Jupiter over the now mute ridge. Pepper, who sat beside him as he fiddled with the focus, suddenly sat up alert, barked once and then loped willfully toward the trees. Virgil had forgotten to leash her and now ran after Pepper calling her. He splashed into the bushes to follow the dog's barking up the ridge's first swell before a shot rang out and he heard Pepper yelp as if in pain. Virgil tore into the dark hillside calling Pepper, who in a small clearing limped weakly toward him. Her left leg bled affluently. Virgil pulled off his jacket and tied it tightly around her and ran with the dog to the house.

"You have to do something about this," Virgil shouted into the phone.

"This is crazy."

"How's the dog?" Deputy Gooch asked from his end of the call.

"Her foreleg was shattered and she lost lots of blood. But the vet says she'll make it. I've got the bullet. God damn it, what do you need to arrest Traxler? This happened on my property!"

"Who says it was Traxler? Did you see him?" the deputy asked.

"Who the fuck else could it be?" Virgil yelled.

"And was the dog on your property? Are you sure? You said she ran ahead of you out of sight. A wild dog is a danger to any rancher.

If you were a rancher, you'd know that and would have kept your dog leashed."

Virgil heard where this was going. The foundation of a fraternity was often a conspiracy, in this case one the deputy shared with his neighbor through an oath of sacred and presumptive privilege. Virgil knew what the deputy did not know. Virgil had begun their conversation seeking justice. Now he wanted revenge.

7

Josie recalled a time when she was free and independent and full of promise. She had a summer job and money of her own and a world of choices loomed voraciously before her. She tried to describe to Virgil how certain strengths and passions were once important and were somehow lost.

Tessa was implicated, and while Josie would never tell her daughter how her arrival presaged the loss of her mother's apparently immortal adolescent vigor, there was no need. Tessa knew. Tessa bore her own intensities, her own regrets-in-training. Even as she awoke to a world outside herself, she held a needy hold of her mother's last breaths, as if Josie's absence might force the daughter out and away on the very same path and with no way back.

"I'm taking her to the ocean," Tessa told the Hospice nurse named Roma, who at first objected and then shrugged her shoulders.

"OK. If she dies, phone me right away," Roma said bleakly.

Tessa dressed Josie and wrapped her in a warm jacket. She packed a snack and a bottle of water. In thirty minutes they were at the beach, Tessa carrying her mother across a sand dune toward a small cove where they sat with a view of the lighthouse.

"I will be the sea. I will be the sky and the clouds," Josie announced shakily, still making plans for her future.

Tessa smiled. There were a few more words before Josie fell asleep and Tessa carried her small frame back to the car, folding her into the front seat as she might a tissue into an envelope.

Josie awoke the next morning and asked for a bath.

"No," Roma said at first.

"Too cold, I mean she might…oh never mind."

Tessa ran hot water in the bathtub while Roma found an old blanket to spread across the bottom to protect Josie's fragile skin. Tessa undressed her mother much as she had been undressed so many times by her. She carried Josie's bony light body like a cushion and slipped her under the water's surface, noting the Caesarian scar at the base of her mother's abdomen that marked Tessa's gateway into life.

Virgil returned at the end of the day to find Josie surprisingly alert, engaged in a conversation with Barbara Nagle, the school principal who hired Josie and who now existed as her only residential friend.

"She seems sharp," Barbara said to Virgil as she prepared to leave.

Virgil thanked her for her visit.

"We just haven't been here long enough to…"

"Yeah," said Barbara.

"This is a tight community. Hard to get in. I know."

Tessa prepared Josie for bed and climbed in next to her. Tessa now slept with her mother while Virgil slept with his gun in the living room, Pepper beside him and on her side to accommodate an extended, heavily bandaged leg that stretched like a fat white club across the rug.

Three French physicians collaborated on the sex journal study Virgil read before he fell asleep on the couch. Among married couples interviewed by the doctors, women were "genitally less active" than husbands "in accordance with the wives' preferences."

Virgil's last sex with Josie was a non-specific memory. He remembered the feeling but could not locate the time. He wondered if his interest in Tessa's journal abstracts was a subtle sublimation of unfulfilled desire. Talking and reading about sex was also sex. Virgil recalled his sexy talks with Josie, especially in the beginning when they did not know very much about each other and could hide their hungers in plain sight.

An intimate life changed all that as they came to know themselves and each other all too well. Sex was no longer a surprise, even though it remained a deeply private experience for Josie, like a hidden treasure buried at a vulnerable core. Virgil did not understand this. Familiarity, he liked to say, breeds attempt, though his active interest seemed at times to confront Josie's pensive, perturbing resistance.

Josie, he realized, was "genitally less active." Virgil loved his cock touched and played with. He loved to touch and taste Josie's vulva. He told her this once and was astonished at how it shrunk her into aversive silence. He thought she would be pleased, knowing that his touch and tongue gave both her and him pleasure. His touch and tongue may have, but his words did not. To his comment about familiarity, Josie responded that many otherwise lovely things were better left unspoken.

Virgil and Josie had married during a time that obliterated any basis for its justification. They were in this way conspirators, seeking an escape into a mutually unsatisfying past, as if what was already awful might be done again and better.

Tessa sensed this and so held herself apart from Virgil, even as she liked him and engaged him in her life's details, even sought his counsel and protection. Now Virgil watched Tessa turn exclusively toward her mother, searching for affirmations Josie had no energy to extend, for dreams Josie no longer shared, for one last chance to restore what was missing, what always went missing when a daughter left her mother behind.

Only now it was Josie who was leaving Tessa, and too quickly and too soon. *I will be a motherless child.* Technically Virgil was a father, but the father of a son who needed nothing, who said nothing, who offered nothing in ways that led Virgil to wonder if he ever had been a parent. Not so with Tessa. A mother, even one who did not wish to be one, was never far from a child that, for the full course of its life, would need to know and hold its ground note.

Gunshots exploded again on the other side of the ridge and angered Virgil who could no longer countenance the barbarous, looming chorus of his neighbor as a brutal accompaniment to his wife's dying. He left Pepper on the rug and burst from the house with his rifle, intent on confronting his savage neighbor. It was enough. It was time, though Virgil had no idea how to coerce a fiend, how to exact revenge from someone even more vengeful.

At the ridge's rocky lip, Virgil looked down into his neighbor's meadow, picking from the darkness a few lighted details. One was the main house. Through a window he saw Traxler's beleaguered wife cleaning up in the kitchen. Two of Traxler's three sons sauntered from the big house to the barn. Virgil could see a workspace at the back, bathed in dark shapes thrown by bright lamps. The shadows of the boys moved across an exterior wall, joined by the long and lanky shadow of their father.

In the collusion of shadows, Virgil grasped the qualities of an exchange as long black arms strained together to maneuver something apparently large and heavy. The youngest, third son emerged from the house and ran toward the barn. Immediately a shorter, thicker shadow joined the others to move within the obscure orbit of a large and incomprehensible shape.

Virgil watched, puzzled by the flickering silhouettes and the quality of a riveting stillness put into motion. What were they doing? For a moment Virgil felt in command, the spy who knew something his subjects did not. Anyone, however powerful, could be a subject. He gave the scene below a long, contemplative look, though his urge to know was thoroughly deflected. He would never know. Seeing was not knowing but within every view there existed an open secret. What was Traxler's?

Virgil watched the barn as he might stars in the night sky or cells through his microscope. He searched for some weak point of entry, some clue that might from the distance of a hundred yards give him an opening for revenge. He saw goats in the field but would never avenge his hurts by harming an animal. He saw a sprawl of vehicles in the driveway. He would not cut brake lines or endanger drivers or passengers. Pouring dirt and rocks into gas tanks simmered momentarily as a way to make a point until Virgil embraced its weak, prankish quality that would leave him to look more foolish than fearsome.

He wanted to break into the barn and shoot his neighbor, shoot him dead in front of his terrified boys, an idea he could indulge because he knew he would never do it. To identify his own misery was to feel the hurt of others, the hurt he knew must be Jedson Traxler's deepest anguish even as it prompted such bad behavior. Virgil continued to search the encroaching darkness for some weak point on his neighbor's property where he might interject an unsettling, harmful disruption. It would not right any wrong but it might arouse fear, which seemed to be Traxler's only guiding motivation.

Later Virgil could not recall entirely what had happened. He knew he had turned momentarily to consider giving up his scheme of revenge and to walk back down the ridge and home. He remembered a flash of bright, blinding light in the trees and then, as he turned, the crush to his ears of a deafening explosion that knocked him to the ground. He climbed to his feet to see Traxler's barn consumed by flames. A woman ran from the house and then ran back in. A figure staggered out of the barn, clothes entirely aflame. Virgil must have dropped his gun to run wildly down the ridge, intersecting the figure as it ran screaming down the driveway.

Virgil tackled the burning man and rolled him into damp, high grass to extinguish the flames. The woman emerged again from the house.

"My boys! My boys! My god!" she screamed as she ran toward Virgil and the now smoking figure writhing in the grass.

The running woman was Traxler's wife and the burned survivor was Jedson Traxler who moaned in his scalded, blistering agony, his flesh a steaming, smoky muck. The woman turned to run toward the barn but could not approach any closer than ten yards before the heat forced her back.

"Josh! Jeffrey! Junior! My boys! No! No! No!"

And she collapsed as the sound of a fire truck rolled over the valley and the first engine speeding over the creek from Mapleton bumped recklessly down the driveway.

Dragged into the open, everything was weakness. Firefighters jumped from the truck and approached the blazing barn with hoses, as helpless in their helmets as the mother in her terror. Virgil stood away as medics ran to Traxler and cradled him cautiously, his energy to survive alive only in his throat as a hungry wail.

Another truck arrived and later another. Virgil remembered standing and telling something to someone before a deputy walked him back to his property where Tessa waited on the porch. She wanted to know what had happened, had worried when she could not find Virgil. The deputy mumbled to Tessa as Virgil staggered past her and into the house where he fell into his chair. He remembered Pepper limping toward him and then a silence that suspended all belief.

8

On a May morning Virgil watched as the penumbra of an anticipated solar eclipse washed the eastern sky in muddy darkness deepest at the edges of his vision. It was a peripheral shadow barely noticeable to anyone not expecting it. But it was a shadow just the same, a shadow over everything and everyone.

He recovered his dream of an infant at the breast of a withered, dying mother, the infant not sucking but spitting back the mother's milk as if to prolong her ugly life and thereby its own. The suckling creature, perhaps himself, was a pathetic wretch and doomed, utterly doomed.

Virgil perused the journal abstract highlighting a study of sexual fantasy and guilt among conservative Christians. It was the last abstract Virgil read. It had been three weeks since the explosion on Traxler's property and a week since the death of Josie. Tessa was gone along with all her editions of the journal. She promised Virgil she would return for a memorial for her mother, that is if one were held. Virgil could not say yet what would happen. He acknowledged Tessa's need to leave. He saw in his stepdaughter's eyes the realization the dead are much less alive but also the hope death was temporary. She needed life to continue.

A favorite professor had invited Tessa back to facilitate a symposium on gender and race. It was the excuse to leave in a hurry, to avoid any coarse, maladroit intimacy with Virgil unmediated by her mother.

Josie's death was easy. Within a day all conversation ceased, her eyes closed, her breathing grew shallower by the hour and in the day's fading twilight she sucked up a last long breath that was not expelled. Tessa sobbed and held her mother's body close. Virgil sat with Pepper at the end of the bed and waited his turn. By morning the bed was empty and made and the room cleaned by the hospice service.

Two days later a deep blue box was delivered that contained Josie's ashes. Virgil set it on the dresser. Josie would become the sea, the sky and the clouds but at a time yet to be determined.

Josie was dead and Traxler was still alive, though just barely, his life held within a shroud of incremated, dying flesh. A second hand report from Bob Ferris, who had traveled to Portland to visit him in the regional hospital's burn unit, rated Traxler's chances of survival at less than half.

"He's in bad shape," Ferris said.

"He barely speaks but his eyes say what he knows. Two of his boys are dead and his youngest is in a room down the hall. Not like the old man, but badly burned. His face. It's not good."

There could have been no sweeter revenge than for Traxler to live with the death by fire of two sons and the horrible disfiguring of a third. Virgil no longer cared, did not wish to imagine such suffering or the thought of someone, anyone he knew, who might have to endure it. No one deserved anything so awful as this. Virgil crumpled under a tormenting guilt each time he imagined wishing any ill on a man who invited to himself so much of his own suffering.

Traxler's property was a crime scene, closed at the gate by heavy chains and wads of yellow tape. Ferris said Traxler's wife was staying with family in Astoria and driving to Portland each day to visit her husband. Traxler's father, increasingly submerged in dementia, was moved to a modest convalescent home in Waldport.

"Guess they had enough fuel to blow up Mapleton," Ferris told Virgil.

"Ammonium nitrate…enough to fertilize 60 acres, which is about 50 acres more than Traxler owns. Think someone would have been suspicious."

Days after the explosion, Virgil was visited by a sheriff's detective who asked pointedly what Virgil was doing on Traxler's property at the time of the explosion. Virgil explained his worries about constant gunfire and the wounding of his dog.

"You can ask Deputy Gooch," Virgil said.

The detective said Gooch was on paid administrative leave during the investigation. Virgil thought to tell the detective about Gooch's presence at Traxler's posse weekend but changed his mind. *Better not to appear involved. And they already know something.*

A week later the regional daily reported the FBI was investigating the Traxler explosion, which an unidentified source said was believed to have occurred during detonation tests for a large bomb. The bomb's purpose and target were not determined, but a separate story reported on the Traxler family's long involvement with extremist paramilitary groups in southern Oregon.

Traxler was described in the article as a self-proclaimed commander in a militia group formed four years previously in Josephine County. In his youth, Traxler's father had been a "Silver Shirt," the name for members of the Silver Legion of America, a pro-Nazi organization with a large Oregon presence prior to World War II. Authorities were questioning several militia members, including a group that regularly attended trainings at Traxler's home.

Days and nights now were absent the gunfire from Traxler's side of the ridge. Virgil heard frogs and crickets, heard the sway of the big trees and the festering gurgle of the creek as a distant slush of comforting white noise. This was what he and Josie had expected from their quiet home, which was now Virgil's quiet home and too quiet without Josie or Tessa.

He sat in the spaces left empty by absence, which he tried to manipulate into a rhythm of words and habits, of departures and returns. Following three days taken as bereavement leave, Virgil went back to work at the Mapleton forestry office. He slipped home at the lunch hour to feed Pepper who limped and did not run and waited through the day for Virgil's reliable arrivals. Each was deeply wounded and, through what Virgil considered a limbic, mammalian loyalty, each took prudent comfort from caring for the other.

In the evenings, Virgil sat with the stars and spoke to Josie. When he became frustrated with her silence, he spoke to Pepper until one night he recognized a wider space for his perpetual investigation and processing. He then described to Josie his discoveries and spoke of his frustration with Tessa and the end of family life. He had searched

Nature for its patterns, understanding now that even the disruptions caused by Traxler's guns and Josie's dying were revelations of a deeper process. He recalled a favorite thought gleaned from the writings of a favorite scientist, that life is a copiously branching bush constantly pruned by a grim reaper of extinction and not a ladder of predictable progress.

On a sunny Saturday morning he walked with Pepper along Sweet Creek, climbing a shallow trail toward the falls. He watched the waters, perceiving their flow and the flow of everything away from him and towards an irresistible bottom. In the weeks that ensued, Virgil made absence an active practice; indeed almost a business through which he could account for fears, reproaches, appetites and despairs.

He catalogued his own feelings the way he might the properties of cellular structure. He examined the surges of his unsettled emotional life as he might the metabolic activity of mitochondria or the variable and invisible atmospheric ridges that create the weather. How could he grasp the meaning of a meaningless existence? How could he make himself understood to himself?

Until one morning the discontinuity of his life no longer appeared as so much trouble and instead impressed him with the privileged way all life made a futile claim to its own mysterious irregularities. What was left for Virgil to observe or explore? He had revered analysis and investigation as tools for understanding. Now they appeared as a means of decoration, a way to embellish experience and to grasp a new beauty beyond anything words might say.

Acknowledgments

Every author or artist of an original work should acknowledge the people that have supported and helped to shape his or her process of creation. I am notably grateful, as always, to my wife Claire and to her thoughtful and honest evaluations of both my process of writing and its many products. My dear son Gabriel was particularly helpful with his suggestions to me about what would best constitute verisimilitude in the story *Tricks of the Trade*. And he's been with me since the beginning. As always, I'm indebted to Robert Bergman for introducing me to this subject matter and to A. Cort Sinnes for his critical and creative book design. A strong and wonderfully readable author in his own right, Cort is a master at presenting my work in a format that is both accessible and beautiful to behold.